THE BOLDEN CYLINDER

THE BOLDEN CYLINDER

A BRUNEAU ABELLARD NOVEL

NORMAN WOOLWORTH

To Mom and Dad
For all the right lessons at all the right times

Praise for The Bruneau Abellard Novels

"Norman Woolworth delivers another beautifully crafted, well-researched story featuring unlikely hero Bruneau Abellard—antiques-dealer, lover of the finer things in life, and accidental detective. What a pleasure it is to once again spend time with this growing cast of colorful, eccentric characters that includes New Orleans itself, which Woolworth masterfully evokes in a plot steeped in the city's rich musical tradition."—Laura Buchwald, *The Coat Check Girl* and the upcoming *The Book of Reservations*

"In his latest novel, *The Bolden Cylinder*, Norman Woolworth delivers a perfect blend of New Orleans culture, jazz history, unique characters, and intertwined mysteries. Bruneau Abellard, New Orleans antique store owner, finds a hidden compartment in a newly acquired piece of furniture that contains a relic of the earliest days of phonographs and recorded music—a 'Edison Cylinder.' When it looks like the cylinder may contain a heretofore unknown recording by jazz legend Charles 'Buddy' Bolden, the cylinder disappears in a house fire. The owner of the house goes missing. Authorities discover a dead body in the walls. And that's just the beginning. Join Bruneau as he works to unravel the mystery behind the so-called 'Bolden Cylinder'—and the secrets of the people he encounters along the way. You won't be disappointed."—Michael Rigg, *Voices of the Elysian Fields, A Jonathan Gray, M. D. Mystery*

The Lafitte Affair, Book One in the Bruneau Abellard series:

A 2024 Best of Indie Selection: "Woolworth's novel is a well-crafted mystery that is beautifully written, educational, and all-around entertaining."—*Kirkus Reviews*

"A savory jambalaya that tempts you to take another bite and keep turning pages."—BookTrib

"*The Lafitte Affair* is set in contemporary New Orleans but vividly evokes the 1820s. The novel is as much about the city's colorful characters as it is about the unfolding mystery. … A fast-paced, edge-of-your-seat read. … Worthy of the big screen!"—*Readers' Favorite*

"Bruneau Abellard doesn't necessarily need a mystery on his hands, but his friends think otherwise. With colonial pirate treasure, grave-robbing, decoding secret letters, and ties to Napoleon, the New Orleans gourmet finds himself tangled in an investigation of international proportions. Wonderfully intriguing; a little gritty and a lot of fun, Woolworth's debut offers good food, great wine and an exceptional whodunit."—Chris Keefer, author of *No Comfort for the Undertaker* and *Tragedy's Twin, the Carrie Lisbon Mysteries*

"Norman Woolworth is a writer with an impeccable eye for detail, and his cleverly plotted novel is infused with the sights, sounds, smells, and tastes of New Orleans. His descriptions of food and beverages alone will leave you eager to book the next flight to the Crescent City."—Proal Heartwell, author of *In Beauty It Is Finished* and *The Boardinghouse*

"*The Lafitte Affair*, exquisitely written and full of delightful plot twists, is peopled with Southern eccentrics drawn with insight, humor, and compassion. Those who love great Southern mystery writers like Greg Isles and John Berendt will appreciate Woolworth's weaving of real-life history with a modern New Orleans flare. Don't miss the first book in this series, featuring gourmand antiques dealer Bruneau Abellard as the quirky, loveable sleuth."—Claire Holman Thompson, author of *The Ring* and *The Blue Water*

"After reading Norman Woolworth's *The Lafitte Affair* we are convinced that this fictional tale could easily have happened. After having experienced our own real-life '*Lafitte affair*' during the research and writing of *Jean Lafitte Revealed: Unraveling One of America's Longest Running Mysteries*, we easily fell into the rhythm of twists and turns laid out in this novel. Knowing the old pirate as we do, we can say with confidence that Woolworth portrays him in a fascinating and yet very believable light."—Dr. Ashley Oliphant and Beth Yarbrough, co-authors, *Jean Lafitte Revealed: Unraveling One of America's Longest Running Mysteries*

Prologue

Colored Male Dormitory
East Louisiana Hospital For The Insane
Jackson, Louisiana
July 1929

Awakened by voices long resident in his head, the man rises creakily from his steel frame bed and pads shoeless toward the soft glimmer of light peeking under the heavy metal door. He pays no mind to the moans and slumberous prattling of his twenty-plus roommates, nor the effluvium of urine, sweat, and industrial disinfectant that permeates the air. Reaching the door, he turns the knob quietly and leans his head into the wide tiled hallway. Seeing it empty, the man turns to his left and blinks as the brightly lit common room at the far end of the corridor comes into focus. Finding his bearings, he begins his advance with small, shuffling steps, his left hand tapping a syncopated beat on the brass handrail that runs along the wall. Taking care to step over every third tile, he proceeds slowly. Emerging finally into the large, oval-shaped communal chamber, he turns left again, still hugging the wall, unnoticed by the room's other three occupants, lost in their own entrancements.

Soon, the man reaches the nearest window. He grabs the heavy iron security bars with both hands, leans his forehead in, and squints into the early morning light. A congregation of moths dart beneath the lamps lighting the walkway that leads to the administration building, and in the nearby shadows he can make out wisps of Spanish moss swaying below the sweeping limbs of the live oaks that line the path.

The man, who they call Charles, speaks quietly to himself.

"Come home, children. Come on home now. The king is callin'. Come home to

da king. Willy C., we gonna play some Funky Butt now. You too, Brock Mumford. Uh-huh. What's that? Oh no, ain't no kid no more. The king now. Still da king. King a Back-a-Town, that's right. Callin' my children home."

He is interrupted by a voice at the far end of the room.

"Why Charles! Good morning! I brought something for you. Thought you might like to give it a try."

The speaker is a large, caramel-skinned man with thick-rimmed glasses. He is well known to Charles as the orderly who works the night shift on the ward. He goes by Clarence, though Charles no longer knows this, if he ever did.

Clarence holds up a coiled metal object for Charles to see and places it on the table beneath his work-station window. He motions for Charles to come take a closer look. Then he turns and quietly exits the room.

Charles maneuvers haltingly toward the object, still clinging to the wall. As he approaches, he discerns an intricate tangle of brass pipes, tubing, keys, and valves. But he is not confused and smiles in recognition. The mouthpiece at one end of the instrument, the tubing that winds snakelike from the mouth and doubles back on itself before emptying into a large conical bore. A cornet. Cautiously, Charles steps away from the wall. He takes hold of the instrument and hoists it. Rubbing it gently from end to end, he begins pressing and releasing the valves, testing their tension. He wets his lips and raises the horn to his mouth. And he blows. Tentatively at first, but then with conviction. Oh, how he blows.

Chapter One

Time was, I enjoyed eating out alone. It was my way of snubbing my nose at the world. Of saying I don't care about appearances or whatever assumptions people want to make about me. I am secure enough in my person that I don't need to lean on the crutch of company.

Lately, I find myself of a different mind. I still dine solo, and I still don't care how it looks, but mainly I just feel bored. Lonesome, even. I guess I'd gotten used to having Sallie Mae Maguire around. It's not that we had such scintillating conversations. Far from it. Mostly we'd talk about work, or the weather, or the food we were eating. Maybe we'd share the latest gossip we'd picked up or compare notes on the news of the day. The point is, the conversation might have been mundane, but we were together, and we talked.

Sallie and I called it quits a few months ago. Sallie likes to say we decided to take a break. But really, there was no *we* about it, and it's been a long break. Fifteen weeks and four days, to be exact; but who's counting? It's not the first time we've split up only to get back together, but this go-round feels different. More permanent. Maybe because we'd both given it our best shot and it still didn't work out. We couldn't say we'd try harder next time.

Now that I'm on my own again, I've returned to my former routines. There is Sunday brunch at Katie's or Atchafalaya, Monday's dinner of red beans and rice, usually at Mandina's but sometimes Liuzza's, and lunch one Wednesday a month at Lilette with my dear friend Charlotte Duval. The difference is that these days I usually invite someone to join me.

My guest for brunch at Atchafalaya on a recent Sunday was Prosper

Fortune, a giant of a man I befriended when he was living as a hermit on Grand Isle, the barrier island that separates Barataria Bay from the Gulf of Mexico. He and Sallie and I helped my childhood friend Bo Duplessis, a property crimes detective in the New Orleans Police Department, solve a grave robbery case that involved the pirate Jean Lafitte, from whose brother Prosper is descended.

Prosper had been a field medic in Vietnam, where he lost the lower part of his left leg to a rocket grenade. He wears a prosthetic now and moves around well for a man his age and size. I don't know all the details, but like so many vets, Prosper returned from combat with a lot of baggage to work through. He spent the better part of three decades wandering from place to place, including a stint in Canada, before erecting a crude shack on Grand Isle, where his only close neighbor was Caliban, a large feral cat. It's a long story, but Prosper and I met when Caliban ambushed Hugo, my French bulldog. While the former medic tended to Hugo, we ended up bonding over a shared fondness for Shakespeare and philosophical musings. Our accidental meeting was at least partially responsible for Prosper deciding to return to civilization.

He lives in Gentilly now, with his sister Irene and brother-in-law Chuck, and we see each other often. Most people would say Prosper has assimilated well, and they wouldn't be wrong. But there is a deep sadness at Prosper's core, a mysterious dark cloud that follows him around that only he can see into. He has told me some things, but I know there is a good deal more he holds back. Having never experienced the horrors of war, there is only so much I can say or do to help or comfort him.

Prosper doesn't drive, so I'd picked him up at Irene's. Arriving at Atchafalaya, we parked in the gravel across the street from the gigantic skillet that is plastered to the side of the building. I'd made a reservation for two, but as we entered the restaurant, the hostess took one look at us and kindly sat us at the last open four-top. I wish I could say it was solely to accommodate Prosper's length and massive, heavy-boned frame, but I imagine my girth also factored into her thinking. I'd lost some weight when Sallie and I were together, but I'd put most of it back on.

Having helped ourselves to the Bloody Mary bar, Prosper and I sat across from each other, menus in hand. He turned his chair sideways, so he could straighten his legs, and I pushed back from the table a bit for some breathing room.

"I know I should be more adventurous, Bruneau," Prosper said, "but I think I'm going to stick with the duck hash again."

Prosper was right that I wished he'd explore more of the menu, but it was hard to argue with his choice. The duck confit with poached eggs, brown butter hollandaise, and bacon vinaigrette stands up to the best Paris has to offer. I considered ordering the same, or the shrimp and grits, which are brothier than most but have an unmatched depth of flavor. But in the spirit of adventurousness, I opted for the Tuscan Eggs, which I'd never tried.

"Shall we split the frito misto as a starter?" I asked.

"Great idea," Prosper said. "I haven't had Fritos in ages."

I groaned, Prosper smiled. Then he fixed me with a look of concern.

"You know I don't like to pry," he said, leaning in, "but you've never really explained what happened with you and Sallie."

"I told you; we decided to take a break."

"I know that's what you decided, but you haven't told me why. It's okay if you don't want to talk about it, but maybe it would do you some good."

"I'm doing fine, thanks."

"You don't look well."

"I've gained a little weight, that's all."

"Your coloring is off, and you seem distracted."

"If I'd known I was going to be subjected to a full-on interrogation, I might have invited someone else to brunch," I said.

Prosper frowned, looked down, and adjusted his table setting.

"You're my friend, Bruneau," he said quietly. "I don't have many friends, so I try to look out for the ones I do have."

Now it was my turn to look down, swallowing hard.

"Sallie thinks I'm controlling and self-involved."

"How so?"

"She says I have fixed ideas about the way things should be, and I don't take her views or feelings into account."

"What kind of fixed ideas?"

"It could be anything. Maybe it's the way I suggest what she should read next, or decide what or where we should eat, or how I plan our weekends. Whatever it is I've said or done, it's always the wrong thing."

"I see," Prosper said. "Was there a final straw? From Sallie's point of view?"

"You'd have to ask her. We did have an argument before she left."

"What about?"

"The house I'd picked out for us to live in."

"I didn't know you were house hunting," Prosper said.

"Yeah, well, Sallie said she could never really think of my apartment as hers, and I get that, so I'd been looking around for a place we could move into as *ours*. Kind of a new beginning was my thinking. I found this charming, raised center hall cottage on Soniat, just a couple blocks off Prytania. It needed a little work, but it had a ton of potential. Oak hardwood flooring throughout, lots of built-in shelving, a spacious kitchen. It even had a fenced-in yard for Hugo. I put a deposit down and everything. It was perfect."

"But not for Sallie?"

"Who knows? She never looked at it."

Prosper didn't say anything, waiting for me to continue.

"The mere idea that I would pick out a place without consulting her made her head explode. Ironic, isn't it? I was doing this all for Sallie, and instead of thanking me she calls me selfish."

"Suppose the reverse had happened."

"What do you mean?"

"What if Sallie found her perfect place, in the Marigny, say, or Bywater. How would you have reacted?"

"Those locations wouldn't make any sense," I said. "My shop is on Magazine."

"And where does Sallie work?" Prosper asked, knowing the answer. Sallie oversees the map and manuscript collections of the Louisiana Historical Center in the old U.S. Mint Building on Esplanade. Basically, the building backs up to the Marigny, and Bywater after that.

"Your point being?"

"I think you know my point," Prosper said.

"We wouldn't fit in those neighborhoods," I said. "They've been invaded by the millennials."

"Which is a bad thing?"

"Just a thing we don't fit into."

"Does Sallie agree with you on that?"

"I don't know, we haven't discussed it. I think so."

"Why do you think so, if you haven't discussed it?" Prosper persisted.

"Because we're of a certain vintage," I said. "The millennials have different values than us. A different culture."

"Right. So, you and Sallie, you agree on all that stuff? Values and culture? You agree on everything, so therefore you're free to make decisions for the two of you? Because you see everything the same way?"

I love the guy but Prosper was starting to annoy the hell out of me. It wasn't like him to badger like this.

"What are you trying to say, Prosper? That I'm some kind of narcissist?"

"Not in the clinical sense, no."

"Jesus! In what sense, then?" I was starting to lose it and Prosper could tell.

"Let's just say that the ability to see things from someone else's point of view isn't one of your shining strengths," he said softly.

I didn't know how to answer that, so I didn't.

Prosper picked the thread back up.

"Look, Bruneau, don't take this the wrong way, but those of us who've lived by ourselves for a long time, after a while, we just naturally become the centers of our own universe. Trust me, I know a thing or two about this. I know you've got a good heart, and I think you love Sallie more deeply than either of you fully understand, but from the outside looking in? Yeah, I have to agree with Sallie. You seem pretty self-involved."

Prosper had never put me down like that, and it stung. I had half a mind to get up and leave, but our waiter arrived with our food.

"Will there be anything else, Mr. Abellard?" he asked.

"No, thank you, James, not for me," I said. "But I don't want to speak for Mr. Fortune here. That would be a self-centered thing for me to do."

The waiter turned to Prosper with a quizzical expression but Prosper sent him away with a polite shake of his head and an apologetic smile.

The rest of the meal passed without incident, though our conversation was perfunctory, bordering on impersonal. The Tuscan Eggs were a tasty mash-up of flavors and textures, but I doubt I'll order them again.

* * *

Monday started like any other weekday. I rose at seven and took Hugo out for his morning constitutional, and then fixed a breakfast of soft-boiled eggs, an English muffin, and a couple cups of French press chicory coffee. I read the papers and showered, and then Hugo and I made our way downstairs to my office. I live above my store, Abellard's Antiques on Magazine Street. We don't open until ten, but I like to catch up on email and bookkeeping before people start drifting in.

Around 9:30, my van pulled up in front of the store. The driver was Henry Wilkins, my pick-up and delivery man, and he had his sometime helper Pablo with him. They were dropping off a pine sideboard I'd purchased at an auction in Shreveport. The piece was a bit of a departure for me. Like myself, my clientele tends to prefer somewhat formal, dark wood furniture with decorative accents. Even if they don't go all in for Louis IX grandeur, they value the craftsmanship behind an intricate carving or a delicate inlay. But my customers aren't getting any younger, sales have been flat lately, and today's market fancies lighter wood, more austere design, and rustic heritage. The sideboard was my nod to the times.

The piece was typical 19th-century farmhouse in its sturdy frame, lack of adornment, and use of material at hand. It had a large bottom drawer and smaller top drawer on each side, and in between there was a shelved cabinet behind a perforated tin door, so that it could perform double duty as a pie safe. The piece had been painted several times, leaving a chipped finish that I imagined the shabby chic crowd swooning over.

As Henry and Pablo carried the sideboard into the store and set it down, Henry commented that it didn't look like my usual style.

"It's an experiment," I told him.

"Oh, okay."

He exhaled and ran his hand through his gray-flecked hair.

"Hey, boss, it's the strangest thing. We can hear something rolling around in there, but we've opened all the drawers and the cabinet and they're all empty."

"Hmm. Let me hear?"

The men picked the sideboard up and jiggled it a few times. We could plainly hear a loose object rolling around. It sounded like it came from the lower right-side drawer. When Henry and Pablo put the piece back down, I opened the drawer and saw that it was empty as advertised. Then I put my hand in as far as it would go, felt around, and found what I was looking for, a cleverly concealed turn button that keeps the drawer from pulling all the way out. I used my thumb to nudge the button to the left and pulled again at the drawer. This time it slid out, revealing a hidden compartment behind a false back.

"Hola!" Pablo said. "How'd you figure that out?"

"Experience," I said. "We've seen secret compartments like this before, haven't we, Henry? They're not all that uncommon."

As Henry nodded to Pablo, I reached my hand into the compartment and pulled out a four-inch cardboard package lined with torn blue paper. The white block letter writing on the paper that remained read, "ISON BLUE AMBEROL." The name Clarence was scrawled on the outside of the box.

"What the heck is this?" I said, not expecting an answer.

"Looks like an Edison cylinder," Henry said.

"A what?"

"An Edison cylinder," Henry repeated. "In the early days, that's how they recorded music."

"And you know this, how?"

Henry and I have worked together for years. In addition to helping out at the store, he's the server at most of my dinner parties. He also plays the trombone in a brass quartet that works the private party circuit, but I wouldn't have thought to consult him on the history of recorded music.

"My granddaddy had a whole collection of these things," Henry said. "Orchestra music mostly. Waltzes, that kind of thing. Some spirituals. He had an old hand-crank phonograph he'd play 'em on sometimes. We used to make fun of him, but he said it brought back memories."

"How does it work?" Pablo asked.

"Well, the cylinder is hollow, see, and it fits over a mandrel on the old phonograph machines," Henry explained. "As the mandrel turns, the stylus skims along the cylinder. I couldn't tell you how that transforms into sound, but it's no different than an LP on a turntable, just a tube instead of a disc."

"Was the sound any good?" Pablo wanted to know.

"Terrible. There was always scratching, and sometimes the speed wasn't right. Course, most of granddaddy's collection wasn't in real good condition either, so that may have had something to do with it."

"What about this one, Henry?" I asked, holding up our discovery. "How do we find out what's on it?"

"You'd have to have the right model phonograph to play it on," he said.

"Where could we find one?"

"I don't know. A museum, maybe? A collector?"

"Alright, I'll ask around," I said. "What about your musician friends?"

"Maybe, but I doubt it," Henry said.

"Mind if I take a look?" he asked.

I handed Henry the tubular package. He popped the cap off the top and pulled out a hollow black cylinder with beveled rims on either end.

"Looks like it's made of hard plastic, which means it must be one of the later models. The early ones were wax. Look here, there's some writing."

Henry handed the tube back to me. The writing was etched into the beveled rim. It said "CBJXHS729."

"A model number or something?"

"No, the series number is on the other end," Henry said, flipping the cylinder to show me the number 5423 imprinted on the other rim.

"This was etched by hand," Henry said, turning the cylinder back over.

"Might be some other kind of label."

Henry rolled the cylinder around between his hands.

"You know, the other thing is, you could buy these things with recordings on them like my granddaddy did, but you could also make your own recordings. Might be that's what this is; somebody's home recording. Clarence's, maybe, whoever that is. Or maybe it's blank. Who knows?"

"Well, whatever it is, I'd like to find out," I said.

Chapter Two

One of the many differences between Sallie and me concerns the way we plan our time. Sallie doesn't like to go to bed until she has sketched out the next day in detail. When unplanned deviations arise, as they inevitably do, it stresses her out. I'm not like that at all. When my head hits the pillow, I may have a general idea of what I'd like to accomplish, but I'm content to roll into the day and see what it has in store for me. For some reason, this is a source of irritation to Sallie. She can't understand how I can be so "anal," to use her favorite trope, about planning my meals and maintaining my quirky rituals, and then be so lackadaisical about other aspects of my life. Basically, she thinks I waste a lot of time. My comeback is that if you're over-scripted, you close yourself off to life's possibilities.

This disagreement spills over into our musical tastes. We both enjoy classical, but whereas Sallie is drawn to the mathematical precision of baroque chamber music, I prefer opera and the majestic symphonies and concerti of the Romantic period. I like that the performers are granted greater interpretive leeway, at least to my untrained ear. Sallie sings along to the repetitive jingles of pop songs that just give me headaches. And while I appreciate the improvisational explorations of jazz, Sallie complains that the music lacks direction and accuses the musicians of "losing the song." One time I tried to argue that as a composer, Duke Ellington may be the equal of Bach. I almost ended up on the couch with Hugo that night.

I guess what it comes down to is that Sallie requires a certain amount of structure and predictability in her life. It's no coincidence that she's a champion puzzler, or that she's a curator by profession, everything in its proper place. Her need to impose order runs deep. And I get it, to an extent. Almost without exception, I'm up at seven and to bed at eleven sharp. Whatever else is going on in my day, Hugo and I take our three walks at the same appointed times. I still eat seafood most Fridays and red beans and rice on Mondays. But when it comes to the things that stir my curiosity and sustain my interest, there needs to be an element of mystery or ambiguity involved. When I come upon an antique that grabs me, for example, it's easy enough to place the period and style. That's the science of my trade. But the art, and the fun, is in uncovering the piece's idiosyncrasies. In discovering, or at least imagining, where it's been and how it was used, and bringing it to life for clients.

The other day, I was listening to Ellington's C Jam Blues, and it struck me how perfectly it underscores the differences between Sallie and me. The song exists as a simple written composition, using just a few chords, that can be played straight up. And it's entertaining enough that way. Sallie would probably even like it. But Ellington's genius reveals itself in the spaces he leaves between the notes, and in what musicians call the "tonal ambiguity" of the chords themselves. That's Duke's way of saying to his interpreters, it could be this, or it could be that, or it could be something else entirely. *Come, explore with me, and join in an act of creation.* And so it is that the piece sounds so different, yet always fresh, in the hands of Johnny Hodges, or Oscar Peterson, or Charles Mingus, or any number of other interpreters. Out of ambiguity comes, yes, order of a sort, but also joy, insight, inspiration, community. Life itself, you might say.

These were the thoughts that occupied me that next morning as I considered where I might turn for information about our Edison cylinder, when my friend Chris Keating wandered into the shop. Chris is a professor of history at Tulane and a frequent lunching buddy. He specializes in the 18th- and 19th-century American South but turns to me as a resource for questions regarding period furniture and design.

"Morning, Chris," I greeted him. "Looking for something, or just in the neighborhood?"

"Morning, Bruneau," he said. "I'm getting my hair cut down the way, but Gus is backed up and running late, so I thought I'd poke my head in and see what's new on the floor."

We exchanged small talk as I showed Chris an antebellum walnut double dresser and burl Victorian bed we'd gotten in recently, before walking him over to the pine sideboard and telling him about the Edison cylinder.

"Never heard of an Edison cylinder," Chris said, "but I'm not really a music guy. Interesting find."

"Any idea who could help me locate a phonograph that could play the thing?"

Chris fingered his goateed chin as he considered the question. With his dirty blond hair pulled back in a short ponytail, and his jeans and Birkenstocks, Chris had the hip academic look down pat.

"No, but I know a couple people in the music department and someone who works in media services at the library. I'll make a couple calls and let you know what I find out."

"Much appreciated, Chris."

"No problem," he said, looking at his watch. "Hey, I need to go check on Gus. Are we on for lunch next week? It's my turn."

"Of course. Where?"

"I was thinking Li'l Dizzy's, if you don't mind a drive across town."

"Fine by me. I can taste that smothered okra now."

"Okay, Li'l Dizzy's it is! See you next week."

* * *

The next few hours passed normally enough for a Monday. We had a few stragglers in the morning, but it was slow, which gave me time to get caught up on paperwork and to review the inventory at an auction I was thinking about attending in Beaumont. I ran down to Stein's to pick up lunch for Henry and me. When I got back, we sat down in my office. Henry got to work on his Italian Hoagie, and I had begun tackling my Reuben, when Angie Duplessis called. Angie is Bo's wife and one of my favorite people.

"Hiya, sweetheart," she said in greeting.

"Well, hello, Madame Duplessis," I said. "To what do I owe the pleasure?"

"I want to run something by you, so you're not blindsided."

"Hmm, that sounds ominous. Go ahead, hit me with your best shot."

"It's about Friday night."

Bo and Angie had invited me for dinner that Friday, in keeping with a monthly ritual we've been following for years. I'm an honorary uncle to their three kids, Little Bo, Sophie, and Monique, and these dinners help me stay in touch with their lives.

"Yes?"

"I've invited Sallie to join us," Angie said in a probing tone. "The kids haven't seen her in a few months, and they miss her. I know I should have asked first, but I'm hoping you're okay with it."

In truth, I was taken aback a bit, but I could think of no reasonable objection.

"Why wouldn't I be okay?" I asked, gallantly, I thought. "It's not like Sallie and I aren't still friends. So long as she's comfortable seeing me in that environment, there's no problem on my end."

Admittedly, this was a bit disingenuous of me. It was true that Sallie and I had vowed to maintain a platonic friendship, but in fact, we'd seen each other only a couple of times since we broke up and had spoken briefly on the phone maybe three or four other times.

"You're a prince, Bruneau," Angie said. "Thanks for understanding. I figured it would be alright, but I didn't want to take you by surprise."

"Not a problem, but thanks for the heads up," I said. "Now, if I may switch to a more pressing topic, what, may I ask, will we be feasting on?"

"You know I can't tell you that, silly. That would spoil the surprise."

The kids have outgrown the convention, but for years, these dinners would begin with me having to name the evening's featured dish simply by smelling the aromas escaping from Angie's kitchen. I was successful often enough that they were convinced I had a superpower.

"Ah, yes, the element of surprise," I said. "Whatever it is, I know it will be sublime."

While Angie and I were discussing Sallie, Henry had gotten up as if to leave me in privacy, but I motioned for him to stay. After I hung up, he asked if everything was okay, which I assured him it was. He heard me say as much to Angie, which made me wonder if my body language had betrayed other feelings. To change the topic, I started to ask him about his musical training, but the phone rang again. It was Chris Keating.

"Any luck?" I asked.

"Maybe," Chris said. "My friend Melissa in media services tells me there's a guy named Izzy Weisman who collects New Orleans music memorabilia. She knows he has some old phonographs, but whether he has one that could play your cylinder, she couldn't say."

"Okay, great, thanks. Did she say anything else about this guy?"

"Just that he's eccentric, but a mensch. Older fellow. Lives in Tremé, a couple blocks off Esplanade. I've got his number for you."

A few minutes later, Izzy Weisman picked up on the second ring, his voice high-pitched and nasal. After I explained what I was looking for he said he'd have to see the cylinder for himself to know for sure if he could play it for us, but he confirmed in a friendly voice that he had a few cylinder phonographs and was optimistic he could find a match. When I inquired as to a good time to visit, he said, "How about now?"

"Want to join me on an adventure?" I asked Henry after I hung up.

"Sure, boss, sounds like fun."

Henry offered to drive, but I hadn't taken Liesel out for a while and figured she could use the exercise. Liesel is my 1979 red Peugeot 604 Turbodiesel. Bo has great fun at Liesel's expense, calling her my frog-box, but she suits my needs just fine. I could tell Henry was a little uncomfortable, looking around for his seatbelt as I engaged the clutch and lurched forward for dramatic effect.

Izzy Weisman lived in a dilapidated Creole cottage on Marais Street, about halfway between Esplanade and the Tremé Community Center at the back end of Louis Armstrong Park. As we approached his house on foot, faded pink paint hung in strips from the façade, and broken slats dangled from the green pastel floor-length shutters.

"You sure this is the right place, boss?" Henry asked, failing to suppress an amused grin.

"I don't know, Henry, why don't you find out?" I smiled back, motioning for him to go first as we reached the steps to the small stoop on the left side of the building.

Henry demurred. "After you, boss."

A faint voice uttered "be right there" when I knocked, but it took at least a minute before we heard footsteps shuffling our way. When the door finally opened, a gust of trapped, foul-smelling air engulfed us like a squall blowing in off the gulf. A slight, elderly man with hunched shoulders peeked out at us. He wore thick glasses strapped to his bald head, and his red-rimmed, bloodshot eyes were wet with a filmy discharge. Black suspenders held up his gray flannel pants, and a half dozen pens and pencils were stuffed into the pocket of his stained white shirt.

"Mr. Abellard? Sorry, I was on a ladder in my library," Izzy Weisman said by way of introduction. I pegged him at eighty-five, but he could have been older. "I don't move as quickly as I used to. Please, won't you come in?"

As Henry and I introduced ourselves and stepped inside the dimly lit front room, there was a lot to take in. Every inch of space was packed with furniture, stacks of papers and pamphlets, and all manner of offbeat curios. Two Siamese cats perched atop a moth-eaten Victorian settee, one clawing intently at the felt upholstery, the other curled in a corner, eyeing us warily. We advanced slowly toward a light at the back of the house, aware of two or more other cats moving in the shadows. There seemed to be no ventilation at all, as the rancid odors of old kitty litter, moldy food, and what might have been a decomposing animal tickled my gag reflex. Henry held a handkerchief to his nose.

"Pardon my mess," Izzy said with a wave of his arms. "I meant to straighten up for you, but I got distracted."

As we inched toward the back room, I could see that it was lined with floor-length bookshelves containing thousands of records. Not just LPs, but 45s, 78s, and reel-to-reel tapes. In the center of the room, there was a large rolltop desk flanked by card tables on either side, on which sat still more records, papers, and books.

"This is some collection you have here," I said. "What inspired you to get started?"

"No one specific thing," Izzy said, shrugging. "There was never any grand design. One thing just kind of led to another."

"There's got to be more to it than that," I said.

"Yeah, I guess. You want the whole sordid tale?"

"Sure."

"Okay, you asked for it," he said, apologetically. "I'll need to start at the beginning."

I was more interested in finding clean air to breathe than Izzy's autobiography, but now that I'd backed us into this corner, there was no easy way out. I could feel Henry's disapproving eyes boring into me.

"I grew up in Brooklyn, in Crown Heights. My family and pretty much everyone we knew were Orthodox Jews, which, as you might imagine, didn't make for a particularly permissive environment to grow up in, especially for a boy with oats to sow. I was my parents' problem child, always after the forbidden fruit. Used to skip school to smoke cigarettes out on Coney Island. Took the train into the city and hung out with the beatniks in Washington Square. I couldn't wait to get away. Signed up for the army as soon as I was old enough and did a tour in Korea as a radio operator. We froze our asses off over there, and when I got back, I just wanted to live somewhere warm. A guy I knew in Korea, I think he was from Mississippi, but he was always talking up New Orleans, so I thought I'd give it a try.

"Soon as I got off the Greyhound, I knew I was going to like it here, despite the shock of Jim Crow, which was appalling. Music was everywhere in those days, and not just jazz. R&B, Doo-Wop, Gospel, you name it. I loved it all. I got in the habit of grabbing flyers off telephone poles and the sides of buildings and just kind of filing them away, and then later, when I had some money, I started buying records and instruments, vintage posters, the whole ball of wax. I didn't think of it as building a collection. It just kind of became that over time."

"How did you support yourself?" I asked.

"Never really had a job in the conventional sense, like with an office or a boss," Izzy said. "I had my pension from the army to start out with and did pretty well with the ponies in those days, out at Jefferson Downs and the Fairgrounds. And then, as I got to know a lot of musicians, some of them would pay me to promote their shows. For quite a few years, I had a pretty good business going. A couple of part-time employees, more clients than we could handle."

"Sounds like you've had a full and adventurous life, Izzy," I said.

"Yeah, I guess you could say that."

"How much do you think your collection is worth?"

"I have no idea, but I did have someone offer me a few hundred thousand a while back."

"I bet it's worth more than that," I said.

"Maybe, but I have no interest in selling. When I die, it's all going to the Tulane library."

While Izzy was talking, I noticed a narrow spiral staircase in the far-right corner of the room. As is the case with many Creole cottages today, a half-second story not visible from the street had been added at some point. Izzy saw my gaze and led us in the direction of the stairs.

"Come on, my phonograph collection is upstairs," he said, motioning for Henry and me to lead the way.

Ascending into what Izzy called his gallery, a spacious cathedral chamber with high vaulted ceilings, our senses were once again overwhelmed. A battalion of cockroaches ran for cover, a blizzard of dust swirled in the shafts of light pouring in from two skylights, and a chirping sparrow fluttered overhead, startling us. Blinking to adjust our sight, we saw that every inch of wall space was taken up by vintage posters, flyers, and album covers. It was immediately apparent that the room contained an assortment of instruments, sound gear, and other objects, but what seized our attention right away was a stunning stained-glass window that covered most of the gable wall at the far end of the room. Studying it, the figure in the large oval center pane was instantly recognizable as Louis Armstrong, cheeks inflated as he blows into his trumpet. Square and rectangular panes featuring all manner of musical performers emanated outward in all directions. I could make out Fats Domino and Professor Longhair at their keys, Snooks Eaglin resting his guitar on his knee, a young, pompadoured Ernie K-Doe, the Meters, Irma Thomas, James Booker with his eye patch, a trombone player I guessed was Kid Ory. There were others who could have been anybody to me but would doubtless be recognizable to the cognoscenti of local music history.

"That is quite a window," I said. "It is absolutely gorgeous, and quite distinctive."

"Yes, it is, isn't it?" Izzy replied. "I had it commissioned back when I had a little bit of money."

"The sacred icons of New Orleans music?" I ventured.

"Or the profane, depending on your point of view."

"I can identify some of the musicians, but not all," I said.

"Who's that?" I asked, pointing to a figure with a cornet.

"Looks like Freddie Keppard," Henry piped up.

"Very good," Izzy said, "not many people get him right. Do you know who this is?"

He pointed to a broad-shouldered Black man holding another cornet.

"Got to be Buddy Bolden," Henry said.

"That's right, the one who started it all," Izzy said. "You a music history buff?"

"No, not really, but I play the trombone, and I've been around the music all my life. You hear older players talking and you take it in, you know? That's how the tradition gets handed down."

"You're a fountain of musical knowledge, Henry," I said. "How did I not know this about you?"

"We mostly talk about furniture," Henry said. I wasn't sure whether to take that as a statement of fact, which it was, or a subtle jab. I decided this wasn't the time to find out.

"Who are some of these others, Izzy?" I asked, turning our attention back toward our host.

Izzy identified King Oliver, Frogman Henry, Bunk Johnson, and a few others, when Henry interrupted him.

"Who is this?" he asked, pointing to one of the larger panes that featured a tall brunette vocalist in a sultry gown.

"Ah, that's Lyla," Izzy said. "Lyla Saint-Clair, or Lady Ly as she was known. One of my favorites."

"I've never heard of her," Henry said.

"She was a rising star in the sixties. Died too young, I'm afraid."

Izzy looked like he was about to choke up, but he changed the subject by asking to see our cylinder, which I handed to him.

"Hmm, a Blue Amberol," he mused, regarding the object with interest. "Edison switched to these around 1912, I think. They're made of celluloid. It's a lot more durable than wax, which is what the early models were made of. You could get more playings out of these, a few thousand supposedly. They provided Edison with a competitive edge for a while, but eventually the disc format won out. By 1930, cylinders were phased out altogether."

"Any idea what this writing means?" I asked, pointing to the etching on the rim.

"Nope, no clue," Izzy said, flipping the cylinder over. "Says here this is number 5423, which puts it near the end of production, probably mid to late 1920s. I think they stopped at 5700 and something."

"Do you have a machine that will play this?" I asked, trying not to seem impatient. I desperately needed to get outside and take in some fresh air, and looking at Henry, I was pretty sure he was thinking the same thing.

"Indeed, I do," Izzy said. "Follow me."

Henry and I trailed Izzy cautiously as he wriggled his way between bass guitars, a box of accordions and blues harps, some old amps, a drum kit, and what may have been a first-generation Moog synthesizer. Finally, we arrived at a phonograph sitting atop a wooden stool, which Izzy unveiled by pulling off a plastic tarp.

"Behold, the Edison Amberola Model 50," he announced proudly. "Notice there's no external horn. The internal horn was a Victor innovation, which Edison incorporated into the Amberola series. The 50 was introduced in 1915 and featured the first double spring direct drive motor, which enabled you to play up to five four-minute recordings on one wind. It was cutting-edge in its time."

As Izzy set about sliding the cylinder into place and priming the hand crank, Henry asked how the stylus worked.

"Same as on a turntable," Izzy said. "Edison even used a diamond, so folks didn't have to keep replacing needles. There, that should do it. Are you ready?"

We nodded, and Izzy gently dropped the stylus into place.

At first, all we could hear was the scratchy static we expected and the muffled noises of what may have been someone moving about or fumbling with an object of some kind. What came next is difficult to describe. There was the muted tooting of what sounded like a trumpet, as if someone was either testing a new instrument or prepping their chops. Then silence, a deep breath, and finally a startling explosion of blaring sound, brassy and screeching. One long, extended note bending up and down before winding sinuously forward. It sounded like the fierce, desperate yowling of an alley cat locked in mortal combat; distorted and cacophonous, but also urgent, plaintive. At first, that's all there was. One note stretched over what during a subsequent playing we timed at twenty-three seconds. Then came something recognizable as a tune, which Henry later told me was "Don't Go Away Nobody," an early standard. But only for a short while before the player severed the melody with an abrupt, piercing note, discordant and abrasive, and then bridged to another long caterwauling length of sound, loud and angry and melancholy all at the same time. Finally, there was a muffled movement and a thud.

After a few seconds, we could make out a distant voice asking, "Is that it, Charles?" A door opens and closes, followed by more shuffling, and, closer now, "Sure you don't want to try some more?" Then silence.

Chapter Three

I t had been a long time since I'd seen Angie so on edge. After talking it over with the kids and me, she had decided to invite Sallie Maguire to our monthly dinner with my childhood buddy, Bruneau Abellard, or "Bru" as I like to call him. I wasn't sure this was a great idea. Bru and Sallie lived together for almost two years, but they broke up a few months back and have had little contact since. Angie's argument was that the kids had grown close to Sallie, and it wasn't fair to them to cut her out of their lives. A fair point, except that we could have simply had Sallie over by herself. My fear, if I'm being honest, was that Angie is so fond of both Bru and Sallie that she may not have been able to see that there are differences between them that may prevent a long-term relationship from ever working. And if Bru thought Angie was trying to play matchmaker, he wasn't going to take it well.

Bru and I grew up as next-door neighbors in Hammond, where our dads both worked for the railroad. He's white and I'm Black, but that was never really an issue for us. We always got along, even if we were very different kids. I was an athlete, and Bru was your basic nerd, so we ran with different crowds at school, but we hung out a lot at home. I'd needle him about this or that, and he always had a sarcastic comeback to crack me up. He still makes me laugh like no one else, even when he doesn't mean to, or maybe especially when he doesn't mean to. Looking back, I can see that we developed our mutual trust early on. Bru had some social anxieties that I helped him through, and I'm not sure I would have made it to Grambling, and NOPD after that, if he hadn't been around to guide me through my schoolwork. We know things about each other that no one else does, except maybe Angie. And if I know one thing about Bru, it's that he does not like to be manipulated.

"Where should we sit them, Bo?" Angie asked as we set the table.

"I don't know. Does it matter all that much? Let's not overthink this, okay?"

"I'm not overthinking anything, just asking a question. Excuse me…"

When Angie is nervous, she gets prickly. After almost twenty years of marriage, I know the signs.

"Come on, you two," came a gently scolding voice from the kitchen. It was Sophie, our middle child, a high school sophomore now, and our star student. Sophie stepped around the island that separates the kitchen from our dining alcove and addressed us calmly.

"It's not that difficult. Mom, you sit at one end, next to Uncle Bru. Dad, you sit at the other end, with Sallie next to you, but on the other side of the table from Uncle Bru. That way, they won't be next to each other, but they can see one another. We'll fill the spaces in between."

"Who gave you the wisdom pill?" Angie asked, hands on her hips.

Sophie shrugged, and Angie and I smiled at each other. Then it was back to boss mama mode.

"They should be here any minute. Bo, how about putting on some music and then seeing if you can get Monique's nose out of her phone, will you? If Bruneau gets here first, we'll put him on drink duty, but if Sallie arrives ahead of him, it would be great if the girls could take her into the living room and start updating her on their lives. Whichever one shows up last, let's not make a big production out of it, okay? Just keep it as natural as possible. We don't want anyone feeling self-conscious."

"Right," I said, careful not to sound sarcastic.

Bru tends to like his jazz on the quiet side, so I teed up some Bill Evans. Then I went to get Monique, our youngest, thirteen going on twenty-five.

Her door was closed, as is often the case these days. I knocked and got no response, even though I could hear a thumping sound inside. I knocked again and poked my head in. Monique was sitting in her bean bag chair, earbuds in, drumming on her thighs with her hands.

"Wow, Dad, anyone ever teach you to knock before entering?"

"I did knock," I said. Monique looked at me blankly. I motioned for her to take her earbuds out.

"I did knock. If you couldn't hear that, you've got the volume turned up way too high. You're going to lose your hearing by the time you're thirty."

"Did you want something?"

"Yes. Your mother would like you and Sophie to greet Sallie when she gets here, which should be any minute now."

"Sure, whatever, as soon as this song is over."

"Make it quick, please."

I'm told the phase Monique is going through is normal for girls her age, but it's new territory for Angie and me. Sophie was too busy with her books to get caught up in gossip games, and Little Bo's a boy, so that was a different set of issues.

As it turned out, Angie needn't have worried about who was going to show up when. Bru and Sallie arrived together in Bru's rickety Peugeot, surprising us all. Even Monique was intrigued by this turn of events.

"Dude, what's the deal? Are they back together, or what?" she asked, peeking through the window as they got out of the car.

"Hush," Angie said. Then she opened the door and headed out to greet our guests. The girls and I followed, acting as though seeing Bru and Sallie together was the most natural thing in the world.

Bru is built like a miniature sumo wrestler, with short arms and bowed legs, a barreled chest, and a protruding gut. When he's in reasonable shape, he moves almost athletically, like an offensive guard. But when he lets himself go, as he has lately, he reminds me of a penguin, gravity tilting him from side to side as he shuffles along. For a while there, Sallie helped Bru slim down, and I could tell he was self-conscious about having put some weight back on. He wore a black short-sleeved Oxford, hanging out over gray slacks, and he was trying hard to pull his stomach in. Sallie, slim and trim, had on a simple cream-colored peasant blouse and capri-style jeans. The natural look suited her.

"Welcome, you two," Angie sang out, opening her arms and running up to embrace first Sallie, then Bru.

"What a wonderful welcoming committee," Sallie gushed as more hugs were exchanged all around.

Bru slapped his forehead, turned around, and walked back to his car. He pulled out two shopping bags. One, I knew, held whatever candy he'd picked up for the kids. The other no doubt contained the ingredients for the cocktail he'd decided to feature. Whenever we have Bru over for these dinners, he takes charge of the beverages.

"What'd you get us this time, Uncle Bru?" Monique wanted to know.

"Get for you? Who says I got anything for you, young lady?" Bru shot back, knowing full well that he had long ago trained the kids to expect a tasty gift of some kind. Monique just cocked her head to indicate she knew better, while Sophie waited patiently.

"Where's your brother?" Bru asked.

"Football practice," I said. "He should be home soon."

"Right, I forgot he's driving now. God, it doesn't seem possible. Here, girls, make sure to leave some for Bo."

Monique rifled through the bag Bru handed her and emerged with a box of mixed fruit jelly slices from Laura's Candies, down in the Quarter.

"Mmm, I love those things," Sophie said.

"There's a box of Mississippi Mud, too," Monique told us, eyes wide. That's the bark with chocolate and caramel-covered pecans the shop is famous for.

"Wait till after dinner, please," Angie said.

When we went inside, the girls made Bru guess what was cooking, a stale old game they used to play with him. For old times' sake, I guess, or because they were nervous and falling back on habit.

"Hmm, it's definitely meat of some kind," Bru guessed, sniffing at the air. "And there's a rich sauce or gravy too. Grillades, maybe?"

"You got it!" Angie said. "Grillades of beef, served over grits. Well done, now go make us some drinks."

"Yes, ma'am, coming right up."

The girls led the rest of us into the living room and proceeded to pepper

Sallie with questions. What has she been up to? How's work? Has she been to any puzzling competitions lately? Everything except what they really wanted to know, which was whether her arriving with Bru meant they were getting back together.

Sallie answered as gamely as she could and then managed to turn the focus back onto the girls, asking for updates on Sophie's driver's permit and the latest additions to Monique's playlists. Then, just as Bru entered the room with a tray of mint juleps, my son pulled up in the driveway. He had a big smile on his face as he came through the door.

"Hi, everyone," he said cheerfully.

"What's gotten into you, Bo?" Angie asked. "That's the friendliest greeting we've gotten since…oh, I don't know, sixth grade?"

"Yeah, I guess I've been a little tense lately. Sorry. Anyway, I've got some news. The guys voted me captain."

Bo beamed as we showered him with congratulations. He's not a Division One caliber athlete by any means, but he's worked hard to become an above-average high school defensive back, and it felt great to see him earn the recognition of his peers.

"This means you've got to handle the coin toss now, right?" Bru asked.

"Yeah, I guess so. Got any tips?"

I answered "heads," and at the same time, Bru blurted "tails." Then we laughed and slapped high fives. We used to play a best-of-twenty-five coin toss game as kids; Bru was always tails, and I was always heads. Even though I'm sure it all evened out in the end, I used to be amazed by how much one or the other of us would sometimes win by. When we got to high school, Bru tried to work it all out with probability equations. I was content to let the coins fall where they may.

When we'd finished reminiscing and were seated for dinner, Bru told us about a recording cylinder he'd found. None of us knew what that was, so he had to explain that folks recorded on them in the old days, before LPs or tape recorders. He showed us a picture, and Little Bo commented that it looked like a cypher, which got a chuckle from Sallie, who decodes cyphers for kicks.

"Wait, where exactly did you find this thing?" Monique asked.

"It was in a sideboard that we brought into the store."

"In a secret compartment?"

"Yes."

"So…*where* was the compartment, exactly? I'm not following this."

"It was in a drawer that had a false back," Bru said. "It was common in those days to build hidden compartments into desks and dressers and such. Not everyone used a bank, or had easy access to one at any rate, so this was how they'd secure their cash or valuables. We come across these things pretty frequently, though usually they're empty."

"So, somebody thought this cylinder thing was valuable?" Little Bo asked.

"Maybe."

Bru told us how he and his helper, Henry, brought the cylinder to a collector of music memorabilia named Izzy Weisman. He had an early phonograph they could play the cylinder on. Apparently, they were in for quite a surprise.

"What was on it?" Little Bo wanted to know.

"It's hard to describe," Bru said. "It's just one musician playing what I initially thought was a trumpet, but Izzy and Henry said it was a cornet. Some of it isn't recognizable as music, or certainly not music you would have heard in the early 1900s."

"Meaning it's more modern sounding?" Sallie asked.

"I guess you could say that, yes. Kind of like Ornette Coleman at his most outrageous, though maybe not as intentional. He starts out just blowing one long screaming note, then there's a brief melody, and then more dissonant blowing. It's kind of harsh the first time you hear it. You want to listen to it?"

Bru explained that he'd left the cylinder with Weisman, who was going to do some research on it, but that he'd recorded it on his phone.

"It's a crude recording of what was already a crude recording, so the sound quality is pretty terrible, but you can get the idea, at least."

The recording quality was even worse than Bru had said, and to me, the cornet sounded like Mrs. Nesbit's fingernails scraping the blackboard in our fourth-grade math class.

"God, it sounds like an exorcism," Angie said.

"Or an animal dying," Monique added.

"I don't know," Sophie said, "I hear what you're saying, but there's something sadly beautiful about it, don't you think?"

"I agree with you, Sophie," Sallie said. "There's an inner struggle to it, like something is fracturing, coming apart, but the musician is trying like hell to hold it together. There's nobility in the struggle. Beauty even."

Bru smiled admiringly at Sallie.

"That's what Izzy Weisman said, but nowhere as poetic as that, Sallie. He said that if the recording was really made in the early 1900s, it could be historically significant. He said he could hear ideas in the music that didn't surface until the 1950s and 60s."

"Does that mean he thinks it was recorded more recently?" I asked.

"He thinks that is a possibility, yes. He said there are plenty of blank cylinders around, and someone could have recorded this last week if they had the right phonograph. That's what he was going to research. He knows someone who he thought could help him figure out when the recording was made."

"What about Henry?" Angie asked. "He's a musician. What does he think?"

"He agrees with Izzy's theory. He thinks it's probably a modern horn player, recorded sometime in the last sixty or seventy years, not in the early 1900s. But not just any player; one with really strong chops. Henry says not many horn players can play that loud for that long without coming up for air."

There was a pause as we all considered the mystery Bru had stumbled upon. Sallie asked Bru to text her the photo of the cylinder. Then Sophie piped up again.

"What do we make of the sound of a door opening and closing and the voice asking Charles if he's done?"

"That the musician's name is Charles, duh," Monique said. What a wise ass my little girl was turning into. Sophie gave her sister the evil eye.

"It's a good question, Soph, and the answer is we're not sure," Bru said.

Bru and Sophie have a special bond. It's normal for him to come to her defense.

"On the one hand, it doesn't sound like they're in a recording studio, but if it's a home recording, it's kind of weird that this person seems to be coming from a different room. The phonograph would have been right next to the musician."

My phone was vibrating nonstop in my pocket, so I left the others to their conversation and stepped into the hallway that leads to our bedrooms to see what could be so urgent. It was Mike Rodiger, my promising young partner in Property Crimes.

"Hi Mike. What's up?"

"Sorry to bother you, Detective, but there's been a fire and the captain wants us on the scene."

"A fire? Shouldn't that be Simpkins?"

"Normally, yes, but he's taking some PTO, apparently," Rodiger said. "Plus, there are some circumstances involved that the captain wants us to have a look at."

After Rodiger filled me in on the details, I made my way back to the dinner table and apologized for having to leave the gathering.

Angie threw her napkin down.

"Really, Bo, on a Friday night? Can't someone else handle this?"

"I'm afraid not," I said. "There's been a fire down in Tremé. They think it's arson, and robbery may have been the motive."

"Where in Tremé?" Bru asked.

"Down near the community center. There's a body, apparently."

Chapter Four

My mind was racing as Bo turned his unmarked Dodge Charger onto Airline Highway, heading toward downtown. When Bo told us the fire he'd been called to investigate was near the Tremé Community Center, and that a body was found, I immediately thought of Izzy Weisman. Bo then confirmed the address on Marais Street was the same one Henry and I had visited just a couple days earlier. When I pleaded with Bo to take me with him, he reluctantly agreed, but only on the condition that I stay behind the crime scene tape and promise to do as I was told. Back when we helped Bo crack the Lafitte case, he thought I overstepped my bounds a couple of times. Ever since, he's kept me on a short leash.

I was filled with dread at what we might find at the scene of the fire, but that's not what Bo wanted to talk about.

"You surprised us, showing up with Sallie like that. Is there something going on we should know about?"

"What, you mean like us getting back together?"

"Well, you know, inquiring minds…"

"No, nothing like that, I can assure you," I said. "Angie told me we were both invited, so I called Sallie and suggested we ride over together. Seemed like a good way to defuse any awkwardness. Plus, it's a bit of a haul out to Kenner, so no point burning extra gas. Sallie thought it was a great idea. It's not like we're not still friends, you know."

"Yeah, makes sense," Bo said. "Good for you that you can be adults about it. It sets a good example for the kids, which I appreciate."

I let Bo's compliment pass in silence, hoping that would put an end to this line of inquiry.

"You miss her?" he asked.

I sighed loudly, for effect.

"Not at the moment, seeing as I just left her after having been in her company for the last few hours."

"You know what I mean."

"Yeah, sure, sometimes I miss her. And sometimes I don't."

"Fair enough, Bru," Bo said. "It's just that Angie and I can't help thinking the two of you are better together than apart."

"Don't you think we should be the judge of that?"

"Yeah, maybe. I guess so, when you put it like that."

Another silence as we crossed Carrolton, and the road turned into Tulane Avenue.

"Talk to Prosper lately?" Bo asked.

"As a matter of fact, I have," I said.

"How's he doing?"

"Fine, so far as I can tell. Why do you ask?"

"Just curious. I took him out for a beer last week. Seems like he's aged since the last time I saw him."

"He's not a young man."

"He thinks you don't seem well."

"So he told me. You two in cahoots?"

"What do you mean?

"I'm just wondering who organized pick on Bruneau week."

Bo laughed. "I don't know what you're talking about."

"No, of course you don't. Mind if we change the subject?"

"Sure. What's on your mind?"

"Izzy Weisman. Why would someone want to burn his house down? With him in it, no less?"

"Whoa, slow down there, big fella," Bo said. "We don't know anything about this fire. Just because somebody says they suspect arson doesn't mean that's what it is. And we certainly don't know that the body belongs to your man Izzy. How about we get a handle on the facts before we start speculating about the Ws?"

"The Ws?"

"Who, what, when, where, why."

"Right, got it. I take your point, but there must be a reason they think it's arson, right? And if it's not Izzy, then who else would it be?"

"I have no idea," Bo said. "That's why we've got to wait on the facts."

"His collections were worth a lot of money," I said. "He told us he'd been offered a few hundred thousand recently, but he said he was going to donate everything to Tulane when he died."

"Bru, the facts! Please! Can we just get the facts straight before we start dealing in conspiracy theories?"

I folded my arms across my chest and leaned back in silence as we turned left on South Broad and then hung a right on Ursulines Avenue, which led to Marais Street. There were no flames visible as Izzy's house came into view, just the flashing lights of fire engines, cop cars, and an ambulance, and the thick, sulfuric smell of smoldering timber doused in firefighting foam. After we parked and began walking toward the scene, we could see that the second story had collapsed, and the back of the house where Izzy kept his music was destroyed, but the frame at the front of the structure was mostly intact. The response team had erected floodlights around the perimeter of the house, which provided good visibility into the scene itself, but had the effect of darkening the surrounding neighborhood. Bo slipped under the police tape and went to join the other investigators, but not before warning me again to stay put.

I took in the scene. A couple dozen onlookers watched from behind the tape, exchanging gossip and taking pictures with their phones. A large woman stood off by herself, holding a toddler to her ample bosom. A TV crew was trying in vain to get one of the investigators on camera. And I caught a fleeting glimpse of a hunched, hooded figure in a raincoat shuffling away from the commotion, before fading into the darkness. There was something familiar in the gait, but I couldn't place it.

I approached a man standing close to the tape and struck up a conversation.

He said he was a neighbor and pointed to the house he lived in two doors down from Izzy's. He told me the crowd had been bigger a couple hours earlier, but that most folks went home when the excitement died down. When I asked him about Izzy, he responded that he only knew him to say hello to. He said he seemed like a nice old man, but mostly he kept to himself and came and went at odd hours.

Looking around to see if there was anyone I knew, I spotted Mike Rodiger, Bo's young partner. He was hanging back from the rest of the investigative team, writing something on a clipboard. I got as close as I could before addressing him.

"Hey, Mike!"

He turned around but did not immediately see me.

"Over here," I said.

"Oh, hi, Mr. Abellard, what are you doing here?" he asked, once he recognized me. Then he walked over to shake my hand.

"It's Bruneau, please."

"Of course, sorry. Bruneau."

I got to know Mike during the Lafitte investigation. He's a smart young man, detailed and thorough in his approach to the job, and a bit more cerebral than Bo, who tends to follow his instincts. The two of them complement each other nicely, I think. The proverbial head and heart.

Whenever I see Mike, which isn't often, I ask him for updates on the global manhunt for Mahdi Toledano, the arch thief we had pursued but ultimately failed to apprehend, who remains beyond the reach of law enforcement. I can't ask Bo about it, because he holds me responsible for looking the other way as Toledano made his escape from New Orleans. It's a long, complicated story, but for Bo, the wounds still fester.

"I tagged along with Bo because I know, or *knew,* I guess I should say, the owner of the house," I told Mike. "Not well. But I visited him here a few days ago."

Mike looked momentarily surprised but quickly recovered his poise.

"In that case, I should probably interview you as a background witness," he said. "Do you mind?"

"No, not at all."

Mike held up the police tape for me to duck under. Once on the other side, I looked around for Bo, who was huddled with a small group of cops and firefighters about ten yards away. He looked right at me, frowning, so I pointed at Mike, opening my arms and shrugging in an exaggerated gesture of helplessness. I told Mike the story of the cylinder and everything I knew about Izzy Weisman and the visit Henry and I paid him.

"Was there anything unusual you noticed that might shed some light on what happened here?" Mike asked.

"I mean, the whole place was unusual, and Izzy was an unusual guy," I said, "but no, not in the way you mean. Like I told you, his collections were worth a lot of money, but that's a motive for robbery, not arson or murder, right?"

"Too early to say," Mike said.

"Have you confirmed that the body is, in fact, Izzy's?" I asked.

"No, not yet," Mike said. "It's a small male; that's about all we know at this point. The remains are charred and fragmented, so we'll have to wait on the lab for identification and cause of death."

"Of course," I said. "Izzy was a small man, so that fits."

Mike smiled grimly, thanked me for my time and held the tape up for me to cross back over the police line. I stood in place.

"One more thing, Mike," I said. "Why is Property Crimes here?"

"A house is property," Mike shrugged. "We always get involved when arson is suspected."

"Got it. No robbery, then?"

"We're still assessing that. It's possible something may have been taken."

"But you don't know what?"

"No, we don't know what. There was a small safe in the main bedroom. The door was left open, and it was empty."

"The door was open because someone left it open or because the heat of the fire caused it to pop open?"

"Like I said, there's a lot we don't know yet."

As Mike again pulled the tape up for me to climb under, a hand clamped firmly on my shoulder, pulling me back. It was Bo, wearing a stern expression.

"I thought I told you to stay out of the way."

"Apologies, Detective," Mike said. "It's my fault. I thought I should ask Mr. Abellard a few questions, seeing as he knows the owner and had visited him recently."

"I understand, Mike," Bo said, breaking into a smile. "Just busting my friend's chops a bit, if you don't mind."

"No, of course not, Detective."

"He give you anything useful?"

"Too early to say. Maybe. Some helpful background at the least."

As Bo and I walked back to his car, one of Izzy's Siamese cats crossed in front of us. It arched its back and mewed loudly, and when we tried to move past it, it followed us, alternately falling back and scooting ahead. It rubbed against my leg as I lowered myself into Bo's passenger seat and then jumped onto my lap. Not knowing what else to do, I stroked the animal and closed the door.

"You're kidding, right?" Bo said as he settled in behind the wheel. "Last time you spent time with a cat, it didn't turn out so good."

Bo was referencing my encounter with Caliban, a large feral cat who co-existed with Prosper on Grand Isle. The beast attacked Hugo and me when we visited Prosper, hoping to learn more about Jean Lafitte. The incident left scars, both physical and emotional.

"Very funny," I said. "Looks like it's a female. Maybe you'd like to take her? The kids could use a pet, don't you think?"

"Not a chance," Bo said. "Sophie's got allergies, and cats give me the creeps. Always stalking around."

"Suit yourself," I said. "So, tell me, what did you learn at the scene?"

"Not all that much, really. The hose jockeys won't let us walk around in the house until all the embers are out and they declare the structure safe."

"Hose jockeys?"

"Sorry. Firefighters."

"Hmm, I wonder what they call you."

Bo smiled.

"I don't know. Nothing good, I'm sure."

I turned the conversation back to the fire.

"You must have learned a few things, right?"

"Yeah, but just basic stuff," Bo said. "The fire was started on the second floor, but there were also traces of accelerant found down below, probably gasoline. The body was found up against the outside wall in the spare bedroom on the left side of the house. We're going to have to wait on the Crime Lab for more details and a reconstruction."

"Mike said there was a safe that was open."

"Yep, that's the main reason we were called in. That and our arson guy being out of town for the weekend. Any idea what Weisman might have kept in there?"

"No, none."

* * *

When Bo and I got back to his place in Kenner, it was late, and only Angie was still awake, enjoying a nightcap on the living room couch after having cleaned up for the evening. She'd kicked off her shoes and was filing her nails.

"Where's Sallie?" I asked.

"Little Bo took her home a couple hours ago," Angie said. "I think he enjoyed chauffeuring a pretty lady around. Good practice for the prom."

"Tell him thank you for me. Sallie wasn't upset, was she?"

"No, not in the least. She said to tell you she understood why you felt the need to tag along with Bo, and not to worry about it."

"Well, that's a relief," I said. "Mind if I join you two for a nightcap before shoving off?"

"Not at all, baby, make yourself at home," Angie said.

"Bo?"

"I'll have whatever you're having," Bo said, squeezing in tight next to Angie.

I poured Bo and myself two fingers each of his Maker's Mark and took a seat in the armchair across from them. Bo and I relayed the details of our visit to the fire scene, and then Angie changed the subject.

"It was nice of you to offer Sallie a ride, Bruneau. I know she appreciated it."

"Seemed like the appropriate thing to do."

"Is that all it was? Appropriate?"

"Oh boy, here we go," I said. "Bo has already interrogated me, Angie. There's nothing going on, okay? Can we leave it at that?"

"Sure, baby, whatever you say."

I thought I detected a note of skepticism in Angie's tone, but I wasn't sure.

"Did Sallie say anything different?"

"Nope. She's like you. Doesn't want to talk about it."

Chapter Five

I'm not in the habit of starting my day with a text exchange from bed, especially not when I have a hangover, which I did, but Sallie's message jarred me awake and grabbed my full attention. Hugo heard me stirring and rose from his slumber to paw at me, but I shushed him away and called Sallie.

"You're kidding, right?" I said when she picked up after the first ring.

"Me? Kidding? I'm not the kidding type, remember? You always tell me I have no sense of humor, Bruneau, and now I'm a jokester?"

Sallie's tone was playful, but we both knew there was a barely concealed edge to her barb. I figured she'd earned the indulgence.

"Good morning to you, too," I said, with as much grumpiness as I could muster.

"Let me get this straight: are you saying Charles Bolden as in Charles 'Buddy' Bolden? That's Buddy Bolden on the cylinder?"

"I'm not saying anything," Sallie said. "I'm just telling you what the inscription might stand for."

"Okay, sure. Mind telling me how you arrived at this little epiphany?"

"I began with the premise that the first two letters were someone's initials, and the numbers represented a date, either July 29th or more likely July 1929. Then I went to Tulane's Music Rising website and looked for trumpet or cornet players with the initials C.B., especially those who would have been active in the late 20s. I was hoping I'd find one named Clarence, since that was the name written on the outside of the box the cylinder was in, but no dice. The only Clarence was Gatemouth Brown. He played about twenty instruments, but not any brass, plus he would've been five years old in 1929. The only C.B. who seemed plausible was Charles 'Buddy' Bolden."

"But he was much earlier than that, wasn't he?" I objected. "It's been a while since I read that book about him, but I thought Bolden was at the peak of his popularity around the turn of the century, and then he disappeared from view."

"That's because he went crazy and was institutionalized at Jackson State," Sallie said. "He spent the last twenty-five years of his life there. He died in 1931."

"Yes, I know. Your theory is that somebody recorded him at the nuthouse two years before his death?"

Sallie sighed, or groaned maybe, and there was a rustling noise, as if she was rolling over in bed. It felt like an intimate moment, even though she was clear across town, and we couldn't see each other. I wondered if she felt the same way.

"You're the theory guy, remember?" she said. "Little ole me, I just solve puzzles."

"Right. Well, you're damn good at it, I'll say that much."

Sallie let out a quiet purr of satisfaction but didn't say anything. The silence felt incredibly awkward and oddly comfortable at the same time.

"How about you come over for lunch, and we can try teasing this thing out?"

My proposition was met with more silence. I was about to apologize for my overreach, when Sallie spoke.

"That's nice of you, Bruneau, but why don't you come over here instead?

I've got some fruit and cold cuts in the fridge that are going to go bad if I don't use them."

This was unexpected. I paused before answering.

"Okay, sure. Is there anything I can bring?"

"A bottle of wine, maybe, and a baguette."

* * *

My talk with Sallie gave me plenty to think about as I went about my morning routine. I tried not to read too much into her invitation, but I couldn't seem to help myself. One minute I was convinced that Sallie had extended an olive branch, perhaps even one that hinted at possibilities. And the next I'd decide that, no, that wasn't right, the invitation was a purely defensive gesture. Sallie's way of ensuring that our encounter took place on her ground, under her terms. Whatever it was, I'd find out soon enough, and in the meantime, there were practical matters to address.

I texted Victoria, my assistant, to let her know I'd open and close as usual, but that she'd need to man the store on her own during the middle part of the day. I called La Boulangerie to reserve a baguette in case they sold out before I got there. And then I turned my attention to the wine. Sallie mentioned cold cuts, but she didn't say what kind, so I decided to hedge my bets, selecting a chilled Vermentino to quench our thirst and cut through any salty ham or bacon, and a tart, low-tannin Barbera to tame a fatty salami or sharp cheese. Neither was going to play well with the fruit, but that couldn't be helped.

Then there was the cat to deal with. When I decided to take Izzy's Siamese home with me, I hadn't thought through what I would feed it or where it would relieve itself. I also failed to consider what Hugo's reaction to a feline interloper might be. As far as I knew, his only experience with cats was his dust-up with Caliban, which could hardly have left a favorable impression. Hugo barked and growled when I walked in the door holding the cat, but lost interest as the animal staked out the high ground beyond his reach. Now, he glared up with a mixture of disdain and dismay as the cat sashayed across the kitchen counter in search of food, or simply to taunt her new adversary. I detected an unpleasant odor coming from behind my living room couch and was on my knees sniffing around when the doorbell rang.

It was my friend Annie Russell, who I'd called the night before in a plea for help. Annie and I go back to our college days at Loyola, where we met in a studio art class. We discovered that neither of us was destined to become the next Picasso, but also that we greatly enjoyed each other's company, and we've remained close ever since. Annie is one of those perpetually upbeat people I usually find annoying, full of energy and always on the go, but she is so authentically who she is that it has never bothered me. We're such opposites, in demeanor and temperament, that for a long time, Sallie couldn't figure out how we became such good friends in the first place. Eventually, she decided that Annie speeds me up, and I slow her down, and in that way, we are good for one another. All I know is that whenever I'm in a jam, I can pick up the phone and Annie will be there for me, and me for her.

"Here we are, your traveling pet shop, at your disposal," Annie proclaimed as I opened the door. She was dressed in a light blue sweatsuit with her curly brown hair pulled up in a bun. She carried a folding crate under one arm, a bag of kitty litter under the other, and she had dropped a litter box and a bag of cat food at her feet. I took the litter box and the food and ushered her upstairs.

"This is awfully kind of you," I said. "I acted on the spur of the moment last night without stopping to consider that I don't know the first thing about keeping a cat."

"Nothing to it," Annie said. "Cats are easy. Just keep the food and water bowls full and scoop out the litter once a day, and then every couple weeks give the box a good cleaning with soap and hot water."

"This may be more of a short-term rental," I said. "Hopefully, I can find a good home for her in the next couple days. Sure you don't want her?"

"Four cats are quite enough, thank you."

Annie spotted the creature watching us warily from the built-in seat below the kitchen bay window, where she lay curled up, soaking in the morning sun.

"Oh, she's beautiful," she said. "What's her name?"

"I have no idea."

"Well, we need to give her one, then."

Naming the cat felt like a step toward ownership. I wasn't sure I wanted to go there, but I didn't want to disappoint Annie either.

"Any suggestions?"

Annie cocked her head and held her chin pensively.

"Well, Siam is Thailand now, so how about Coconut or Pad Thai or something Thai related?"

"Hmm. Coco?"

"Sure! That works. Coco it is."

"Good. Can I interest you in a cup of coffee?"

Annie said she had a half hour to burn before her yoga class, so I poured us both a cup and we sat across from one another at the kitchen table. We hadn't seen each other for a couple weeks and spent a few minutes catching up. After telling me about a party she was planning, Annie confided that she worried her older husband, Bert Kingsley, might be showing signs of early-stage dementia, something Sallie and I had suspected for a while. She asked about the status of Sallie and me, and whether I would mind if she included Sallie on her invitation list. And then I told her about the cylinder, the fire, and Buddy Bolden. Though her tastes run more toward Dixieland and Swing than any of the later genres, Annie is a jazz enthusiast and knew all about Buddy Bolden.

"If you're right about it being Buddy Bolden, that would really be something," she said. "There aren't any known recordings, are there?"

"Nope. But there's a problem."

"What's that?"

"I left the cylinder with Izzy. It probably burned in the fire."

Annie just stared at me with a crestfallen expression, so I let her know about the recording on my phone, and she perked up and asked to hear it. As it was playing, she winced like the rest of us at the more jarring sections.

"Well, that was kind of painful," she said. "It doesn't sound like any early jazz I've ever heard. If the recording weren't so primitive, I'd say it was from the Avant-Garde or Free Jazz era. Don Cherry, maybe, the way he bends those notes."

*   *   *

This was the first time Sallie had had me over since our split, and I was anxious to make a good impression. I went back and forth on what to wear, finally settling on poplin khakis, a salmon-colored short-sleeve button-down, which I wore untucked, and leather sandals. Casual and comfortable, but not unkempt.

I ran a bit late getting there because I first had to take an Uber out to Bo and Angie's, stopping on the way at La Boulangerie to pick up the baguette I'd reserved. The night before, Angie had insisted that I was in no condition to drive, and she was probably right, so I let her call me a driver.

When I arrived to pick up Liesel, Angie was watering the flower bed in front of the house. She was barefoot and had on gym shirts and a tee-shirt, but even though she wasn't done up, she was as vivacious as ever.

"Look who the cat dragged home," she sang out. "How you feeling, baby?"

"I've felt better, thank you."

"Coffee?"

"No thanks, I have an appointment and I'm running late."

Angie turned off the water and made a show of looking me over.

"I'm impressed," she said, "you've pulled yourself together pretty nicely. Is this appointment with a lady friend?"

"Strictly professional," I said, not wanting to get into it.

Angie eyed me suspiciously but didn't force the issue.

"Where's Bo?" I asked, to change subjects as artfully as I could manage.

"Professional appointment," Angie said dryly.

I laughed, thanked her again for dinner, and headed for the Marigny, where Sallie lives.

Sallie owns a cute yellow single-barreled shotgun. We didn't spend much time there when we were a couple. Looking back, I can see that Sallie hanging on to her house meant that she hadn't completely bought into the idea of me as her life partner. I couldn't see it then, though. I just figured she had accumulated furniture and other possessions that wouldn't have fit in my place, but that she didn't want to part with. That's one of the reasons I wanted to surprise her with our house.

It is a nice place, I must admit, brightly lit and attractively appointed in a white lacy motif, but I always feel a little cramped there, as I do in the Marigny more generally. I used to call the neighborhood "The Shire" until Sallie made it clear that she didn't appreciate the implication that she lived among Hobbits.

It's hard to find parking on Sallie's Street, so I pulled into a spot a few blocks away. Beads of sweat were beginning to form on my mostly bald head by the time I reached her door, which she'd left slightly ajar. I rapped the brass knocker anyway.

"Come in, it's open," Sallie's voice sang out from the kitchen. Entering, I saw that she wore a red striped apron over a sleeveless white t-shirt and lightweight olive cargo shorts. Clearly not done up for me, but fetching, nonetheless. She was squeezing lime juice into the fruit salad she'd made.

"That looks yummy," I said.

"I hope so."

Sallie offered me her cheek, which I pecked as I handed her the baguette and placed the wines on the counter.

"No Hugo?" Sallie asked, making a pouty face. "I forgot to tell you to bring him along. I miss the little mug."

"At least you miss one of us," I said, and immediately regretted my words.

Sallie shot me a doleful glance but otherwise let my comment go.

"Actually, Hugo and I have a new housemate, at least for the time being," I said. I proceeded to tell her about Coco the cat, which, for some reason, she found hysterical.

"You left the two of them alone in the apartment?"

"Yes. Why? Was that not a good idea?"

"You know what they say about cats and dogs…"

"I can't imagine there'll be a problem," I said. "Even if Hugo wanted to pick a fight, he'd never be able to get to her. She stays well beyond his reach."

"It's not the cat I'd worry about," Sallie said, snarling and pantomiming a cat's claws.

"Okay, change of subject," I said, affecting annoyance. "Did you have a good time at Bo and Angie's?"

"Lovely. You?"

While we shared our impressions of the current health and well-being of each of the Duplessis children, Sallie sliced the baguette, slathered it with a pesto she'd made, and layered slices of prosciutto, salami, and provolone, which she topped with arugula. I uncorked the Vermentino, which wasn't a perfect match, but worked better than the Barbera would have.

"Your sandwich is delicious," I said, meaning it.

Sallie nodded, smiling. Then she took our conversation in a new direction.

"Tell me what you know about Buddy Bolden," she said.

"What do you want to know?"

"Anything I didn't learn in a ten-minute scan of the Internet. I remember you read that book a few years ago."

"Yes, *In Search of Buddy Bolden, First Man of Jazz* by Don Marquis."

"Was Bolden really the first man of jazz?"

"So legend would have it, although without any recordings, nobody really knows," I said. "He was 'King Bolden' in his brief prime, that much everyone agrees on. Those who remembered him said he wasn't all that technically proficient and he didn't read music, but that he blew louder and dirtier than anyone else, and he was wildly popular. Supposedly, he could start playing in Congo Square or Lincoln Park with no one around, and within minutes, folks would pour in from all around to hear the king. He'd say he was 'callin his children home.'"

"That makes him the *loudest* man of jazz, not the first," Sallie said.

"Good point."

"I've never heard of Lincoln Park."

"It was near where Earhart Boulevard crosses Carrolton. There's a little league field and a playground there now, but in Bolden's day, there was a large pavilion that housed all kinds of entertainment, mainly for the neighborhood Black population."

"Interesting. You still haven't told me what made Bolden first."

"His contemporaries said he was the first to take the rhythms of ragtime and marry them to the emotional expressiveness of the blues, and that without that union we wouldn't have what we now call jazz. They called it raggin' the blues."

"You mean I have him to blame?"

"Maybe so."

I spent some time sharing what I remembered about Bolden from the Marquis book, which wasn't as much as I'd thought, and I made a mental note to reread it to refresh my knowledge. Then Sallie changed the subject again.

"Sorry about the fire and this Izzy fellow," she said. "It must have been an awful scene."

"Yes, it was. Sad and kind of grisly."

"If the cylinder burned in the fire, do you think you can get anywhere with the recording on your phone?"

"You mean in trying to establish that it's really Bolden?"

"Yes."

"I don't know, I haven't really thought about it. I imagine it might be a tough sell."

Sallie nodded in agreement, took a sip of her wine, and considered the challenge.

"Maybe if we could find out more about Jackson State and whether there were other recordings made."

"We?"

"I mean, if you want my help."

"Of course, I want your help. I'd be a fool to turn it down."

When I left Sallie's place an hour or so later, I smiled all the way home.

1927

East Louisiana Hospital For The Insane
Jackson, Louisiana
April 1927

*D*r. E.M. Robards stands on the front steps of the administration building, arms folded across his chest, observing the patients entrusted to his oversight as they gather in the vicinity of the large six-sided gazebo that stands twenty yards in front of him. Some mill about in their loose-fitting wool flannel tunics, staring vacantly into the distance, or at their feet. Others wander, causing Clarence, the ward attendant, and Sebe Bradham, the chaplain, to herd them back toward the assembly. But a dozen or so gravitate to the musical instruments Robards has arranged on the gazebo's bandstand, and begin to experiment with all manner of toots, trills, drum rolls, and cymbal crashes. The effect is cacophonous, but Robards, the newly appointed superintendent, does not seem to mind.*

"You think this is going to work, sir?" the chaplain asks him. "Doesn't sound like much so far."

"It all depends on your definition of 'work,' reverend," Robards replies. "I am under no illusion that we are recreating the New York Philharmonic."

"No, I didn't think so. You believe, then, that music has a curative application?"

"Again, reverend, I would challenge you to define your terminology," the superintendent says. "Do I believe music can cure these men of the demons that afflict them? No, sir, I do not. But if music can calm a troubled mind, even a little bit, or for only a short while, as research suggests it can, shouldn't we afford these

tortured souls some measure of solace?"

"That is a noble sentiment, sir, and I commend you for it," the chaplain says. "You are a musician yourself, are you not?"

"I play the violin," Robards says. "Classical style, mostly. I trifle with the jass piano, or 'jazz' as they call it now, but the violin is my first love."

"Perhaps you will privilege us with a concert."

"Perhaps, reverend, but I am not today's featured attraction."

With that, the superintendent descends the steps and walks to the bandstand. He has noted that there are a handful of patients with at least rudimentary knowledge of the instruments they have chosen. He recruits from this group, and over the course of fifteen minutes, manages to coax a nearly coherent version of Oh, Susannah *from a subset of these players.*

"Would anyone else like to try an instrument?" he asks those who have not yet returned to the ward.

There is no response. He is about to call an end to the session, when he notices a broad-shouldered man stutter-stepping toward him. When the man reaches the bandstand, Robards asks him which instrument he would like to try. The man regards him blankly, and nods toward the cornet.

"Very well, sir. Here then, let's have a go at it."

Accepting the instrument, the man nods obliquely at the superintendent. He inspects the cornet closely, turning it over in his hands, and puts it gently to his lips. As he begins to blow, his cheeks expand like the throat of a croaking bullfrog, and the horn emits a flurry of impossibly loud staccato notes, unrecognizable as song, yet discernibly musical. Gradually, the notes begin to slow, and he transitions to a familiar melody.

Robards, who has stepped from the rostrum and stands next to Clarence, smiles as the patient launches into "Go Down, Moses."

"Well, Clarence, it appears we have a musician in our midst," he says. "What is his name?"

"Charles, sir. Charles Bolden. Used to be King Bolden."

Chapter Six

It was way past our bedtime when Bruneau finally left. One nightcap had turned into three, and after telling us he didn't want to talk about Sallie, all he did was talk about Sallie.

"That was quite a scene last night," Angie said the next morning. She was getting the coffee started, and I was rummaging for Tylenol.

"What was?"

"Bruneau. What else?"

"Right, sorry," I said, "for a minute there I thought you meant the scene of the fire. Yeah, once the alcohol kicked in, he was on a roll, wasn't he? I'm glad you called him an Uber. He was in no shape to drive."

"The poor man is lovesick, Bo. He's a total mess."

"He is, isn't he? Too bad Sallie doesn't feel the same way."

"But she does, though! That's the thing. She misses him terribly."

"What? Are you sure about that?"

"Yes, of course, I'm sure," Angie said. "She told me so herself after you and Bruneau left to see about the fire."

"So, what's the problem?" I asked. "Why doesn't she just tell him how she feels so they can patch things up?"

"It's not that simple, Bo," Angie said.

"Seems pretty simple to me. Bru misses Sallie, and Sallie misses Bru. All they have to do is tell each other how they feel and, boom, problem solved."

Angie looked at me and shook her head like she was talking to the village idiot.

"It's a matter of principle," she said.

"Principle? Really?"

"Yes, principle. Sallie knows that if Bruneau isn't willing or able to change certain behaviors of his, and by that she means really and truly change, there's no point getting back together, because they'll just fall back into the same patterns that made her unhappy in the first place."

Angie looked down and shook her head sadly.

"The thing is, Bo, I just don't know if he can do it. He's so set in his ways; it's like this stuff is hardwired. It's just part of who he is."

"Newsflash! Bru's eccentric! I mean, who knew? Not exactly a new development, Ange. It's what we love about him, isn't it? Sallie can't accept him for who he is?"

"The eccentricities aren't the problem," Angie said. "It has more to do with his insensitivity to her needs. It's not deliberate, I don't think. It's just that, as an only child and a lifelong bachelor, he doesn't know what it means to be a partner. Not really."

"Maybe we can help him with that."

"We can try."

I thought about what Angie had said and realized she was right. But it also seemed a little unfair, as if Bru's relationship with Sallie was a one-way street and he was the only one who had to make a U-turn.

"What's the litmus test?" I asked. "What does Bru have to do to demonstrate that he's evolved into a sensitive modern male? Make a speech? Go to confession? Ace a multiple-choice test? How does Sallie decide if he passes inspection?"

"She'll know when she knows, Bo."

It was my turn to look at Angie like she was the one who was crazy. She just shrugged her shoulders and turned back to the coffee. Time to change the subject, I figured. Or get the hell out of Dodge.

"Hey Ange, I know it's Saturday and we've got stuff to do, but I need to run over to the lab for a bit. Doctor No is working today, and I want to see what she's turned up on the fire."

Doctor No is Minh Ngo, in my opinion, the best tech at the NOPD Crime Lab. Most of us call her Doctor No because her last name is a bitch to pronounce.

"So long as it's quick," Angie sighed. "The gutters need cleaning, and Monique's chorus concert starts at three."

* * *

I try not to let work interfere with my weekends, but sometimes if I've got a big case or a hot lead, there's no avoiding it. This wasn't either of those things, not yet anyway, but there were a few things about that fire scene that bugged me. The empty safe and the location of Izzy Weisman's body, for starters, not to mention the unanswered question of motive and why on earth someone would start the fire upstairs when everyone knows flames travel upward.

The seagulls were making their usual racket, but otherwise the lakefront was quiet as I made my way to our Crime Lab and Evidence building out by UNO. There were no more than a dozen cars in the lot when I pulled in, and other than the guards at the security checkpoint, I didn't see a soul until I reached Doctor No's lab. She was peering into a microscope when I knocked and let myself in.

"Hello, Detective," she said without looking up. "What brings you out on a Saturday morning?"

"The fire in Tremé," I said. "A couple things aren't sitting right with me. I thought I'd come see what you've got. Oh, and good morning to you, too, Doctor."

A faint smile crossed Minh's lips as she turned away from the microscope and looked at me briefly before returning to her work. Minh rarely holds eye contact for long.

"There's still a lot of work to do, Detective," she said. "There's much we don't know yet."

"Of course, that's to be expected. Can you tell me what you do know?"

"The fire was started upstairs, which you have probably already heard, but still, it's unusual. There were traces of petroleum downstairs, too. The corpse that was found in the bedroom is a juvenile male, in his early teens, most likely. The coroner is still running tests, but I'd be surprised if he hasn't been dead for at least twenty years."

"A boy? Really? I didn't see that one coming. How can the coroner tell he's been dead that long?"

"Why the interest in the corpse, Detective? Have you transferred to homicide?"

"I'm investigating the possibility of arson and whether robbery might have been the motive. I'd say our dead body bears on both of those questions, don't you think? And don't worry, I'll be talking to the Homicide boys soon enough."

"Of course, Detective, I did not mean to impugn your motives," Minh said demurely.

"To answer your question, the first thing the crime scene team noticed was that the corpse was not in the boxer pose."

"What does that mean? I'm not following."

"When we die from intense heat, such as that caused by prolonged exposure to fire, our soft tissue contracts, causing our skin to rip apart and our muscles and our internal organs to shrink. As our muscles contract, our joints flex, and we contort into what we call the boxer pose. If you've seen pictures of the bodies at Pompeii that were preserved in volcanic ash, you'll notice that most of them were positioned this way."

"Most, but not all."

"Correct. Which is why we also look for changes to the surface of the bone caused by the fire, as well as to the microstructure inside the bone."

"Microstructure? What do you mean by that?"

"The architecture of the bone, basically. We tend to think of bones as static, non-living objects, but in fact, they are animate, ever-changing structures made of cells and blood vessels, and water and minerals of various types. When living bones burn, or the bones of a recently deceased subject, we see U-shaped fracturing throughout the skeleton, but if decomposition has already occurred, there are grid-like fracture patterns instead. That's what we have here, Detective. The coroner is examining those fractures and the density of the microstructure to determine an estimated time of death."

"How specific will he be able to be, do you think?" I asked.

"The PMI is complicated by the fire damage, so it is hard to say," Minh said.

"PMI?"

"Sorry. The post-mortem interval, or the time that has elapsed since the cessation of life."

"Right, got it. You said earlier that you thought the deceased had been dead for at least twenty years. Can you give me a more specific estimate?"

"Not really, Detective. It's been decades rather than years; that much I can say. Based on where the body was found and the position it was in, we think it had probably been placed inside the wall of the guest bedroom. The house was built in the 1840s, so we can safely say that it hadn't been there for more than two hundred years."

"Thanks for narrowing things down for me."

Minh looked up briefly, her face a blank canvas, then returned to her microscope.

"Somebody in more recent years could have torn out a section of wall and placed the body inside, right?"

"Yes, that is one hypothesis, certainly."

"Can you tell how this person died?"

"No, not yet," Minh said. "It wasn't anything obvious like a blow to the head or a bullet wound. We may never know."

This case had started out as a mild curiosity because of Bru's connection to Izzy Weisman, but the information Minh provided took it to the next level. Still, I'm in Property Crimes, not Homicide, and I knew to stay in my lane.

"Why would someone set the fire in the upstairs room?" I asked.

"I don't know," Minh said, pausing briefly.

"This is just speculation, but maybe there was something in that room that the perpetrator wanted to destroy. Perhaps an object of some kind, or a piece of evidence. Or maybe it had to do with an emotion connected to that room in some way. Anger, remorse, a memory maybe. We don't always think logically when our emotions get the best of us."

So said the most relentlessly logical thinker I know.

"What about the safe?" I asked. "Any clues there?"

"No, not really. It wasn't damaged other than some minor warping and cracking of the exterior. It hadn't been forced open, so either it had been left open or whoever opened it knew the combination. We have no way of determining if anything was taken from it. We did recover a set of prints, but I expect we'll find that they belong to the owner."

Which raised two questions: First, if the corpse wasn't Izzy Weisman, who the hell was it? And second, where in god's name was Izzy Weisman?

* * *

As I drove home following my visit to Doctor No, I gave Bruneau a call.

"Hey, Bo," he answered on the third ring. "I was going to call you in a bit. What's up?"

"Why were you going to call me?"

"Because Sallie cracked the code."

"What code?"

"The letters on the cylinder, CBJXHS729," Bru said. "We think it stands for Charles Bolden, Jackson Hospital, July 1929."

That didn't mean anything to me, so I waited for an explanation.

"Charles was Buddy Bolden's given first name, and Buddy Bolden was still institutionalized at the Jackson insane asylum in 1929. He died a couple years later. We think that may be him playing on the cylinder."

I knew who Buddy Bolden was and realized the significance of the discovery.

"Wow, Bru, Buddy Bolden? That cylinder of yours might be worth something. As I recall, there are no known recordings of Bolden."

"That's true, but unfortunately, I left the cylinder with Izzy, so it probably got destroyed in the fire."

"Maybe not," I said.

"Why, do you know something I don't?"

"The reason I called is to tell you that the body we found in the fire isn't

Izzy Weisman."

Bru went silent as he processed this piece of news.

"If it isn't Izzy, who is it?" he asked after a few seconds had gone by.

"And where is Izzy?"

"The answer to both questions is we don't know, but we're working on it."

"I'll be damned," Bru said. "If Izzy is alive, maybe he's still got the cylinder."

"Could be."

"This was all pretty weird to begin with, Bo, but it just got a whole lot weirder, didn't it?"

"It did," I agreed. "Any chance you're free for lunch on Monday? I'd love to kick around some theories, plus there's something else I want to talk to you about."

"I can be, sure. Where and when?"

"You choose."

"Okay, how about Cochon Butcher? Haven't been there in a while. Meet you at 11:30 to beat the crowd?"

"Deal. See you then."

Chapter Seven

When I returned home and let myself in following my visit to Sallie's, I was greeted not by the yipping and yapping to which I am accustomed, but by pronounced silence. I called Hugo's name. No reply. More curious than concerned, I climbed the staircase to my living room two steps at a time. The first sign of trouble, the shattered remains of a vintage Murano vase given to me by Charlotte Duval, lay on the floor beneath the bookshelves built into the opposite wall. Reaching the top step and looking around, I saw the torn remnants of one of the pillows from the sofa lying on the glass coffee table. The pair of small botanical prints that hang next to the bay window dangled cock-eyed, and my antique Imari bowl rested precariously on the edge of the bombe chest positioned beneath the window.

Hearing a low growling, more hum than snarl, I entered my bedroom cautiously. Hugo sat at the base of the mahogany armoire where I store my bed sheets and linens, looking up toward the ceiling with murderous intent. The object of his ire was Coco the cat, who perched sphynx-like atop the armoire, looking down at his canine adversary with something less than apprehension. Both animals ignored my cursing.

Reconstructing the scene as best I could, I saw that there had been a chase, spanning not only the living room and bedroom, but also the kitchen and salon, where a small carafe of Armagnac had been knocked over, spilling onto my prized Persian silk rug. I stormed back into the bedroom, screaming loudly enough this time to command Hugo's attention. Avoiding eye contact, he relinquished his post and slinked into a somber trot of shame back to the living room. Coco appeared unfazed, licking her paws from the safety of higher elevation.

I called Annie and explained the situation.

"Goodness, Bruneau," she proclaimed, "it sounds like you have a veritable *cat*-astrophe on your hands."

"This is serious, Annie," I said. "I can't leave these two alone if this is going to happen. What do I do?"

"I'd say finding a new home for poor Coco is your first order of business," Annie said.

"Poor Coco?"

"Why yes, imagine how traumatized she must be, abandoned in a strange apartment, and chased around by a savage beast, poor thing."

"Savage beast? Somehow, I don't think Coco is the traumatized one."

"No, of course you don't," Annie said. "You men are forever closing ranks." Annie paused for effect.

"Anyway, to answer your question, when you leave, put the cat in the crate I left you. Just make sure to put it in a high place where Hugo can't get to her."

* * *

After hanging up with Annie, I cleaned up the mess from Hugo and Coco's shenanigans, cued up Chet Baker's soothing *The Art of the Ballad*, and sat down with a bowl of cashews and a small glass of sherry to begin re-reading the Marquis book on Buddy Bolden. I ended up skimming most of it, as the basic contours of what can be learned of Bolden's life came back to me with surprising ease.

Buddy Bolden was born in 1877 to Westmore and Alice Bolden. The family moved around a bit but lived for most of Buddy's early years on St. Andrews Street, near where it crosses Magnolia. It was around the corner from the popular music and dance venue Turners Hall, and just off a common parade route, putting young Buddy in regular proximity to some of the more established brass and string bands of the day.

Westmore Bolden died of pneumonia in 1883, and when Buddy was ten, his mother moved the family into one half of a double shotgun on First Street, near its crossing with Lasalle, in what was then a mostly German and Irish neighborhood. Buddy attended school at least into his early teens, and the family worshipped at St. John's the Baptist about a dozen blocks away, where Buddy would have internalized the swaying gospel rhythms that informed the music he would later pioneer.

Marquis provides little information as to when Buddy began playing, or why he settled on the cornet as his instrument of choice, but he documents that Buddy did receive some basic instruction from a family friend and started sitting in with neighborhood string bands as early as 1894. Within a year, he regularly fronted his own lineups. He was "Kid Bolden" in those first years and still finding his way, but from the outset, he showed little interest in imitation or in playing correctly, like the trained "reading" musicians in the popular bands of the day. From the get-go, he chased his own sound.

Exactly what that sound was, and how it came to be, remains an elusive question for jazz historians. Because no known recordings of Buddy Bolden have survived, if they existed in the first place, Marquis and others are left to speculate, or lean on documented accounts from Bolden's contemporaries, some of which may be compromised by jealousy or self-serving agendas. There is broad agreement that Buddy's musical gumbo contained a bountiful assortment of ingredients, culled from the many styles and traditions swirling around New Orleans in the closing years of the 19th century. But precisely how he assembled those elements to fashion something at least nominally new, and distinctly his own, is anybody's guess.

There is no disagreement regarding Buddy's popularity. By the early 1900s, he was "King Bolden," and the undisputed top draw among the city's Black audiences. The personnel in his band fluctuated, but the core group was Buddy on cornet, his closest friend Willie Cornish on trombone, Brock Mumford on guitar, Frank Lewis and Willie Warner on clarinet, Jimmy Johnson on bass, and Cornelius Tillman on drums. They played all over town, at dance halls, picnics, and parades, drawing huge crowds wherever they went. Their set lists included the usual waltzes, marches, and rags of the day, but they played them in a grittier, bluesier style than other bands, and with more embellishment. Their signature tune was "Funky Butt," which resulted in Union Sons Hall, where the band often played, becoming better known as Funky Butt Hall to ardent followers.

Louis Armstrong's mother, with whom he sometimes lived, resided at the corner of Liberty and Perdido, across the street from the Funky Butt. Satchmo claimed to have heard Buddy when he was five years old and decided then and there that he was going to play the cornet. He called Buddy "a one-man genius that was ahead of them all—too good for his time."

Buddy's popularity peaked around 1905, but within a year, his hard-driving lifestyle, fueled by a packed booking schedule that sometimes included as many as three or four gigs in a day, and the twin pursuits of women and alcohol, caught up to him. His behavior grew increasingly erratic. He missed or showed up late to gigs, lashed out at friends and bandmates, and began experiencing terrible headaches. He continued drinking heavily and by the spring of 1907 had succumbed to full-blown dementia, no longer recognizing friends or family members. His mother and sister, unable to control him, had the police pick Buddy up. They detained him and charged him with insanity. After a few days in jail, Buddy was examined by a Dr. J. O'Hara, who declared him insane by reason of alcoholism and committed him to East Louisiana Hospital for the Insane in Jackson, Louisiana, or Jackson State, as it is colloquially known.

Once admitted to the asylum, two-plus hours northeast of New Orleans near the Mississippi border, Buddy was diagnosed with dementia praecox, or "precocious madness," a term then used to indicate rapid deterioration of cognitive functioning. Today, Buddy's condition would likely be classified as schizophrenia. Though he would remain institutionalized until his death in 1931, hospital records indicate that Buddy grew more docile over time and less communicative. In response to a 1925 letter from Buddy's mother, Dr. S.B. Hays wrote of Buddy that "on the ward, he insists on going about touching each post and is not satisfied until he has accomplished this at least once. He causes no trouble and cooperates well."

The section of the Marquis book that interested me most concerned the arrival of Dr. E.M. Robards, who took over as superintendent of the asylum in the late 1920s. A musician himself, Robards introduced music to Jackson State. He brought in bands of various types to play for the patients, who he encouraged to try their own hand at playing an instrument. According to Marquis, there are accounts of Buddy playing a horn during this period. He quotes Sebe Bradham, the hospital's protestant chaplain at the time, as saying of Buddy that "you could tell he was better than the rest. He played over the rest and louder than most people." I couldn't help but wonder if our cylinder recording of Buddy, if indeed it was Buddy, might have been recorded at Jackson State during this period, as Sallie had speculated.

I was lost in these thoughts when my phone vibrated loudly on the cocktail table beside me. It was Sallie.

"I'm calling to invite you to lunch tomorrow," she said after we'd exchanged greetings. "I thought we could map out our strategy for researching the cylinder."

"Oh, how nice," I said. "But you just fed me today, and tomorrow is Sunday. How about you join me for brunch at Katie's?"

"I wasn't calling because I want to join you for brunch."

I remembered my conversation with Prosper and wondered if this was a test.

"Okay, sure," I stumbled. "What did you have in mind?"

"There's a cute little place that just opened on Esplanade," Sallie said. "I thought we could try that. They do bowls."

"You mean like soups and salads?"

"Yeah, salads anyway. You make your own. They have grains, vegetables, and different protein options. It looks nice."

It may look nice, I thought to myself, but it sounded dreadful. I've observed this trendy "bowl" phenomenon. As far as I'm concerned, it's just another millennial affront to civilized dining. Chefs around the world spend centuries refining the classic dishes of their regions, and these kids come along, toss a bunch of tasteless health food ingredients in a bowl, and think they've invented the next great cuisine.

"Sounds wonderful," I lied.

We agreed to meet at Sallie's place at 11:30 and walk to lunch from there. It was only a few blocks away, she said. After we hung up, I opened the refrigerator to make sure I had enough eggs and bacon to feed myself a proper breakfast before heading off for my indeterminate "bowl." Then I got up and walked into the kitchen to open a bottle of wine and begin making the carbonara I had planned for dinner.

No sooner had I entered the kitchen than I was presented with the sight of a large ball of fur curled up on the counter next to the fruit bowl. Coco had found the lone ray of late afternoon sunlight still pouring in through the kitchen window. I shushed the cat away and spent the next few minutes sweeping up hair and sanitizing the counter. Then, as I was considering what to do about Coco, the doorbell rang. I was in no mood for company but got up anyway and trudged downstairs. All I could see through the peephole was the top of a bald head and a couple tufts of white hair, but I knew who it was.

"Izzy?"

"Hello, Mr. Abellard. Apologies for showing up uninvited like this."

Izzy Weisman looked awful. He wore a grungy white t-shirt that was at least two sizes too big, clumsily tucked into ridiculously baggy chinos held up by a belt fastened to its last hole. His skin was mottled, and his eyes were puffy.

"Please, come in," I said, and led Izzy upstairs. "This is quite a surprise. What is it that you want? Are you aware that you've got half of NOPD looking for you?"

I handed Izzy the newspaper, which I'd kept open to the page with a short story about the fire. He requested a glass of water, which I went to pour for him as he read the article.

Body Found Amid
Tremé Fire Rubble

(Newsbrief)—New Orleans police and fire personnel discovered the dead body of a juvenile male Friday night in the fire that burned down a house on the 1100 block of Marais Street.

The cause of the fire and the identity of the victim have not been determined, although police said arson is suspected. According to a spokesperson, NOPD expects to release additional information once crime scene analysis has been completed.

Property records indicate the house on Marais Street has been owned since 1961 by Isadore J. Weisman. Police have not commented on Weisman's whereabouts.

"We thought it was you in the fire, Izzy," I said as I delivered his water. "I'm glad that it wasn't, but what happened?"

"I'm not sure," Izzy said. "I think someone might be trying to kill me. I saw you at the fire scene and wanted to let you know I was okay, but I didn't know if it was safe."

I remembered the short figure in a raincoat shuffling into the shadows and thinking there was something familiar about him.

"Why would someone want to kill you?"

"I don't know exactly. Maybe because of something I have. I told you that someone offered to buy my collection. Maybe it's connected to that."

"If someone wanted your collection, why would they destroy it by burning your house down?"

"I don't know. Maybe because they were just after one specific thing, such as your cylinder, perhaps."

I thought about that.

"Is that why you came here?"

"Yes. That and the fact that I don't really have anyplace else to go."

"Do you have any money?"

"I've got a few thousand in my checking account, but everything else was tied up in the house."

"What about insurance?"

"Yes, I have a homeowner's policy, but if they're saying it's arson, who knows when they'll pay out."

I thought about that.

"Where were you when the fire started, Izzy?"

"Out running an errand. When I got home, the fire engines were already there."

"Do you remember leaving your safe open when you left the house?"

"No, but it's possible that I did."

"Well, it was left open by somebody, and it was empty. Can I ask what you kept in the safe?"

"Just some documents. And your cylinder. I put that in there for safekeeping."

That jolted me.

"Why would you put it in the safe? Did you think it might be valuable?"

"I wasn't sure, but I had a theory I was going to follow up on. If the theory proved correct, it might be quite valuable, yes."

"Did your theory have anything to do with Buddy Bolden?"

There was a pause.

"As a matter of fact, it did," Izzy said.

"Why didn't you tell us you thought it might be valuable when we visited you?"

"Like I said, it was just a theory. I didn't want to get you all excited for no reason."

We stared at each other in silence. Then Izzy caught sight of Coco wandering into the room.

"Is that my L'il Queenie?" he exclaimed, more stating than asking.

"She was wandering around outside your house and followed me to the car."

"Thank goodness she's okay. Come here, girl. It's so good to see you."

"L'il Queenie? Did you name her after Leigh Harris?"

"Yes. Did you know her?"

"No, but I used to catch L'il Queenie and the Percolators from time to time, at Tyler's Beer Garden mostly, on ten-cent oyster night. She was something."

"Yes, she was. It never seemed possible that such a tiny body could belt out so much sound. This cat and her sister were hanging around Leigh's memorial service and didn't seem to have a home, so I took her in, and she kind of named herself. I called her sister Mahalia. I hope she made it out, too."

Izzy's eyes grew misty as he cradled his cat, gently stroking her fur. It seemed like a good time to shift the conversation back to more pressing matters.

"Izzy, you know you're going to have to talk to the police, right? I can help set that up if you'd like. They're going to want to know about the safe and the cylinder, and even more about the body that was found. Do you have an explanation for that?"

"No, I don't," Izzy said. "It must have been some neighborhood kid poking around my stuff. Maybe that's who started the fire."

"I don't think so. Whoever it was had been dead for several years."

"Oh, I see. That is odd, isn't it? I wonder how that could be."

Izzy's words expressed surprise, but it seemed to me that his tone and body language did not. He agreed to speak with Bo if I would set up a meeting. I told him I would make that call, but he looked like he could use a good meal, so I told him I'd wait until after dinner. I poured Izzy and myself a glass of Dolcetto, separated a couple egg yolks, and was rendering some pancetta and grating a wedge of Pecorino when the doorbell rang again, setting Hugo off as usual.

As I descended the stairs to see who it was, I was trying to figure out how to send whoever it may be away, cognizant that I had a person of interest in a major crime investigation sitting at my kitchen counter. It was Prosper, and he had a container of soup in one hand and a baguette and a bottle of wine in the other.

"I come bearing gifts, Bruneau, and an apology. I feel bad about the way our last conversation went. I was way out of line."

"Water under the bridge, Prosper," I said. "Thank you for all this. I have a guest upstairs, and we're about to eat, but you are welcome to join us. There's plenty of food, and we can sop up my carbonara with the baguette."

"Oh, I'm sorry, I didn't mean to intrude," Prosper said. "I should go."

"Nonsense. Come join us, please."

"Are you sure?"

"Positive."

I had gone against my own better judgment, but the truth is I was feeling awkward about being alone with Izzy, and I welcomed Prosper's company.

I ushered him in and followed him up the stairs. I was about to introduce my guests to one another when Prosper stopped in his tracks in front of me.

"Izzy?"

"My God. Andre? Is it really you?"

1895

Odd Fellows Hall
New Orleans, Louisiana
September 1895

Charley Galloway had known Buddy Bolden since he was three or four *years old. His father Wes, dead ten years now, was a coachman. He used to drop by Charley's barbershop on South Rampart to drink beer and shoot dice between fares, and sometimes he'd have young Buddy in tow. In those days, as now, the shop was a gathering place where musicians from the neighborhood could meet band leaders trying to pull together a lineup. They'd bring their instruments with them to audition, or maybe to work out a new arrangement. Charley remembered that when a group was playing, young Buddy would drum along with his hands on a chair, or a countertop, or whatever was available. He played loud, even then.*

When Buddy was in his early teens, Charley's friend Manuel Hall got close with Buddy's mother, Alice. He got Buddy started on the cornet, and then Buddy began stopping by the shop on his own. He wasn't good enough yet to get himself hired out, but Charley noticed that he listened closely to everything he heard, soaking up whatever he could. It wasn't long before Charley felt comfortable inviting Buddy to sit in with his string band.

On this night, Charley on the guitar is joined by Albert Glenny on bass, Wallace Collins on fiddle, Bill Willigan on drums, Frank Lewis on clarinet, and seventeen-year-old Buddy Bolden on the cornet. It is a larger crowd than the band is used to, younger and better dressed. Shiny black faces look up in eager anticipation, the troubles of their day forgotten for a few carefree hours. But as the band runs through its standards, Charley senses a lack of enthusiasm. He calls for "Ride On, King," a lively number sure to get the party started.

They begin with an acapella treatment of the spiritual's opening statement, belting out two stanzas of "Ride on, King Jesus; no man can-a hinder me" in their higher registers. Then Frank's playful clarinet leads the strings through a sprightly first turn through the melody, his delicate syncopations accenting the rhythmic vocal line. The audience taps along politely, while a dozen or so couples on the dance floor swirl and twirl to the bouncy beat. Charley nods to Buddy, letting him know it is his turn to lead.

The youngster steps to the front of the stage and hits the opening notes on cue, the way the band has practiced. But soon something goes wrong, and Charley is not sure what to do. Buddy blows too loudly, and he loses the melody, if only for a moment. The refrain returns but is barely recognizable due to the thunderous clamor of Buddy's horn. The other musicians turn toward Charley, terror in their eyes. Buddy is thrusting and gyrating now, contorting himself as his instrument honks and groans and howls. Charley knows he must shut him down. He resolves to do so, but when he catches sight of the dance floor, he is startled to find bodies spinning, dipping, and grinding with newfound energy. Couples mingling in the background join hands and flood the dance floor. Elsewhere heads bob, feet stomp, and hands clap.

When Buddy finally finishes his solo, the audience roars in appreciation, and begins chanting "kid, kid, kid." They do this for the rest of the evening, and Charley obliges by calling Buddy's number as often as he is able. Buddy does not disappoint. His playing is far from perfect, but no one seems to notice. The feral scream of his horn and the libidinous coaxing of his movements course like electricity through the crowd, unleashing torrents of ecstatic frenzy.

Later, after the band has left the stage, Charley feels as though the ground underneath him has shifted. He cannot know that in just a few years' time, Buddy Bolden's honky-tonk sound will rule the city. Or that many years later, folks who claim to have been there that night will swear that Buddy blew the tuning slide out of his cornet so forcefully that it landed twenty feet away. All he knows is that the world has changed, and in a way he cannot yet apprehend.

Charley wants to take Buddy aside and tell him there is no place for showboating in a band; that he is just one player among equals. But there is no hope of reaching Buddy now. The crowd has surrounded him. Women grab hungrily at his clothing. Men slap him on the back and offer him drinks.

"Not sure what I just heard," Frank Lewis says, stealing up behind Charley. "But whatever it was, the young folks sure liked it."

Charley nods.

"Looks like life is about to change for that boy," he says. "I just hope he's ready for it."

As the two men walk back out to the stage to pack up their instruments, they catch a final glimpse of their young bandmate as he exits the hall. His arms are draped around two young women. In one hand he clutches his cornet; in the other a bottle of whisky. He turns and looks over his shoulder, smiling broadly as he nods at the men on the stage. Then he steps out into the warm embrace of the bright and welcoming night.

"Won't be Buddy Bolden no more," Frank says.

"Nope. It's Kid Bolden now."

Chapter Eight

My mind was still racing from Izzy Weisman's surprise visit, and the revelation that he and Prosper knew each other, when I climbed Sallie's stoop and knocked on her door.

"I'll be right there," came her call from inside.

A moment later, I heard the hurried slapping of sandals against a hardwood floor, followed by the clicking of the doorknob. As the door swung open, a flood of sensations washed over me. Her scent registered first. Orange blossom perfume mixed with sandalwood shampoo and traces of fresh, clean soap. Her strawberry hair shimmered in the late morning sunlight, and her pink lips formed an amused smile as she recorded my reaction to her appearance.

"Good morning!" she beamed.

"Hi," I stammered, stepping back for a better view. Sallie wore a loose-fitting coral linen shirt over pleated white shorts and white strap sandals. Her painted fingers and toes matched her shirt, and her dimpled cheeks were abloom with the warmth of a new day. She was radiant.

"Aren't you perky today," was the best I could come up with.

"Perky?" she considered, cocking her head and making a face. "I guess I'll take Perky. I'd have preferred stunning. Or vivacious."

"Perky and stunning and vivacious and beautiful and gorgeous and all those other superlatives I'm too tongue-tied to come up with."

"Bruneau Abellard, tongue-tied?"

"Only around the most beautiful woman in the world."

"Oh, stop," she said, playfully punching my arm. "The truth is, I am feeling kind of perky today. I've been needing a new project, and Buddy Bolden's cylinder has me feeling energized."

Sallie took hold of my arm, and we headed off in the general direction of Esplanade. As we walked, more briskly than I prefer, I told her about Izzy and Prosper.

"You're kidding. How do they know each other?"

"I haven't gotten the whole story yet, but from what I can gather, they ran in some of the same circles back before Prosper shipped out to Vietnam. Mid to late sixties, I think."

"Were they friends?"

"More like acquaintances, from the sound of it."

"If they recognized each other after so many years, they must have been more than just acquaintances, don't you think?"

"That's the feeling I got, but they both downplayed the extent of their relationship. In fact, I'd say neither seemed particularly happy to see the other. Izzy knew Prosper as Andre, of course."

Prosper's birth name is Andre Coulon. He started going by Prosper Fortune around the time he moved to Grand Isle.

"Where is Izzy now?" Sallie asked.

"At Prosper's. I'm bringing him in to talk to Bo tomorrow morning, but in the meantime, he had no place to stay. Much to my relief, Prosper offered to put him up."

"Why relief?"

"The man stinks to high heaven, Sallie. Even Hugo couldn't stand to be in the same room with him."

"But Prosper could?"

"He didn't smell much better than Izzy back in his Grand Isle days, so maybe he's desensitized to it."

True to form, Sallie's "just a few blocks" turned out to be closer to a mile, and though our route was shaded by Esplanade's oak-lined canopy, the calescent mid-day sun made its presence felt. By the time we arrived at our destination, I was dripping. Fortunately, I'd stuffed a small washcloth into my pocket and was able to towel off to a degree, though I couldn't do much about the moisture spreading beneath my armpits and behind the buttons of my shirt.

Sallie was entertained by my toweling off routine, though it wasn't anything she hadn't seen before.

"You'd think you'd run a marathon."

"Just a few blocks, she said."

"Oh, stop being grumpy. Exercise is good for you."

"As I've told you many times, it's not the exercise that gets me, it's the sweat. I can't help it if I am blessed with superior pores."

"It's superior pores now, is it?"

"Studies have shown, people who sweat more have better pores and are healthier in the long run."

"I see. In that case, let's make you even healthier by getting you some healthy food."

The restaurant was exactly as I expected. Small, vaguely industrial feeling, and filled with young people with their noses in their phones or tablets. Whatever happened to the communal meal? Or the solitary nosh focused on food, rather than a device?

A short line led to the counter, where you are expected to instruct a server on the other side of a glass partition which ingredients you'd like in your bowl. They did offer some pre-made pita sandwich rolls, but I was pretty sure I'd fail Sallie's test if I ordered one of those.

She went first, choosing quinoa as her base grain and layering in an assortment of vegetables, leafy greens, tomatoes, and avocado, before topping the mash-up with falafel and a lemon vinaigrette. I met her halfway, opting for a healthy mix of brown rice, cauliflower, corn, arugula, cherry tomatoes, olives, and avocado, but adding a protein of grilled chicken and covering it all with some pita chips and tahini dressing. We both ordered a Perrier, and Sallie insisted it was her treat.

"What do you think?" she asked after we'd taken a few bites at the outdoor table we'd found.

"It's edible," I said in a neutral voice.

That drew a smirk.

"For something that's merely edible, you seem to be digging in with quite a bit of gusto."

"Studies have shown, it's important to refuel after exercising."

Sallie laughed. Not that I was going to admit it, but my bowl wasn't half bad. Crisp vegetables, flavorful chicken, and creamy dressing made the whole thing feel more substantial than I had expected.

"Alright, let's get down to business," Sallie said. "How are we going to prove that's Buddy Bolden on your recording?"

"I don't know that we're going to be able to prove anything, especially without the cylinder," I said. "But we can start by looking into the history of the sideboard that we found the cylinder in."

"Agreed. We can also research Jackson State during the time Bolden was locked up there. If that's him on the recording, whoever made it had to have been given access to him."

"Could have been somebody who worked there."

"Yes, and we could start by finding out if they employed a 'Clarence' in 1929. If the cylinder belonged to this Clarence, maybe he made the recording."

"True. I also wonder if there's anybody still around who can tell us more about Buddy than was in the Marquis book," I said.

"If he died in 1931, people who are in their late nineties today would have been children then, and they certainly wouldn't have visited Jackson State," Sallie said. "And there won't be anybody left who would have seen or heard him when he was popular around the turn of the century."

"No, but lore gets passed down through generations of musicians. I'll ask Izzy about it when I take him to Bo. Henry might know something, too."

"Henry? What would Henry know?"

"More than me."

* * *

When I picked Izzy up at Prosper's place Monday morning to take him to see Bo at NOPD headquarters, I was disappointed, though not surprised, to learn that he had not showered. He said it was because he didn't have any clean clothes to change into, so he didn't see the point. Prosper said his sister Irene was going to take him clothes shopping when she got home from work.

As Izzy made his way gingerly down the outdoor stairs that led to and from Prosper's studio apartment, above Irene's detached garage, I pulled Prosper aside.

"Is he okay?" I asked.

"I think so. Frail, but still feisty in his way."

"I'm looking forward to a full explanation of your relationship."

"Not sure I'd call it a relationship."

"What then?"

"Let's just say we had a lady friend in common and leave it at that."

I had no intention of leaving it at that, but Izzy was calling from the bottom of the stairs and Prosper had turned back into his apartment. I was left with little choice but to table the matter for the time being.

"It's been a long time since I've been in one of these," Izzy said as he slid into Liesel's front seat.

"Hey, I deal in antiques."

Izzy smiled. I got in and rolled down my window to let some breathable air in.

"Prosper says you had a lady friend in common, back in the day."

"Prosper. Interesting name, that."

"He's had an interesting life, Andre has."

"Yes, I suppose he has. He shared some of his story last night. I knew him when he was finishing up med school, before he went to Vietnam. It's been almost fifty years."

"Who was this lady friend you two had in common?" I asked.

"Ah, Lyla. Dear sweet, troubled Lyla," Izzy sighed wistfully. "Lyla Saint-Clair, or Lady Ly as we called her. She was a singer I managed for a time. She and Andre had a thing for a while."

"She was in your stained-glass window, wasn't she?"

"Yes, that's right."

"What happened to them? Andre and Lyla?"

"He went off to Vietnam, and she died not long after."

"You said she was troubled. Did she take her own life?"

"That's what the coroner said."

"And you have your doubts?"

"No, not really. I don't know if she meant to kill herself, but I guess you could say she killed herself all the same. The drugs, you know. Was it suicide? Depends on your definition, I suppose. It's just semantics, at the end of the day."

"Who found her?"

"I did. It wasn't the first time she'd overdosed, but it was the last."

"Did it have anything to do with Andre going off to war?" I asked. "Her killing herself, intentionally or not?"

"It might have been a factor, but there was other stuff going on with her."

I thought I heard a slight break in Izzy's voice, and as I turned to look at him, he was staring out the passenger side window. I figured I'd pushed the Lyla Saint-Clair envelope as far as I could.

"Can I ask you something on a different subject, Izzy?"

"Sure."

"What made you think it might be Buddy Bolden on the cylinder?"

"Just a hunch," Izzy said. "If the cylinder was recorded in the 1920s, the only cornet players I'm aware of with chops like that were Freddie Keppard and a young Louis Armstrong, but it didn't sound like either of them.

"What we heard on that recording was so fractured and atonal, it made me think the player must be disturbed or in the midst of a psychotic break, even. And then I thought of Buddy Bolden, locked up in that nuthouse, whose real first name was Charles, by the way. Whoever is doing the recording wants 'Charles' to keep going, remember? There had always been rumors of Buddy having made recordings, but none have ever surfaced."

"You said you were planning on following up on your theory," I reminded Izzy. "Who were you planning on talking to?"

"A handful of people. I started making a few calls but hadn't made much progress. I played it over the phone for Professor Martin at Southern Miss, and he was interested enough that he was going to stop by the next time he was in town. He's a musicologist who specializes in the origins of jazz. He visited me a few weeks ago because someone told him about my collection. I think he was impressed."

"Anyone else?"

"I hadn't gotten around to it, but I was going to suck it up and see if I could get Mose Adler to talk."

"Who is Mose Adler, and why would you need to suck it up?"

Izzy chortled quietly.

"Mose is one of the all-time characters," he said. "You probably think I'm eccentric. Let me tell you, you ain't seen nothing."

"Tell me more," I said.

"Mose lives in a shack in the Lower Ninth Ward. He sells voodoo paraphernalia now, but in the old days, he used to play African drums for some local bands. He's older than dirt, probably my age, or even a few years older."

"Why would you consult him about Buddy Bolden?"

"Because he's an amateur folklorist of sorts and he's got an encyclopedic memory. He's spent most of his adult life around musicians down here, and anything anybody's ever told him, he's going to remember."

"I'm still not getting why you'd have to suck it up to talk to him."

"Because he's a pain in the ass, that's why," Izzy said.

"How so?"

"First of all, he's never liked me. Second, he never gives a straight answer. And third, he'll probably make me buy some voodoo crap before agreeing to talk."

I filed that information away and turned to more pressing matters. We were passing the criminal courthouse on Tulane Avenue, and were about to turn onto South Broad, a block away from NOPD headquarters.

"You nervous about this, Izzy?"

"Should I be?"

"Not if you've got nothing to hide, I wouldn't think."

Izzy smiled ruefully.

"Not many people get to be my age without having something to hide."

I let that comment go and then, once we parked, I escorted Izzy to Property Crimes, where Bo works. On the way, Izzy asked me if I thought he should have a lawyer with him. I told him my understanding was that this was an interview, not an interrogation, but if at any point he felt uncomfortable, he should stop the proceedings and demand an attorney.

When we got to Property Crimes, Bo was nowhere to be found, and neither was Mike Rodiger. I had met Bo's boss, Captain MacLaren, a couple of times before, so I rapped my knuckles on the window next to his door. He looked up from his desk and motioned for me to enter.

"Hello Captain," I said, "my name is Bruneau Abellard, I don't know if you remember me."

"I remember you."

"Ah, excellent. This gentleman is Izzy Weisman, and he's come to talk to Detective Duplessis about that fire in Tremé. Mr. Weisman is the owner of the house that burned."

MacLaren had seemed uninterested in me, but once he realized who Izzy was, he snapped to.

"I see," he said. "Thank you for coming in, Mr. Weisman. Detective Duplessis is around here somewhere. Why don't we get you settled in our interview room, and I'll go find him for you."

MacLaren led Izzy and me across the squad room to a stark, glass-enclosed chamber with a table and a few chairs in it. I started to follow Izzy into the room, but the captain held out his forearm to stop me.

"I thought I'd sit with Mr. Weisman until Detective Duplessis arrives," I said.

"That's quite all right, Mr. Abellard," he said. "We can take it from here."

"But—"

"I assure you he'll be in good hands. Thank you for bringing Mr. Weisman in. From here on, this is police business, okay? I'm sure you understand."

There didn't seem to be any room to argue, so I waved to Izzy and bid MacLaren a good day.

Chapter Nine

When I got to work Monday morning, Mike Rodiger was waiting for me in the hallway.

"Morning, Detective," he said.

"Hi Mike. What's up?"

"Bit of a stink, sir. Gator Guidry dropped in on the captain to bitch about you poking around in his homicide investigation. You know how the captain is. Folded right away. Said he'd make sure you mind your own business."

Joe Guidry goes by Gator because before he became a cop, he made his living guiding alligator hunting trips out of Breaux Bridge. He's as good a homicide detective as we have, but more than a little uptight about protecting his turf. A few years ago, I collared a car thief who I later discovered was responsible for a murder Gator was investigating. I got all the credit, and Gator's held a grudge ever since. Any chance he gets to even the score, he's going to take it.

I thanked Mike for the warning and headed into the squad room to take my poison. Captain Hugh "Mac" MacLaren was leaning against the door to his office with his arms crossed, waiting for me to pass.

"A word, T-Bo."

Mac calls me T-Bo because my full first name is Thibodeaux. We've known each other since long before I started reporting to him. We get along fine, but the man is image-conscious to a fault. It didn't surprise me in the least that he gave in so easily when Gator lodged his complaint. Whether it's padding our stats or staying out of turf wars, he's all about polishing the Property Crimes brand.

"Gator got his panties in a twist, Mac?" I asked.

"Not without reason from the sound of it," Mac said, taking a seat behind his desk. "I sent you and Rodiger to investigate a fire, not a homicide, T-Bo. He said you've been poking around the lab, asking questions about the corpse."

"You don't think the two things could be related? The fire and the corpse? Can't investigate arson without looking into motive, now, can we? Does murder not qualify as a possible motive?"

"Guidry said that the victim's been dead for years, T-Bo. That poor kid, whoever he was, he wasn't killed in no fire."

"I didn't know that when I started asking questions, now did I? Either way, the fact that the body was in a house that burned is still relevant to the arson investigation."

Mac took a deep breath and swiveled his chair around to look out his window.

"Alright, I take your point. I'll speak to Rooster and explain that you and Guidry need to work together on this. Can I assure him you'll play nice in the sandbox?"

Captain Jack "Rooster" McCutcheon is Gator's boss in homicide. His nickname comes from his long neck and flaming red hair.

"I'll play nice if Gator will," I said. "Takes two to tango, Mac."

"Right, whatever. Go on, get out of here. You've got work to do."

Leaving Mac's office, I poured myself a coffee and took a seat beside Rodiger's desk.

"Captain wants us to work with Gator on this," I said.

"Gator doesn't work *with* anyone," Mike said. "Not in my experience, anyway."

Rodiger did a stint in Homicide as part of a management training program he was in. He knew all about Gator Guidry.

"Mine neither," I said, "but let's keep an open mind."

I leaned back and clasped my hands behind my head.

"What we got here, Mike?"

Rodiger shrugged and turned his chair toward me.

"I've got to believe it was an amateur who lit the fuse. A pro wouldn't start upstairs. The fact that there were traces of gas found downstairs, too, suggests the suspect realized his mistake, but either he ran out of fuel, or it was getting hot, so he panicked and ran."

"He may have been an amateur, but he got the job done in the end," I said.

"True. I'm guessing the ceiling beneath the upstairs room collapsed, and when those beams fell, they set things off downstairs. That would explain why the front of the house was in better shape."

"Makes sense, but let's wait on the Fire Department report before jumping to any conclusions," I said. "What about from a robbery standpoint. Think anything was taken?"

"Hard to say. Weisman's music collection may have been valuable, but it was almost completely destroyed. If anything was taken, it would have to have been one or two specific things, maybe from that safe. No way of knowing at this point. We need to find Weisman."

"Agreed. What do you make of his disappearance and the decades-old corpse?"

"I'm not sure what to think, but there are lots of possibilities," Rodiger said. "Maybe he got scared and ran off. Maybe he was kidnapped. Maybe he set the fire himself. And as far as the corpse goes, maybe he knew about it and maybe he didn't. I checked the property records, and he bought the place in 1961. It's possible the body was there before he moved in."

"Good point," I said. "Finding Weisman needs to be our focus. I'm guessing Gator is thinking the same thing. Let's suck it up and talk to him. Maybe we can divide and conquer."

As we walked over to Homicide to break bread with Joe Guidry, I quizzed Rodiger about his former colleague.

"What's Gator's rep within Homicide, Mike?"

"More respected than liked, I'd say. Respected and feared."

"Yeah, I've seen him in the gym, he's pretty ripped."

"I think it has more to do with his manner. The man is intense. I mean, we're talking all business all the time. He doesn't do small talk at all."

"He have any friends in the unit?"

"Not really. The other detectives keep a polite distance. He seems to get along with the captain, but that's about it."

"Rooster gives him some rope?"

"Yep. But in fairness, he's earned it. Whatever else you want to say about him, he gets results."

"You ever work with him directly?"

"No."

We stopped talking as we reached the Homicide offices. Rodiger waved to a few of the guys while I scanned the room for Guidry. He was standing by a printer, shuffling through some papers. He didn't see us coming until we were almost on top of him.

"Afternoon, Gator," I said.

I'd taken him by surprise, but once he realized who it was, his expression darkened. His eyes darted to Rodiger and then back to me, taking us both in.

"What do you want?"

His body language was tense and coiled, like a cobra.

"I don't know if you've been told yet, but Mac and Rooster want us to work together on the arson in Tremé," I said. "I thought we could compare notes."

"What for? I'm looking into a suspected cold-case homicide. It's got nothing to do with your fire."

"You don't know that. The two things could be related."

Gator was about to respond when something over my shoulder caught his attention. I turned and saw the tall, red-headed figure of Rooster McCutcheon approaching, a friendly smile on his face.

"Well, well, Detective Duplessis, it's been a while since we've seen you around these parts," he said, extending his hand to me and nodding at Rodiger.

"Hello, Captain. Good to see you. I was just explaining to Gator that you and Captain MacLaren would like us to work together on the fire in Tremé."

"Yes, that's right. Mac made the case that your arson might have something to do with our fossil of a corpse. Not sure I see it that way, but a little inter-departmental cooperation couldn't hurt either of our images. Gator, I expect you to keep detectives Duplessis and Rodiger informed of all new developments, and I know Captain MacLaren expects the same from you two. Are we all clear on this?"

Rodiger and I nodded our agreement, but Gator made no response.

"Gator? We good here?"

"Yes, sir, we're good," Gator said finally.

"Very well then. I'll leave the three of you to your work."

Rooster started to walk away but stopped abruptly and spun back around.

"Where are my manners?" he asked, looking at Rodiger.

"Mike, shame on me for not having asked how it's going for you in Property Crimes. I hated to lose you but it's important that talented young officers like yourself find the best homes for themselves. Did you make the right choice?"

"Yes, Captain, I believe so," Rodiger said. "But I have fond memories of my time in Homicide, and I learned a lot from you and your team. I appreciate you asking, sir."

"That's good to hear, son, you're a class act and Mac is lucky to have you."

Rooster patted Rodiger on the shoulder and headed back in the direction he came from. I turned to face Gator, who pretended to go back to his papers.

"What do you say, Gator? Do you have a few minutes now, or should we schedule a meeting?"

"I don't do meetings," he said, still staring at his papers. Then he looked up and fixed me with a glare.

"What do you want to know? My understanding is you've already interrogated the lab folks about my corpse."

"I did ask some questions, that's true," I said. "I apologize if you think I was stepping on your toes. That wasn't my intention. I was expecting the corpse to be the owner of the house, not a kid who's been dead for twenty-plus years."

"More like fifty."

"What's that?"

"The coroner's latest estimate is the kid died fifty to seventy years ago," Gator said.

I whistled. Gator shrugged.

"What about the placement of the body, Detective?" Rodiger asked. "Has the lab determined whether the corpse had been stashed inside the wall of the spare bedroom?"

Gator looked at Rodiger like he'd just caught a whiff of a foul smell. Instead of answering him, he turned to me.

"This pup follow you wherever you go? Detective Ringding, or whatever his name is?"

"Mike Rodiger is a good cop, Gator," I told him. "Might be our boss one day, the way he's going. You probably want to stay on his good side."

Gator smirked at that and looked Rodiger over.

"Don't worry kid, not many cops can make it in Homicide. There's worse consolation prizes than Property Crimes, I suppose. Kind of slow from what I hear, but it beats writing parking tickets. What was your question again?"

"I asked about the location of the body."

"Oh yeah, the body. The lab tells me the deceased was inside that wall for a mighty long time. No skeletal signs of foul play, but the fact he was packed into the wall suggests somebody didn't want him found. We're going through missing persons reports from the fifties, sixties, and seventies, see if anything matches up."

"Sounds like you've got things under control, Gator," I said. "You need our help with legwork, just let us know. We'll be in touch."

I motioned to Rodiger, and we started to leave.

"Hold on, Detective," came Gator's voice behind us. "What about you? Aren't you going to tell me about your fire? Seeing as we're supposed to be a team and all?"

"I thought the fire had nothing to do with your cold case, Gator?"

"Might as well cover all the bases, now that you're here and on the case," Gator said. "Make you feel useful."

I smiled.

"There's not much to tell until we get the NOFD report. The fire was started upstairs with petroleum, which suggests an inexperienced arsonist. There was a safe that was left open, and it was empty, so obviously that's got our attention."

"I'm not seeing any connection to my corpse."

"Nothing obvious, I agree, but if we can find the homeowner, this Weisman guy, maybe we can get some answers. He's owned the place since 1961, which fits into your window."

"Yeah, I know."

Rodiger and I told Gator we'd be in touch and headed back to Property Crimes. As we walked, I apologized for Gator's "Ringding" dis.

"Water off a duck's back, Detective. Typical alpha fare. Gator's probably the worst, but that's the culture over there."

"Everybody in Homicide have an animal nickname?"

Rodiger laughed.

"Well, let's see, there's Goose Gallagher and Rhino Reineke. I think that's it."

"It was nice of Rooster to ask after you," I said. "You choosing us over Homicide was a major coup for Mac. It had to be tough to swallow for Rooster."

"Speaking of which ..." Rodiger said, his eyes pointing down the long hallway. I looked up and saw Mac walking toward us at a fast clip and motioning for us to hurry.

"What is it?" I asked when we'd drawn close enough to talk without shouting.

"Christ, T-Bo, your friend the antiques dealer just showed up out of the blue with the owner of your torched house in Tremé."

"Izzy Weisman?"

"Yeah, that's the one. Wait till you get a load of this guy. He's waiting for you in the toaster. You might want to bring a clothespin or some nose plugs."

The toaster is what we call the interview room because when circumstances merit, we've been known to turn up the heat.

"Where is Bruneau, and how did he find Weisman?" I asked.

"I sent him home. Thanked him and told him this was police business. I don't know how he found the guy, but so help me God, you are not going to let him get involved in another investigation. We clear on that, T-Bo?"

"Absolutely, Captain," I said.

Bruneau played a role in a high-profile case I handled a few years ago involving a grave robbery and the pirate Jean Lafitte. The truth is, we wouldn't have solved it without Bru and his friends, but Mac chafed at their involvement and reamed me out about it more than once.

"Good," Mac said. "You two ready to talk to this guy, or do you need some time to prepare?"

"We're as ready as we'll ever be," I said, and began walking toward the toaster. Mac headed back to his office.

"Excuse me, Detective, haven't we forgotten something?" Rodiger asked.

"What's that?"

"Gator Guidry. Shouldn't we invite him to join us?"

Rodiger was right, of course, much as I didn't want him to be.

"Yeah, I suppose we should," I sighed.

No sooner had I said that than Gator darted through the door, looking a little out of breath.

"Oh, hey Gator, we were just about to call you."

"Your captain beat you to it," Gator said. "He called Rooster right after you left. Said he was heading out to find you."

"It's good that we're all here then. I'm thinking we start with the fire and gradually work our way to the corpse. That work for you?"

"Suit yourself."

Before entering the toaster, we stopped briefly to watch Weisman through the one-way mirror. He was a tiny, shrunken shell of a man. His stringy white hair and filthy clothing were disheveled, and he had some kind of rash on his arms and face. His elbows were propped on the stainless-steel table in front of him, and he held his forehead in his hands. A plastic cup of water he'd been given sat untouched.

When we opened the door, we were knocked back by the stench Mac had warned us about. It was like popping the lid of a garbage can with rotting fish inside, with piss and sweat mixed in for good measure. Rodiger and I managed to stifle our reactions, but Gator uttered a disgusted "Jesus!" and buried his nose in his forearm.

"Good afternoon, Mr. Weisman," I said. "My name is Detective Bo Duplessis, and these gentlemen are Detectives Mike Rodiger and Joe Guidry. Thank you for coming in. As you know, we have some questions for you, and to be honest, we were worried you might have left town."

"There's little chance of that detective. I have no place to go. I've just been a bit disoriented, trying to make sense of what's happened. I hope you understand. Everything I owned in the world was in that house."

I read Weisman his rights, which surprised the old man.

"I thought this was an interview, not an interrogation. Do I need a lawyer?"

"You have the right to have an attorney present, Mr. Weisman. Would you like to exercise your prerogative?"

"No, not at this point. I'll let you know if I change my mind. Please, proceed."

Weisman's voice was stronger and clearer than I had expected based on his appearance.

"Of course, Mr. Weisman. May I call you Izzy?"

"Yes, I'd prefer that."

"Excellent. Izzy it is then. As it happens, Izzy, we're interested in the same thing as you. Making sense of what's happened, that is. We're wondering, now that you've had some time to reflect, what is it that you think did happen?"

Weisman didn't answer right away. He looked for a second like his mind had left the room, and his thoughts were far away. Then he spoke.

"I really don't know. I'd been gone for a couple hours running errands, and when I came back, the house was in flames, and police and firefighters were everywhere. I got scared and walked away. I didn't know if there'd been a gas leak, or if I forgot to turn off a burner on the stove, or what. But then I wondered if maybe someone was trying to kill me. And then I read in the paper that arson is suspected, so now I'm really wondering."

"Does someone have a reason to want you dead?"

"Not that I know of. As you probably know, I had a large collection of music memorabilia. It was worth a lot of money, I'm not sure how much. People have been trying to get me to sell it, but I've refused. Maybe it had something to do with that."

"If someone was trying to kill you, why would they set the fire when you weren't in the house?"

"I don't know, but I see your point, Detective. It was just a feeling I had."

"Was your collection insured, Mr. Weisman?" Rodiger asked.

"Only as part of my homeowner's insurance. There was no policy covering the collection itself that would recoup its true value."

"If someone was interested in owning your collection, Izzy, why would they destroy it?" I asked.

"I don't know. Out of spite, maybe. Or maybe there was one specific thing they were after. When they found it, they covered their tracks with the fire."

"Like what?"

"Again, I don't know."

Rodiger asked Weisman for the names of people who tried to buy his collection, and for the specifics of the errands he said he ran at the time of the fire. Then Gator butted in, which I knew was coming. His body language had been getting antsy.

"Mr. Weisman, are you aware that a corpse was found in your house?"

"Yes, I read that in the newspaper. A juvenile male, it said. I can't imagine who it could be."

"Are you aware that the boy had been dead for several years?"

"That's what Mr. Abellard told me, yes."

"Who is Mr. Abellard?"

"Bruneau Abellard is the man who escorted Mr. Weisman to the station," I told Gator. "In full disclosure, he is a friend of mine. My understanding is that he made Izzy's acquaintance just a few days ago when he brought him a recording cylinder he had discovered in a piece of furniture that had come into his antiques store. Do I have that right, Izzy?"

"Yes, that's correct."

Gator had clearly been knocked off balance by this revelation, and he shot me a look that said we'd be discussing it later, and not in a friendly way. The momentary pause in the interview gave Rodiger an opening.

"Mr. Weisman, is it possible that the cylinder is what the arsonist was after?"

"I suppose it's possible, yes. Not many people would have known about it."

"But one or more people besides yourself did?"

"Yeah, I guess."

"We're going to need those names."

"Okay, sure. I played it over the phone for Paul Martin, who is a music professor at Southern Mississippi University. Other than that, it was just Mr. Abellard and his friend."

"His friend?"

"Yes, he had a friend with him when he visited me. Henry, I believe his name was. He was knowledgeable about music."

"Henry Wilkins?" I suggested.

"Yes, that sounds right."

I knew Henry Wilkins, but not well. He helps Bruneau with pickups and deliveries and as a server at some of his fancy dinner parties. He seemed like an honest, trustworthy sort to me, but I made a note to follow up with him. Gator leaned forward to resume his questioning about the corpse, but I held out my arm to let him know I wasn't done.

"Izzy, why might someone be interested in the cylinder?"

Weisman took a deep breath and scratched the top of his head. Bits of dead skin fell to his shoulders.

"It's only a theory, but I think it's possible that it might be Buddy Bolden on the cylinder. If that could be proven, the cylinder would be worth a good deal of money."

"Who the hell is Buddy Bolden?" Gator asked, annoyed.

"The man who some say invented jazz," I told him.

"That might be a bit of an overstatement," Weisman corrected me, "but he was certainly an early pioneer and an important influence. There are no known recordings of Bolden, which is why the cylinder would be so valuable if it really is him."

"Where is the cylinder now?" Rodiger asked.

"I don't know. As a precaution, I put it in my safe. Mr. Abellard told me the safe had been left open and that it was empty. Is that true?"

Gator shot me another angry look, and I silently cursed Bru for yet again overstepping his bounds.

"Did you leave the safe open, Mr. Weisman?" Rodiger asked.

"I don't think so."

"You don't think so?"

"It's possible. I can be forgetful sometimes."

"Did anyone else know the combination?"

"No, I don't think so. Did somebody open it using the combination?"

"We're not at liberty to release details of the investigation at this time," I said.

That gave Gator his opening.

"Back to the corpse," he said, facing Weisman. "Are you aware of where in your house the corpse was found?"

"No, I am not."

"It had been concealed behind the wall of your guest bedroom. Do you have an explanation for how that could be?"

"No, I'm afraid I do not," Weisman said, looking surprised. "All I can think of is that it was already there when I bought the house and moved in."

"That would have been in 1961, correct?"

"Yes, that's right."

"According to the coroner, the boy had been dead for twenty to thirty years, not seventy," Gator lied. "It would seem that the math doesn't exactly support your theory."

Weisman shrugged his shoulders but did not respond.

"You have no explanation then?" Gator pressed on.

"No, I don't," Weisman said. "All I can think of is that your coroner is wrong on his timeline or maybe somebody broke in and hid the body when I was out of town."

"Do you go out of town often?"

"When I was younger, I used to travel from time to time. Sometimes I'd be away for a few weeks."

"Where would you go?"

"To visit friends and family back in Brooklyn, where I grew up. Occasionally, I'd accompany musicians I was promoting when they'd go out on tour. I've traveled to Europe a few times, for pleasure."

Gator drummed his fingers on the table, plotting his next move, I assumed, and letting Weisman stew in the story he'd spun.

"Mr. Weisman, you should know that we're investigating this corpse of yours as a cold-case homicide," he said. "It's only a matter of time until we discover the identity of the boy who died. We don't have enough to hold you here, but if there's something you know that you're not telling us, I strongly suggest you do so now."

"Are you saying I'm a suspect in this homicide, Detective?"

"Let's just say we consider you a person of interest."

"That goes for the arson, too," I added.

Weisman looked especially feeble as he crossed his arms, and his shoulders sagged.

"In that case, I have nothing more to say."

1967

The Dew Drop Inn
New Orleans, Louisiana
May 1967

Gliding down Louisiana Avenue on his Ducati Scrambler, the warm wind ruffling his shoulder-length hair, and the sweet smell of gardenia and honeysuckle tap dancing in his nostrils, Andre Coulon is at peace. Med school is behind him, and his future is settled, at least for now. In a few months' time he will be off to war. He doesn't know what that means yet, or where he is going, exactly. He imagines it won't be pleasant. But he has a plan, and that counts for something, even if it isn't of his own making.

He turns right on LaSalle, and as he crosses Seventh Street, and then Sixth, he cranes to his left and takes note of the streetlights at the edge of the Magnolia Projects, and the bleak brick complex behind them on the far side of Freret. In the middle of the next block, he pulls his bike to the curb and parks a couple buildings down from the Dew Drop. He hasn't been to the club since catching a James Booker show a few years earlier. He remembers that the opening act was a female impersonator, and that he had found it strangely entertaining.

Andre arrives early in hopes of grabbing a seat close to the stage. Only a couple dozen people mill about as he pays the two-dollar cover and makes his way to the bar, depositing himself on a stool at the far end, as near to the action as he can get. He orders a Dixie long neck and turns around to take stock of the room. At first, he thinks he is the only white man present, but then he catches sight of the promoter angling toward him from the backstage area.

"Hello Andre," the man says.

"Izzy."

"I don't suppose you've seen her?"

"No. I thought it was your job to get her places on time."

"I did. She was here a few minutes ago. We did a sound check and then she disappeared."

The men look at each other, an unspoken understanding passing between them.

"She'll be back in a bit, I'm sure," the promoter says.

Andre doesn't much care for Izzy Weisman. He's always working an angle, and Andre doubts he is as well-connected as he pretends to be. He told Lyla that he thought another promoter could get her bigger bookings, but he has since come to understand that Izzy is more to Lyla than a manager. He is her protector and her enabler, her scold and her confidant. And maybe the only person in her tangled world she can fully trust. Lyla had cast her spell on Izzy, and he was in her thrall. That is the bond the two men share, fellow captives in a confusing web of seduction, dependency, and deceit.

Standing at the bar, they form a curious sight, the hulking giant and the diminutive promoter. Andre in jeans, work boots, and a faded green henley, studded leather bracelets on his wrists, long hair and mutton chop sideburns framing his heavy features. Izzy in pointed city shoes, tight fitting nylon pants, and a brown and white collared sweater shirt, his curly auburn hair neatly trimmed.

"Lyla tells me you got drafted," Izzy says.

"That's right."

"I'm sorry to hear that. When are you heading out?"

"I'm supposed to be at Fort Benning in July."

"You going as a doctor?"

"Field medic."

Izzy whistles.

"You're going to see some shit, Andre."

"Yeah, that's what they tell me."

"You know, I was in Korea. Did I ever tell you that?"

"No, I don't think so."

"Yeah. I was a radio operator. Cold as hell over there. I don't guess you'll have *that problem."*

"No, I wouldn't think so."

Izzy's eyes look past Andre and without turning, he knows she is there.

"Hey baby," she purrs from behind him. Before he can shift, she has draped herself over him, her raven hair falling about his chest. She nibbles at his neck, her breath warm and sickly sweet, a stale mix of nicotine and gin. Andre's entire body tingles with pleasure, but his bliss is tempered by the suspicion that she has been using again. He turns around to face her, and her glassy eyes confirm his assessment. He smiles anyway and pulls her in for a kiss.

Andre first laid eyes on Lyla Saint-Clair, or "Lady Ly" as Izzy bills her, four months earlier. He'd closed out a long intern's shift at the Charity Hospital emergency room, and headed over to Club Tijuana, where Earl King was scheduled to play. Lyla was the opening act and when Andre arrived, she had already begun. From the first, he was spellbound. He had heard better voices, and seen prettier women, but never had he felt such a visceral pull. She was Circe, and he was a drunken sailor.

Lyla stood at the edge of the stage, tall and arresting in her low-cut emerald gown, black hair tumbling about her chest in long cascading waves. She swayed hypnotically as her accompanist, a piano player, steered her through a bluesy number. Her voice was deep and throaty, and Andre knew without asking that she was a smoker. But it was her phrasing that mesmerized him. The breathy way she exhaled. Her languid holding of a note. The way she punctuated an ending with the vocal equivalent of an ellipse. Lyla didn't so much finish a song as release it tenderly into the night.

Afterward, when the set had ended and the crowd was waiting for the main act to appear, he stood at the bar, the singer's voice still playing in his head. Then she was there, a soft tug on his elbow, looking up from clouded obsidian eyes.

"Buy a girl a drink?"

Chapter Ten

I met up with Bo at Cochon Butcher that Monday afternoon, as planned. It was a beautiful day out, so we got our sandwiches to go and took them out to St. Mary's Park around the corner. Bo ordered the Cubano and a Barq's, and I went with the Porchetta on focaccia and water.

I knew that Bo had interviewed Izzy that morning, and I also knew he wouldn't want to tell me about it, so I tried a sideways tack.

"Your captain doesn't much care for me, does he?" I asked once we found a place to sit.

"It's not that. He doesn't know you. And he really doesn't want civilians getting involved in police investigations."

"I wasn't trying to get involved. I just wanted to keep Izzy company."

"Uh-huh."

So much for the sideways approach.

"What did Izzy have to say?"

"About what?"

"The fire, the corpse, where he'd been."

"What did I just say about civilians getting involved in police business?"

Plan B wasn't going well either, so I tried one last tack.

"He told me he thinks someone may have been trying to kill him."

"Uh-huh, he told us that, too."

"You believe him?"

"If you were trying to kill someone, would you start a fire when he wasn't in the house?"

"Right. Good point."

Bo looked at me uneasily.

"Look, Bru, I'll tell you some stuff when it's appropriate, but this case is extra sensitive, alright? I've got to work with a hard ass from Homicide, and there's departmental politics involved. I need you to let me do my job."

"Okay, sure, no problem," I said. "I understand. Any reason I can't keep researching the Buddy Bolden angle?"

"No, not that I can think of. You're the one who found the cylinder, after all, and I doubt it's related to the fire anyway. Keep me posted on what you find."

We took bites out of our sandwiches and grunted our approval. Then Bo changed the subject.

"So, how're you doing?" he asked me in an almost paternal tone.

I wasn't sure where he was going with this, so I just looked at him quizzically.

"I mean, how's your life? You and Sallie have been living apart for a while now. Are you okay with that? Are you resigned to it being a permanent split?"

"We're good. We spent the afternoon together yesterday and had a delightful time. I think maybe we're better as friends than partners."

"She feels the same way?"

"I don't know. I think so, yeah."

"Angie thinks maybe she doesn't."

"Meaning what?"

"Meaning, maybe she'd like to get back together if she thought you were serious about changing some of your ways."

I'd heard this before, and frankly, I was tired of it.

"You mean my eccentricities? We've been down this path more than once, Bo."

"No, that's not what I mean. Angie thinks your eccentricities are part of what Sallie loves about you. Sounds like it has more to do with your being kind of self-absorbed sometimes and not always being tuned into what's going on with her."

"I've heard that before, too. It seems whatever it is she expects of me, I can't live up to."

"It can be hard, Bru. Angie and me, we have these issues too. It's easy to get wrapped up in your own stuff, you know? But sometimes you've got to remind yourself that the other person's got stuff going on too. Maybe your priorities aren't always the same. What helps is just to check in with each other sometimes. Maybe find some areas to compromise."

"Thank you, doctor, that's very helpful. What's your hourly rate?"

Bo smiled at me dolefully.

"Ever think maybe it's not just me who could stand to make some changes?" I asked.

"Sure. I said as much to Angie. What are your gripes with Sallie, if you don't mind me asking?"

"She's always judging me. I eat too much. I don't exercise enough. I'm too set in my ways. I don't like bowls."

"Bowls?"

"Never mind. Bad joke. But the pressure gets to you after a while, you know?"

"Sure, I get it. But that nagging, you know it's because she cares about you, right?"

"Yes, I do understand that, and I'm grateful for it up to a point. But I can't walk around on eggshells all the time."

"You tell her that?"

"Sometimes I'll snap at her when it gets to be too much."

"Maybe pick a time when you're both in a good place and introduce the topic gently."

I looked at my friend. The carefree jock of our youth was still there, but so was the consummate police professional, the husband of a lovely but sometimes combustible woman, and the father of three wonderful children with disparate needs. Sometimes I don't give him enough credit for all the hats he wears and the jobs he juggles.

"Thanks, maybe I will," I said.

* * *

Bo's advice was still swimming around in my head that night when Sallie called me with the surprise suggestion that we both take the next day off to drive to Jackson, home of East Louisiana State Hospital, two hours north of New Orleans. She had called ahead and found someone in Human Resources who agreed to meet with us and review employment records from the 1920s. It felt like another test, but also a win-win. An opportunity to spend quality time with Sallie, and a long shot chance to draw us closer to solving the mystery of Buddy Bolden's lost cylinder, if that's what it was.

Naturally, I offered to drive, but Sallie said she didn't want to take Liesel. She didn't mind putzing around town in the old girl but didn't like the idea of taking her out on the highway. An earlier version of me might have objected, but I told her that I understood her logic, even if Liesel's feelings would be hurt.

"Liesel has feelings?" she asked.

"Of course she does. A man and his car spend thirty-plus years together, you develop feelings."

"In that case, you'd better break it to her gently."

The next morning, Sallie picked me up in her Toyota Prius. She asked me to drive because she'd been up late learning everything she could about Buddy Bolden. She handed me her key, which isn't really a key at all, just a fob that enables you to push a button to turn on the ignition.

"What was wrong with keys?" I asked.

"What?"

"What was wrong with keys? I don't get what problem automakers think they solved with these fobs."

"Seriously, we're going to debate keys versus fobs for the next two hours?"

"I'm just saying, I don't get it. You lose this thing; you've got the same headache as if you lost your key. You get out of your car, your key is always in the ignition; this thing, you've got to remember where you put it. A key doesn't have a battery that's going to die on you someday. Does it take less work to push a button than turn a key?"

"I see you've put a lot of thought into this topic."

"It's just that this whole fob thing is a solution in search of a problem, if you ask me."

"I didn't."

"Didn't what?"

"Ask you. But if I say I agree with you, can we move on?"

I can tell when I'm being patronized, so having made my point, I decided to cut my losses. I briefed Sallie on Izzy Weisman's situation and the status of the police investigation. I also told her about Lyla Saint-Clair.

"Prosper had a girlfriend?" Sallie mused. "How interesting. I've always wondered. That heaviness he carries around, I know it's from Vietnam, but it always seemed like it was more than that."

"I haven't had a chance to talk with him about it, so I don't know. Might have been just a fling."

"Or maybe she was the love of his life."

"Yeah, could be that too."

"How do you plan on approaching it?" Sallie asked.

"Delicately. Don't want to open any old wounds."

Sallie nodded her agreement, and then we talked about Buddy Bolden. Most of what she had learned I already knew, but she did share a theory I hadn't heard, which is that it wasn't his boozy lifestyle that drove Buddy mad, but pellagra.

"What's that?"

"It's a disease caused by a deficiency of niacin, or Vitamin B3. They didn't really know about it until a few years after Buddy got sent away, but once it was diagnosed, it became an epidemic throughout the rural south, where diets were low in protein and heavy on corn. People called it sharecroppers' disease, but it was prevalent in the cities, too. Wherever people were living in poverty, basically."

"What are the symptoms?"

"The three D's: Diarrhea, dermatitis, and dementia, and they come on in that order."

"Did Buddy have diarrhea?"

"His signature song was Funky Butt, wasn't it?"

I had to laugh at that, and Sallie flashed a self-satisfied grin. That gave me an opening.

"You know, it's been good spending time with you the last few days," I said, patting her knee. "I've missed you."

"Yes, it has been nice. I've missed you too."

"I've been doing a lot of thinking, you know."

"That sounds dangerous."

"No, I'm being serious. I used to think it was all my little quirks that got on your nerves, but it wasn't really that, was it?"

Sallie didn't answer right away. Then she turned to face me, leaning back against her door.

"No, I suppose it wasn't."

"It was more that I can be kind of overbearing, right?"

"That's one way of putting it."

"How would you put it?"

Sallie looked away and sighed.

"I don't know. Smothering, maybe. Hovering. Arrogant, sometimes."

"That's fair, I guess. I can see it now, looking back. I couldn't at the time."

"Knowing others is intelligence; knowing yourself is true wisdom."

"Who said that?"

"Lao Tzu."

"Impressive. You're into Taoism now?"

"I'll take wisdom wherever I can find it."

Sallie turned again and looked out her window.

"I guess I should tell you, I've been doing a little soul searching of my own."

"And what have you found?"

"Maybe that I can be a little overbearing too, in my way. Too judgmental. A bit of a nag."

"You, a nag? Never."

"Very funny," she said, smiling and gently punching my arm. Then she looked at me again, a pensive expression on her face.

"What is it about people that we're always trying to change those closest to us?"

I thought about that.

"People you care about, you want them to be the best version of themselves. But maybe they're happy with who they are or have a different idea of who their best self is. And anyway, can you ever really change someone? People have to change from within; it seems to me."

* * *

The approach to Jackson State looked more like a college campus than any image of a mental hospital I'd had in my mind. A large, well-kept lawn stretched out before a magnificent white Greek Revival building with a grand three-story central portico and matching colonnades on each wing. It was the administration building, we would learn, surrounded by clusters of smaller buildings that housed the patients.

"A bit more grandiose than I was expecting," I said.

"They built it a few years before the Civil War," Sallie informed me. "They told the architect, name of Gibbens, not to make it look like a prison."

"Well, he succeeded on that score."

"In every other way it was a prison, though. Or worse. A *Times Picayune* reporter wrote a big exposé back in the eighties, and he uncovered all kinds of corruption and negligence. They chained patients to the walls, apparently. It had to be just an awful place. Probably still is."

"Is there anything you do without researching it first?"

"I like to be prepared, okay?"

"Really? I didn't know that about you."

Sallie punched me in the arm.

"There's no need to resort to violence," I complained.

"When I decide to get violent, you'll know."

I parked under the shade of a stately live oak, and leaving the cool comfort of the air-conditioned car, we stepped out into the late morning humidity. A long walkway and two flights of stairs led to the main entrance of the imposing edifice. By the time we made it to the top, I was short of breath and sweating. I tried to hide it, but Sallie was on to me.

"How's that workout regimen going?"

I bent over, hands on my knees.

"I'm all about incremental gains," I gasped. "Today, Jackson State. Tomorrow, the Empire State."

Sallie smirked, grabbed my shirt, and pulled me inside to the front desk, where she notified the receptionist of our appointment. Soon we were in the office of Marilyn Rogers, head of HR, a cordial middle-aged woman dressed in a gray button-down shirt and pleated black skirt.

"Our records prior to the 1950s are spotty," she explained. "I couldn't find a list of employees from 1929, but I did find one from 1926. The only Clarence listed was a Clarence Burkett."

She slid a fraying canvas ledger in front of us, pointing to the handwritten name on faded yellow paper.

"Do you have any way of knowing when he was hired or if he was still employed here three years later?" Sallie asked.

"I'm afraid not. If it helps, the next year we have records for is 1931, and his name does not appear."

"Do the records say what his job was?" I asked.

"Yes. He was an orderly on what they called the colored ward in those days, so he would have had contact with patients, including Mr. Bolden."

"What about an address or any other kind of identifying information?"

"It says he was an African American male and that he was thirty-four years old."

"Colored, you mean."

"Yes, colored."

* * *

Burkett is a common name in the deep south, but at least it wasn't Smith or Jones, and Clarence was a lot easier to work with than Tom or John. Sallie thought that if she spent some time with her databases at work, she could find a Clarence Burkett living in or near Jackson in the 1920s, or at least narrow him down to a handful of candidates.

As we rolled through Baton Rouge on the way home, with Sallie driving this time, I took advantage of the strong cell signal to place a call to Billy Collins, the owner of Arklatex Auctions in Shreveport, which he named after the tri-state area that Shreveport anchors. I left a voicemail with Billy the day before, asking for the name of the previous owner of the sideboard that contained the cylinder, which I had purchased at one of Billy's auctions. Once again, he didn't pick up, and I left another message. A few minutes later, I got a text from Billy.

Bernadette Ledet, Natchitoches, 318-767-9281

I tried the number, and a woman's voice answered on the third ring. I put us on speaker so Sallie could listen in.

"Hello, is this Ms. Ledet?" I asked.

"Who is this?"

"Apologies, ma'am. My name is Bruneau Abellard, and I own an antiques store in New Orleans. I recently purchased a sideboard at a Shreveport auction that I believe may have belonged to you. Does that ring a bell?"

"Yes. What about it?"

"The sideboard contained an object that I'm trying to trace the history of. It's a recording cylinder, from the 1920s I believe."

"I don't know nothing about that."

"I understand, ma'am, but I wonder if you could tell me about the sideboard. Was it a family piece or something you purchased?"

There was a pause during which I supposed Bernadette Ledet was deciding whether to engage with me. Curiosity got the better of her.

"Well, let me see now. I reckon it belonged to my ex-husband's family. He passed away some years ago. I'm getting ready to move into assisted living now, so I'm in the process of 'downsizing,' as my daughter likes to say. That's how come the sideboard was in your auction."

"I see. I'm sorry about your ex-husband, ma'am. He didn't want the sideboard, I take it?"

"No, sir, he never much cared for things like that. Just his football and his drinking buddies."

"I see. I hate to be nosy, ma'am, but if I may ask, do you know how long the piece had been in his family?"

"Oh my, I'm afraid I couldn't rightly say. A good many years, I should think."

"Where was your husband from?"

"He grew up in St. Francisville, over on the Mississippi. He moved to Baton Rouge as a young man. That's where we met and where we raised our family. I came to Natchitoches about twenty years ago, after our divorce, so I could be close to my daughter and my grandchildren."

"St. Francisville. That's near Jackson, isn't it?"

"Yes, sir, it surely is."

"Again, I don't mean to be nosy, but may I ask you your husband's name?"

"Hollis."

"His last name?"

"Burkett. Hollis Burkett was his name. I went back to my maiden name when we divorced."

"I don't suppose Hollis's father's name was Clarence, by any chance?"

"Why yes, how did you know?"

I gave Bernadette a high-level summary of our Buddy Bolden saga, and she confirmed that Clarence Burkett worked at Jackson State when Hollis was little. Bernadette couldn't have been sweeter, but she didn't seem all that interested in her father-in-law. She said she didn't know Clarence well, as he died a few years after she and Hollis were married. She didn't remember any talk of Buddy Bolden or a recording cylinder either. I asked if her ex-husband had any siblings who were still living, and she gave me the name of her former sister-in-law, Henrietta Thomas, who lived in a retirement community in Mandeville.

"Well, that was something!" Sallie exclaimed after I'd thanked Bernadette and hung up.

"I guess I can forget about running down Clarence Burkett for you. One phone call and you've found the man. How's a nosy girl supposed to have any fun?"

"Sorry to ruin your sleuthing fix, but we're getting somewhere," I said. "Let's hope Henrietta Thomas still has her wits about her and can tell us about her father."

Chapter Eleven

We all had different takeaways from our interview with Izzy Weisman. To me, he was a frightened old man overwhelmed by what had happened to him. I thought he answered our questions as truthfully as he could. And it seemed plausible that his flight instinct would have kicked in as he watched his life go up in flames. Admittedly, it wasn't hard to imagine Weisman as a sleazy operator in his younger years. But a murderer? No way. An arsonist? I couldn't see it. And anyway, if his collection wasn't insured, what would his motive have been? No. To me, Weisman was the victim of a crime, not a perpetrator.

Rodiger wasn't so sure. He was bothered by the missing cylinder and the open safe, and he wanted to check Weisman's alibis and the names of the people he said offered to buy his collection. Beyond that, he felt that Weisman was holding something back.

"I can't put my finger on it, but something is off," he said. "Why would somebody torch the house of a harmless old man and destroy the one thing he had that was of value? What would the motive be?"

"Maybe it wasn't about money," I said. "Maybe it was personal. What if someone held a grudge against him? Maybe that's why Weisman thought somebody might be trying to kill him. Because he knew he had an enemy."

"Could be. But why didn't he tell us about this enemy if that was the case? Couldn't it also be that he started the fire himself, to hide something he didn't want found?"

"Like, gee, I wonder what?" Gator Guidry interjected. "Oh, I know, how about the remains of a kid he killed fifty years ago?"

"You really think the old man could kill somebody?" I asked.

"He wasn't always an old man. You do this job long enough, you realize killers come in all shapes and sizes."

"I'm sure that's true, Gator, but if he didn't want the corpse found, why would he burn the house down? We wouldn't have the corpse if it wasn't for the fire."

"First of all, it's my corpse, not yours. We clear on that?"

"Of course. Crystal."

Gator held eye contact until he was satisfied that I meant what I said. Then he answered my question.

"Maybe he thought the skeleton would disintegrate in the fire. Or to your point, maybe somebody else torched the place for reasons we don't understand yet. One thing I know. If that kid was killed after 1961 when Weisman bought the place, the corpse would've stunk to high heaven for a long time. So, whether he was away on vacation or not, he would've known about it."

It was hard to dispute Gator's logic.

"The coroner said fifty to seventy years, right?" I asked.

"Yeah. What of it?"

"According to my math, sixty-one is right in the middle of your window, Gator. Kid could've been killed after sixty-one, for sure. But he also could've died in the fifties, before Weisman owned the place."

"It's possible, yes," Gator admitted. "That's why we've got to identify the corpse, so we can narrow this down."

* * *

The day after our debrief, more information trickled in.

The fire department report didn't tell us much we didn't already know. Petroleum was the arsonist's fuel of choice. The torcher started the fire upstairs, then descended to the main floor and set off another blaze in the room at the back of the house that contained Weisman's music. He or she may have intended to marinate the front of the house, too, but probably the heat and flames were spreading so quickly, they panicked and fled. There were no identifying markers left behind that NOFD could find.

Rodiger checked on Weisman's alibis. He said he'd been to the Rouses on North Carrolton and the CVS just up the way before returning home to the fire. In-store video confirmed both accounts, but there was a forty-five-minute gap between Weisman's appearance at the drug store and the onset of the blaze.

"Enough time for him to drive home, start the fire, and leave again," Rodiger said.

"You think so? Hard to imagine the old man moving that fast," I said. "How does he account for those missing minutes?"

"I don't know, we'll have to bring him back in to find out."

I changed the subject.

"What about the folks who Weisman said offered to buy his stuff?"

"He said there were three of them and I've talked to two."

"What've you learned?"

"I talked to Carla Goodson first," Rodiger said. "She's the widow of Dean Goodson, the fat cat oil man who died a few years ago. She confirmed that she'd been in touch with Weisman but said she never made a firm offer. She was only interested in the jazz recordings and memorabilia, which she was going to donate to the jazz museum."

"Not the whole collection?"

"Nope. She said a lot of Wiesman's stuff was crap. In her mind, he was more of a hoarder than a collector."

"Interesting. Who's next?"

"Dominick Martello."

"*The* Dominick Martello?"

"Is there more than one?"

Dominick "The Dandy Duca" Martello is a big-time commercial real estate developer and patriarch of the local Sicilian Creole community. It's also widely known that he runs large-scale loansharking and prostitution rackets, but despite the best efforts of NOPD, it's never been proven. The feds got him on tax evasion a few years back, and he served a few months in a minimum-security facility, but NOPD has never been able to pin a thing on him.

"Why would Martello be interested in Weisman's collection?"

"Turns out he's a connoisseur of early rock and roll. You should see his house. He's got a vintage juke box filled with old 45s, a huge oil painting of Fats Domino, clothing that belonged to Professor Longhair and Ernie K-Doe, one of Buddy Holly's guitars, all kinds of stuff. Plays a little bass guitar himself when he wants to blow off steam."

"You went to his house?"

"Yeah. I couldn't get past his secretary the first couple calls, but once she relayed what I was looking into, he called me personally and invited me over."

"Wait until Vice gets a load of this," I laughed. "They've been trying to get a peek inside Martello's place for years, and you get yourself invited over for a chat with the big man himself. Nice work, Detective."

"Dumb luck, I guess."

"What did Martello have to say about Weisman and his collection?"

"Just that he was sick about the fire. He said Weisman was an eccentric pain in the ass, but there was no doubt he had one of the finest collections of recordings and memorabilia around, even if not many people knew about it. He said there were a lot of one-of-a-kind items in that house, and now they're lost to history."

"Did he say what he thought the collection was worth?"

"I asked him that. He said he couldn't hazard a guess but that he had offered Weisman four hundred grand. He said he turned him down without blinking an eye."

"You think maybe he's been leaning on Weisman?"

"That's not the sense I got, but anything is possible."

I made a mental note to talk to Joe Bailey about Martello. Joe is my long-time buddy in Vice, and if anybody knows Martello's M.O., it would be Joe.

"Remind me who the third one is, the one you haven't spoken to yet?" I asked Rodiger.

"Paul Martin, the guy Weisman played the cylinder for over the phone. Weisman said he's a musicologist at Southern Miss, but the music department there says there's no such person on their faculty or staff. I need to check back with Weisman. He might have gotten the department confused."

"Alright, keep trying. If it comes to it, we can ask Hattiesburg P.D. to poke around."

* * *

I left work early to swing by Bruneau's store. I'd called Bru earlier in the day to see if Henry Wilkins was there, and he said he wasn't, but that he expected him to roll in with a delivery around four. He said he'd make sure Henry stuck around until I got there.

When I walked in, there was a familiar scene. Bru was in a back corner of the store with a customer, talking up a fancy-looking desk. We waved at each other. His assistant, Victoria, was at the counter talking to someone on the phone, and Bru's French bulldog, Hugo, was curled up at her feet. When he saw me, Hugo growled, roused himself, and waddled over to sniff my leg suspiciously. I don't know what that dog has against me, but I get the full treatment every time.

I found Henry Wilkins on a ladder outside Bru's office, changing out a fluorescent lighting tube.

"Hello, Henry," I greeted him.

"Oh, hi there, Detective Duplessis," Henry said, looking down from his ladder. "It's good to see you. How you been?"

"I am well, thank you."

"And Mrs. Duplessis?"

"Angie's doing great. She sends her regards."

We exchanged a few more pleasantries as Henry stepped off the ladder, and then I got down to business.

"Henry, did Bruneau tell you that I was hoping to speak with you for a few minutes?"

"Yes, sir, he did. About Mr. Weisman, whose house burned down?"

"Yes, that's right."

"What a shame that was," Henry said. "A lifetime of collecting and it's all gone, just like that. He had some amazing stuff."

"That's what I'm told. Any idea why someone would want to destroy it all?"

"No, I can't imagine why someone would, unless they were angry about something, and they wanted to punish Mr. Weisman. It doesn't make any sense otherwise."

"What about that cylinder, Henry? Weisman said he put it in his safe, but the safe was open and there was nothing in it. Do you think maybe someone was after the cylinder and set fire to the place to cover their tracks?"

"I wouldn't know about that, Detective. I guess anything is possible."

"You're a musician, Henry. Do you think that was Buddy Bolden on the cylinder?"

"I couldn't say for sure, but that wasn't no ordinary 1920s trumpet player. The way that cat was blowing loud and long and bending those notes? He was way ahead of his time, whoever it was."

"Bruneau tells me you thought maybe the cylinder was made more recently."

"Yes, that was my first reaction because I never heard anyone from back then play like that, but then after Ms. Maguire cracked the code on that inscription, it seemed like it must have been Buddy. People who remembered him said there wasn't nobody could blow like him. I guess maybe they were right."

"Who would want a recording like that?"

"Oh lordy, could be anybody. Collectors. Somebody out to make a buck. Musicians. There'd be lots of people interested."

"Wouldn't it be hard to sell, if it was known to be stolen?"

"You'd know more about that than me, Detective," Henry said. "Some folks, they just like having stuff, especially stuff nobody else has got."

"I guess you're probably right about that. Henry, when you visited Izzy Weisman's house, was there anything that jumped out at you?"

"You mean besides the smell?"

"Yeah, besides the smell. As a musician, especially. Anything you saw that Bruneau might not have noticed?"

Henry put his hands on his hips and looked down at the floor, like he was trying to retrieve a memory.

"I'm sure he told you about the stained-glass window," Henry said. "I guess I kept staring at that, trying to identify all the musicians, and didn't look around as much as I should have. There was one thing kind of strange about that window, though."

"What was that?"

"Well, each pane was of a different legend of New Orleans music. All the ones you'd expect: Louis, Fats, Irma, Toussaint, Longhair, the Nevilles, you name it. But there was one I never even heard of. A female singer, and she had one of the two or three biggest panes. She just seemed out of place in that company."

"Who was she?"

"I can't remember what he said her name was. Lady something. Liza? Layla? Lilly? Something like that. Leggy white woman with long black hair. Seemed like it was kind of personal for Mr. Weisman. He got a little choked up when he talked about her. Said she was a rising star in the sixties, but she died young. Drugs, I think."

"Interesting. I'll have to ask Weisman about her. Anything else you noticed, Henry?"

"Upstairs, he had lots of old instruments and equipment, and the walls were full of posters from the Dew Drop Inn, Club Tijuana, Jed's, The Safari Room. Brought back a lot of memories."

"All closed now, right?"

"Yes, long gone, although I hear somebody's trying to bring back the Dew Drop."

"Yeah, I heard that too. What about downstairs, where he kept his music collection? Anything catch your eye down there?"

"No, not really. He had a lot of music, that's for sure, but we didn't really stop to look at it. I do remember that even though the house was a mess, the music seemed to be carefully organized. To be honest, the place smelled so bad, I just wanted to get out of there."

***

The next day, I was back at the station, shooting the breeze with Rodiger, when Gator Guidry walked up behind us.

"Got a probable I.D. on our corpse, boys. It's against my better judgment, but Rooster thought you should know."

"Aw, Gator, it's so kind of you to share. You're a team player all the way."

Gator ignored my barb.

"We're still running down the details, but we think the kid was named Arnold Jesse. Thirteen years old. Disappeared in June of sixty-seven."

"What makes you think it was him?"

"Kid grew up in the Magnolia projects, a couple blocks from the old Dew Drop Inn. According to the case file, he used to hang out around the club, doing odd jobs and tap dancing for tips. He was treated kind of like a mascot by the servers and some of the musicians and entertainers."

"And the significance of that is…?"

"One of the people the detectives on the case interviewed was Izzy Weisman."

"Okay, now you've got my attention. Why did they interview Weisman?"

"Apparently, he would pay Arnold to put up posters around town, advertising his clients' shows. Kind of took the kid under his wing from the sound of it."

"Was he considered a suspect at the time?" Rodiger asked.

"No, but that's because they thought Arnold was a runaway, and they treated the case as a missing person with no foul play suspected. Arnold's mother was a hooker and an addict, and there was no dad around. Kid was on his own pretty much all the time. Street savvy, everybody said. Cops just figured he lit out for greener pastures."

"Path of least resistance?"

"Looks that way."

"These detectives still around?" I asked.

"No. One of 'em was before our time, a guy by the name of Wells; the other was Hank Peterson. You remember Hank? Died probably ten years ago."

"Yes, I remember him. Not one of our finest, as I recall."

"Nope. This was a lazy investigation all the way around. The mother insisted Arnold wouldn't run away, and the people they talked to at the Dew Drop said he always seemed like a happy kid. They had the impression that he was devoted to his mom and looked out for her."

"What did Weisman say?" Rodiger asked.

"Not much. Just that Arnold was a good kid and that he hadn't seen him for a couple weeks."

"The mother still alive?" I asked.

"No. She OD'd a couple years after her son went missing."

"Are there any relatives we can talk to?"

"We're working on that. There's a reference to a half-sister in the file. If we can find her, we can take some DNA, see if we have a match."

"What about dental records?"

"Nada."

"Sounds like you're gonna have a hard time proving Arnold is our corpse," I said.

"Yeah, but if the shoe fits…"

"It does seem to; I'll give you that."

"There's one more thing."

"Yeah? What's that?"

"According to Hank's notes, when they called Weisman to talk to him, they were just a few blocks from his home, but he insisted they meet him at the Dew Drop instead. Said he had a client meeting there that he was running out the door to. But when they met him there, they talked for fifteen minutes, and no client ever showed up. When they asked about that, Weisman said his client must have forgotten about their meeting."

"And you're thinking he didn't want to meet at his house because…?"

"Because something smelled rotten in Denmark."

Chapter Twelve

When I got back to my place after dropping Sallie off from our Jackson trip, I saw that I had a text from Bo, asking me to call him. I let Lil' Queenie out of her crate and put Hugo's leash on him. Then we headed out for a walk, and I gave Bo a ring. I told him about Clarence Burkett, but he seemed only mildly interested. He was excited to tell me that the cops had a likely ID on our corpse and that Izzy was looking more and more like the prime suspect in a sixty-year-old homicide.

Swearing me to secrecy, Bo told me a thirteen-year-old named Arnold Jesse disappeared in 1967 and was never heard from again. The cops at the time treated it as a missing persons case, not a homicide. The catch that had now drawn the interest of Bo and his colleague in Homicide was that, before he disappeared, Arnold Jesse did odd jobs for Izzy, and Izzy had been interviewed about his disappearance. Mere coincidence? Bo thought not.

I asked about the arson investigation, and Bo let me know that Izzy's alibi was less than airtight. Did he think he was a murderer *and* an arsonist? Bo wasn't prepared to go that far, but he said it couldn't be ruled out.

"I find this somewhat hard to believe," I said. "Izzy's no saint, but he doesn't strike me as violent."

"Appearances can be deceiving," Bo said. "This was almost sixty years ago, Bru. A lot can change in sixty years."

"I guess. What are our next steps?"

"Our?"

"Your next steps?"

"Rodiger's on his way to pick up Weisman. Apparently, some insurance money came through, so he's holed up at the Residence Inn in Metairie. We're bringing him back in, and this time he should probably have a lawyer."

"That bad, huh?"

"Afraid so."

"Why would Izzy kill this kid or burn down his own place?"

"That's what we've got to nail down," Bo said. "In both cases, we've got opportunity. Means shouldn't be hard to establish. Motive is the big unknown."

"You realize what this means, Bo?"

"What's that?"

"If you lock Izzy up, you're turning me into a cat owner."

"Hah! It's good for you to step outside of your comfort zone, Bru."

"I bet Sophie would love to have a pet."

"Whoah! Easy there, partner. We've got enough mouths to feed."

Bo and I traded a few more barbs and were about to hang up, when he remembered something.

"I almost forgot, when I talked to Henry, he mentioned something he thought was strange about Weisman's stained-glass window. He said he knew every musician except one, a female singer named Lady something. You remember that?"

"I do," I said. "Her name is Lyla Saint-Clair. Izzy was her manager. Her stage name was Lady Ly. She died young, of a drug overdose from the sound of it. I got the impression Izzy was quite fond of her. He choked up when he talked about her."

I figured I owed it to Prosper not to mention his connection to Lyla Saint-Clair until I had a chance to talk with him about it.

* * *

I offered to pick Sallie up and take her to Annie Russell's party, but she declined on the grounds that I'd be going far out of my way. This was true, of course, but I'd hoped that we could resume our strategizing about how to gain an audience with Henrietta Thomas, Clarence Burkett's daughter. If

I was being honest with myself, what I really wanted was simply to spend more time with Sallie, but I took solace in knowing I'd see her at the party.

The party was classic Annie. As guests approached her magnificent State Street home, soft interior light refracted through fifteen-foot lead glass windows, and flickering lantern flames danced about the lacquered portico. Footmen in period clothing greeted us at the open doorway and escorted us through the foyer into the grand hall that leads to the double parlor at the back of the house, where servers offered us flutes of Veuve Clicquot. Bubbly in hand, we trickled outside. Purple and gold torches lined the pathway through the cloistered courtyard as we made our way to the well-lit tent that covered most of the lawn area. Inside the tent, Henry and his quartet, Harmony Brass, dutifully worked their way through Dixieland standards, as well-dressed couples shuffled about the portable parquet dance floor.

I drained my Champagne and made a beeline for the bar that was set up in front of the pool house. Kenny, the bartender, informed me he was pouring large batches of French 75s and satsuma margaritas, in addition to the wines and beers on display. I went for the French 75, which was better than I expected, though lacking the refinement of an individually mixed drink.

Bert Russell was holding court nearby with our mutual friends, John and Pamela Roseberry. I joined the group for a spell while scanning the crowd for familiar faces. Bert is older than Annie and has slipped some in recent years. Annie worries that it's early-onset dementia, but on this night at least, he seemed in fine form.

"Annie tells me you've become a cat man, Bruneau," he said.

"I can assure you, Bert, rumors of my feline fidelity are greatly exaggerated."

"Really? A cat, Bruneau? Whatever has gotten into you?" Pamela wanted to know. "How has poor Hugo taken to this change in circumstance?"

"The cat is a temporary boarder, Pamela, nothing more. I am simply helping an acquaintance during a difficult time. Hugo is less than pleased, but making do. I'm sure he appreciates your concern."

"Bully for you, Bruneau," John offered. "A damn fine thing to do, helping out a friend."

Sensing that this prattle could go on for a while, and a bit troubled by the thought of Izzy Weisman as a friend, I spied a welcome face near the tent and excused myself.

"Well, hello, darling!" Charlotte Duval greeted me in her husky smoker's voice, offering first one cheek and then the other.

"Hello Charlotte," I said, "quite a spectacle Annie has created, is it not?"

"As usual, my dear, Annie will have pulled off the social event of the season, although I do wish she'd do something about those dreadful footman outfits."

"Yes, they are a bit much."

In her eighties now, Charlotte remains a leading arbiter of style and opinion among the older Garden District and Uptown set. An unapologetic snob, she was an early champion of my store and remains an instrumental guide to navigating the petty jealousies and shifting alliances of moneyed New Orleans' social strata. We've been friends and confidants going on twenty years now, and still lunch together at least once a month, usually at Lilette.

Though she remains sharp-witted, Charlotte is not the vital force she once was. A couple years ago, she became entangled in our Jean Lafitte grave robbery case when she unwittingly assisted Mahdi Toledano, the criminal mastermind we were chasing. The experience shook Charlotte's confidence, and she has never fully recovered, though she still talks a good game.

As Charlotte and I compared observations of Annie's gathering, I became dimly aware of a tall, dark-haired man wearing a fitted black suit over a white t-shirt, with a scarlet scarf slung flamboyantly over his shoulder. He was talking animatedly to a petite woman in a pink dress whose back was to us. There were people between us, but what I could see of her body language and hand gestures suggested she was entertained by his shtick. She seemed familiar, but before I could get a good look, Charlotte took hold of my arm.

"Why look, dear, they've set out the buffet. Shall we strike while the iron is hot?"

"Ladies first," I said, holding out my hand to signal that she should lead, and I would follow.

The spread was impressive. Besides the obligatory shrimp remoulade and oysters on the half shell with mignonette sauce, there was crabmeat ravigote, a crawfish and andouille tart, slices of beef filet with bearnaise, Brabant potatoes, blanched asparagus, a leafy salad, baguette sections, and an assortment of dips, cheeses, and meats.

"Who's the caterer?" I asked Charlotte once we'd filled our plates and seated ourselves.

"It's Calcasieu, Donald Link's outfit," chirped a voice from behind us. Before we could turn, Annie's smiling face was sandwiched between us, and her arms were draped across our shoulders.

"How is it?" she asked.

"Everything is sublime, my dear," Charlotte exulted. "You have outdone even your past triumphs."

I added my congratulations, and we exchanged brief small talk before Annie continued her hostess rounds.

"I don't know where she gets her energy from," I said.

"Some people are born that way. I do worry, though," Charlotte confided.

"What about?"

"Annie and Bert were always cut from different cloth, but as they age, their differences become more pronounced. I fear he can't meet her halfway anymore. That can be hard on a couple."

"I know she worries about Bert," I said, "but I talked to him a while ago and he seemed fine to me."

"I hope so, dear."

As I leaned back to sniff the Gigondas I'd been poured, deeming it serviceable, I again caught sight of the tall man on the other side of the tent, still holding forth. I had a better view now, and I realized with dawning horror that his rapt audience of one was not just any woman but my very own Sallie Mae Maguire.

* * *

I left the party early that night. I'd been knocked off kilter but managed to put on a cheerful face as I made my round of goodbyes. Annie gave me a kiss and apologized for not spending more time with me, which, of course, I dismissed as nonsense. We made plans to get coffee later in the week.

I ran into Henry as I was leaving. He was on a break, sitting on the front steps, sipping a beer. He told me about his talk with Bo. He didn't think he'd been very helpful, but I assured him every detail matters.

When I got home, my forehead and cheeks were burning, my throat was dry, and there was a fluttering in my stomach I couldn't suppress. It catches me unawares sometimes, and hits me hard, when I am reminded that I am not alone in my attraction to Sallie's understated beauty. If I am not as attuned as I should be to the pervasive appeal of her charms, it is because she wasn't always this way. When we first met almost twenty years ago as fellow assistant curators at the Cabildo, Sallie dressed like she belonged in a 1950s secretarial pool, with uniforms of cat glasses, plaid skirts, penny loafers, and frumpy cardigans. She was shy and withdrawn in those days and projected an air of indifference to social life. Somewhere along the way, that changed. Gradually at first, but then more dramatically a few years ago, when, with the help of Angie Duplessis, she "rebooted" herself, as she likes to say. She cut her hair in a stylish bob, started dressing more fashionably, and began carrying herself with a cheerful confidence. Sallie's makeover had the effect of re-awakening my interest in her, but alas, I am now far from her only admirer.

Earlier, I had tried to join the conversation between Sallie and her raconteur, introducing myself to the latter. Sallie's reaction wasn't cold exactly, but I sensed annoyance that I was interrupting her tête-à-tête. Her friend was a Brazilian whose name I was given but promptly forgot. How the hell he got himself invited to Annie's party, I had no idea. We talked for a bit, but our conversation was stilted. Eventually, I excused myself, pretending to spot a long-lost friend.

Back at my apartment, I felt empty and confused. I thought our trip to Jackson had been a success, but now I wondered if I had deluded myself. I took Hugo out, poured myself an Armagnac, and sat on the couch, staring out the window. I don't think I formed a coherent thought. I just sat there like a zombie for probably twenty minutes until I was awoken from my stupor by a light knock and Hugo's barking.

"Hey," Sallie said as I cracked the door open.

"Hey," I said, surprised.

"I came to apologize."

"What for?"

"For being rude and insensitive."

"You're a grown woman, Sallie. You can talk to whoever you wish. It's not like I hold a claim over you."

Sallie looked up at me with a furrowed brow.

"May I come in?"

"Of course."

Sallie pecked my cheek, gently took my hand, and walked me up the stairs. She placed me on the couch and dropped down beside me, gazing intently into my eyes.

"You're hurt, aren't you?"

"Maybe a little."

"Jealous?"

"Very."

"Oh, Bruneau, my dear sweet knight. You've got nothing to be jealous about, I promise you."

Sallie pushed my head back and gave me a long, slow kiss on the lips. Then she held my cheeks in her hands and regarded me with a loving smile.

"I was working, you big dummy!"

"Working?"

"Yes, on our case! I've uncovered a suspect in the case of the missing cylinder."

Chapter Thirteen

Bruneau called me as I was heading back to the office after a late lunch at Parkway with Angie. He and Sallie had taken a two-hour trip to Jackson to visit the asylum where Buddy Bolden had been a patient. He was excited because he thought they may have discovered who made the cylinder recording that they believed was of Bolden. It was a guy named Clarence Burkett who worked as an orderly at Jackson State during the later years of Bolden's time there. Bru's funny that way. He's got that grumpy act going most of the time, but when he picks up the scent on one of his little historical treasure hunts, he's like a little kid who can't wait to tell his parents about what he's found.

"You'll never believe it, but we found his daughter-in-law in Natchitoches," he told me. "She's the one who put the sideboard up at auction. She had no idea about the cylinder or Buddy Bolden. Said she didn't know Clarence well, but she told us his daughter lives in a retirement community on the North Shore. We're going to try to talk to her next."

I complimented Bru on his detective work, but in truth, I didn't care much about the whole Buddy Bolden thing. Sure, it was interesting, and maybe it was loosely related to our Izzy Weisman investigation, but I couldn't see how it could be connected to a sixty-year-old homicide, and I doubted it had much to do with the torching of Weisman's house either.

That morning, I paid a visit to my buddy Joe Bailey in Vice, to see what he could tell me about Dominick Martello. Joe and I started at NOPD around the same time and worked a beat together for a few months before I landed my promotion to Property Crimes detective. A few months later, Joe also made detective and landed in Vice. He's a lieutenant now, and we remain friendly. Angie and Joe's wife Simone enjoy each other's company, and every now and then we get together as couples to go bowling or catch a movie.

Joe is built like the Texas Southern all-SWAC nose tackle he used to be, with broad shoulders, iron-plated pecs, massive arms, and tree-trunk quads. I used to know a guy who played center for Alcorn State and faced Joe a couple times. He said you couldn't move him anywhere he didn't want to go. That sums up his personality, too. Joe's a gentle giant in most respects, but you cross him at your own peril. And when Joe sets his mind to doing something, it's going to get done. Which is why Dominick Martello is such a touchy subject.

"You get something on Martello, you're gonna let me know, right?" Joe asked when I told him what I'd come to talk about. "Been chasing that son of a bitch forever."

"What makes him so hard to nail, Joe?"

"The man's smart, Bo. Crooked as all get out, but smart and slippery as they come. He's built layers within layers within layers of deniability. We pick his people up all the time, but we can't ever get to the inner circle. To be honest, we're not even sure who the inner circle is."

"You try undercover?"

"Of course. Same result."

When I told Joe about Martello inviting Rodiger into his house, he was dumbfounded.

"Who is this Rodiger kid?"

"An up-and-comer, Joe, young and hungry, just like us back in the day."

"He get anything?"

"A lesson in early R&B mostly."

Joe let out a low rumbling laugh.

"Oh yeah, a regular patron of the arts, Martello is. That's how he got started, you know."

"No, I don't know. Tell me."

"Martello grew up working class out in Westwego. At some point, hanging around the neighborhood, I guess, he learned how to play the bass. He got good enough to where he could pick up some nightclub work. We're talking early to mid-sixties. I asked Art Neville about him one time. He said he was just a guy. Not somebody you'd recruit for your group, but if you needed somebody to sit in for a few gigs, he could do that. There were a lot of guys like that back then, apparently. Still are for all I know."

"What does his playing the bass have to do with him getting his start?" I asked.

"Well, big surprise, but the music scene in those days was full of women and drugs. Martello was never into drugs himself, but he was part of that world, knew everybody. Some of these women, just like now, they get into drugs, they get hooked, they need their next fix, but they don't have the dough. Meantime, there's men coming in off the docks or wherever, they've got their paycheck, and they're looking for some action. Martello, he sees the demand, so he builds the supply, starts pimping these girls out."

"And gradually he builds his empire."

"That's right. And then the other thing about musicians and addicts, they're always short on cash, so Martello sees another opportunity. He gets into the banking business. Starts lending money, at interest. Customer can't make a payment, interest rate rises. Can't make the next payment, he starts foreclosure proceedings, if you catch my meaning."

"I do. After a while, he gets big enough, he starts some legitimate businesses, right?"

"Bingo. Real estate, a couple restaurants, some shipping, companies within companies, you name it. He's got accountants, lawyers, all kinds of white-collar types working for him. But the meat and potatoes? It's still coming from the street."

The story Joe told was a familiar one. There are Dominick Martello's in cities all around the country. Guys who started out as small-time crooks but had outsized ambition and a ruthless determination to make it big. They built their empires on the backs of the people they exploited, but are they any worse that way than the owners of factories or social media empires? Who's to say?

"What about Martello the person, Joe? What's he like?"

"I've only met him a couple times. In person, he's confident and relaxed. Outwardly, he's friendly, but behind that smiling face, you know you're dealing with a stone-cold killer. With us, he knows he's playing a cat and mouse game, and it seems to amuse him."

"You think he's personally violent?"

"If he is, I've never heard about it. You talk to some people; they'll tell you he's got a good side. By all accounts, he's faithful to his wife, dotes on his kids, supports various causes. A regular pillar of the community, the Dandy Duca."

* * *

Rodiger had gone to pick up Izzy Weisman and was due to return soon, so on my way back from Vice, I stopped by Homicide to check in with Gator. He was sitting with his feet up on his desk, reading through some papers, when I caught his eye. He smiled and waved me over.

"Your man back with Weisman yet?" he asked.

"Should be here any minute. Your toaster or ours, Gator? It's your call."

Gator swung his feet down and sat up.

"Yours probably works better, since Weisman's been there before. We want him to feel comfortable. The sooner he's comfortable the sooner we get him talking."

"Alright, let's head on over then," I said.

"You gonna let me lead this time?" Gator asked. "We're further along on my cold case than your arson."

"Sure, no problem."

On our way back to Property Crimes, I told Gator about my talk with Joe Bailey. He seemed to already know most of what Joe told me about Martello, except the music part. He briefed me on his efforts to locate Arnold Jesse's half-sister, which so far had led nowhere. Our conversation was friendly and flowed naturally, as though maybe the grudge Gator held against me had finally run its course. When we turned the corner into Property Crimes, Rodiger was pulling a bottle of water out of the refrigerator.

"Weisman's waiting for us in the toaster," he said. "He asked for water. He also called his lawyer, who hasn't arrived yet."

"How does he seem?" I asked.

"Nervous. Tired, weak, stressed, confused. All the things you'd expect of an eighty-four-year-old man going through what he's going through. On the positive side, he's cleaned himself up."

"Thank God for small mercies," Gator cracked.

As we were talking, a large, jumbled mess of a woman lumbered through the door and scanned the room.

"May we help you?" I asked.

"Yes, Officers, I'm looking for Isadore Weisman," she said in a deep but polite voice. "I believe he's been brought in for questioning; I'm not sure what about. Do you know where I might find him?"

"And you are?" Gator asked.

"Bella Gurwitz. Izzy has asked me to advise him during the interview process."

"Are you a lawyer?"

"Yes, or at least I used to be, but not the jailhouse kind. Mostly, I work on contracts. I've known Izzy for years. I think he just wants someone around he trusts."

"I see. Well, we are just heading in to talk to Mr. Weisman ourselves, and you are welcome to join us."

"Follow me, ma'am," Rodiger said, ushering our guest to the toaster.

Bella Gurwitz looked to be in her mid-seventies. She was more heavy-set than fat, with wide shoulders, big bones, and a mop of gray hair sitting atop her six-foot frame. She wore a billowing cotton jumpsuit with heavy leather sandals and large silver bracelets and necklaces. I sized her up as an ex-hippie or, as Bruneau would say, a seasoned counter culturalist.

"Ah, Bella, so good of you to come," Weisman said softly as we filed into the room. He appeared even more shrunken and defeated than the first time we brought him in, although, as Rodiger had noted, he did have on a clean set of clothes and looked as though he'd showered recently.

"Nonsense, Izzy," Bella replied. "You know I'm always here for you. What have you gotten yourself into this time?"

Weisman shrugged his shoulders and looked down at the table in front of him.

"Hmm, that bad? Officers, would you mind giving my client and me a few moments alone? If I'm to represent him, I need him to bring me up to speed."

"Of course," I said. "Take as much time as you like. We'll be just outside."

As Gator, Rodiger, and I watched through the two-way mirror, Bella Gurwitz and Izzy Weisman made for an interesting sight, the towering woman and the little man. At one point, Weisman said something sheepish, and Bella slapped her forehead dramatically. She leaned over, grabbed his chin, and made him look at her as she addressed him sternly, like she was barking out instructions. Then she walked over and opened the door for us.

After we introduced ourselves, and Rodiger let Izzy and Bella know the interview would be recorded, Gator got us started.

"Mr. Weisman, you may recall that when we last talked, we hadn't identified the corpse that was found in your house."

"Yes."

"We believe we now have a positive ID. Would you care to hazard a guess as to who we think it might be?"

"No. I mean, how would I possibly know?"

"Indeed, how could you? Is the name Arnold Jesse familiar to you, Mr. Weisman?"

"Um, Arnold Jesse? No, I don't think so. Should it be?"

"Let me see if I can refresh your memory. Arnold Jesse was thirteen years old when he disappeared in 1967, never to be seen again. According to their case notes, the officers who investigated his disappearance, Detectives Wells and Peterson, interviewed you about Arnold. Do you remember now, Mr. Weisman?"

"Oh yes, of course, you must mean Arno," Weisman said. "Pardon me, Officer Guidry, I'd forgotten Arnold's last name. We all knew him as Arno. It's been so long; I should have made the connection sooner. Bella, you remember Arno, don't you?"

"Of course I do," Bella said. "Such a sweet boy. He used to hang around the Dew Drop all the time, hustling for errands and tap dancing for loose change. Everybody loved Arno."

Gator was caught momentarily off guard by Bella's chiming in. Rodiger filled the void.

"How is it that you knew the deceased, Ms. Gurwitz?" he asked.

"I was part of the scene in those days, Officer. I helped Izzy and other agents negotiate deals with the clubs and with the studios in some cases. Sometimes I represented the musicians directly. I was around the Dew Drop a lot. So was Izzy, and so were a lot of people. If you were part of the scene, you knew Arno."

Bella's answer gave Gator time to regain his balance.

"Mr. Weisman, I take it then that you do remember being interviewed about Arnold's disappearance?"

"Yes, vaguely. It was a short discussion, as I recall. The detectives just wanted to know when I'd last seen Arno and if I'd noticed anything unusual about him in the weeks leading up to his disappearance."

"And do you remember what you told them?"

"Just that he seemed normal to me. Arno was always talking about how, when he grew up, he was going to go west to make his fortune. I just figured he decided to get an early start on his dreams."

As Weisman spoke, Bella Gurwitz nodded sympathetically.

"Except that he also felt a duty to take care of his mother, didn't he?" Gator asked.

"Yes, he did talk about wanting to provide a better life for his mother," Weisman said. "That's what he wanted to do, strike it rich and buy his mother a house. I never met her, the mother. Did you, Bella?"

"No, I never did."

"What about a half sister?" Gator asked. "Did he ever mention her?"

"Not that I recall," Weisman said.

The formalities over, Gator was ready to get down to business.

"Mr. Weisman, do you remember where your interview with officers Wells and Peterson took place?"

"Oh my, it's been a long time, Detective, but if I'm not mistaken, we met at the Dew Drop Inn."

"You have an excellent memory, Mr. Weisman. Do you recall why you met at the Dew Drop?"

"I'm afraid I don't. I may have had some business there, I suppose."

Weisman cast a quick glance at Bella, who nodded discreetly.

"According to Detective Peterson's notes, Mr. Weisman, you were at home when they called you, the same home where Arnold Jesse's remains were found; but you insisted on meeting at the Dew Drop, even though the officers were just a few blocks from you when they called. Does that sound familiar?"

"I really don't remember, but if that's what the notes say, I'm sure they're right. I probably had an appointment at the Dew Drop that I didn't want to be late to."

"Yes, that's exactly what the notes say, that you had an appointment. But according to those same notes, when you did meet the officers at the Dew Drop, your appointment never showed up. Does that strike you as odd, Mr. Weisman?"

Just as Weisman's body language was beginning to show signs of anxiety, Bella snorted loudly.

"It is obvious, Detective, that you haven't spent much time around musicians," she said. "Let's just say that punctuality and follow-through are not regarded as strengths of the musical class. My rule of thumb was to expect three missed appointments for every actual meeting. I can assure you that Izzy's appointment not showing would have been in no way unusual."

"I see," Gator said calmly. "Thank you for educating me on the finer points of the musical class, as you say."

Gator paused and exchanged poker-faced glances with Rodiger and me, before continuing.

"Is it true, Mr. Weisman, that Arnold Jesse worked for you?"

"He wasn't an employee, if that's what you mean. But, yes, I used to pay him a few bucks to distribute flyers and hang posters around town."

"Did he ever come to your house? To pick up these flyers and posters?"

"Sure, sometimes."

"I'm not sure where you're going with this, Detective," Bella interjected. "We all gave Arno small change to run errands and do odd jobs for us, and everybody was in Izzy's house at one time or another. It was a gathering place."

"Thank you, Ms. Gurwitz," Gator said. "I was simply establishing that Mr. Weisman's house was known to Arnold Jesse and that the relationship between Arnold and Mr. Weisman had a financial aspect to it. Sometimes, where money is involved, there can be disagreements."

"I never had any disagreements with Arno," Weisman said.

"No, I'm sure you didn't," Gator said. "Perhaps it's time to get down to the heart of the matter, Mr. Weisman. Do you have an explanation for how Arnold Jesse's body may have come to rest between the walls of your spare bedroom?"

Weisman looked at Bella, who nodded.

"I'm afraid I'm as befuddled as you are, Detective."

"Yes, of course you are. The thing is, Mr. Weisman, when you stop to think about it, it would have taken some time to knock out a hole in the wall, stuff a body inside, patch the hole back up, and then plaster and paint over it until it looked as good as new, don't you think?"

"I wouldn't know, Detective, I'm not a carpenter. But if you say so, yes, I imagine it would take some time."

"Do you have a theory as to how someone could have done all that while you were living in the house? It would have been noisy, don't you think? And smelly too, for quite a while. The decomposing of a human body takes several weeks. And trust me, as someone who has dealt with more than his share of corpses, you would have noticed that smell."

"As I told you last time, Detective, I did have occasion to travel from time to time. It's possible I was out on the road when this was going on."

"When you were on the road, did other people have access to your house?" Gator asked.

Fatigue and worry were written all over Weisman's face, and I had the sense he was close to cracking.

"I can answer that, Detective," Bella said. As she spoke, she handed Weisman his water bottle and motioned for him to drink.

"I had a key, so I could stop by to feed Izzy's cats and water his plants when he was away, and I wasn't the only one. Bands had a hard time finding places to practice in those days, and Izzy was famously generous in letting folks use his space. I can think of three or four people with keys just off the top of my head."

"Such as?" Gator asked.

"Bobby Reade, for one. Truman Peychaud, Alphonse Romero, Lyla Saint-Clair. Probably there were others."

Bella looked at Weisman for confirmation. He shrugged in acknowledgement.

Bella Gurwitz might not have been a criminal defense attorney, but she was finding a way to rescue Weisman at every turn, and I could see it was starting to wear on Gator. The mention of Lyla Saint-Clair gave me an opening to spell him for a bit.

"You mentioned Lyla Saint-Clair, Ms. Gurwitz," I said. "What can you tell us about her?"

"What do you want to know? She was a singer of modest talent who Izzy managed for a time."

"But she was part of this scene you've been describing? The local nightclub circuit?"

"Yes, I suppose so. She was a loner. Didn't really hang out with us much, but she was around, usually with a man. She had a drug problem, and sometimes she'd disappear for days at a time, miss a show or two, but Izzy always took her back in and went to bat for her."

"Is that the way you remember it, Mr. Weisman?" I asked. "Wasn't one of the panes in your stained-glass window dedicated to Lyla Saint-Clair?"

"Yes, that's right."

"Ms. Gurwitz said Lyla was a mediocre singer. Wouldn't she have been a little out of place in your window, surrounded by immortals?"

"Not to me," Weisman said. "Bella never cared for Lyla."

Weisman cast a side glance at his attorney.

"I think Bella may have been jealous of Lyla," he said quietly, but loud enough for us all to hear.

"You wish," Bella spat under her breath.

"Why would Ms. Gurwitz have been jealous, Mr. Weisman?" Gator asked.

"Because of Lyla's talent, I imagine, and all the attention she got from men."

She didn't say a thing but from the way Bella looked at Weisman, it was clear that his jab had hit home. She turned away from him and addressed me.

"Are we through discussing Lyla Saint-Clair, Detective? I fail to see what she has to do with Arnold Jesse, and frankly, if we continue down this path, Izzy may soon find himself without a lawyer."

"As you wish, Ms. Gurwitz," I said.

I nodded to Rodiger, who informed Weisman that he had checked his alibis and that we did have video of him at Rouses and CVS, but that the time signatures left a forty-five-minute gap before the onset of the fire at his house.

"I move slowly these days, Detective," Weisman said. "I think I may have pulled over in City Park for a spell. Sometimes I do that, just park there and watch the young couples on their evening strolls. You get to be my age, you get nostalgic."

"Were you and Lyla Saint-Clair a couple, Mr. Weisman?" Rodiger asked.

Weisman and Bella Gurwitz exchanged glances, and Weisman smiled ruefully.

"No, Detective, we were not. I wasn't exactly Lyla's type."

"Lyla was about my height, Detective," Bella added. "She and Izzy would have made for an odd pairing, not that Izzy wouldn't have been up for giving it the old college try."

Weisman sighed and rolled his eyes.

"Whatever you say, Bella."

There was obviously friction between Weisman and his lawyer when it came to the subject of Lyla Saint-Clair, and I made a mental note to bring it up in our debrief. Rodiger let it go and moved on to a different subject.

"Mr. Weisman, last time we met, you said that three people had offered to buy your collection: Carla Goodson, Dominick Martello, and Paul Martin. I've spoken with Mrs. Goodson and Mr. Martello, who confirmed your accounts, but I haven't been able to locate Mr. Martin. According to my notes, you said he was a musicologist at Southern Mississippi University and that you had played the cylinder recording for him. Is that correct?"

"Yes, that's right."

"The music department at Southern Miss says there is no Paul Martin on their faculty or staff."

"That's strange. Mr. Martin visited me at my house, and we spent about three hours going through my things, so I can confirm that he exists, Detective. He was very knowledgeable, especially for one so young. That's why I called him about the cylinder. I wonder if maybe he's connected to a different department, such as History, for example?"

"I'll look into it," Rodiger said. "In the meantime, do you have a phone number for Mr. Martin?"

"Yes, I do."

Weisman looked up Martin's number on his phone and gave it to Rodiger.

"How old would you say Mr. Martin was?" I asked.

"Late thirties? Forty, maybe. He was tall with a dark complexion, and he spoke with a bit of an accent."

"What kind of accent?"

"Spanish, I think, although there was something odd about it. Maybe a dialect of some kind. Could have been Portuguese, even."

"Did you have any further communication with Mr. Martin?"

"Yes, he called me the day after he visited to make me his offer. It was about half of what Nico offered."

"Nico?"

"Oh, sorry. Dominick Martello. Nico was his nickname back in the day."

"I take it you've known Mr. Martello a long time?" Rodiger asked.

"Fifty going on sixty years."

"And you know him well?"

"Oh, I don't know, well enough, I guess. We're not close or anything, but like I said, we've known each other a long time. He used to play the bass, you know?"

"Yes, so we have learned."

"What does Nico have to do with all this?" Bella asked.

"I take it you also know Mr. Martello, Ms. Gurwitz?" Gator asked.

"Yes, of course. We were all part of the same scene."

Gator took that in and nodded at Rodiger to proceed.

"Mr. Martello confirmed to me that he offered to buy Mr. Weisman's collection, for quite a large sum of money," Rodiger said.

"You weren't going to tell me this, Izzy?" Bella asked.

"I wasn't interested in selling. You know that."

Bella shook her head in exasperation.

"You could have set yourself up for the rest of your life, you idiot. Whatever happened to your common sense?"

"I'm surprised you think I ever had any."

It was becoming increasingly clear that "attorney-client" didn't begin to describe the relationship between Bella Gurwitz and Izzy Weisman.

"If we could return to the subject of Dominick Martello, did he take no for an answer, Mr. Weisman?" Rodiger asked.

"You mean, did he badger me about it?"

"Yes. Or lean on you."

"No, I wouldn't say that. He'd check in every few weeks to let me know his offer was still on the table, but there wasn't any nastiness. Usually, we'd just end up reminiscing about old times. Not so much recently, but it used to be that occasionally, he'd come over and we'd listen to something together, or I'd go to his place."

"I'm sure you're aware that Mr. Martello has a reputation for getting things his own way?"

"Yes, I'm aware, but things between us have always been friendly."

I had a thought.

"What about you, Ms. Gurwitz? Do you remain friendly with Nico?"

"I haven't seen him in years, Detective."

"Were you close, once upon a time?"

"I don't know about being close, but we spent some time together. You could tell, even back then, that he was going places. He didn't have a lick of talent as a musician, but he understood people. He was never one you worried about."

"But there were others you did worry about?"

"Sure, lots of them."

"Bella was sort of a den mother, Detective," Weisman interjected. "She'd tend to all the lost souls. We were similar in those days in that we did a better job taking care of other people than we did taking care of ourselves."

"That's the first thing you've said in a while that I actually agree with," Bella said. Then she put her hands on the table and pushed herself up to a standing position, towering over us.

"It seems to me that this conversation has wandered off course, Detectives, and I can see that my client is tired. I know I am. Unless you plan on charging Izzy with something, I suggest we call it a day."

"That would be fine, Ms. Gurwitz, and no, we are not in a position to bring charges at this time, so your client is free to go," Gator said. "But I do have one last question, if you'll indulge me."

"Yes?"

"Did Arnold have any friends his own age? Kids back then who knew him well, who might still be around to talk to?"

"No, not that I recall," Weisman said. "Sometimes there were other kids around, from the project, I assume, but I never got the sense he was particularly close to anyone. Just his mother, I think."

"Do you remember any names?"

"No, I'm afraid I don't."

"Me neither," Bella said, "although I do remember a couple times he had a younger boy with him. The reason I remember is because the boy's mother got wind of her son hanging around the Dew Drop with Arno, and she threw a fit. I remember it clear as day. A few of us were passing a joint in the alley next to the club, and Arno and this kid ducked in like they were hiding from somebody. Next thing you know, the kid's mother turns into the alley, cussing up a storm, not just at Arno and her son, but at us too.

Said we should be ashamed of ourselves, smoking in front of children. She grabbed her kid's collar and hauled him off. Never saw him again after that."

"When was this?"

"Probably a few months before Arno disappeared."

"This boy have a name?"

"Henry, I believe. Henry Wilkins, to be precise. The only reason I remember is when she took him away, she said, 'Henry Wilkins, you are in a world of trouble, young man!' It was a command performance, and it's stuck with me all these years."

Chapter Fourteen

It was both wonderful and strangely awkward to have Sallie sleep over. When we lived together, we had our morning routines. I'd get up first, make coffee and walk and feed Hugo. Sallie would roll out of bed fifteen minutes later, grab her cup of joe, and head straight for the shower. By the time she reappeared, I'd have my nose in the morning papers, having already consumed a full breakfast. She'd cut up a piece of fruit, pour a second coffee into her Yeti mug, plant a peck on my forehead, and dash off to work.

Now, we weren't sure what to do. It was a Saturday, so we stayed in bed longer than usual, waiting for the other to make the first move. I could hear Hugo beginning to stir in the living room, which meant he'd soon be pawing at me to get up. I rolled over to look at Sallie. A tangle of fine strawberry hair obscured her face, and red imprints from where she'd been resting pocked her ivory skin. When I parted a few strands of hair, her sky-blue eyes looked up at me with a mix of sheepishness and contentment.

"Shall I make coffee?" I asked.

"That sounds wonderful," she purred, muffled by her pillow.

I rolled out of bed, slipped on my robe, and padded into the bathroom. I placed an unopened toothbrush from a recent visit to the dentist next to the sink, along with a clean towel and washcloth. Then I made my way to the kitchen, where I found L'il Queenie's latest debris field. The cat had pried open the spice cabinet and knocked over several containers. The Paprika had shattered on the counter, and the cap had come off the Oregano, spilling half of the contents. I thought I had cat-proofed the kitchen, but not for the first time, I had underestimated this feline's capacity for destruction.

When Sallie finally made her appearance, she wore the XXL Abita Turbodog tee-shirt Bo's kids had given me for my birthday. It hung down past her knees like a potato sack. I had already taken Hugo out to do his business, cleaned up the counter, and made a pot of coffee. Sallie poured herself a cup and sat down next to me on the living room couch.

"Last night was lovely, but it was just that, a night, okay?"

"Okay."

"I just don't want to rush things."

"I understand," I said, though in truth I really didn't. It felt so right just then, sitting shoulder to shoulder, strands of morning light warming us, Hugo curled up at our feet. But I knew better than to force the issue.

"Shall we discuss your suspect?" I asked.

"Sure."

The night before, Sallie had briefly explained that a Brazilian researcher named Paulo Martins had for several days been combing her archives for information about early to mid-20th-century New Orleans. This was the tall, dark interloper she'd introduced me to at Annie's party. He said he was a post-doctoral student at the University of São Paulo, and he was exploring the origins of jazz and R&B in New Orleans. He seemed particularly interested in Buddy Bolden. When Sallie asked what he knew about Bolden, he told her everything there was to know and speculated that long-running rumors of extant recordings were likely true and that whoever unearthed them would stand to make a lot of money.

"Why did this Paulo come to you?" I asked. "I would think he'd find more relevant information at the Jazz Museum or the Tulane archives."

"He said he'd spent time at both, but that now he was looking for maps and deeds to chart where musicians were born and lived, and the venues where they played."

"And how exactly did his scholarly pursuits earn him a date with the Crescent City's sexiest archivist?"

Sallie smiled, and color rushed to her cheeks.

"He'd been kind of flirty with me. I figured if I could get a little alcohol in him…well, you know…his lips might loosen."

"And did they?"

"Not as much as I was hoping, but some."

"Uh-huh. Was he the only one flirting?"

"Let's just say, there are times when a girl's gotta do what a girl's gotta do."

I stiffened at that, visibly, I guess. Sallie leaned in, put her chin on my chest, and looked up at me.

"Even if she'd rather be with someone else."

I inhaled deeply, for effect, and rolled my eyes.

"What did you talk about?"

"He asked me a lot of questions about myself, but eventually I got him going on Brazil and how he got interested in the history of our music."

"And?"

"He said he grew up in a musical family. His grandfather was a bossa nova percussionist who toured for a while with João Gilberto. Paulo said his interest is in how forms collide and morph into entirely new genres. He equated the way the blues and ragtime came together to form jazz to how jazz and samba fused into bossa nova and how gospel, blues, and jazz coalesced into rhythm and blues."

"The blues had a baby and they called it rock and roll?"

"Something like that. Muddy Waters, right?"

"Correct. There may be hope for you yet."

Sallie smiled, and we each took a sip of coffee.

"True confessions?" I ventured.

"By all means."

"Maybe Bo is rubbing off on me, but I'm not getting what makes your Paulo a suspect. Where's your evidence? The fact that he knows who Buddy Bolden was and believes that a recording of him exists is hardly remarkable."

"There are some other things."

"Such as?"

"When I asked him about the aims of his research, Paulo said they were twofold: he's writing what he hopes will be the definitive book on the origins of R&B; and he aspires to create the world's foremost depository of what he calls 'uncharted origin recordings,' by which he means informal recordings of consequential artists experimenting with new forms."

"Such as the Buddy Bolden nuthouse sessions?"

"Exactly. Nothing a label would have put out, but experimentations containing the germs of what would emerge later."

"Interesting, but that still doesn't scream suspect."

"Perhaps not, but when I asked him where one finds recordings like this, he said in private collections, primarily. By way of example, he told me about this amazing collection he'd found in New Orleans, but that it had been destroyed in a fire."

"Okay, now you're getting warm."

"Was that supposed to be a pun?"

"No, actually."

"Alright, I'll give you the benefit of the doubt."

"Is that it?" I asked.

"Not quite. I surprised Paulo by asking if he was talking about Izzy Weisman's collection. He confirmed that he was and said he'd been in Izzy's house a couple of weeks before the fire. He described it as a pigsty but also a musicologist's goldmine."

"True enough, but any visitor would have said that."

"I know. It's just that when I asked him if there were any highlights of the collection, he mentioned a cylinder recording that Weisman thought might be of Buddy Bolden."

"Okay, so Izzy mentioned the cylinder to him. That still doesn't make him a thief or an arsonist."

"Except that he said he visited Izzy a couple weeks before the fire. You gave Izzy the cylinder on a Monday, and the house burned down four days later."

I let that sink in.

"I guess I better call Bo."

* * *

We'd swung by Sallie's so she could shower before our appointment with Henrietta Thomas, and as she did, I sat on her porch, called Bo, and told him about Paulo Martins. He said he'd see what he could find out about him, and then, after I prodded him, filled me in on his latest go-round with Izzy. He said Izzy was cagey in the beginning but eventually admitted to having employed Arnold Jesse as an errand boy around the time of his death. According to Bo, Izzy couldn't produce a plausible explanation for how Jesse's corpse came to rest inside the walls of his house.

"You still don't know for sure that Arnold Jesse is your corpse, do you?" I asked.

"Technically, no. But it's got to be him. Too many pieces fit for it not to be."

"So, you're proceeding under the assumption that it's him?"

"Yes. If we can find the sister, we can test her DNA for an official confirmation, but there's not really any doubt in our minds."

An interesting twist Bo let slip was that both Izzy and the quasi-lawyer who accompanied him, a woman named Bella Gurwitz, said they knew Dominick Martello when he was a journeyman musician in the 1960s nightclub scene. He also said the name Lyla Saint-Clair came up again, which reminded me that I needed to talk to Prosper.

Sallie emerged from her bedroom in a soft pink crewneck, a pair of white linen slacks, and straw-colored espadrilles. As she bent down to kiss my forehead, she smelled like morning in Provence. I held her there, greedily inhaling lemon rind and lavender. Then she pushed herself away and said, "Come on, you, get up, it's time to hit the road."

Once again, Sallie insisted on taking her Prius, and as she drove, her oversized black sunglasses rested snugly on her button nose. I found myself admiring her effortless posture and the way her lips in the sunlight matched her hair. She didn't want to rush things, she said. We'd have to see about that.

I know people who think the Causeway is fun to drive and a great way to see Lake Pontchartrain. They rave about the 360-degree views and the aerial acrobatics of the gulls, pelicans, and ospreys as they dive for their meals. I think it's the most boring twenty-four miles in America. Just a straight line with no change in the scenery other than the gradual coming into view of the North Shore. Which is why, even as Mandeville and Covington have their merits as commuter havens, the drive makes them non-starters for me.

As I relayed Bo's account to Sallie, we reached the end of the causeway and made our way to Pat's Rest Awhile, the sprawling restaurant and watering hole on the Mandeville lakefront. We were both in the mood for a seafood lunch, so we'd built in an extra hour before our appointment with Henrietta Thomas. We found a table on the deck, and I ordered a dozen oysters on the half shell for us to share as a starter. For entrees, Sallie went for the trout almondine, and I got the shrimp and corn bisque. It was a beautiful, crisp day with a pleasant breeze, and as we sipped iced tea, a colorful patchwork of billowing sails glided across the lake's whitecaps.

"The Dandy Duca started out as a musician? Seriously?" Sallie asked, amused.

"Apparently. And now he's a big collector."

"I mean, who knew? The Duca, a closet Renaissance man. Are they looking at him for the fire, the murder, or both?"

"I think more the fire, but I don't really know. He'd certainly have the means for either, but I'm not sure what his motive would be."

"That's the problem with all our theories," Sallie said. "There's no shortage of people who might have been interested in buying or maybe stealing Izzy's collection, but who would want to destroy it and why?"

Sallie's question triggered a thought that had been slowly forming in the back of my mind, unarticulated until now.

"What if they didn't destroy everything?" I asked.

"What do you mean?"

"Suppose there was a particular part of Izzy's collection they wanted, but they didn't care about the rest of it. If they took what they wanted and then burned the place, no one would be the wiser about what was taken."

Sallie looked at me with dawning recognition.

"Of course! That could be it, Bruneau!"

"It's just a theory, Sallie."

"Yes, but one that fits. Whether they were after the cylinder or a particular part of the collection, the fire would cover up the robbery."

"Precisely."

* * *

It turned out that Henrietta Thomas had an acute case of emphysema and was confined to a wheelchair. She did her best to cooperate, but it was painful listening to her cough and wheeze as she tried to talk, pausing frequently for hits from her oxygen tank. Henrietta confirmed that her father was Clarence Burkett and that he had worked at Jackson State, but she didn't remember anything about Buddy Bolden or a cylinder. The only nugget she provided that was of any interest was that her father made occasional reference to a life insurance policy he'd taken out for his family, but when he died no such policy was found.

"Do you think maybe the cylinder was Clarence's insurance policy?" Sallie asked as we left Henrietta's assisted living unit.

"It's possible. Henrietta said Clarence died in a car accident when he was still in his forties. Maybe he didn't tell anybody about the cylinder because he didn't see himself passing away anytime soon."

Henrietta tired quickly, so our meeting only lasted for half an hour. That freed up time for another engagement I had put on the back burner. I told Sallie about Mose Adler, the African drummer turned voodoo merchant Izzy had mentioned and suggested we swing by his store in the Lower Ninth Ward.

"The Ninth Ward?" Sallie exclaimed mockingly. "My, my, aren't we the bold adventurer."

What Sallie calls my "geographic glass bubble" has long been a favorite target of her barbs. She maintains that my concept of New Orleans is bound by the crescent-shaped bend of the Mississippi that frames the French Quarter to the east, Mid-City to the north, and Uptown to the west. In my defense, I do make it out to Metairie from time to time, and of course, I visit

Kenner every month for my dinner with Bo and his family. But Sallie does have a point.

"Always up for a new adventure," I professed.

"Uh-huh."

I'm embarrassed to admit that before Katrina, I barely knew where the Ninth Ward was. Like a lot of folks, I left the city the day before the storm hit and didn't return for almost two years. I rented a small apartment in St. Augustine, Florida, and ran a pop-up there with the help of dear friends in the local antiquing business. Sallie stayed with her cousin in Beaumont, Texas. She worked remotely from there to improve the digital accessibility of her archives and drove back to the city from time to time to keep an eye on their safekeeping. Bo's job required him to stay in New Orleans, but he set Angie and the kids up in a rental in the Atlanta suburbs and visited as frequently as he could. It was an awful, disorienting time for all of us, cast adrift from the rhythms and routines of the lives we had made for ourselves.

I'd seen the TV footage of the Ninth Ward completely overrun by floodwater, the result of breaches in multiple levees, but it wasn't until I returned to New Orleans and Bo gave me a driving tour of the neighborhood that I truly appreciated the extent of the devastation. It was like Atlantis arose from centuries of submersion, its basic contours preserved, but all vestiges of the lives that had once sustained it, gone. Even now, as Sallie and I crossed the Industrial Canal and looked lakeward from the Claiborne Bridge, we could see that for every newly built subsidized home on stilts, with its rooftop solar panels, there remain dozens of vacant lots, many of them overgrown by weeds or used as illegal dumping sites.

"I haven't been over here for quite a while," Sallie said.

"Me neither. There's been progress. All these NGOs, it's a long slog they've signed up for. I admire their commitment."

"Me too. Even so, the folks who are moving in now, they're not the ones who left. The neighborhood that was here, it's not coming back."

"Nope. In ten years, maybe less, this will be the next Bywater. The stampede of gentrification halts for no man."

Izzy had jotted directions to Mose Adler's place on a small piece of notepaper I had given him, but as we turned left onto Tupelo Street and made our way toward its terminus at Florida Avenue, I grew increasingly skeptical. We were just a few blocks from the end of the road, and there was no sign of a store or any other structure, really. Sallie slowed to a crawl and pointed to our right, down North Dorgenois Street.

"There," she said. "Did you see that?"

I couldn't see anything, but Sallie said she caught a flash of light through a gap in some trees. She turned right, and a small wooden sign came into view. A hand-painted arrow pointed to a narrow footpath leading into a thicket of shrubs and small trees strangling in kudzu. Sallie parked across the street, and as we approached on foot, we saw that an elaborate cross formed from odd shapes and figures was carved into the sign.

"That's the symbol of Papa Legba, the guardian of the crossroads," I said.

"What? How do you even know that?"

"One of Prosper's teachings."

Prosper served with a guy in Vietnam who taught him the basics of Haitian Vodou. The way he explains it, Vodou is a proper religion, with a coherent theology and an elaborate set of rituals. What passes for "Voodoo" in these parts is more a hodgepodge of folk practices than a religion per se.

I took Sallie's hand, and we advanced tentatively into the small jungle. After fifteen yards, we came to a clearing, and it took our eyes a few seconds to adjust to what we were seeing. Straight ahead of us was a crude A-frame shack fashioned from sheets of plywood and fiberglass. Inscrutable writings and occult-looking drawings were scrawled in white paint across haphazard splotches of red, green, and yellow. A sign above the door read "Mose's House of Mistè." Behind the store to the left, a triangular tarp anchored by three metal posts covered a large patch of dirt, in the middle of which sat a rotting wooden rowboat. In the boat, a three-foot statue of a male figure with an outlandishly massive erection stood sentry, surrounded by an assortment of charms and figurines. To the right of the store, a stone altar with animal skulls ringing its base stood before six small wooden benches.

"I don't know about this, Bruneau," Sallie whispered, fear in her voice.

"It'll be okay," I said. "Let's see if anyone is inside."

I tugged at Sallie gently, and she followed me up the path to the open door. I knocked.

"Hello! Anybody home?"

Receiving no answer, we edged inside. Incense filled the dimly lit air, and chimes made of small animal bones rattled as we brushed against them. Every inch of the cramped space was filled with voodoo paraphernalia, from dolls and masks and amulets to musical instruments and goat heads. As we took it all in, we were startled by a loud creaking noise and some grunting coming from directly above us. Sallie and I exchanged worried glances. There was a thud, another grunt, and then the sound of shuffling feet. Finally, a filthy sandaled foot appeared on the top rung of a ladder leading to a small loft, and gradually, step by creaky step, Mose Adler came into view.

He was a large man, maybe six-one, with a wide chest and protruding waistline. The top of his head was bald, but curly white hair formed a thick ring above his ears. A long bushy beard and a thick nest of chest hairs augmented the hirsute profile. He wore an old tie-dye tee shirt that was at least a size too small, and painter pants that may have once been white but were now mottled by stains. As he stepped off the ladder, scratching at his crotch, I could see that he wore the glassy-eyed look of one recently roused from slumber.

"Mose Adler?" I asked.

The man nodded ever so slightly.

"My name is Bruneau Abellard. I was given your name by Izzy Weisman. This is my friend Sallie Maguire."

I extended my hand, but the gesture was not returned.

"Cachimbo?" Adler asked gruffly.

Seeing our blank expressions, he turned to his right and pulled a small clay pipe from a shelf. It was filled with something; I wasn't sure what. He held it out for us to see.

"Cachimbo?"

"Sure," I said, with some trepidation.

Sallie dug her fingernails into my hand. Mose struck a match, took a toke from the pipe, and handed it to me. The sweet smell of the smoke told me the substance was closer to tobacco than cannabis, but really, I had no idea what I was inhaling. Cloves, maybe? I offered the pipe to Sallie, but she waved me off.

Mose took the pipe and set it down, still burning. He looked at me expectantly.

"Izzy is in some trouble," I said.

I went on to explain about the fire and Arnold Jesse's corpse. Mose listened silently.

"Make trouble; expect trouble," he muttered finally.

I wasn't sure what that meant but opted not to ask.

"Do you remember Arnold Jesse?"

Mose's expression remained impassive, but I thought I detected a slight nod.

"So, you knew him?"

"I remember many people. I know none."

Izzy had warned me that Mose didn't like to give straight answers. He also told me I'd probably have to buy something to get him talking. Mose picked up a straw doll version of the statue we'd seen outside and pointed its erect wooden penis at Sallie.

"For you, eh, cher?" he grinned lecherously.

Sallie gasped, flushed red, and averted her eyes.

"Perhaps something more functional?" I suggested.

I pointed to the chimes.

"These are nice, Sallie. Don't you think they'd work well on the balcony?"

"If you say so," Sallie mumbled, still looking down at the dirt and sawdust floor, her body tensed for flight.

"How much?" I asked.

Mose shrugged. I gave him a twenty-dollar bill. He looked at me blankly. I handed him another.

"Arno danced," Mose said, stuffing the bills in his pocket. "This, I remember."

"Do you remember him working for Izzy, running errands, and posting flyers?"

Mose shrugged again.

"What about a sister? Arnold had a half-sister. Do you remember her?"

Another shrug. I began to consider the possibility that I'd just spent forty dollars to learn that Arnold Jesse could shake his booty. I decided to try a new tack.

"How about Lyla Saint-Clair?" I asked.

Mose maintained his disinterested countenance, but I caught a momentary flash of apprehension in his eyes, and he saw that I had noticed.

"Man-eater," he spat under his breath.

"She went through a lot of men. Is that what you're saying?"

"Chew 'em up; spit 'em out. Ptooey."

"What was Lyla's relationship with Izzy like?"

"Someone makes a mess; someone cleans mess up."

"Izzy cleaned up Lyla's messes?"

Mose didn't answer. He crossed the room and leaned against a table filled with totems and gris-gris. As he moved, I recalled Izzy saying that Mose was his age, maybe older, but seeing him in person, he seemed much more vital and spry than his contemporary, despite the extra weight he carried. And there was a twinkle in his eye that told me he enjoyed playing the enigmatic riddler.

"What do you think happened to Arnold Jesse?" I asked. "How could he have ended up between the walls of Izzy's house?"

Mose ran his fingers through his beard.

"Maybe bad luck, eh?"

"You mean wrong place, wrong time?"

"The spider spins for one fly but catches many."

I had no idea what that was supposed to mean but tried to play along.

"Arnold got caught in a spider's web? I'm not sure I follow."

"Beware the woman scorned, eh, cher?"

Mose leered at Sallie, who flinched, tearing her nails into my forearm.

"Who was scorned?" I pushed him. "Lyla?"

Mose shook his head.

"Eezz-abella."

I was beyond confused.

"Who is Eezz-abella?" I asked. "Are you referring to Izzy Weisman or a woman named Isabella?"

"Maybe neither, maybe both, eh? Eezz-a-he? Eezz-a-she? Ha, ha!"

I looked at Sallie to see if she was making any more sense of this than I was. She wasn't. Nor was she amused when Mose picked his doll back up by its penis and dangled it in front of her, smirking and arching his eyebrows suggestively.

"Do you mind?" she seethed.

Mose put the doll back down, still smiling. Sallie looked at me as if to say it was time to leave, but I wasn't ready to give up quite yet.

"Before his house burned down, Izzy came into possession of a cylinder recording he thought might have been of Buddy Bolden," I said. "We think it was from the 1920s, when Bolden was confined at Jackson State. Do you know anything about that?"

As Mose considered my question, his expression changed, becoming more serious. He took his time before answering, and when he did, he spoke slowly and directly, giving us a glimpse of the encyclopedic memory Izzy had told me about, and revealing that he was capable of speaking in coherent sentences.

"There have been many claims about recordings of King Bolden, some full of guano, others maybe not. Willie Cornish said there was a recording made in 1898, but it has never been found. There was a guy named Oscar Zahn who owned a bar near Rampart and Perdido, where Buddy used to play. Supposedly, he made some wax recordings and kept them in a shed where they would have been damaged by heat and humidity. The shed was torn down in the 1960s."

"What about recordings from the Jackson State years? Ever hear anything about that?"

"No, but there could have been recordings made. There was a guy who ran the place for a while, name of Robards, I think, who thought music could help the poor souls locked up there. He brought in some instruments, supposedly. If that was the case, Buddy might have had opportunities to play."

"Out of curiosity, what would Buddy have sounded like, do you think?"

"Loud," Mose said. "More loud and energetic than virtuosic, was what some said. Brash, cocky, in your face."

I dug my phone out of my pocket.

"Do you think this could be him?" I asked. Then I played the recording I had made.

Mose listened intently, his eyes alert and discerning.

"Well?" I asked when it was over. "What do you think?"

"Maybe yes, maybe no," he said.

"Can you give me a little more?"

Mose looked at me pensively.

"There is pain blowing through that horn. Buddy would have known great pain, but he was not alone in that. Being a 'nigra' in the Jim Crow South, that was some scary, painful shit. You didn't have to be locked away to feel it."

I shifted gears.

"Before the fire, Izzy was planning on talking to you about the cylinder," I said. "Why you, do you think?"

Mose considered the question. Then, maddeningly, he slipped back into riddle mode.

"Blessed are the eyes, for they see, and the ears, for they hear."

Sallie took a step toward Mose.

"Is there a reason you feel compelled to answer every question with a riddle or non-sequitur?" she asked pointedly.

"I will open my mouth in parables. I will utter things kept secret from the foundation of the world."

"Oh, I see. You're the Messiah now, is that it?" Sallie bristled. "Bruneau, we're wasting our time here. I think it's past time for us to go."

"So soon, cher?" Mose asked, dangling his horny doll again and smiling lewdly. "No more questions for Mose?"

"Actually, I do have one, if you'll give me a straight answer," Sallie said.

Mose opened his arms in invitation.

"Do you think Buddy Bolden invented jazz?"

"Ah, cher," Mose responded, laughing.

"Which came first, eh, the music or the instrument?"

1967

New Orleans, Louisiana
June 30, 1967

Rolling over, Andre Coulon knows it has been some hours since the sun announced the dawn of a new day. Its bright light seeps through the drawn blinds of his one-room apartment. Rising slowly from sheets drenched in sweat, his sleeveless undershirt plastered to his back, he rests his elbows on his thighs and places his throbbing head between his hands. He is awash in self-loathing. At that moment, he doesn't know which he hates most, the stale aftertaste of Cutty Sark lining his parched mouth, the monotonous hum of his electric table fan, or the way he'd bungled his breakup speech.

The phone rings so loudly that the entire room seems to vibrate, and a half dozen roaches scurry for cover. The stabbing pain in Andre's head almost brings the big man to his knees. He lurches for the receiver before it can ring again, but fumbling, he knocks it to the floor. He grabs at the chord angrily and yanks the receiver to his ear, bouncing the phone along the floor.

"Hello?"

"Andre, it's Izzy Weisman."

Andre says nothing.

"I've got a situation here, and I don't know who else to call."

Andre sighs.

"What kind of situation?"

"The usual, but much worse."

"I'm sorry, but I can't be of help. We're over, Lyla and me, okay? I'm off to Fort

Benning tomorrow. It's better for everybody that we keep this a clean split."

"I understand, Andre, but this is serious. Like, life-and-death serious. We need your medical expertise, and I can't call an ambulance. You'll understand why when you get here. Please hurry."

Hanging up, Andre rises unsteadily to his feet, kicks the wooden chair in front of him, and then curses, hopping on one foot, as a searing pain radiates through his big toe. He splashes cold water on his face, forces down a slug of warm orange juice, and struggles into his clothes from the night before, still reeking of cigarettes and whisky. He shields his eyes from the blinding sun as he opens the door and walks down the outdoor staircase to the side street where he has parked his bike. Reaching it, he lifts the seat to check the small storage compartment where he keeps his first-aid kit. He is out of aspirin and makes a mental note to stop at a K&B on his way to Weisman's place. He pulls his silver aviator glasses from his shirt pocket and mounts his Scrambler, throttling up and peeling out onto Leonidas Street, heading left toward Claiborne and a scene he cannot yet imagine.

It is a fifteen-minute trip to Izzy Weisman's house in Tremé, and as he rides Andre turns over the prior night's scene in his head. He had tried to play the virtuous warrior card, explaining that he couldn't expect Lyla to wait for his return when that return was by no means guaranteed, but she had seen right through his deception. He wonders if it would have gone better if he had simply told her the truth, that her drug use and mood swings had exhausted him, and that he was looking forward to basic training and the chance to regain a sense of balance in his life. As it was, she threw a fit, swinging at him wildly, gouging at his chest, calling him weak and cowardly, "just like the rest of the lying bastards." The words stung, both because he couldn't disavow their truth and because he could feel the depth of her anguish behind them.

Lyla had thrown herself face-down onto her bed and screamed at Andre to leave and never come back. The last words she'd spoken to him were, "I hope you die over there!"

Now, as he pulls up to the house he'd visited only once before, Andre is filled with foreboding. He knows Lyla is capable of extreme behavior and he'd heard the raw panic in Weisman's voice. He parks and grabs his first-aid kit. As he crosses the street, he catches a fleeting glimpse of a beat-up green VW Beetle turning onto

Esplanade two blocks away. He thinks he recognizes it, but he's not sure.

"Thank god, you made it," Weisman says as he meets Andre at the door.

"Follow me."

As Weisman leads him through a sunlit front room, Andre is struck again by the promoter's diminutive stature and the contrast it presents to his own hulking frame. He does not know Weisman well, or particularly like him, regarding him as an enabler of Lyla's unhealthy indulgences. But he has spent enough time around him to understand that his affection and concern for the singer are genuine.

"She showed up a couple hours ago, strung out as can be," Weisman explains. "I laid her down on my bed and watched over her until she crashed. Then I went out to get something for her to eat when she woke up, but when I got back, I couldn't rouse her."

This is not the first time Andre has had to revive Lyla, but he knows that no two overdoses should be assumed to be alike.

"Do you know what she took?"

"Pills, I think, and smack, but there's probably some alcohol too. I don't know exactly."

"Do you know what kind of pills?"

"No, but it's usually the downers when this happens. I couldn't find anything in her purse."

Weisman leads Andre into the bedroom where Lyla lay on her back in her underwear, her long black hair strewn about her. Andre kneels, leans over her, and listens to her breathing. Then he takes hold of her wrist to check her pulse and look for fresh track marks.

"Well?" Weisman asks.

"Her pulse is racing, and her breathing is shallow," Andre says.

"Will she come out of this on her own? Is there anything you can give her?"

"It's hard to say. She's in what we call respiratory depression, which can result from mixing depressants, like barbiturates and alcohol, with opioids. Depending on what exactly she has in her system, she could be heading for cardiac arrest or brain damage."

"Oh god."

Andre reaches into his kit and removes one of the vials of Naloxone he had filched from the E.R. for just such an occasion. The FDA has not yet approved the drug, but because of the high volume of street junkies it treats, Charity Hospital had been chosen to participate in a clinical trial. Andre has never seen the drug not work

Tenderly, Andre scans Lyla's delicate wrists and arms for easy entry points. He sees only a few indications of recent injections, bolstering his belief that she had been mostly clean until recently. But the telltale signs of past overuse remain; darkened veins, scabbing, old puncture marks turned white or a pale pink, some bruising. Worried about collapsing a vein, Andre moves to Lyla's groin. He probes with his fingers until he has located the object of his search. Carefully, he loads a syringe, swabs the surface of the femoral vein with alcohol, and injects the drug.

"This is what we call an opioid antagonist," he tells Weisman. "Unless I've misdiagnosed the problem, we should see an effect within a minute or so."

As the two men hover anxiously, Weisman clears his throat.

"Andre, Lyla is not our only problem. When she wakes up, I need to show you something else."

Andre nods but doesn't really process the words. He waits nervously, caught in the fraught limbo between dread and hope. Then, as though shot through with electricity, Lyla's body convulses to life. She bolts upright and flails her arms at imagined attackers, her eyes wild with animal terror. Andre easily deflects Lyla's blows and restrains her as gently as he is able, engulfing his ex-lover with heavy arms. He pulls her to his chest and holds her close. She pants, frantically at first, but then more easily. Soon, he feels her body relax. He leans in and is relieved to hear her breathing beginning to normalize. She pushes herself away softly and looks up at him, just now gaining her bearings.

"Andre, what are you doing here?" she asks.

"Shh, you need to rest," he whispers.

He places his hand on her forehead and gently pushes back her damp hair. Taking her elbow, he helps her to her feet and into the armchair Izzy has pulled up next to the bed. Sitting up should make it easier for her to breathe, he reasons, and if she throws up, she won't choke on her vomit.

Andre knows he must monitor Lyla for the next few hours and that she should not be allowed to fall into a deep sleep, but she does need to rest.

"We'll be right outside if you need us," he says.

Lyla nods and leans back on the pillow Weisman had wedged behind her head.

Stepping out of the bedroom, Andre tells Weisman that he intends to stay for at least a couple hours so that he can monitor Lyla's condition.

"Okay, thanks, I appreciate that," the little man says.

There is a brief pause before Weisman speaks again, his tone solemn.

"Andre, you need to brace yourself, okay?"

"Okay, if you say so. Why?"

"I need to show you our other problem. It's a really, really big one and I don't know what to do about it."

Andre says nothing but nods uncertainly.

"Come, follow me," Weisman says. "He's in the kitchen."

"He?"

Cautiously, Andre trails the promoter as he turns right toward the back of the house and then right again into his small galley kitchen. As soon as Andre enters the narrow room, he sees a dark mass on the floor. Seconds pass before it comes into focus, and he realizes that he is looking at the curled-up lifeless body of a skinny, light-skinned Black boy. He is perhaps twelve years old, and he looks vaguely familiar.

Stunned, Andre glances at Weisman, who rubs his brow, eyes averted from the horrible scene before him. Then he drops to his knees and presses his ear to the boy's heart. He hears nothing.

Chapter Fifteen

Sallie was in fine form as I took the wheel and drove us back to my place after our visit with Mose Adler. I don't think I've ever seen her so furious, not even at me.

"What a disgusting pig!" she raged. "The nerve of the man! Waving that disgusting penis at me? All that nonsense about a spider's web, a woman scorned, Eezza-frickin-bella? Give me a frickin' break!"

"I think you underestimate the man's charms," I quipped.

"Don't you even!" Sallie roared.

"And you! Did you defend my honor? Voice an objection? No! Instead, it's 'oh gee, Sallie, wouldn't these revolting chimes look nice on the balcony. They're so FUNCTIONAL.' Really, Bruneau? What could you have been thinking?"

I was getting a kick out of Sallie's performance and couldn't help but chuckle.

"Glad you think it's funny," she scowled, red-faced, arms folded across her chest.

"Come on, Sallie. Seriously, I had to humor him to get the answers we needed."

"And what did we learn? That Arno could dance and may have run into some bad luck? Major scoop right there."

"We learned that the ill-named Lyla 'Saint' Clair's hagiography won't be coming out anytime soon. From the sound of it, she was high maintenance, and Izzy schlepped around after her, cleaning up her messes. Probably enabled her too. And we learned about an administrator named Robards who brought music to Jackson State. All in all, I'd say our visit with Mose Adler was a productive use of our time."

Sallie harrumphed, kicked the glove compartment, and glared out her window.

I decided to press my luck just a little bit further.

"Unfortunately, there is one important question we still don't have an answer to," I said.

I waited for her to take the bait.

"What?" Sallie sighed, exasperated.

"Eezz-a-he or Eezz-a-she?"

* * *

The next morning, having eventually soothed Sallie's ruffled temper, I got an early visit from Bo, who swung by unannounced on his way to work. These matinal drop-ins are not regular occurrences, but they're not all that unusual either. If there's something Bo wants to talk about, he knows he can catch me before he starts his day. Mostly, I think he enjoys disrupting my routine, but this time the joke was on him.

"Oh…uh…hello Sallie," he stammered when Sallie opened the door and Hugo rushed to confront him, snarling at his feet.

"I'm sorry, I wasn't expecting. Hugo, stop that! Am I interrupting? Should I come back another time?"

"Nonsense, Bo, come on in," Sallie said. "We're just finishing breakfast. Can I get you a cup of coffee or anything to eat?"

"No, that's alright. I was just…. Well, now that you mention it, a cup of coffee would be great. Thank you, Sallie."

As Bo crested the stairs, Hugo's nose still affixed to his pant leg, I peered over my newspaper, trying without success to conceal my amusement.

"Good morning, Detective. To what do we owe the pleasure?"

"I just came by to update you on the Izzy Weisman case, and to get your take on something."

"I see. Well, we're all ears."

While Sallie served Bo his coffee, we told him about our visits with Henrietta Thomas and Mose Adler. He seemed vaguely interested in Mose as someone who was around the music scene in the sixties and said he'd pass the name along to the homicide detective he'd been working with.

Once we were done with our updates, Bo let us know that Rodiger had been unable to locate Paulo Martins, here or in São Paulo. The number Izzy had given him was assigned to a burner phone paid for with cash two months earlier. He suspected that the Paulo Martins Sallie met was the same person who passed himself off to Izzy as Paul Martin, a musicologist at the University of Southern Mississippi. Neither Southern Miss nor the University of São Paulo had any record of the man.

"He is definitely a person of interest," Bo said. "Thank you, Sallie, for putting us onto him. Your instincts were right on the money."

"I'm glad I could be of some help," Sallie said. "I'm confused, though. Who is this man, really? It sounds like he isn't Paulo Martins, or Paul Martin, for that matter. And maybe he's not a musicologist either, although he certainly sounded like one. Who is he and what is he after?"

"We don't know, and we have the same questions," Bo said.

There was a brief silence as Bo leaned forward and addressed Sallie.

"I need to ask, Sallie, do you have contact information for Paulo Martins? The number Izzy Weisman gave us was for a burner phone."

"I don't have a phone number, but I do have an email address."

"Would you be willing to email him to set up a meeting?"

"Whoa, hold on there," I jumped in. "You've just said you don't know who this guy is, but you suspect him of being an arsonist, and now you want to use Sallie as bait to lure him out? I don't think so."

"We'd be there to meet him, Bru," Bo said. "Sallie would never be alone with him."

"I don't like it. Not one bit. Completely out of the question."

"Oh, relax, Bruneau," Sallie said. "I'm happy to help, Bo. I can't promise it will work, but I can give it a try."

"Are you crazy?" I cried. "There are too many variables you can't control, Sallie. This is a terrible idea."

"It'll be fine. Paulo is harmless, at least where I'm concerned, and Bo will be right there if anything goes wrong. Bo, what pretense should I use?"

"Maybe that you've found something in your archives that you think he'd be interested in?"

"Should I be specific?"

"That's up to you. Whatever you think works best. But you do need to be specific about a time and place, so we can be sure to be there."

"That would be awkward," Sallie said. "He knows I'm in my office most of the day. He'd expect to be able to just drop by."

"Huh. I didn't think about that."

"I can't believe this!" I objected again. "What if he does show up at work? Who's got your back then?"

Sallie ignored me.

"How about I suggest we meet for a drink? He fancies me, I think. Whatever it is, I can say I'll bring copies with me."

"I am really not liking this," I said.

"Oh, stop it, Bruneau. What's the big deal? All I have to do is get him there, and Bo and his team will take over."

"That's right," Bo said. "We would be there with you, posing as customers. The second he walks in, we grab him, escort him out, and take him to the station for questioning."

That was it. Just like that, Bo and Sallie cut a deal. My opinion on the matter seemed to be of little consequence.

Sallie grabbed my laptop off the kitchen counter and took it back to the bedroom. Once Bo and I were alone, I took advantage of the opportunity to register my displeasure, in case he hadn't already gotten the message.

"I don't appreciate you pimping out my girlfriend. At least you could have come to me first."

"Sallie's a big girl, Bru. I promise you we'll take good care of her. She won't be in any danger at all. Besides, you said yourself you've got to stop trying to manage her every move."

"When I said that, I wasn't thinking about the moves a handsome Brazilian arsonist might try."

Bo chuckled at that.

"I didn't expect Sallie to be here this morning," Bo said, a sly grin forming. "Did you just call her your girlfriend? You guys hooking up again or what?"

"We're taking things one step at a time."

"If you're having sleepovers, I'd say you've taken more than a step."

"Very funny."

Just then, Sallie emerged from the bedroom, cradling L'il Queenie in her arms.

"Message sent," she announced. "I told Paulo I found some architectural drawings for some of the torn-down buildings in the Rampart-Perdido area, where Buddy Bolden used to play and hang out. I said I took pictures of them to show him and suggested we meet at the Royal Frenchman to go over them."

"Perfect. Is that the place across from Washington Square?" Bo asked.

"Yes. They have a nice patio area. I told him we could meet there tomorrow at 5:30, for cocktails and maybe a snack."

"Okay, great. As soon as you hear from him, please let me know."

As Sallie and Bo made their plan, I listened intently, looking for flaws. Sallie interpreted my silence as sulking and made an effort to prop me up.

"Bo, we should discuss a theory that Bruneau came up with," she said. "He made the point that whoever burned down Izzy Weisman's house, whether it was Paulo Martins or someone else, might have done so to cover up another crime."

Bo nodded knowingly.

"You mean he, or they, were only after one thing, or maybe a few things, which they took, and then they torched the place so we wouldn't know what was taken?"

"Yes, exactly."

"That is one of our theories, too."

L'il Queenie jumped off Sallie's lap and then hopped up onto the windowsill she claims for her daybed. Sallie leaned forward.

"Okay, so let's say Paulo Martins is the thief, and he stole the Bolden cylinder or some specific part of Weisman's collection. What would he hope to gain?"

I took a stab at that one.

"Well, for one, he may not have known that we know about the cylinder if that's what he was after. And no one other than Izzy knows exactly what he had in his collection. If there was any documentation of his inventory, it went up in flames, too. Izzy is an older guy who's probably not going to be around a lot longer. If the thief is smart, he waits for Izzy to pass, and then, to great fanfare, he reveals Beethoven's lost symphony, or whatever it is he has."

"Are you assuming he is an academic after all, and this is the 'find' that's going to make his career?" Sallie asked.

"Not necessarily," Bo jumped in. "It might just be about money. It usually is, in my experience. Something like this, there are people out there who are prepared to pay big bucks."

"People like Dominick Martello?" I asked.

"Maybe."

There was a pause in the conversation, which I took advantage of.

"You said that was one of your theories. What are the others?"

"Well, let's begin with the obvious one," Bo said. "Weisman torched his own place. His alibi has holes in it, so he had the opportunity, even if his motive isn't clear. My colleagues like him for the cold case homicide, too. I'm not all the way there on that, but he definitely knows more than he's telling us."

"I have a hard time seeing it," I said.

"Are there more theories?" Sallie asked.

"Sure. It's hard to ignore the name Dominick Martello. What the man wants, he's accustomed to getting, no matter what it takes. If there was something he had his eye on that he couldn't convince Weisman to sell, maybe he had one of his henchmen do the deed."

We all agreed that it was a plausible scenario. Then Bo commented that the cops had more leads in the cold case than for the arson investigation. He said Lyla Saint-Clair keeps coming up. And the name Henry Wilkins was also mentioned.

"Henry? As in, our Henry?" I asked, surprised.

"I think so."

"What possible connection could Henry have to all this?"

"He may have been childhood friends with our victim," Bo said. "I'd like to talk with him before my buddy in Homicide tries to haul him in."

"Haul him in? For what?"

"It's a power play. He likes the people he interviews to be nervous, whether they're a suspect or not. And to be clear, Henry is not a suspect. But it's possible that he may remember some things that could be useful to us."

"Can I be present when you question him?"

"Why?"

"I don't know. Just curious, I guess."

Bo sighed.

"Fine, whatever. But I'm the one asking the questions; are we clear on that?"

"Yes, of course. Henry might be downstairs now. Let me check."

I called Henry, who said he was at District Donuts with Pablo. They had a pick-up in Bogalusa and were fueling up for the ride. When I explained that Bo needed to speak with him, he said to give him ten minutes. By the time he arrived, coffee in hand, Sallie had already left for work.

"I really appreciate you stopping by, Henry," Bo said as the three of us took our seats in the living room.

"No problem. Is this about that cylinder again?"

As he spoke, Hugo rubbed up against Henry's leg, and Henry scooped him up onto his lap. Hugo panted eagerly, his bright red tongue hanging out as he scanned the room.

"No, not exactly," Bo said. "Henry, does the name Arnold Jesse mean anything to you?"

"Yeah, sure," Henry answered without hesitation. "We were friends growing up. Arno was a couple years older than me, but we'd hang out sometimes. Until he disappeared, of course. Why do you want to know about Arno?"

"It was Arnold's body in Izzy Weisman's house," I said.

That took Henry back. He looked at Bo.

"Just to clarify, Henry, we don't know for sure that it was Arnold Jesse behind the wall. We think it was, but we don't have proof yet."

"I never did believe he just ran away," Henry said. "None of us did. Arno never seemed unhappy, and he was devoted to his mother, who he took care of more than she took care of him. It never made sense that he'd split town, like the police said he did. Now we know. How in the world did he end up in Mr. Weisman's house?"

"That's what we're trying to find out," Bo said. "What do you remember about Arnold, Henry?"

"He was a great kid. Looking back, I can see that he had to grow up faster than the rest of us. My folks and most of the other families in the neighborhood…we weren't rich, but there was always food on the table. Sure, we'd do stuff to earn some spending money whenever we could, but Arno, he *had* to make money, on account of his mother. She was deep into drugs, and he couldn't count on her for anything. They lived in the Magnolia projects. I remember going to their apartment one time. It was pretty bad."

"You grew up nearby?"

"Yeah, on South Liberty, a few blocks away."

"Did Arnold have a job?" Bo asked.

"No, not a 'job' job, I don't think, but he was always hustling up work of one kind or another. He'd hang around the Dew Drop and run errands for the folks who worked there."

"How did you and Arnold come to know each other?"

"I don't really remember. He was just a kid who was around. There were a lot of us in those days. It might have been through his sister. She was my age, and we went to school together."

"What was her name?"

"Cheryl."

I was about to ask a follow-up question about Cheryl, but Bo motioned for me to hold off. He was getting ready to speak, but Henry beat him to it.

"How in the world did you find out that I knew Arnold?" he asked.

"From someone who was part of the Dew Drop scene back in the day,"

Bo said. "She had a distinct memory of you being with Arnold and getting hauled off by your mother because you were hanging around with some musicians who were smoking a joint."

"Yeah?"

"Yeah. She remembered your mother saying, 'Henry Wilkins, you are in a world of trouble, young man!' And it stuck with her all these years."

Henry laughed, a big smile on his face.

"That sounds like Mamma, alright. She was a force, bless her soul. If you heard her, you'd remember her too."

"Getting back to Arnold, Henry," Bo said, "do you remember the last time you saw him before he went missing?"

"No, I'm sorry, that was a long time ago. Probably I'd seen him around that time, but I can't remember any specifics."

"Did you ever get the sense that he was in trouble of any kind or that something was bothering him?"

"No, not that I remember. Like I said, he always seemed like a happy kid even though, looking back, I can see that he had a hard life."

"Do you remember the name Lyla Saint-Clair from those days?"

"You mean the singer in Mr. Weisman's window?"

"Yep."

"No, that was the first I ever heard of her."

"What about Dominick Martello?" Bo asked.

"Well, sure, everybody knows who Dominick Martello is, but I didn't know the name back then," Henry said.

"And you hadn't heard of Izzy Weisman either?"

Henry shook his head.

"What about Bella Gurwitz?"

"Nope. None of these names mean anything to me."

There was another name I was curious about.

"How about Mose Adler, Henry? Ever hear of him?"

Henry put his hand to his chin.

"That name does sound familiar," he said. "I think there was a Mose who was around the Dew Drop sometimes. Bit of a character. He was a big red-haired guy with a long beard and a serious afro for a white dude. The only reason I remember him is he used to play these drums that Arno and a couple other kids would tap dance to. The bunch of 'em went down to the Quarter a few times and made out pretty well with their hat line."

"Interesting," Bo said, shooting me a sidelong glance. "Henry, did Arnold have any close friends who might still be around?"

"Not that I can think of. Cheryl would be the main one. They were close. She looked up to him, and he was very protective of her."

"She was his half-sister, right?"

"Yes. She had a different last name. Robinson, Cheryl Robinson. Goes by her married name now, Cheryl Bertrand. I think she got divorced a few years back. No kids, I don't think."

"Is she still in town? Do you keep up with her?"

"Oh yeah, she's around. We don't keep in touch, but I saw her at a party a couple years ago, and one time we ran into each other on a second line for a childhood friend of ours. Last I heard, Cheryl runs the drug treatment center over on Saint Claude."

"Open Arms?" Bo asked.

"Yes, that's the one."

"I know that place. They do God's work. My wife used to volunteer there."

"Yeah, they save lives," Henry said. "Growing up the way she did, with her mom and all, Cheryl's made it her mission in life to help folks with addictions."

"If you can't save the ones you love," I said, "save the ones you can."

"Something like that."

Chapter Sixteen

It was almost ten o'clock by the time Bo and Henry left, and I had a lot to think about. I was more than a little bothered by Bo's use of Sallie to lure Paulo Martins into the open and couldn't help but think about all the things that could go wrong. Learning from Henry that Mose Adler and Arnold Jesse were busking partners caused me to wonder if I'd asked enough questions of the lecherous old coot. And Henry's revelation that Arnold Jesse's sister had dedicated her life to helping drug addicts like her mother tugged at my heartstrings. But it was an unsettling conversation I had with Prosper the night before that dominated my thoughts.

I had called my friend to set a time and place for a long-overdue conversation about Lyla Saint Clair.

"I knew this call would come sooner or later," he said. "What took you so long?"

"I've been busy and distracted," I said. "Sorry if you feel neglected."

Prosper chuckled softly.

"I've got a lot to tell you, my friend, and I'm afraid you're going to have to brace yourself. It would be good if we found a private setting."

"How about an outside table at Bacchanal?" I suggested.

"That would work."

"Are you free on Wednesday? I could pick you up at five."

"It's a date."

For the three years or so I've known Prosper, he has alluded to skeletons in his closet, but I've never pushed him for details and assumed that most of them stemmed from his time in Vietnam. As I hung up the phone, I had the strong feeling that I was about to find out differently.

I was slouching on my couch, stroking Hugo's head on my thigh, lost in my thoughts, when it suddenly occurred to me that I had a lunch appointment to prepare for. Chris Keating and I were supposed to meet at Lil' Dizzy's, but Chris had called a couple of days earlier to notify me of a change in plans. He found an adjunct professor of music history at Tulane who he thought might have some insights into Buddy Bolden and his times. His name was Orville Whitlock, and according to Chris, he wasn't exactly a Lil' Dizzy's kind of guy. Chris told me apologetically that he'd made a reservation for three at Commander's Palace, and offered to split the tab. I thanked him for the gesture but declined his offer on the grounds that he was doing me a favor. I can't say I was thrilled about footing what was sure to be a significant bill, but on the other hand, a meal at Commander's is always something to look forward to, no matter who is paying.

A couple hours later, as I was hurrying along the ruptured banquette that runs parallel to the Lafayette Cemetery, I took a misstep and turned my ankle badly enough that I had to lean against the cemetery wall for a couple minutes to collect myself and let the stabbing pain subside. Not for the first time, I cursed the condition of New Orleans' streets and sidewalks, a widely acknowledged civic disgrace. Phoneless, limping, and in pain, I arrived at my destination in a less-than buoyant mood. Chris stood under Commander's iconic teal- and white-striped awning, dressed casually in jeans, an open-collared oxford, and a tan linen jacket, his shoulder-length hair pulled back in a neat ponytail. Next to him stood a tall, raptor-faced man in a black suit and pencil-thin black tie, peering self-importantly over wire-frame glasses.

"Bruneau, this is Orville Whitlock," Chris said cheerily as I approached.

"Pleased to meet you," I said, extending my hand.

Whitlock nodded and smiled faintly. His hand was cold and fleshy.

Chris had requested the Garden Room, where we had the good fortune of being seated next to the wall-length window that overlooks the magnificent courtyard. When our waiter, Vincent, handed us our menus, Chris ordered a Campari and soda, and I opted for a Mojito. Whitlock eyed us skeptically and asked for a Diet Coke.

"So, Bruneau, our friend tells me you have discovered a long-lost recording of Buddy Bolden, first man of jazz," Whitlock said, sounding bored.

"You say that as though this is an everyday occurrence," I said.

"People come to me from time to time. The common assumption seems to be that any unlabeled recording found in grandpa's attic must be of historic importance."

"They might be important to them."

"Yes, undoubtedly that must be true," Whitlock said loftily. "Tell me, Bruneau, what makes you think you've found the genuine article?"

Our drinks arrived in the nick of time. I took a healthy slug before embarking on the tale of our cylinder. Whitlock listened patiently.

"I must say, your story is a good deal more intriguing than most," he said when I had concluded. "You say you've got the recording on your phone?"

"Yes, although I didn't bring it with me."

"Naturally."

I made eye contact with Chris to let him know I didn't appreciate Whitlock's condescending insinuation.

"You are welcome to check it out at my apartment," I said. "It's a short walk from here."

Just then, Vincent appeared, a pencil and notepad in hand. Grateful for the interruption, Chris wasted no time ordering the turtle soup and the bronzed redfish. Whitlock followed with the romaine salad and the jerked tenderloin, which he asked for well done. Stifling an impulse to comment on the man's misguided palate, I asked for the soft-shell crab bisque and the lacquered quail. Then, summoning the captain, I asked his opinion of an Alsatian pinot gris as an accompaniment to the seafood and poultry. He signaled his approval and went off to retrieve our bottle. I had assumed Whitlock would continue to nurse his soda, but when the captain returned to uncork and chill our wine, he ordered a twenty dollar glass of cabernet.

Determined to re-establish our conversation on a more equal footing, I asked Whitlock to tell us a bit about himself and how he came upon his reputation as a jazz aficionado. He seemed to appreciate the question and told us that he grew up in St. Louis, the only child of an Irish pub owner and his German wife. The family lived above the pub, which had a jukebox that featured a steady diet of big band swing and Tin Pan Alley crooning. He took to the former more enthusiastically than the latter, and on his seventh birthday received his first clarinet. He practiced daily, and by the time he was in high school, he was accomplished enough to sit in with some of the city's better ensembles. He went on to study at the Jazz Institute of Berlin and described his time in Germany as formative.

"European audiences get it," Whitlock said. "They appreciate jazz, in all its forms. Ironic, isn't it? Our greatest cultural gift to the world continues to thrive overseas but is on life support here in America."

"So, you decided to dedicate your life to spreading the gospel of jazz here in the States?" Chris asked.

"Something like that. I'm no evangelist, but I teach those who are open to learning."

"Do you teach anywhere other than Tulane?" I asked.

"I've got a dozen or so clarinet students, and I teach a jazz history class at the Ellis Marsalis Center. In the summer, I pitch in at the Louis Armstrong Jazz Camp. I've got a radio show, a group I gig with from time to time, and a blog. Special projects here and there."

"Is there a core message you impart to your students?"

"There are many messages, but the big one is that the story of jazz is the story of race in America. Today, we think of modern jazz as cerebral music, and scholars like me chart its every mutation with academic detachment. I'm not sure if we're keeping the music alive or killing it, to be honest. But in its earliest days, jazz was a music of ecstatic release. It offered long-suffering people the prospect of liberation through freedom of expression. When Buddy Bolden started playing hot, the children he called home didn't marvel at his virtuosity or scrutinize his every note. They came for a feeling; a deliverance, however temporary. It would have been a distinctly visceral and uniquely African American experience."

"And then our white ancestors took note of what was happening and appropriated the music?" Chris asked.

"Yes, of course, eventually. That's what we do, right? But in addition to disseminating the music to a wider audience, white musicians made important contributions of their own. And as white and black musicians began playing together, tossing ideas back and forth, and appearing before mixed race audiences, jazz music acted as a bridge between races and cultures, long before the sports leagues got into the act."

I don't know if it was the alcohol kicking in or his warming to his subject, but the more Whitlock talked, the more I found my initial aversion to the man softening. What struck me first as arrogance may just have been a mask he assumes to hide social awkwardness.

Working our way through the appetizers and then our entrees, we continued to discuss the intersections of race and music and society. The absurdity of three white guys opining on these topics was not lost on me, and I found myself wishing Bo or Henry were with us to lend a perspective born of lived experience. Eventually, I brought us back around to our original subject.

"Getting back to Buddy Bolden, if I may, what I've been told is that he was the first to bring the blues and ragtime together, and by doing that, he created something entirely new. Is that how you see it?"

"That's the party line," Whitlock said.

"With which, I take it, you disagree?"

"Not disagree, no. It's just an oversimplification."

"What's your take, then?"

"Before Buddy, the guys who made their living as musicians were schooled. They could read, keep time, play different styles. They were downtown guys, Creole mostly, and they were genteel."

"But that wasn't Buddy."

"No, not at all. Bolden came out of what we now call Central City, but in those days was known as Back O' Town. It was a hardscrabble place, where maybe Buddy heard some ragtime, and certainly the blues, but he would have heard a lot of other things too, and in my imagining, he played what he heard."

"Are you talking about church music and military marching bands? That kind of thing?" Chris asked.

"Sure, those things, but also funeral dirges, the hawking of vendors, foghorns on the river, the hissing and chugging of steam locomotives pulling in and out of Union Station, the squawking of backyard chickens, the clopping of hoofbeats, and the creaking of wagon wheels. The sounds of the city would have been a lot different in those days, and I envision Buddy with his instrument playing them all."

"That doesn't explain the attitude," I said.

"You mean loud and aggressive?"

"Yes."

"In those days, bands would sit in the back of horse-drawn wagons that would wind through the neighborhoods, advertising dances or nightclub acts. When rival bands came across each other, they would stop their wagons and compete to see who could win over the crowds that spilled out of nearby homes and bars. Buddy would have seen and heard a lot of that, too."

"Kind of like a musical version of the dozens," Chris said.

"Yeah, exactly."

"The dozens?" I asked.

"It was a game of verbal jousting that was popular in the Black communities of the time," Chris said. "Combatants would trade escalating series of insults, egged on by a raucous crowd, until one party gave up."

"That sounds like a blast," I said. "I think I was born in the wrong century."

That drew a chuckle from Chris and a wan smile from Whitlock, and as we devoured the order of pecan pie à la mode that Vincent had cut into three equal pieces, we exchanged small talk and friendly banter. I did manage to ask Whitlock if he knew a Paul Martin at Southern Miss or a Paulo Martins from Brazil. He said he did not.

Later, when we said our goodbyes outside the restaurant's front entrance, I asked Whitlock if he'd like to swing by my apartment to listen to the recording on my phone. He said he had an appointment he had to get to but gave me his number so I could text it to him. Then he left me with a parting thought.

"I wish you luck, Bruneau, in finding your cylinder and authenticating its contents," he said. "Even so, I can't help but wonder if some things mean more to us because of what we don't know about them than what we do."

1907

Black Storyville
New Orleans, Louisiana
March 1907

Louis Jones is cutting hair in his shop when the news reaches him that they've taken Buddy Bolden away. It is Jimmy Johnson who lets him know, poking his head in on the way to work at the furniture factory. Neither man is surprised at the news, having known for some time that this day would come. But both are saddened, remembering the time not long past when King Bolden reigned supreme.*

Jimmy had played the bass in Buddy's best bands, but like so many others, he'd fallen out with his erstwhile leader.

"It sure was good while it lasted," Jimmy says, shaking his head. "I've seen the whisky ruin more than one good man, and the women some others, but I ain't never seen no man fall so low, from so high, so fast."

"Who'd he hit this time?" Louis asks.

"I don't know. His women couldn't handle him no more, I think is what it was. Can't blame 'em for being scared."

Even though he isn't a musician, Louis is, or was, one of Buddy's closest friends. He and Willie Cornish used to stay up all night with Buddy after the band stopped playing, sharing whisky, and sometimes women too. But then the headaches started and the lashing out at bandmates, even though it was Buddy who was missing the notes and failing to show up on time, if he bothered to show up at all. He'd gotten himself arrested for hitting his mother-in-law over the head with a water pitcher, convinced she was trying to poison him. He got into fights with his wife, Nora, and sister Cora, and any stranger he didn't like the look of. He let himself go physically too, no longer caring about his appearance. When Louis tried to visit him a couple months ago, Buddy didn't even know who he was.

Closing up shop that evening, Louis is too despondent to go straight home. He decides to walk over to the Cornish residence three blocks away and see if Willie is in. As he approaches the single barrel shotgun Willie shares with his wife Bella, he can hear the trombone playing low and sad from half a block away. He mounts the stoop and pushes the screen door open. The big man is in a sleeveless white undershirt, leaning forward in his rocker. He looks up at Louis, his face a dark shadow.

"I guess you heard the news?"

"Yes."

"I got me a bad case of the blues, Louis."

"Yeah, me too."

"Drink?"

"Sure."

Louis steps toward Willie's liquor cabinet, but Willie stops him.

"Not here," he says, gesturing over his shoulder at the kitchen, where Louis can smell chicken frying.

"Deichmann's?" Louis suggests.

"That works."

Seated in a booth at William Deichmann's grocery store saloon, a bottle of gin between them, Louis and Willie clink their glasses and take a deep swill of the bracing spirit.

"They always said he was going to blow his brains out from playing too loud," Willie says.

"Maybe he did, if you think about it that way," Louis says.

Willie nods, pours himself another gin, and leans back, a smile of reminiscence slowly forming.

"Remember that time we were out at Johnson Park and the Robichaux band was playing over at Lincoln?" he asks.

"Hard to forget. Buddy says, 'come on Cornish, stick your horn out that window,

put your trombone out there, I'm going to call my children home.' And sure enough, he does, and here they come, damn near all of 'em. Wasn't nobody left for Robichaux's boys to play for."

Willie folds his thick, heavy arms across his wide chest, shakes his head, and chuckles at the memory.

"He might've been the king already, but that was the night it became official. All hail King Bolden."

"1902, wasn't it?"

"Yeah, I think so."

"Three, four, maybe five years at the top," Louis says. "Not many can say they had that."

Willie picks up his glass and pounds the table three times, mimicking the way Buddy would stomp once with his foot and then knock on the floor with his horn to set the beat. Then he poured himself and Louis another drink.

"To King Bolden," he says, lifting his glass.

"To the king."

Chapter Seventeen

I told Angie about dropping in on Bruneau and being greeted by Sallie, and she seemed to think it was just about the funniest thing she'd ever heard. The kids had left for school, and she was fixing my favorite breakfast of freshly baked buttermilk biscuits with sausage gravy, a rare treat.

"You did what?" she howled. "What time was this?"

"I don't know, maybe 7:30."

"And Sallie just opens the door like it's the most natural thing in the world?"

"Pretty much."

"Was she even dressed?"

"Fully."

"What I would have given to have seen your face!"

"Poker face, all the way."

"Yeah, right, I bet. After a losing hand, maybe. Serves you right for just dropping by at that ungodly hour without any notice. What in the world were you thinking?"

"I do that sometimes. I get a kick out of throwing Bru off his routine."

"Sounds like he wasn't the one who got thrown off."

"Nope, the joke was on me, I can't deny it. But it's pretty cool that they're back to spending nights together, don't you think?

"Yeah, but I'm not surprised," Angie said, bending down to pull the biscuits out of the oven. They were light and fluffy, the way I like them, and the buttery steam that escaped made me even hungrier than I already was.

"Let me guess. Your woman's intuition?"

"No, not this time. I met Sallie for lunch the other day. She told me she and Bruneau were starting to do things together again."

"Well, yeah, I'd say so."

"Very funny. Sallie's theory is that things go best when they're working on something together."

"Uh-huh."

"Bo Duplessis! You get your head out of the gutter, you hear?"

"Right. Working together. Like on the Buddy Bolden cylinder?"

"Exactly. They're a team then, figuring stuff out together, and Sallie feels valued."

"I guess we'll have to line up more projects to keep them busy," I said.

Angie's biscuits were perfect, and it was one of her better batches of gravy, thick but not pasty, with a bit of kick from the spicy sausage she uses. As we ate, we discussed the meeting Angie set up for us with Cheryl Bertrand, Arnold Jesse's half-sister. Turns out Angie knew Cheryl well, having processed Medicaid payments at the Open Arms treatment center ten hours a week for several years. She stopped volunteering when she went back to work, once Monique could fend for herself when she came home from school.

Angie gave me the rundown on all the things Open Arms does, and it's a lot more than I realized. They run an opioid treatment program for addicts, which is the part I knew about, but they also provide care management services such as helping patients find affordable housing or navigate the criminal justice system.

"You think highly of Cheryl and her work, right?" I asked.

"Oh yeah, she's amazing," Angie said. "A total dynamo. And a really good person."

"How do you think she's going to take this?"

"I don't know. I'm sure it will be a jolt, but she's strong. It might come as a relief to finally get some closure."

"What about your buddy, Gator?" Angie asked me.

"What about him?"

"Is he okay with us doing this without him?"

"At first, he got a little bent out of shape, but when I told him about your relationship with Cheryl, he came around. The way we left it is we're just going to break the news to her, and then set the expectation that, once she's over the shock, Gator will follow up with questions from the investigation."

* * *

I'd been to Open Arms before, to drop Angie off or to pick her up, but I'd never been inside or met anyone who worked there. Judging by the no-frills entrance in the corner of an aging steel warehouse that also housed a boxing gym and a body shop, I assumed it was a bare-bones operation. I was surprised, as we entered the spacious waiting room, to see long hallways branching off in three directions and an elevator leading to a second floor. In the hall directly ahead of us, three lines of patients waited at dispensary windows. In the waiting room, two patients slept slumped in their chairs, a heavily tattooed amputee in a wheelchair flipped through a beaten-up issue of *Us* magazine, and an emaciated young woman paced about, visibly agitated.

If I had come a day earlier, by myself, I might have described some of the Open Arms clientele as "addicts" or "street junkies." But I'd gotten an education from Angie on the ride over. She told me that people in what she called "the recovery community" view those terms as degrading. She went on to talk about the history of U.S. drug policy and its impacts on urban Black communities. Communities like the one Cheryl Bertrand and Arnold Jesse grew up in.

"Language like that stigmatizes people, Bo," Angie said. "You don't hear the lily white, pill-popping suburban housewife who drains a fifth of vodka a day called an addict, do you? We don't call the hedge fund manager with a cocaine problem a junkie, either."

"No, I guess we don't," I said. "Thanks for the lesson."

Angie approached the reception desk.

"It's Gladys, isn't it?" she asked the large middle-aged woman typing into a computer.

"Yes, that's right," the woman said, looking up for the first time.

"Hey, I remember you. Angie, right? How you been, girl?"

"You've got a good memory, Gladys," Angie said. "I've been well, thank you. This is my husband, Bo. We're here to meet with Cheryl. She's expecting us."

"Oh, okay, sure, let me buzz her," Gladys said. As she spoke with her boss on the phone, informing her of our presence, I got the feeling Gladys thought we were there for a clinical visit, and she was sizing me up as the likely patient.

"She said to go on up," Gladys told us after hanging up the phone. "Hang on while I get someone to escort you."

Within seconds, a well-built staff member appeared, introduced himself as Bill, and led us to the elevator, where he swiped a fob to open the doors. He rode with us to the second floor, where he showed us into a suite of eight offices connected by a common area. An attractive, graying woman in a brown pant suit came out of the largest one, arms outstretched and a warm smile on her face.

"Angie Duplessis, it has been too long!"

"It has Cheryl, I know," Angie said as she and Cheryl Bertrand hugged.

"Cheryl, this is my husband, Bo," Angie said, turning toward me. "I don't know if you remember, but Bo is a detective with the Property Crimes division of NOPD."

"Of course I remember," Cheryl said, extending her hand to me. "It's a pleasure to meet you, Bo. Angie talked about you and your kids often when she worked here."

"I'd love to catch up, Cheryl," Angie said, "but to be completely open with you, we're here on police business."

"Has one of our patients gotten into some trouble?"

"No, it's nothing like that," I said. "Do you think we could talk in private? It's a personal matter we'd like to discuss with you."

Cheryl led us into her office, closing the door behind us and taking a seat opposite Angie and me. I'm not the best at delivering bad news, but I have found that it goes better if I get right to the point, so that's what I did. When I finished, Cheryl was silent, and tears welled up in her eyes. She put her head in her hands and wept. Angie crossed to Cheryl's side of the desk and wrapped herself around her.

"I'm sorry," Cheryl gasped, her shoulders shaking and her chest heaving.

"It's okay," Angie said, leaning in close and squeezing hard. "You have yourself a good cry, baby. We understand. We know this comes as a great shock, and we can't imagine what you're feeling. Would you like us to leave you alone?"

"No, no, please don't. I've got so many questions. Just give me a minute."

"Of course," I said. "Take all the time you need."

After another half minute or so, Cheryl took a couple tissues from a box on her desk and blew her nose. Angie stepped back around to her chair, and as she did, Cheryl pulled another tissue from the box and dabbed at her eyes. Then she spoke, managing a forced smile and sniffling between sentences.

"I've always known this day was going to come. Now that it's here, it feels surreal. I never believed for a minute that Arno ran off on us like the police said. I always assumed he ran into foul play somehow, but it's been so long, I figured maybe I'd never find out for sure what happened to him. Do you know how he died and how he ended up in this house?"

"The answer is no on both counts," I said. "The coroner hasn't been able to determine a cause of death, only that there are no signs of violence. No broken bones, bullet wounds, or blunt force trauma."

"Well, that's something to be grateful for, I guess. He wouldn't have died of natural causes, though, right? I mean, he was only thirteen years old."

"It doesn't seem likely, I agree, but anything is possible."

"If it was natural causes, why would someone hide his body behind the walls of a house?"

"We don't know. We're trying to find out."

"Whose house was it?"

"The owner's name is Izzy Weisman. He's been in that house since 1961. He was a small-time music promoter who did some business at the Dew Drop Inn. Does that name mean anything to you?"

"No, I don't think so."

There was a pause in the conversation. I was about to say our goodbyes and explain to Cheryl that Gator would be following up with her when Angie spoke.

"Tell us about Arnold, Cheryl. What do you remember about him?"

Cheryl smiled, blew her nose again, and wiped a couple new tears from her cheeks.

"I remember everything about him. He was my hero. My protector. Neither of us knew our fathers. And Momma, she loved us, but we couldn't count on her. So, Arno, he and I, we just had each other. He was almost like a father to me, and he took care of Momma more than she took care of him. He'd make some money, feed us sometimes when Momma's food stamps ran out. He'd even make sure I did my homework and put me to bed some nights."

"Was he ever able to just be a kid?" Angie asked.

"Oh yes, he had his fun. He could be the life of the party when he wanted. He was a charmer, you know, always smiling. Everybody loved Arno. Which is why this never made any sense. Why would anyone want to hurt Arno?"

"That's what Bo is trying to figure out. Arnold used to hang around the Dew Drop, didn't he?"

"Yes, that's right. He made some money by tap dancing out front and running errands for some of the musicians there."

"Did you ever go with him?"

"A few times, maybe, but no, not really. I was only nine years old when Arno went missing. When I wasn't in school, I was playing with kids my own age."

"Like Henry Wilkins?" I asked, smiling.

"Yeah, sure, Henry and other kids in the neighborhood. How do you know Henry? I had a schoolgirl crush on that boy."

We all laughed at that.

"Henry is a friend, or a friend of a friend anyway," I said. "He's the one who helped us find you."

Cheryl smiled and pulled another tissue from the box. I sensed an opportunity to say our goodbyes, but Angie pressed on. There was going to be hell to pay with Gator, not to mention Mac, if I let my wife conduct a full-on interview.

"Cheryl, did Arno ever seem afraid or worried about anyone?" Angie asked. "Someone at the Dew Drop, maybe, or an associate of your mother's?"

"Not that I remember, but again, I was only nine. He definitely didn't like the men who'd come around looking for Momma, and he'd try to shield me from them, but I don't remember anything specific. One thing I do remember is when he'd head off to the Dew Drop, Momma used to tell him to stay away from someone named Nico. 'You listen to me, young man,' she'd say, 'don't you go getting mixed up with that Nico. He's bad news, that one.' Does that mean anything to you?"

"Possibly," I said, remembering that Dominick Martello was known as Nico back in the day. I made a note to tell Gator to look into that angle. Then I tried to head Angie off at the pass.

"Cheryl, our main purpose in coming here today was to tell you about finding the body we think is Arnold's, and we figured it would be best if you heard it from someone you knew. As you might imagine, Arnold is now the subject of a cold-case murder investigation. My colleague in Homicide, Joe Guidry, is going to ask you some questions. And we'd like to take a swab from you so we can check for a DNA match. Would that be alright with you?"

"Of course, Bo, however I can be of help. I appreciate the two of you bringing me the news."

Angie reached across the desk for Cheryl's hand and squeezed it tightly. Cheryl smiled gratefully, a new round of tears beginning to well up. She started to get up to see us out, but Angie held her grip.

"Cheryl, can I ask you one more question?" she asked.

"Of course, honey. What do you want to know?"

"It's just that, learning what we have about your childhood, it seems remarkable to me that you became the person you are. What happened to you after Arnold disappeared, and then your mother died a couple years later? You were, what, eleven or twelve years old, and you were all alone in the world."

"Not completely alone. I had my grandmother, who I went to live with in the Seventh Ward. And I didn't know it yet, but I had a guardian angel."

"A guardian angel?"

"Yes. Not long after I moved in with Granny, I started being sent to see tutors after school. I didn't understand at the time that the tutors were paid for by someone other than the school. And then a few years later, when I was ready to graduate high school, our principal told me that I had a full scholarship to LSU, paid for by a benefactor."

"Did you find out who this benefactor was?"

"Yes, but not until I was out of school and working as a social worker here in the city. I'd been meeting with banks about starting Open Arms, and I was getting nowhere. Somehow, my angel found out. She introduced herself to me one day and invited me to lunch. She said she learned about my situation through what happened with Arnold, who she knew from the Dew Drop, and decided to do what she could to help me succeed in life. She told me how proud she was of me and that she wanted to help me fulfill my dream of opening a treatment center for people like my mother. I never could have gotten this place off the ground without her help."

"That's incredible," Angie said. "Does your angel have a name?"

"Yes, her name is Bella. Bella Gurwitz."

* * *

"Look, I understand why you're upset, but put yourself in Bo's situation," Mac told Gator Guidry and Rooster McCutcheon as the three of us stood around his desk, behind closed doors.

"His wife and the presumed victim's sister are friends. It's natural that Angie is going to ask some questions. The fact that those questions produced some new information isn't Bo's fault. What's he supposed to do, pretend he didn't hear what the woman had to say?"

"This isn't the first time your man has hidden the ball, captain," Rooster said, tensed and leaning over Mac's desk.

"Hidden the ball? What did he hide? First thing Bo did was tell Guidry here what he found out. That's called teamwork where I come from."

Mac has a reputation within Property Crimes for folding easily in disputes with other departments. I appreciated him going to bat for me.

Rooster stood up and relaxed his shoulders. He looked at Gator, who shrugged.

"I apologize for any misunderstanding," I said. "I did tell Gator that Angie and I would break the news to Cheryl Bertrand and then leave it to him to do the questioning. Our conversation with her went in a direction I wasn't anticipating. I'm sorry. But the fact is we got two leads to follow up on."

"Which are what again?" Rooster asked.

"That the victim's mother told him to stay away from Dominick Martello, who went by Nico in those days," Gator said. "And that Izzy Weisman's lawyer, Bella Gurwitz, has been Cheryl Bertrand's fairy godmother all these years."

"Exactly," I said. "She didn't even volunteer that she knew Cheryl when we asked Weisman about her."

"Right, got it," Rooster said. "Both of those leads go to Gator's cold case, so he's in charge. We clear on that?"

Mac and I made eye contact, and he nodded ever so slightly.

"Yes, crystal," I said.

"Where are you with your arson investigation?" Rooster asked me.

"We're setting a trap for our leading suspect later this afternoon," I said. "With any luck, we'll have him in for questioning tonight."

"You helping Bo with that?" Rooster asked Gator.

"Yes, sir."

"Yeah, but Bo's in charge," Mac said. "We clear on that?"

* * *

It had been a while since I'd been involved in a sting operation, and I was nervous. This wasn't a sting exactly, because we weren't baiting Paulo Martins into committing a crime, just luring him into the open, so we could arrest him. It was a stretch, but with Mac's help, we had obtained a warrant, based on a probable cause argument Rodiger had cobbled together that leaned heavily on the discrepancy in the timeline Martins gave to Sallie. It would never stick, but it was enough to haul him in for a few hours of questioning.

Gator and I arrived at the Royal Frenchman hotel bar twenty minutes early. The courtyard where Sallie set the meeting was an attractive space, with a mix of lounge seating and well-spaced metal tables with red umbrellas. But for our purposes, it was less than ideal. There were two entrances and exits, a door from inside the hotel and an open gate leading to and from Royal Street. The two tables closest to Royal were both occupied, one by a group of four loud soccer moms and the other by a goateed artist in a beret and sunglasses who was sketching behind an easel. We grabbed the table closest to the hotel bar, near the fountain that flanked the seating area, and then I called Rodiger, who was shadowing Sallie on her walk from work in case Martins tried to intercept her in transit. I told him when he got to the hotel to station himself across from the Royal Street entrance, so that if Martins tried to escape that way, he'd be there to grab him. When a waitress stopped by, I ordered a sparkling water with lime, figuring it could pass for a gin and tonic. Gator got a Coke.

Sallie arrived at 5:25 and took a seat two tables away from us, on the Royal Street side. She made brief eye contact with me but otherwise played it cool. She ordered an Aperol spritz and made a show of flipping through texts on her phone. As we waited, a young couple claimed the table between us and Sallie. It's not the way we would have drawn it up, but there was nothing to be done by that point.

It was another ten minutes before Paulo Martins showed up. A tall, athletic-looking man in capri-style black pants, white sneakers, and a tight white polo strode past us and approached Sallie's table. As she smiled and rose to meet him, he must have caught her eyes darting toward us. He looked over his shoulder, saw us getting up, and took off running toward the Royal Street entrance.

What happened next was a blur. There was a crashing of metal and glass, and panicked high-pitched screaming, as the artist who'd been sketching launched into Martins, shoulder to rib cage, and drove him into the table with the four women. The entire table toppled over, along with two of the women. The heavyset artist landed on top of Martins, who was pinned beneath him, tangled up in the furniture and screaming in pain, his right arm jutting out at an unnatural angle. As Gator rushed in and pulled the artist off his victim, his beret had fallen off, and his goatee hung to one side of his chin. It took me a second, but then it hit me.

"Bru?"

Chapter Eighteen

"Behold, my knight in shining stupidity!"

That was how Sallie introduced me when we arrived home after my visit to the Touro emergency room and were greeted by Angie and Sophie Duplessis, Charlotte Duval, and Annie Russell, who had conspired to prepare a dinner for Sallie and me when they heard about my kerfuffle at the Royal Frenchman. Annie knew that I kept a spare key inside the lantern by the front door and had organized the effort.

I received heartfelt hugs and a healthy dose of tut-tutting from each of my dear friends, and a few loud yelps from Hugo, but it was young Sophie who touched me most deeply. She had insisted on coming, Angie said, and fretted about the extent of my wounds the whole way in from Kenner.

I assured everyone that I was fine, despite hobbling in on crutches and no doubt looking like a car wreck, but Sallie ran through my list of injuries anyway. They included a broken left thumb, bruised ribs, and a sprained ankle, the same one I had turned the day before. Then the ribbing began.

"Little Bo says they should make an action hero movie about you," Angie said.

"The Amazing Adventures of Antiques Man!" Annie proclaimed.

"Or Perils of a Bull in a China Shop," Charlotte chimed in. "Dearest Bruneau, whatever possessed you?"

"He was protecting Sallie," Sophie said solemnly.

"Aw, that's sweet of you, Soph," Sallie said, giving Sophie a gentle hug. "And you're right, of course. I do appreciate Bruneau's caring about me, but don't you think he could have been a little more civilized in the way he went about showing it?"

"Maybe," Sophie frowned, "but I think it's romantic. I hope someone will be willing to lay it on the line like that for me someday."

"Don't you worry, dear," Charlotte said. "There will be a long line of volunteers. Of that I am certain."

"Sallie's right, Sophie," I said. "My credo in life is that discretion is the better part of valor. I lost sight of that today."

"Falstaff says that in Henry IV, Part One, but you got it wrong, Uncle Bru. It's 'valor is the better part of discretion.'"

"Touché, grasshopper! I stand corrected."

"Oh dear," Angie sighed. "How about helping me serve the lasagna, young bookworm of mine?"

With that, the crew sprang into action. Angie and Sophie began doling out servings of lasagna, Annie tossed a salad she had prepared, and Charlotte poured a Chianti for everyone except Sophie and me. We were served ice water. Despite my protestations, I was denied alcohol on account of the oxycodone I'd been given for my pain.

"Bruneau, please tell us, what inspired your turn as the goateed artiste?" Annie asked playfully, drawing hoots from around the table.

"I wanted to be close by in case anything happened to Sallie, but I couldn't allow myself to be recognized," I said simply.

"Did you think to take a photo, Sallie?" Charlotte wanted to know. "If there's a picture of Bruneau Van Gogh, I insist on receiving a copy."

"Honestly, Charlotte, everything happened so quickly, I could hardly process it," Sallie said. "There was the sound of crashing metal and all this screaming, and the next thing I know, there's Bruneau, explaining himself to Bo and looking like he'd just survived a cyclone."

"Bo says if he knew Bruneau could tackle like that, he would have recruited him for the high school football team," Angie said. "He says you should have seen the other guy."

When Bo visited me in the E.R., he told me that Paulo Martins had a dislocated elbow and a chipped front tooth. He was probably interrogating him at that very moment, either at the station or in the hospital.

"You make it sound like we had some kind of knockdown, drag-out brawl," I said. "It was nothing like that. I tackled the guy, and we got tangled up in the table and chairs. There were no punches thrown. The furniture did all the damage, not me."

"What about the women sitting at the table you knocked over?" Sallie asked. "Are they okay?"

"Bo said one of them had a small scrape or a bruise, but nothing serious," Angie said. "They were scared, mostly. Bo smoothed things over with them, and he doubts they'll press charges."

"Charges?" I hadn't thought of that.

"Yeah, for assault," Angie said. "You're not out of the woods yet, you know. Martins could still file a complaint."

"Just let him try," Charlotte said, vowing to personally lobby our chief of police, with whom, to my knowledge, she had absolutely no relationship.

"I could plead mitigating circumstances—"

"Like temporary insanity due to romantic hero complex?" Angie smiled.

"Mom!" Sophie barked.

"Easy, dear," Charlotte said soothingly, "your mother is entitled to a little bit of fun at Bruneau's expense. We all are, don't you think?"

Sophie looked at me, and I smiled at her, nodding my approval.

"I guess so, as long as Uncle Bru is okay with it," she smiled back demurely.

Our dinner continued like that, expressions of sympathy and concern interspersed with jokes at my expense. I maintained a posture of mock crankiness through most of the meal, but really, I was basking in the warmth of my friends' affection. And when it came time for everyone to pack up and head home, I fought back tears as we exchanged hugs and goodbyes.

When everyone had gone, Sallie sat down beside me on the couch.

"You do have your share of female admirers; I'll give you that."

"As befits a gallant romantic hero."

"Ah, yes, my hero."

Sallie sighed and snuggled up against me.

* * *

After spending most of the next morning resting and icing my ankle, I was due to pick up Prosper for our tête-à-tête at Bacchanal. I left early so I could swing by City Park to meet Bo and get an update on his investigations. He'd asked me not to call, text, or email him about his work because he was worried the Homicide cops were keeping tabs on him, so I texted him asking if he was done with the drill bits I'd lent him. He replied by saying he was, and if I was going to be in the vicinity of City Park, he could return them to me there.

"Drill bits, really?" he teased when we met in front of the sculpture garden. "I'm surprised you even know what a drill bit is."

"I'm a man of hidden talents," I said.

"Uh-huh. How are your wounds? Everything healing okay?"

"I think so. I can get around without the crutches, at least."

"Good. I still can't believe you pulled that one over on us. What the hell, Bru? You could've gotten hurt a lot worse than you did, not to mention screwing up our investigation."

"But I didn't, did I?"

"I wouldn't be too sure about that. Your victim's lawyer is raising a stink and not without some justification."

"Is that right? In that case, maybe you'd better tell me what you've learned about my supposed victim, so I can defend myself."

Bo shook his head.

"I'm going to tell you some stuff, Bru, but since you're now an actor in this investigation, you've got to keep this to yourself, even more so now than before, okay?"

"Okay."

Bo told me that Paulo Martins was actually Eduardo Alves, a forty-one-year-old U.S. citizen of Brazilian descent. He had lived in the New Orleans area for the past twenty years and was employed as a procurement manager for a hazardous waste management company called EcoNico Waste Services. His lawyer advised him not to answer any questions and made noises about suing the city for entrapment, reckless endangerment, excessive use of force, and a litany of other outrages.

"We're going to have to drop the charges and let him go for now," Bo said, "but we did pick up a few useful pieces of information."

According to Bo, Mike Rodiger's research uncovered that Alves' grandfather was indeed a bossa nova musician and that Alves himself was enrolled for a time as a music major at the University of Miami, though he didn't graduate. More interesting was that EcoNico is owned by Blueberry Hill Holdings, which in turn is owned by none other than the Dandy Duca himself, Dominick Martello. And the attorney who represented Alves, Gino Randazzo, has acted on Martello's behalf in the past.

"The plot thickens!" I said.

"You could say that," Bo agreed. Then he told me about the meeting he and Angie had with Cheryl Bertrand, Arnold Jesse's half-sister, at the drug treatment center she runs. Their discussion yielded two interesting revelations. One was that Arnold's mother had warned him to steer clear of someone named Nico, which Bo reminded me was Dominick Martello's nickname back when he was an aspiring musician. The other was that Bella Gurwitz, Izzy Weisman's lawyer, had been Cheryl Bertrand's anonymous benefactor, dating from roughly the time Arnold disappeared.

"Bella Gurwitz?" I asked, surprised. "It seems there are coincidences on top of coincidences."

"In my line of work, there's no such thing, only connections and complications," Bo said.

* * *

Leaving Bo and heading to pick up Prosper at his sister's place in the Gentilly neighborhood, I gave Orville Whitlock a call. He picked up right away.

"Did you play the recording?" I asked him straightaway.

"I did, yes."

"What do you think?" I asked.

"You've piqued my curiosity, Bruneau, I'll say that much."

"Do you think it could be Bolden?"

"It seems unlikely, but if it's really from 1929, it's of interest no matter who the player is. Unfortunately, you're not going to get anywhere with a recording on your phone. If you can locate the cylinder, and can authenticate it, you might have something."

I thanked Orville for his words of encouragement. After hanging up, I again went through all the possibilities of what could have happened to the cylinder. Had it been destroyed? Lost, somehow? Or had it been taken? And if the latter, by whom and to what end?

As I arrived at Irene's, I snapped out of my reverie. Prosper was waiting outside when I pulled up, and as he squeezed his massive frame into Liesel's tight passenger seat, he took note of the splint on my thumb and the crutches I'd thrown into the back seat in case I needed them. He'd heard about my dust-up from Sallie, who had called him to invite him to dinner the following evening.

"So, you've been mixing it up again, Bruneau," he said, alluding, I took it, to the unfortunate run-in Hugo and I had with his wildcat Caliban, which occasioned our first meeting.

"Yes, well, it turns out Brazilians go down easier than feral felines."

Prosper smiled and pointed at my wrapped ankle with the cane he'd started using recently. He pulled up his pant leg to show the prosthetic he's worn since getting blown up by a rocket grenade in Vietnam.

"We could race."

"No thanks. I might lose, and I could never live that down."

We exchanged small talk as we made our way down Franklin Avenue to St. Claude and eventually to the nondescript corner of Bywater where one of the city's most unlikely hot spots has thrived for almost a quarter century now. Part wine shop, part live music venue, and part outdoor restaurant, Bacchanal is an unlikely success story if ever there was one. Despite its out-of-the-way location, the place draws a steady stream of locals every day of the week.

After browsing our options, we built a small cheese plate, to which we added mixed olives, some prosciutto, a couple small salamis, and a baguette. I picked a refreshing Bandol rosé to wash it all down with and paid the bill; then we made our way outside to where a jazz trio was playing. We found a table in the far corner of the courtyard where we could talk freely.

"Okay, Prosper," I said, "we've put this off long enough."

Prosper sat up straight, a pained expression on his face. Then he spoke with a pronounced sadness, but a seriousness of purpose.

"I owe you an apology, Bruneau. The information I'm about to share is long overdue. Shamefully overdue, in fact. I fear you will think a great deal less of me after I'm done with what I have to tell you."

I shrugged, as if to say I thought that was unlikely.

"You have asked about Lyla Saint Clair more than once. The plain fact I have withheld from you is that Lyla and I were lovers. More than lovers, really. We were passionately in love."

"I had an inkling that might be the case."

"Yes, well, we weren't together long. Just six months. But our relationship was intense; unlike anything I've experienced before or since."

"How'd you meet?"

"At Club Tijuana. I was doing my internship at the old Charity Hospital E.R., and I'd go there sometimes after my shifts, to blow off some steam. This one night, Earl King was playing, and Lyla was the opening act. She was incredible. I mean, I was spellbound. I stood near the stage and was taller than everyone else, so maybe it was inevitable that we made eye contact. More than once, she smiled at me and gave me a come-hither look, and I smiled back. Afterwards, Lyla approached me at the bar and asked me if I'd like to buy a girl a drink. The way she said it; it was the sexiest thing I'd ever heard. She said she'd been watching me from the stage and thought I must have an interesting story to tell. Which I didn't, by the way; not then anyway.

"Suffice it to say, there was an instant attraction. We were all over each other in those early days, and it wasn't just the sex. Lyla had a wonderful sense of humor, and we'd laugh and laugh, about almost anything. And we bared our souls to each other. Lyla told me about her rough childhood in Milwaukee, running away from home, living on the streets of Chicago. That's where she got her first taste of heroin."

"How did she end up in New Orleans?" I asked.

"She hopped a train with a couple other street musicians. Winter was coming on, and their only plan was to go someplace warmer."

"Riding on the City of New Orleans?"

"Yeah, exactly, just like Arlo. Anyway, those first few months, life was great. Lyla's career wasn't taking off exactly, but she had a growing following, and her drug use was mostly limited to grass, the occasional sleeping pill, and a bit too much alcohol. I was working hard but enjoying what I did and loving coming home to Lyla every night. If she didn't have a gig, Lyla would have dinner ready when I got home. She was a terrible cook, but I didn't care. And when she did have a show, sometimes I'd go straight home and make a late supper for her. Other times I'd catch her act, and we'd grab a bite somewhere afterward."

"From the sound of it, things went south at some point?"

"Yes. Not south exactly, not at first, but there were strains. We both felt that Lyla's career should have been further along. I blamed Izzy, who I didn't know very well, but who I thought wasn't trying hard enough to get her bigger bookings. But Lyla was devoted to Izzy and would get defensive when I criticized him. Then one night, I ran into an ex-girlfriend at the Dew Drop. That ex-girlfriend was Bella Gurwitz, who is now Izzy's lawyer, apparently."

"Whoa! You dated Bella Gurwitz?"

"Yeah, for a couple years. We got along well enough, but she was more into me than I was her, and eventually I broke it off. She didn't take it well. And that night, she was drunk and kind of came on to me, and Lyla saw it and became enraged. There was a big scene, and all three of us ended up getting kicked out of the place."

"Have you seen or been in touch with Bella since?" I asked.

"Not since the morning I left for Fort Benning. She showed up at the bus station and made a big deal about how she knew she'd made some mistakes but that I was the love of her life, and she'd be waiting when I got back."

"How did you respond?"

"I just said I hoped we could stay friends, but that I didn't see romance in our future. She said time might change my perspective, and then she tried to kiss me. I gently held her off, said I was sorry, and went to find my bus."

"And when you returned, you didn't come across her?"

"No. Not then and not now. Until Izzy mentioned that she was representing him, I didn't even know she was still around."

"Interesting. Sorry for interrupting you. Please, back to your story."

"Right. The real trouble started when I got my draft notice. We both knew it was coming, but when it did, it knocked Lyla off the rails. She became almost pathologically clingy and increasingly unstable. She would say things one minute, like she didn't think she could live without me, and then the next minute she'd accuse me of not caring about her and run out of my apartment in tears, slamming the door behind her. When I'd find her later, she'd be at some bar, strung out and drunk."

"Heroin?"

"Yes, when she could get it. Or pills. Amphetamines to get her up before a show; booze, and Valium to bring her down afterward. She was a walking mood swing, and there were ugly public incidents that made it harder for Izzy to find work for her. And of course, Lyla's solution to that problem was just more drugs. I tried to help her, but looking back, I don't think I knew how. I was young and stupid, too. Anyway, it got to where we were fighting all the time, and by the end, I was just exhausted and ready to be done with the whole thing. I actually looked forward to going to war, as awful as that sounds."

"I'm sorry, Prosper, that must have been a terrible time for you," I said. "But why are you telling me this now?"

Prosper looked down, smiled ruefully, and took a sip of his wine. I got the feeling he was trying to figure out how to phrase what came next.

"And so, we arrive at the meat of our story." He paused and looked directly at me.

"Early on, Lyla and I had talked about remaining committed to each other while I served out my tour and making a life together when I returned. I thought maybe I'd go into family practice in a bucolic small town somewhere, and we'd have our white picket fence, and our golden retriever, and raise our perfect children. It was all so delusional. I wasn't any more cut out for family practice or parenthood than Lyla was for small-town life. But we were young, and we could dream."

"I think you sell yourself short," I said.

Prosper smiled politely, but sadly.

"I was due at Fort Benning on the first of July, and as June wound down, I just wanted out, not because I didn't still love Lyla, but because watching her decline was taking more toll on me than I thought I could bear. Two days before I was to leave, I told her we were through. I tried to let her down easy by sugar coating it with a chivalrous narrative about how it wouldn't be fair to her for me to expect her to wait for me, but she saw right through my bullshit and exploded, saying she never wanted to see me again and that she hoped I'd die in Vietnam."

"People say stuff when they're upset. I'm sure she didn't mean it."

"No, perhaps not, but her words stung all the same. When I left her, I knew she might hurt herself, with drugs or some other way. I should have called Izzy. But I didn't, to my everlasting shame."

"Did Lyla have anyone besides Izzy she could lean on?"

"No, not really. She had her musician friends, some of whom she liked and got along with, but nobody she was truly close to. At least I don't think so. I didn't know any of them well. They were just people I'd meet when Lyla performed."

"Do you remember a Nico?" I asked.

"That sounds familiar, but I can't say for sure. Why?"

"Never mind. Just a thought I had. Please, go on."

"Like I said, I should have asked someone to keep an eye on Lyla, but I didn't. The next morning, the day before I was supposed to leave for basic training, I get a panicked call from Izzy telling me he's got a situation with Lyla, and he needs my help. I tell him Lyla and I are through, but he says it's a matter of life and death. So, I go to his house, and Lyla is lying unconscious on his bed in respiratory depression, and close to death. Izzy said she'd shown up a couple hours earlier, more strung out than he'd ever seen her. Thankfully, I had some Naloxone I'd swiped from the hospital in the event something like this might happen and was able to revive her."

"Thank goodness Izzy called you," I said.

"Yes, well, what happened next may change your mind about that. I'd gotten Lyla back to resting comfortably. She had some tremors and vomited a couple times, but she was on the road to recovery. But Izzy had been acting strangely. Now he lets me know we have another problem. I could tell from his face that it was a bad one. He leads me into his kitchen, and there on the floor lies the lifeless body of a boy, who Izzy tells me is a neighborhood kid named Arnold, who I vaguely recognized from the Dew Drop. Izzy is hysterical. He says he doesn't know what happened, that he'd gone out to get some groceries, and when he got back, Lyla was unconscious and Arnold was lying dead in his kitchen. That's when he called me."

"How did he die? Were you able to tell?" I didn't like where this was going. I didn't like it one bit.

"No, not definitively, but there were no signs of violence, and thirteen-year-old boys don't often just drop dead, so we both assumed that somehow he had ingested some of Lyla's drugs."

"Were there drugs lying around?"

"No, and that seemed weird. There were no traces of heroin or empty pill vials anywhere, which led us to believe that whatever she took, she took it before she got to Izzy's place."

"Then how did Arnold get drugs into his system?" I asked.

"I don't know," Prosper said. "The only thing we found that was remotely suspicious was an empty Coke bottle with a straw in it on the kitchen counter."

"Suspicious because it might have been spiked?"

"I mean, maybe. I didn't see any evidence of that."

"What was Arnold doing in Izzy's house to begin with?"

"Izzy said it wasn't unusual for him to stop by and raid the refrigerator, maybe hang out for a while."

"Okay, so you've got a dead boy on your hands. Now what?"

Prosper had gotten this far; I figured I owed it to him to let him finish.

"I said we needed to call an ambulance, but Izzy freaked out. He said that would get the police involved and given Lyla's condition and the drugs in her system, they were bound to blame her. I suggested we move Lyla out of the house, but Izzy thought there was too much evidence of her presence for that to work, plus he didn't want them arresting him either."

"So, you decided to just stick the kid in the wall? What the hell were you thinking?" I glared at Prosper, and he dropped his eyes in shame. Then he looked up again.

"I really don't know. I've asked myself that question many times since. But initially, at least, I wasn't on board. Izzy suggested dumping the body somewhere, like in the river or the lake, or worse yet, a dumpster. I was like, 'are you crazy, this kid must have a family, and people who care about him.' Izzy said there was just his mother, and she wasn't much of a mother at that. He said he felt terrible about it, but he'd been thinking about the options ever since he found the body, and none of them were good, but getting rid of the body was the least bad choice. I told Izzy I refused to be a part of whatever he was going to do. That I was heading off to war and leaving all this behind me. But then he played the Lyla card."

"Meaning he'd have no choice but to let the police pin the blame on Lyla?"

"Yes, and that Lyla wasn't strong enough to weather something like that. He told me I was consigning her to a death sentence. I told him I didn't care and that that was her problem, and then I stormed out of the house. When I got outside, I leaned against my bike and pretty much melted. I was crying and hyperventilating. I walked around in circles for a while. At one point, I looked up and saw Izzy standing on his stoop, watching me. It was like he was waiting for me to work through the agony I was feeling, like maybe he had earlier. I saw in his eyes the same pain and sadness and worry I felt, but not the confusion. He had arrived at something like clarity."

Prosper stopped to collect himself and take a drink of wine.

"Eventually, I went back inside. I told Izzy I'd help him, for Lyla's sake, but that I was leaving town the next morning and whatever consequences followed were for him to bear. He said he understood. Then we discussed options for getting rid of the body, so matter-of-factly that it makes me sick to think about it now. It was my idea to wrap it in a tarp, with some lye to combat the odor of decomposition, and stash it behind the wall. I'd worked on a construction crew during the summers when I was in high school, and I knew how to break through plaster and patch it back up again. I sent Izzy to the hardware store with a list of supplies I needed. When he got back, the whole thing didn't take me more than a few hours. Izzy said he would repaint the entire room the next day, once my patchwork had dried."

I didn't know what to say.

"Bruneau, I understand the ramifications of what I did, and I want you to know that I am fully prepared to face the consequences, legal and otherwise, however belatedly," Prosper said. "I am ashamed of myself beyond measure, not just for what I did back then, but even more so for sitting on this all these years. There are simply no excuses."

"Consequences are a topic for another day," I said, "but you do realize you're going to need to tell Bo what you've told me, right?"

"Yes, I understand. I'm prepared to tell him everything."

Prosper looked down, silent.

"Prosper," I asked, "was Lyla aware of what you and Izzy were up to? Breaking through a wall and placing Arnold's body inside? There had to be a lot of noise and dust."

My large friend looked up slowly, as though trying to retrieve a memory.

"No, I don't think so, not until near the end anyway. She was kind of out of it and resting most of the time. At one point, when I was almost done patching the wall, she called from the bedroom asking what we were doing out there. Izzy went in and told her I was helping him with a small carpentry job."

"When did you find out Lyla had died?"

"I was still at Fort Benning. I received a letter from Izzy, just a few days before we shipped out, telling me Lyla had overdosed. I wish I could say I was devastated by the news. That would make me seem more human, to myself at least. But honestly, it all felt so inevitable, and I was so wracked with guilt, I just compartmentalized it. The grief came later, during long nights in the jungle. But at Fort Benning, I was just focused on preparing to be the best field medic I could be. I think I thought, in some confused moral calculus, that if I could save some lives, it would somehow balance out the awful thing I had done."

"Before leaving Izzy's house or heading off to Fort Benning, did you speak with Lyla?"

Prosper smiled wistfully.

"Yes. I remember our conversation almost word for word. I sat by her bedside, rubbing her thigh and telling her she was going to be okay, but the next time I wouldn't be around to help. She said not to worry, that there wouldn't be a next time. She said it so convincingly that I almost believed her. I told Lyla I would miss her, and she said she'd miss me too and that she was sorry for saying she hoped I would die. And that was it."

At last, Prosper had unburdened himself of his story. I was at turns horrified, disgusted, and strangely sympathetic.

"I need to think about this, Prosper."

He nodded.

I got up and walked out, leaving him alone at the table.

Chapter Nineteen

Once I was over the shock of Prosper's confessing to his role in hiding Arnold Jesse's dead body, the revulsion I felt began to fade. Rather than abandon him at Bacchanal, I waited inside Liesel until he stepped out onto the street ten minutes later. I swung around and picked him up, and we rode wordlessly back to his sister's place.

"I'll get over this," I said finally, as he was getting out of the car. "I just need some time."

"I understand," he said solemnly.

He closed the door, turned, and limped away slowly, slouching under the heavy weight of recrimination and regret.

The next day, I tried to reflect on what I had learned. On a personal level, I could understand the actions Prosper took, repugnant though they were, based on the circumstances in which he found himself. He was a young man heading off to war who, in the face of a dilemma, chose to protect the woman he loved, who, in theory, still had a full life in front of her, rather than doing right by a boy whose time on this earth had already ended. I now had a fuller portrait of the man, but contrary to Prosper's prediction, I did not find myself thinking less of him because of something he did sixty years ago. Like the rest of us, he is a flawed human being who has never pretended otherwise.

Despite my personal sentiments, I recognized that Prosper and Izzy must now step forward and give an accounting of themselves, not only to NOPD's cold case investigation, but to the sister the men didn't know Arnold had. The question was how best to accomplish this. Sallie thought I should call Bo and dump it all in his lap, which would have been the simplest solution, but I worried that would result in Prosper having to stare down the homicide cops in a lengthy interrogation. Worse, they'd probably isolate Izzy in another room so they could pick apart discrepancies in the two men's stories and play them off against each other.

Since Prosper was coming for dinner anyway, I suggested we add Bo and Angie to the guest list and let Prosper recount his tale in a less threatening environment. Sallie thought the disposal of a human corpse was an inapt subject for dinner table conversation, and she had a point. She also made a convincing case that the person who really needed to hear what Prosper had to say was Cheryl Bertrand.

Finally, I called Prosper to see how he wanted to approach his official confession, only to learn that he'd taken the matter out of my hands.

"I called Bo and gave him the headline," he told me. "He's picking me up in a few minutes. I spoke to Izzy, and he's coming in, too."

"I'm glad you took the initiative," I said. "Do you have a lawyer? If not, I strongly suggest you retain one."

"I was hoping you could represent me during the interview."

"Me?"

"Yes, if you'd be willing. You know me better than anyone, and I trust your judgment."

"Thank you for that, but I don't know the first thing about criminal law. This could get complicated, Prosper. There may be statutes of limitations involved, depending on what charges they decide to bring against you. And the homicide detectives are going to push you on what they believe was Arnold Jesse's murder, not just on your cleaning up the scene and disposing of the body after the fact."

"I'm not really worried about that," Prosper said. "I'm just going to tell the truth as I know it and let the chips fall where they may. If they decide this old man should go to prison for his crimes, I won't have a problem with that."

"Don't be ridiculous, Prosper. It's one thing to come clean about all this. Engaging in deliberately self-destructive behavior is another matter entirely."

"Then it would be useful to have you alongside me to help sort out the difference."

"What if I say no?"

"Then I go in solo, and that's okay. I understand if you're not comfortable."

"You need someone to protect you from yourself."

Prosper chuckled ironically.

"That's been evident for a good many years now, Bruneau. Maybe if somebody had told me that when I was younger—"

"Okay, okay, enough! Fine, I'll do it."

I flung my head back and sighed loudly.

"Don't let them start the questioning until I get there, understand? And Prosper, if this thing starts to go sideways, promise me you'll let me stop the proceedings until we can get an attorney on board."

"Whatever you say."

When I hung up, my thoughts were scattered. I called Sallie, told her what was going on, and explained that I didn't know when I'd be back home. She was still reeling from what I'd told her about Prosper the previous evening and didn't take this latest piece of news well.

"Is he crazy? He needs a lawyer, not a friend."

"I tried to tell him that. He said it was me or nobody."

"I really don't think you should get involved in this, Bruneau. It's not just Prosper. Think about your relationship with Bo. You'll be adversaries."

"Bo and I have been through plenty of awkward situations in our lives. We'll be fine. Plus, I imagine it'll be the homicide guy in charge. Look, I agree with you, Sallie. Prosper should have an attorney, no question. But he's refusing to go down that path, so I'm all he's got."

There was a long silence on the other end of the phone.

"What about dinner?" Sallie asked tersely.

"What about it?"

"Should we call it off? Given what's transpired?"

"Let's play it by ear. Forget the pasta and the salad we were going to make; we can have those tomorrow night. If Prosper isn't going straight to jail, and he feels up to it, maybe we can order a pizza or something."

"Fine, whatever. Just let me know."

* * *

When I arrived at the station, Bo and Mike Rodiger were standing outside the interview room conferring with a colleague they introduced as Joe "Gator" Guidry, a homicide detective. I could see Prosper through the one-way glass, leaning back in his chair, his arms crossed, a bottle of water in front of him.

"You sure you want to do this, Bru?" Bo asked. "Don't you think he'd be better off with an attorney?"

"That's what I told him," I said. "This is the way he wants to roll."

"Did he tell you that he requested that Cheryl Bertrand be present when he tells us his story?"

"No, but it doesn't surprise me. Will you allow it?"

Joe Guidry cleared his throat and stepped forward.

"It's against my better judgment, but yes, we've agreed that she can sit behind the glass. He also wanted Izzy Weisman to join us, but we said no to that. He's down the hall in another room, with his lawyer."

"Bella Gurwitz?"

"Yes."

As we spoke, an attractive, professionally attired Black woman entered the room and waved uncertainly at Bo.

"Hello, Cheryl," Bo said. "Thank you for coming in. These are my colleagues Joe Guidry and Mike Rodiger, and my friend Bruneau Abellard, who is going to sit in with us on behalf of Mr. Coulon."

"Hello, gentlemen," Cheryl Bertrand said. "I understand that Mr. Coulon requested my presence?"

"That's right," Bo said. "Prosper, or Andre I should say, is going to tell us what he knows about your brother's death and disappearance. As you listen to what he has to say, please understand that until a few days ago, he didn't know that Arnold had a sister."

"Okay, sure," she said hesitatingly. "I guess I get that."

"A couple other things you should know before we get started," Bo said. "Detective Guidry is with Homicide, and Arnold's death is his case, so he'll be leading the interview. Also, I need you to know that Andre Coulon is a social acquaintance of mine, and Bruneau a close friend since childhood. We know Andre as Prosper Fortune, a name he started going by later in life, so if we slip up and call him Prosper, you'll know what that's about."

"That seems a little unorthodox, doesn't it, Bo? You being friends with Mr. Coulon?"

"Yes, it is, which is another reason Detective Guidry is in charge, and I won't be saying much. Detective Rodiger and I are investigating a possible arson and burglary at the house where Arnold's body was found, so Mr. Coulon's testimony is potentially relevant to our case."

"Okay, I understand. That makes sense."

Just then, Angie Duplessis poked her head in the door, harried and out of breath.

"Why, Angie! What are you doing here, girl?" Cheryl asked.

"Hey, Cheryl," Angie gasped. "Sorry I'm late, everybody. Bo only called me half an hour ago. I got here as fast as I could."

"Cheryl, some of what Mr. Coulon has to say may be upsetting to you," Bo explained. "I asked Angie to come by, thinking maybe you'd like her to sit with you."

"Why, thank you, that is very thoughtful of you, Bo. I'd love for Angie to keep me company."

Angie stepped toward Cheryl and gave her a comforting hug, and Cheryl returned the gesture. Then Angie took Cheryl's hand in hers, patted it tenderly, and guided her to the two seats that had been set up for them. Mike brought the women some water, and we filed into the interview room.

When Guidry informed Prosper that Cheryl and Angie were behind the glass, he nodded approvingly and waved sheepishly in the general direction of the window. The account he gave varied little from what he'd told me the day before. He was remorseful, unsparing in his self-criticism, and from time to time, he would look up apologetically toward the window

Cheryl Bertrand sat behind. The cops let him talk with few interruptions, maintaining their professional poker faces throughout, although I did notice Bo sighing softly.

There was one digressive exchange, when Prosper mentioned Bella Gurwitz.

"Wait, I just want to be clear about something," Guidry interjected. "You're saying you dated Bella Gurwitz prior to becoming involved with Lyla Saint-Clair?"

"Yes. Bella was in law school at Loyola when I was in med school at LSU, here in New Orleans. We met then and were together for a couple years."

"When did you break up?"

"Not long after she graduated law school and passed the bar. I was beginning my internship, and she was trying to start an entertainment law practice. From my perspective, at least, it wasn't working out."

"She felt differently?"

"Yes."

"How much time passed between your breaking up with Bella and becoming involved with Lyla Saint-Clair?"

"I don't know, a year, give or take?"

"Did you see Bella much during that time?"

"No. I tried to avoid her, to be honest. There was a stretch of a few weeks where she'd show up in the same places I'd frequent, almost like she was stalking me, but that stopped after a while."

"And what about after you and Lyla became a couple? Other than the one run-in at the Dew Drop, did you see her after that?"

"I remember a couple days after that incident she was waiting outside the hospital when I got off my shift. She said she wanted to apologize for making a scene, but before long, she was going on about how Lyla was bad news and what did I think I was doing with her? I just shut her down and walked away, and I think that was the last time I saw her before the day I shipped off to Fort Benning, which I told you about."

"What about Bella and Lyla? Did they have a relationship with each other outside of your triangle?"

"I wouldn't call it a triangle, Detective. I was devoted to Lyla. There was nothing going on with Bella."

"Right, but you understand my question."

"Yes, I think so. I was only vaguely aware at the time that Bella was becoming part of the music scene that Lyla was involved in, and to be honest, it never occurred to me that they would know each other outside of their relationships with me. But in talking to Izzy these past few days, I guess they did come across each other. According to him, there was no love lost."

"Okay, thank you for clarifying that," Guidry said, casting a sidelong glance at Bo. "Please continue with your story."

Prosper did as instructed, and when he was finished, Guidry spoke again.

"That was a thorough accounting of your actions post-mortem, Mr. Coulon. I appreciate the level of detail you provided. Now I'd like to talk about what happened during the hours leading up to Arnold Jesse's death."

"There's not much I can tell you on that front," Prosper said. "I only know what Izzy told me."

"Humor me, please. You said you recognized the deceased from the Dew Drop Inn. What was your relationship with him?"

"There was no relationship. I don't think I ever spoke to Arnold or even knew his name. He was just a kid who hung around the place. I do remember that he was a tap dancer, and a good one. And he smiled a lot. That's about it."

"What about Lyla Saint-Clair? Did she have a relationship with Arnold?"

"I really don't know. I guess she probably knew him, at least casually, because she spent a lot more time around the Dew Drop than I did, but I have no memory of her talking about him."

"What about Izzy Weisman?"

"Izzy definitely knew Arnold, as I imagine he's told you. He paid him to do odd jobs, and he said that Arnold would sometimes hang out at his house."

"Did you?"

"Did I what?

"Hang out at Weisman's house?"

"No. I'd only been there once before, with Lyla. She and Izzy were going over some business stuff together, and I was a third wheel. If I remember correctly, Lyla and I were going out somewhere after she and Izzy were done."

"Did you believe Weisman when he said he'd left the house to buy groceries before returning to find Lyla unconscious and Arnold dead?"

"I didn't have any reason not to. He didn't act or sound like a guilty man if that's what you're getting at."

"You'd been through medical school and worked in an emergency room, Mr. Coulon. I imagine you'd seen your share of corpses. Did you have any theories as to how Arnold had died?"

"No, not beyond what I've told you. Like I said, there were no external signs of trauma, and no odors or discoloration or vomit that might have suggested poisoning. Given Lyla's condition, Izzy and I landed on the assumption that he must have consumed some of whatever she took."

"Which was a cocktail of heroin and pills of some kind?"

"Yes, most likely a depressant. High doses of that combination are known to lead to respiratory depression, which is the condition Lyla was in. Alcohol could have been a factor as well."

"But there were no signs of drug use in the house? No syringes, pills, empty vials, traces of white powder? Nothing like that?"

"Nope. And we did look for those things."

"Did you look in the garbage?"

"Yes. We didn't pour out all the contents and sift through it all, but we did poke around. Didn't see anything unusual."

"Heroin in those days was always injected, wasn't it?"

"Yes, so far as I know."

"Did Arnold have needle marks?"

"Not that I noticed."

"Then, if he was drugged, how did these drugs get into his system?"

"I don't know."

There was a pause as Guidry considered the impasse at which he had arrived. Then Mike Rodiger spoke up.

"Tell us more about the Coke bottle you mentioned, Mr. Coulon?"

"All I know is what I told you. There was an empty bottle of Coca-Cola on the counter near where Arnold had collapsed, and it had a straw in it."

"Did you inspect the bottle? For drugs or poison?"

"Not thoroughly, but yes, sort of. It didn't smell unusual, and I didn't see any residue of a foreign substance, but I didn't look all that closely. If you'll remember, the bottles were green in those days, and not very transparent."

There was another pause as Guidry looked at Mike and Bo to see if they had anything else they wanted to ask. Neither seemed to.

"I think we are done for today, Mr. Coulon," Guidry said. "You are free to go, for now. I am sure you understand that the actions you have confessed to have serious ramifications; accessory after the fact to murder being just one possible charge. I'll be conferring with the district attorney's office regarding how best to proceed, but in the meantime, we need you to stay close to home. Normally, we would take you before a magistrate for a bail hearing, but Detective Duplessis has vouched for your character and agreed to assume responsibility for your whereabouts. Considering your age and the initiative you took in contacting us, I am comfortable with this arrangement for the time being."

"Thank you, Bo, and you too, Detective Guidry," Prosper said, "that is more consideration than I deserve. And yes, Detective Guidry, I fully understand that I will doubtless be charged with a crime or crimes, and I am prepared to face the consequences."

As we gathered our belongings and began filing out of the room, the mood was nearly funereal. For Bo and Mike and me, and maybe Joe Guidry too, there was the unsettling knowledge that a good man had done a terrible thing. And for Prosper, there was the dreadful premonition of the worst being yet to come, as around the corner waited the ghost of Arnold Jesse incarnate, revivified in the form of his still grieving sister, Cheryl Bertrand.

I made sure that I walked out ahead of Prosper, thinking that if Cheryl tried to accost him, I could help diffuse the situation by stepping between them. But as we left the toaster and turned into the room where Cheryl and

Angie had been seated, there was only Angie, standing by the door to the hallway with an anguished expression on her face.

"She left a few minutes ago," she said. "I'm sorry, Prosper, I know you wanted to apologize to Cheryl directly. She just wasn't up to it, I'm afraid."

"I understand, Angie, thank you," Prosper said sorrowfully. "I wouldn't have wanted to talk to me either."

* * *

As we stood outside the police station after saying goodbye to Angie, Prosper accepted my offer of a ride, but declined to join Sallie and me for pizza. He was quiet in the car, lost in his thoughts.

"Does it feel like at least somewhat of a relief to have gotten it all out?" I asked him.

He shrugged.

"I don't know, maybe. No, not really."

Then he paused, but in a way that made it clear he had something else he wanted to say.

"You know, it's only coming back to me now, after that line of questioning about Bella, but there's a detail I left out of my story. It might be nothing, but I should probably mention it to the police."

"Really? What's that?" I asked cautiously, not sure I wanted to hear the answer.

"When I arrived at Izzy's house that night, there was a car. It was a couple blocks away, turning onto Esplanade. I only saw it for a second or two in my peripheral vision, but I thought I recognized it."

"How so?"

"It was a beat-up green VW bug. I think it may have belonged to Bella."

"Jesus, Prosper. The cops are in with her and Izzy as we speak. They might be interviewing the wrong person, for all we know. You should try texting Bo right now."

"Okay, sure, I will."

* * *

After dropping Prosper off, I called ahead and swung by Katie's Mid-City to pick up a large Iberville, Sallie's favorite pizza, a vegetarian offering of garlic butter sauce, grilled eggplant, spinach, red onion, and feta. As a sucker for pulled pork, I personally prefer the Boudreaux, piled high with garlicky cochon de lait, but that's a mere quibble. Sallie and I are in agreement that even among an increasingly diverse and crowded field of excellent pie shops in town, most with Italian-sounding names, Katie's has no equal.

As we sat down to eat and I briefed her on the day's events, Sallie was unusually quiet. When I asked her what was wrong, she said she just felt sad for everyone involved, Arnold Jesse and Cheryl Bertrand most of all, but also their mother, Lyla Saint-Clair, Prosper, Izzy, and even Bella Gurwitz, though we didn't yet know her full story. She only ate one slice of the pizza; then she retired early after helping me clean up.

I poured myself an Armagnac and sat down on the couch with my phone, exhausted but not yet sleepy. Hugo jumped up and snuggled beside me. Then, to my surprise, L'il Queenie appeared over my shoulder and crawled down my chest to my lap, where she curled into a ball. Hugo appeared unconcerned that his mortal foe had come to rest mere inches from his jaws. I could only wonder at the strange détente these two creatures had somehow arrived at.

Shaking my head, I called Bo.

"Hey, buddy," he answered.

"Hey."

"Some kind of day, huh?"

"Yeah, I'll say. How'd it go with Izzy and Bella? I'm assuming we can talk freely on the phone now?"

"Yeah, we're good," Bo said. "Izzy's story matched Prosper's almost exactly. Gator made some noises about them having had the opportunity to compare notes beforehand, but I think he believes them."

"What about Bella?"

"Prosper's text came in just in time. Gator had already started leaning into her pretty hard about all the Prosper stuff and her strained relationship with Lyla Saint-Clair. The car was just another piece of anecdotal evidence working against her. She deflected and denied, knowing that we can't prove anything, but she's definitely hiding something."

"Like what?"

"I'm not sure, but Angie told me that Cheryl got emotional when Prosper was talking about his relationship with Bella and her not being able to let go."

"Are you going to follow up with her?"

"Gator is."

"It feels like you're getting close on the cold case," I said. "What about the arson and the possible burglary? Any progress?"

"We had to let Eduardo Alves go for now, Bru, sorry. I told him to steer clear of Sallie, but I've taken the added step of having a uniform keep an eye on her workplace for the next few days."

"You think he's dangerous?"

"I doubt it, especially not with his elbow in a cast, but better safe than sorry."

"Indeed. Thank you for that. I'll let Sallie know you're keeping an eye out."

"Don't scare her but tell her I said it's probably best if she avoids walking alone in places where there aren't other people around."

"She wouldn't do that anyway, I don't think. But you believe Alves might try to get even with Sallie for setting him up?"

"Not if he's smart, but you never know. I just think she should be extra careful."

Now that Bo had planted the thought that Alves might seek retribution, it was just the kind of thing I was likely to obsess about, no doubt annoying the hell out of Sallie in the process. For now, I buried the thought and changed the subject.

"You know, there are two things I don't understand."

"What's that?"

"If Alves visited Izzy a few weeks before the fire, but I didn't give the cylinder to Izzy until a couple days before the fire, and Izzy and Alves didn't have any more contact, how did Alves know about the cylinder when he mentioned it to Sallie?"

"I think Izzy said he'd called him, thinking he was Paul Martin the academic, and told him about it. I'll have to check my notes on that. What else don't you understand?"

"Why was he poking around Sallie's archives?"

"We don't know the answer to that one either, but I have a feeling I know someone who might be able to help us on both fronts."

"Who's that?"

"The Dandy Duca."

1967

New Orleans, Louisiana
June 30, 1967

Rolling out of bed in the cramped room he shares with his still sleeping younger sister, Arnold Jesse steps barefoot into the narrow hall and strains to listen over the hum of a whirring fan. He is startled by two loud snorts in the bedroom across the way but reassured by the low rhythmic rumbling that follows. Satisfied that his mother is asleep, he pads on into the small kitchen, where a mountain of greasy dishes spills out from the sink and insects carry away the detritus from discarded food wrappers. He opens the refrigerator and reaches behind a container of weeks-old milk to a small bundle he has concealed in the back corner of the bottom shelf. Removing it, he unfolds the dish towel in which the packet is wrapped, and smiles at its contents, a perfect yellow banana, a box of Frosted Flakes, a bologna sandwich on white bread he made at Izzy Weisman's house, and a small Tootsie Roll. He finds Cheryl's battered Flintstones lunchbox in its usual spot on the small table by the door and fills it with his bounty. Then he returns to his room, rouses Cheryl, and prepares for the day ahead.

Half an hour later, Arnold and Cheryl walk side by side on their way to the Lafon School, just a few blocks away.

"I can hear at least three things moving around in there, Arnold," Cheryl says with eager eyes, shaking her beat-up tin container. "Can I peek?"

"You know the rules. Not until you're in school."

"You're no fun."

Arnold smiles and rubs the top of his younger sister's head. When they reach *the school, he watches Cheryl run up the ramp that leads to the front entrance, stop at the top, open her lunchbox, and peer inside. She flashes a broad, toothy grin and waves excitedly. Arnold waves back, smiling, and heads off in search of his own sustenance.*

Arriving at his usual post outside the Dew Drop Inn just a few minutes later, Arnold is surprised to find his friend, the drummer Mose Adler, sitting slumped on the bench in front of the building. Like most musicians, Mose rarely shows his face during the morning hours. As Arnold approaches the large man with the bird's nest of curly hair and flowing red beard, he can see that he is half asleep.

"What are you doing up so early, Mr. Mose?" he asks.

"Whoa, Arno!" Mose shouts, snapping awake. "You scared me, man."

"Sorry."

Mose slaps his face twice and shakes his head from side to side. Then, settling down, he regards Arnold with a conspiratorial look.

"Just so you know, Ace, I got me some business to take care of this morning, That's why I'm up early."

"What kind of business?"

"The kind of business that ain't none of your business, you dig?"

"Yeah, I guess so. You got some work for me today, Mr. Mose?"

"Not today my man, but maybe tomorrow, okay? I'm s'posed to meet Isabella. You seen that slug bug of hers?"

"That's it right there, isn't it?" Arnold asks, pointing up the road toward Sixth Street as an aging green VW Beetle comes into view.

"Right on! Good set of peepers you got there, Arno!"

The rickety car, scratched and dented from end to end, coughs to a stop in front of Arnold and Mose, its exhaust fumes fouling the hot, humid air. The driver leans across the passenger seat to open the door for Mose to get in. She is a large, heavy-boned young woman, cloaked in a floral-patterned cotton maxi dress, a matching headband that harnesses her long brown hair, and an assortment of beaded bracelets and necklaces. She peers out at Arnold over blue-tinted bug-eye sunglasses, the smoke from a cigarette in the car's ashtray curling around her face.

"Hello sweet boy," she coos, her voice husky but gentle.

"Morning Miss Bella," Arnold says.

"It's going to be a hot one, Arno. You be sure not to stay out in the heat too long and drink plenty of fluids, you hear?"

"Yes, Miss Bella."

As Mose squeezes his ample frame into the small car, he asks Bella if she knows where she's going.

"To Nico's, right?"

"No cher, Nico doesn't do business at his place, okay? You should know that."

"I don't do business with Nico, remember? That's where you come in. Just tell me where to go."

Mose sighs loudly and shakes his head.

"Just head down to Jackson and hang a left. I'll tell you where to go from there."

As Mose and Bella sputter out of sight, Arnold picks up a small rock and flings it at the telephone pole across the street, missing his target by at least a foot. He has a feeling it is going to be a slow day, and he is not wrong. After two hours of nothing more lucrative than a few idle conversations with the Dew Drop's cleaning crew, he sets off on the hour-long trek to Tremé, where he hopes Izzy Weisman will have work for him. If he doesn't, at least he can get out of the heat for a while and grab a bite to eat.

By the time he reaches Marais Street, Arnold's mouth is as dry as the Sahara and his throat feels like coarse sandpaper. Peering into the house he thinks of as a second home, he sees that Izzy is not there, but as usual the door is unlocked. He lets himself in, and remembering Bella's admonition to stay hydrated, he heads for the refrigerator. But as he passes Izzy's room, he catches sight of a long, thin form stretched out on the bed. Looking closer, he sees that it is Lyla Saint-Clair, the pretty singer who sometimes treats him to doughnuts or a sno-ball. She is asleep, sprawled out on her back in her underwear, her long black hair splayed about, a bottle of Coke with a straw in it sitting on the table beside her.

"Miss Lyla?" he whispers softly.

Receiving no answer, he calls her name again, louder this time. Still no answer.

Deciding to let Lyla sleep, Arnold moves on to the refrigerator. He finds a half-full carton of milk and a large bottle of Seven-Up that has gone flat, neither of which appeal to him. He is about to pour himself some water, when he remembers the Coca-Cola. He walks softly back into Izzy's room, careful not to wake Lyla.

He picks up the bottle and feels that it is still cold. It will be warm by the time she wakes up, he reasons to himself, and besides, she won't notice if a few small sips are missing. He puts the straw to his lips and drinks. His first sip is just that, a sip. But his thirst is so great, and the icy sweetness of the soda so enticing, that he is unable to resist. He drains the entire bottle.

Slightly embarrassed by his lack of self-control, Arnold carries the bottle into the kitchen. Placing it on the counter, he resolves to fill a glass with ice water and place it next to Lyla's bedside. But a wave of nausea washes over him, and he feels suddenly cold and dizzy. He leans on the counter and rests his head on his arms. His vision blurs, his legs turn to Jello, and the world goes dark.

Chapter Twenty

When we debriefed after interviewing Prosper, and then later Izzy Weisman and Bella Gurwitz, Gator and I agreed that we both had an interest in talking to Dominick Martello. Gator liked Bella Gurwitz as a suspect in Arnold Jesse's death, especially after I told him about Prosper mentioning to Bru that he'd seen her driving away from Weisman's house as he arrived. If Bella had been jealous of Lyla Saint-Clair, she had motive; and if she was at Weisman's house around the time of Arnold's death, she had opportunity. The means was still unclear, but Gator's theory was that Bella tried to off Lyla, and Arnold was collateral damage.

"Before I really put the screws to her," Gator said, "I want to see what I can get from the other players around that scene. The ones who knew Gurwitz, Weisman, and the victim. That means Martello and the Adler guy, and maybe Weisman without Gurwitz being present."

"Makes sense," I said. "I want to talk to Martello too, about the arson. If Eduardo Alves is our torch, and I'm betting he is, and if the company he works for is owned by Martello, and they have the same damn lawyer, there's no way he isn't involved or at least doesn't know something. Should we tag team?"

"Works for me," Gator said.

"With Adler too, if that's okay."

"Why?"

"He's knowledgeable about music, he knows about the Bolden cylinder because Bruneau played it for him, and he would have known Martello."

"Okay, sure. But my case takes precedent."

"Naturally."

* * *

We started with Mose Adler.

When Rodiger found him at his shack in the Lower Ninth and explained that he wasn't a suspect in any crime, but that we wanted to talk to him about the Sixties music scene, he came willingly.

Mose Adler is not a guy you'd pass on the street without noticing him. He's big and barrel-chested, with a gut, like Bru had described him, but what stood out most was his hair. It was like somebody had pulled a hollowed-out fuzzy frisbee down to just above his ears, so that the bald top of his head looked like a halo, or maybe a dinner plate surrounded by a wreath of snow. His massive white beard reached down to his chest and held evidence of a breakfast that might have been scrambled eggs. He wore faded jeans, an old Procol Harum t-shirt, and worn leather flip-flops.

"We appreciate you coming in, Mr. Adler," Gator said when we'd all been seated in the Toaster.

"We Fuzz got to stick together, eh?" Adler smiled, playfully puffing up the hair on both sides of his head.

"Yes, well, be that as it may," Gator hemmed, "as Detective Rodiger may have told you, we're interested in your memories of the music scene you were part of in the 1960s. The reason for our interest is that the remains of Arnold Jesse were found in the ashes of a house that burned down recently. Do you remember Arnold Jesse?"

"Arno," Adler nodded.

"What do you remember about Arnold?"

"Sweet boy. He danced."

"You two busked for money in the Quarter, right?"

"I drummed. Arno danced."

"Izzy Weisman, Bella Gurwitz, Dominick Martello, Lyla Saint-Clair, Andre Coulon. You remember all these people?"

"Not the last one."

"He was Lyla's boyfriend at the time of Arnold's disappearance."

"Hmm, maybe. Big man?"

"Yes."

"I remember."

Gator nodded and then continued.

"Do you keep in touch with any of these people, Mr. Adler."

"Izzy, when he wants something. Nico sometimes."

"By Nico, you mean Dominick Martello?"

"The Duca."

"What is the nature of your relationship with Mr. Martello?"

"Old friends. Help each other sometimes. Listen to music."

"How does he help you?"

"With money."

"And how do you help him?"

"Advice. Protection."

"What kind of advice?"

"Musical, eh. What to buy, what not to buy. What is real, what is not."

"That's when you listen to music together?"

"Sometimes we just listen. Talk about the old days."

"Yes, of course. You said you help Nico with protection. What kind of protection?"

"From bad juju, eh. Enemies lwa, police."

"I'm sorry. Lwa?"

"Spirits."

"Okay," Gator said, shooting me a quick look. "How do you protect Nico from his enemies and these, um, lwa?"

"It depends, eh. Gris-gris, vèvè, prayers."

"Vèvè?"

"Signs, symbols."

"So voodoo, in other words?"

Adler smiled mischievously.

"Hoodoo voodoo whoo-dunit, eh?"

Mose Adler was one strange dude. I wasn't sure how much of his act was a put-on, and how much was the eccentricity of an old man who'd been living by himself for too long. Either way, Gator looked like he could use a break.

"Mose," I said, "may I call you Mose?"

"Mose do. Heh, heh."

"Right. I'm wondering, Mose, did you and Nico ever listen to Buddy Bolden?"

Adler let out a loud laugh, and then he started to sing.

"*I thought I heard Buddy Bolden say, you're nasty, you're dirty, take it away.*"

Weirdly, I knew where that came from. My dad was a Jelly Roll Morton fan and used to play the song around the house.

"Buddy Bolden's Blues, right, by Jelly Roll?"

I could tell I'd impressed Adler. Gator and Rodiger just stared at me, expressionless.

"*Open up that window and let that bad air out,*" Adler sang. "*Open up that window and let that foul air out.*"

"That's the problem with funky butts," I said. "Bad air, right? But you haven't answered my question. Did you and Nico listen to Bolden."

"Not Nico, but maybe me, eh."

"When Bruneau Abellard played you a recording on his phone?"

"Fat man and pretty girl."

"Did you think it really was Bolden?"

Adler shrugged.

"Possible, eh."

I pulled a mug shot of Eduardo Alves out of the folder I'd brought in with me.

"Ever seen this man, Mose?"

Adler picked up the photo and looked it over closely. He shook his head and handed the photo back.

"Let me ask you something, Mose. If Nico knew about that recording, would he have wanted it for his collection?"

"What Nico wants, Nico gets, eh."

"That's his reputation. Did you ever talk with him about Bolden or the recording?"

"Only fat man and pretty girl."

"Martello has quite a music collection, though, doesn't he?"

"Got some rhythm, got some blues."

"And you help him with his collection?"

"When he asks."

"What does he ask about? Whether a recording is authentic?"

That got him talking in full sentences. Finally.

"Sometimes. Look, Detective, collectors like Nico, they're after the stuff nobody else has got, eh. Garage recordings, first cuts, songs that were never released. The people that sell that stuff, you don't always know if they're on the level, you dig?"

"Yeah, I dig. So how do you figure out if a recording is legit?"

"There's science and there's art. Nico, he's got people to help with the science, run down provenance, that kind of thing. Could this performer have been in this place at that time, with that band, eh? Me, I help with the art. Me and Nico, we listen together. Does this sound like it could be Fats or Ernie or Fess? Is it just another take or is there something special about it?"

"I imagine the only known recording of Buddy Bolden would be quite a feather in Martello's cap."

"Maybe," Adler shrugged, "but Nico, he's not really a jazz guy. Early rock and R&B, that's his thing."

I decided to circle back around to the fire.

"What did you think when you heard about the fire that destroyed Izzy Weisman's house?"

"Unlucky," Adler shrugged.

"Maybe. Did Izzy have any enemies you were aware of? Someone who'd have a reason to burn his house down."

"You live a long time, probably you have enemies, eh."

"Like who, in Izzy's case?"

"Beats me."

"Did you have business dealings with Izzy?"

"Me?" Adler laughed, pointing at himself and leaning back in his chair. "Maybe I sold him a gris-gris one time, I don't know. Sometimes I'd sit in with one of his acts. Always took a couple weeks of nagging at him to get paid."

"When was the last time you were in his house?"

"Long time. Forty, fifty years. We'd rehearse there sometimes if we couldn't find anyplace else."

Gator cleared his throat to let me know it was time to change the subject. He turned his chair toward Adler, glanced at his notes, and spoke.

"What about when you heard about Arnold Jesse's disappearance?" he asked. "What did you think at the time?"

Adler played with his beard while considering the question.

"People said he must have run off," he said. "Never sat right with me. Arno was always looking after his kid sister. His momma too. He wouldn't have run out on them."

"What did you think happened to him?"

"Figured he ran into trouble of some kind. Never could find out what."

"It wasn't long after Arnold disappeared that Lyla Saint-Clair died, was it?"

Adler nodded and waited to see if there was more to the question.

"It was ruled a suicide," Gator said. "That seem legit to you?"

"Sure, could have been. She was up and down, up and down, and when she was down, she was really down."

"You knew her well?"

"Well enough. We played together sometimes."

"You and Nico, too?"

"Sure."

"And Izzy was her manager, so he'd be around, right?"

"Yeah, of course."

"You said Lyla was up and down. What was she like when she was up?" Rodiger asked.

"She was great. Friendly, good sense of humor, easy to work with."

"And when she was down?"

"Terrible. Self-absorbed, needy, temperamental, completely unreliable."
Gator jumped back in.

"Looking back," he said, "now that you know that Arnold's body was found
at Izzy's, do you think there could be a connection between his death and
Lyla Saint-Clair's?"

"Connection?" Adler asked, surprised. "Like what?"

"I don't know. They were both in Weisman's orbit, right?"

Adler frowned and shook his head.

"Izzy and me, we were never close, okay? Never really jibed, you know?
But he was devoted to Lyla, and he treated Arno real good, like a father
almost. What you're implying, I don't see it."

"What about Bella Gurwitz?"

"Eezabella? What about her?"

"Is Bella short for Isabella?"

"I don't know, it's what I used to call her," Adler shrugged.

"Were you friends?"

"We knew each other well."

"But you weren't friends?"

"Bella was nice enough. We weren't enemies or anything. But she was
sneaky, you know? You could never really trust her. She had it out for Lyla,
too."

"How so?"

"Jealous. We all saw it. I think maybe she had a thing for that boyfriend of
Lyla's. The big guy. What's his name again?"

"Andre Coulon."

"Yeah, that one. Lyla, she'd been through a lot of men, but she seemed
pretty stuck on him, and it was obvious that Eezy didn't like it none."

"You said she was sneaky. In what way?"

"Well, lawyers, you know, you always got to read the fine print, find
the weasel words. But there was this one time…oh, never mind, it's not
important."

"How about you let us be the judge of what's important and what's not.
What were you going to tell us? This one time…?"

Adler ran his hand through his hair and exhaled loudly.

"Eezy was never into drugs, see. I mean, she'd take a few tokes, knock back a beer or two, but that was about it. One day, she catches me alone and asks me if I know where she can get some Quaaludes. I'm like, what? What do you want Quaaludes for? She says they're for a friend. So, I say okay, I know a guy, who she knows too, but she doesn't want to do the deal herself. She pays me to buy the ludes for her, while she stays off in the distance. The whole thing was weird."

"When was this? Was it around the time of Arnold's disappearance or Lyla's death?"

Adler fiddled with his beard again, making a show of thinking hard.

"Yeah, in that general timeframe. Always wondered what she did with them."

"Did you think maybe she gave them to Lyla?"

"I have no idea. The thought never crossed my mind, but I suppose anything is possible."

Gator and I locked eyes. He saw that I had a question and nodded for me to go ahead and ask it.

"Mose, this guy you bought the Quaaludes from, who Bella also knew, I don't suppose that was your buddy Nico by any chance."

"You didn't hear me say that."

* * *

Mose Adler's comments about Bella Gurwitz buying Quaaludes around the time of Arnold Jesse's death strengthened Gator's feeling that she was involved in some way.

"You can see how it fits," he said, as we stood near Rodiger's desk after we were done with Adler.

"Lyla Saint-Clair is lights out, maybe from the drugs Bella Gurwitz gave her. Weisman leaves the house. Arnold Jesse shows up and takes whatever Quaaludes are left. By the time Weissman gets back, Arnold is dead."

"Why would he take the drugs?" I asked.

"I don't know. Curiosity, maybe."

"He'd had to have taken quite a few, wouldn't he?"

"I was just looking that up," Rodiger said. "Quaaludes, or Methaqualone, were usually sold in 300-milligram tablets. Two pills would lead to strong sedation, but fatality doesn't become likely until about 8,000 milligrams, which would be like twenty-five pills."

"He was a kid, though, and probably a first-time user, so maybe he didn't need that much," Gator said. "Plus, maybe they were poor quality or laced with something else."

"Okay, sure," I said, "but even then, it would be Lyla's negligence that killed Arnold, not Bella's, right? If she gave the drugs to Lyla, maybe she bears some responsibility, but she wouldn't have had any way of knowing Arnold would come into contact with them."

"I get it, we're not there yet. I'm just saying there's a picture that's starting to come into focus," Gator said. "The fact that Bella Gurwitz has been Arnold's sister's fairy godmother all these years suggests she may feel guilty about something where Arnold is concerned. The pieces are falling into place, it's just that we're still missing a few."

"Think the Duca can help us?"

"It's worth a shot."

Chapter Twenty-One

Rodiger's luck in getting a meeting with Dominick Martello didn't hold the second time around. He got the run around from the Duca's personal assistant and was told to speak with Martello's lawyer, Gino Randazzo. Gino and I go way back, and we have a pretty good relationship, so I offered to make the call.

"Detective Thibodaux Duplessis!" Gino greeted me. "To what do I owe the pleasure, my friend?"

"How're you doing, Gino? It's been a while."

Gino started out as a criminal defense lawyer about the same time I joined the police force, and we've had many dealings since, most recently when he represented Peter Burns, Mahdi Toledano's accomplice in the Jean Lafitte case. People say Gino has mob ties, but I've never seen evidence of that. He's got a bit of that Sicilian American braggadocio, but in my experience, he's a man of his word who does right by his clients, no matter who they are.

"We tried to speak with a client of yours, Gino, and were told to go through you."

Gino laughed.

"You don't say? I heard you were out hunting elephants, Bo. That's not your usual style. Why do you want to speak with Mr. Martello?"

After I explained that we wanted to question Martello about Eduardo Alves, as well as his memories from the 1960s music scene, Gino said he'd run it by his client and get back to me. He also let me know he no longer represented Alves.

"How come?" I asked.

"It became apparent to me that I had a conflict of interest."

"You mean because you also represent Martello?"

"Those details are between me and my clients, Bo, you know that."

When I hung up with Gino, I gave Angie a call because I knew she'd been planning to drop in on Cheryl Bertram during her lunch break.

"How'd it go?" I asked her.

"She's a bit of a mess, but she'll get through it," Angie said.

"She angry at Prosper and Izzy?"

"No, not really. Just sad, I think. She saw how torn up Prosper was and understands that he and Izzy were young men at the time and were trying to protect their friend. She's pretty upset with Bella Gurwitz, though."

"Yeah?"

"Yeah. It sounds like there's a lot that Bella never told her about the Dew Drop days. Bella offered to meet and hash through it all, but Cheryl said she needs some time to cool down first."

As Angie and I were talking, my phone started to vibrate, and I saw that it was Gino calling me back. I told Angie we'd catch up later and switched over to Gino.

"Today is your lucky day," he told me. "You've been invited to the Villa Martello."

* * *

Dominick Martello lives across the river in Algiers Point, on a double corner lot just off Pelican Avenue. I wouldn't describe his complex as beautiful in any way, but it is impressive. Surrounded by small cottages and shotguns, the "Villa Martello" is a sprawling two-story red brick fortress surrounded by twelve-foot-high brick walls in all directions. I'm not an architecture guy, but I'd guess it was built in the seventies, around the same time as our house. Bruneau would probably turn up his nose and call it "nouveau" or "gauche," but I could see the attraction. For a man with enemies, it offers security, privacy, and peace of mind.

When we arrived, a security guard met me, Gator, Mike, and Joe Bailey, and led us through a side gate into a large courtyard behind the house. Palm trees surrounded a fountain in the middle of the outdoor space, and looking around, I recognized bronze statues of Fats Domino, Little Richard, James Booker, and Professor Longhair. A raised porch looked out at the courtyard, and behind the porch an enormous window ran almost the full width of the house.

Martello's butler, "Enzo," greeted us. He was probably in his early sixties, but fit-looking, with slick-backed white hair. He was dressed in a formal uniform, with tails and white gloves. The whole get-up.

"Welcome to Villa Martello, gentlemen," he said. "Please, follow me. Your host is expecting you."

Enzo showed us into what he called "the soggiorno," which Bruneau later told me means "living room." He told us to make ourselves at home and that "Mr. Martello" would be with us shortly. He offered us something to drink, but we declined.

The soggiorno was like nothing I'd ever seen. It was probably a thousand square feet, painted Mardi Gras green with purple trim, and had a two-story ceiling and a balcony overlooking the courtyard. Vintage guitars, trumpets, saxophones, and accordions hung on the walls on both sides of the room, along with framed photos and album covers signed by various stars of the fifties and early sixties. The juke box Rodiger had told me about stood against the back wall, next to a double door leading to the front of the house. A huge purple sectional sofa and oversized purple and gold lounge chairs surrounded a large white marble table shaped like a bass guitar.

While we were still taking it all in, the Dandy Duca himself entered the room, leaning on a cane. He wore a simple polo shirt and shorts, white socks, and tasseled loafers. I was shocked by how hunched and fragile he seemed compared to his larger-than-life public image. He walked unsteadily, and his skinny legs were covered with scaly skin and varicose veins.

"Good afternoon, gentlemen, and welcome," he said, his voice surprisingly strong and clear. "You must pardon my diminished appearance. I have not been well of late."

Looking around, Martello gave a friendly nod to Rodiger, and then to

Gator and me, who he didn't know. He smiled when he saw Joe standing in the far corner of the room.

"Well, well, if it isn't Captain Vice himself. I wasn't expecting you, Detective. Are you and your merry band of puritans rounding up the usual suspects for yet another witch trial, or are you here on other business?"

"I was invited to tag along as a professional courtesy," Joe said, icily.

"Ah, how nice," Martello said, seating himself and handing his cane to Gino, who had followed him in. "If I'd known you'd be joining us, Joe, I might have arranged for some entertainment. Perhaps a lap dance or two, Detective?"

"That won't be necessary," Joe said.

Martello smiled and turned to the rest of us, asking us to introduce ourselves. After we had done so, he scanned the room before speaking.

"So, gentlemen, how may I be of assistance today? I understand music is on the agenda. As you can see by looking around, it is one of my favorite subjects."

"Not so much music as the music scene you were part of during the nineteen sixties," I said.

"Ah, yes, the halcyon days," Martello said, smiling. "We didn't have much, but we had everything. We just didn't know it. Those were good times, gentlemen, and I miss them. As a man begins to glimpse the end of his days, his mind returns to his formative years."

"Then you won't mind reminiscing for us?"

"Certainly not."

"That's good to hear. Do you remember Arnold Jesse, Mr. Martello?"

"Of course, Detective. Arno, we called him. Arno was a fine lad. He had one of those smiles you couldn't help but smile back at. I was told that his corpse turned up recently. I figured it would eventually, though I never imagined it would take this long. At least his sister will finally have some closure. None of us at the time believed the police narrative that Arno ran away, but it must have been hard to close the book on a missing loved one without knowing for certain that he was really gone."

"You know Arnold's sister?"

"I know of her."

"You went by Nico in those days, right?"

"Yes. I still do, to my oldest friends."

"Does your list of old friends include Mose Adler, Bella Gurwitz, and Izzy Weisman?" I asked.

"It does. I've seen more of Mose than the other two in recent years, but they all hold a special place in my heart."

"Are you aware of where Arnold's corpse was found, Mr. Martello?" Gator asked.

"In the walls of Izzy's house, is what I heard. It's a shame about that fire."

"Any theories as to how Arnold's body ended up where it did?"

"I have no earthly idea. I will only say that Izzy Weisman is many things, Detective, but he's no killer. Of that I am quite certain."

"One of the things he is, or was, is a collector," I said.

"Hmm. Yes, I guess you could call him that. He's more hoarder than collector in my estimation, but perhaps that's just semantics."

"How do you see the difference?"

"Sometimes people who can't throw things away end up with valuable collections. Not because they started out with a plan or because they have a knack for spotting value, but because if you have enough stuff that sits around long enough, odds are some of it will age well."

"Yet you wanted to buy his collection?"

Martello smiled.

"Izzy had a lot of junk but some genuine treasures, too. I'm not sure he knew the difference in a lot of cases. My plan was to sort through the mess, keep what I wanted, and donate the rest."

"Were there particular items you had your eye on?" I asked.

"Well, let's see, one that comes to mind is a recording of outtakes from Lloyd Price's 1952 J&M Studio sessions that produced 'Lawdy Miss Clawdy.'"

"I remember that song. What makes these outtakes so valuable?"

"Ah, good question. This is not well known, but Dave Bartholomew produced those sessions for Specialty Records, and he brought Fats Domino in to play the piano in place of Cosimo Matassa's usual studio man. If you can think of the keyboard intro to 'Miss Clawdy,' in what we musicians call rolling triplets, that's actually Fats playing."

"Huh. That's an interesting bit of trivia."

"Not many people know it. The best parts of some of those cuts are just Fats goofing around, playing with ideas. I've had Izzy play them for me on many occasions. They never get old."

"Any other items of note?"

"There were many, and undoubtedly some I wasn't aware of. Ever hear of Smiley Lewis?"

"Sounds familiar, but I can't place him."

"He was Fats before Fats. Similar voice, similar style; just came along a little too soon. His biggest hit was 'I Hear You Knocking,' which Bartholomew wrote and produced at J&M for Imperial. Izzy had a couple fantastic cuts from those sessions with Huey Smith on piano and Frank Fields on bass."

I smiled politely. Then I got us back on track.

"Why do you think Weisman turned you down?"

Martello shrugged.

"Hard to say. I tried him a few times over the years. He always said he had no interest in selling and was going to donate everything to Tulane when he died. It's not like he couldn't have used the money. Maybe it was just the hoarder in him that couldn't bear to part with his possessions."

"Things ever get heated between you two?"

"Woah! Easy there, Detective," Gino interjected. "This is supposed to be an informational interview, not a fishing expedition."

"It's alright, Gino," Martello said.

"Heated is way too strong a word, Detective. If you've spent any time around Izzy, you know he can be an irritating little twit. Between the hygiene and his eccentricities, he can get under your skin. We've had our share of little spats over the years, but in the end, Izzy means well. What's that Yiddish word for a good guy?"

"Mensch?" Rodiger suggested.

"Yes, that's it, mensch. Thank you, Detective. Izzy is a mensch. I've always liked that word. There's nothing quite like it in English or Italian."

CHAPTER TWENTY-ONE

Gator cleared his throat and leaned forward.

"Are you aware that Arnold's mother warned him to stay away from you, Mr. Martello?"

Gino started to object again, but Martello shut him down. He answered Gator calmly, but I thought I saw his expression darken ever so slightly for just an instant.

"No, I am not, Detective. That strikes me as rather unlikely, seeing as I never met the lady. I can't imagine who your source could be for such a scurrilous aspersion."

"Arnold's sister remembers her mother telling Arnold to stay away from 'Nico,'" Gator said. "She didn't know who Nico was, but she remembers her mother's warning."

"Cheryl said that, really?" Martello asked, leaning back in his chair and stroking his chin. "I've never known her to be anything but honest. Maybe her mother was referring to another Nico? She was reputed to run with some rough customers."

"I thought you didn't know Arnold's sister; just 'of her.'"

"Good catch, Detective," Martello said, smiling again. "I should clarify. I have never met Cheryl Bertram, but I have followed her and her good works closely for some time. Many years ago, after I'd given up music and had begun accumulating my fortune, I helped put her through college and establish her treatment center. All anonymously, of course. I continue to make modest annual donations to Open Arms, sometimes in my name, sometimes not."

"We were under the impression that it was Bella Gurwitz who was her fairy godmother," I said.

Martello chuckled.

"And so she was, and is, Detective. It was Bella who first came to me way back when. She explained Cheryl's situation to me. No parents, no siblings, no resources, but lots of potential. She let me know that she'd been paying to get Cheryl some tutoring but didn't have the money to send her to college. She asked if I'd loan her the money, which I agreed to do."

"Let me get this straight," Joe butted in. "Your 'philanthropy' consisted of collecting interest on money you *lent*, rather than *donated*, to the cause?"

Gino once again started to object, but Martello howled in laughter. Then he had a coughing fit that seemed like it was never going to stop. Enzo had a glass of water at the ready, which Martello accepted.

"Please excuse me, gentlemen," he said when his throat had begun to clear. "This happens a lot these days. It's the cancer talking, I'm afraid."

"I'm sorry," I said.

"Thank you, Detective, but there's no need for pity. I've lived a good, long life, and I may still have a few years left, if the chemo doesn't kill me before the cancer. It doesn't matter who we are or who we've been; Father Time plays no favorites. Now, where were we?"

"Your philanthropy," Joe said sarcastically.

"Ah, yes, of course! You truly are a piece of work, Detective. Far from being the sinister usurer of your imaginings, Joe, I'm a sentimental softie at heart. I'm surprised you don't know this about me. The fact is, Bella kept me apprised of Cheryl's progress, and I was impressed. Bella was an old friend trying to do a noble thing, and she didn't have a lot of money, so I forgave the loan. She did what she could for Cheryl financially, and I lent a helping hand whenever it was needed. Cheryl has more than repaid me with her many good deeds. From what I can see, she does honor to her brother's memory every day of her life."

Joe looked like he was about to come back at Martello, but Gino butted in.

"Alright, gentlemen, it seems to me we're getting a bit off track here, and Mr. Martello doesn't have all day. Is there anything else you'd like to know about my client's memories from his time as a musician, or should we move on to Eduardo Alves, the other topic you wanted to discuss?"

"I do have one more question," Rodiger spoke up.

"Please," Martello said, turning toward Mike.

"What are your recollections of Lyla Saint-Clair?"

"Now there's a name I haven't heard in a while," Martello said, leaning back in his chair.

"Lyla was a talent, I'll say that. One of many from those years who left us way too soon. It was a damn shame. Lyla had a chance to make the big time,

I thought. With the right song, the right band, and the right promoter, she just might have. Of course, that was before the drugs took over."

"Were you close with her?"

"Other than Izzy, I probably knew her as well as anybody, but I wouldn't say we were close. Lyla wasn't an easy person to get close to."

"From what we've been told, Weisman was a bit of a father figure to Lyla. Would you agree with that?"

"Yes, that sounds right. Izzy managed Lyla's career, as you undoubtedly know. Not very well, in my opinion, but he did what he could, I guess. He spent a lot of time putting out fires. Lyla's behavior could be erratic, to say the least."

"Yes, we've heard that. What about Lyla and Bella Gurwitz? What do you remember of their relationship?"

Martello paused before answering, as though trying to pull back a memory.

"I don't recall them being around each other much, to be honest," he said. "Lyla was one of those women who didn't have many female friends. She seemed more comfortable hanging out with the guys. Why the interest in Lyla, Detective?"

"Just curious," Rodiger said. "It's a name that has come up a few times."

Martello nodded, but I could tell he didn't buy Mike's explanation.

"Okay, are we ready to move on to Alves?" Gino asked.

"Sure," I said, shifting in my seat. "I presume you are aware of who Eduardo Alves is, Mr. Martello?"

"I am, yes," Martello said. "As you surely know, he's been employed by one of my companies for a few years now, although I only became aware of him relatively recently."

"And how was that?"

"I had attended a meeting at the EcoNico offices, and as I was leaving, I walked by Eduardo's office. He had 'Honey Hush' by Big Joe Turner playing on his phone. The original from 1953, not the watered-down version he recorded several years later. It's not every day one hears someone Eduardo's age playing my kind of music, so I poked my head in and struck up a conversation."

"And was that it, just one conversation?"

"Oh no. We talked for quite a while. I was surprised by how knowledgeable Eduardo was about early R&B and the history of American popular music generally, so I invited him out here. Naturally, he was impressed with my collection, which I was happy to share with him. He was writing a book, and some of my possessions were helpful to his research."

"I see. It sounds as if you got to know Alves pretty well."

"I'm not sure how well I got to know him, Detective, especially knowing what I know now."

"I'm not sure I follow," I said.

"How well do we know anyone, Detective? Joe Bailey over there thinks he knows me. But what does he know, really? He knows me in the context of a label people have applied to me, and perhaps I bear some responsibility for that. But we are all more than the sum total of the roles people expect us to play, are we not? Even Joe, I imagine."

Joe chuckled quietly, shaking his head.

"You said 'especially knowing what I know now,'" I said. "What did you mean by that?"

"Yes, well, the truth is, I have a confession to make, Detective."

Martello paused to gauge the reaction in the room. We all kept our poker faces, except for Joe, who raised his eyebrows.

"Now don't go getting all excited, Joe. I won't be surrendering myself to your meddlesome carabiniere anytime soon. No, my confession, gentlemen, is that it was me who sent Eduardo to see Izzy."

"I'm not sure I understand," I said.

A look around the room told me I wasn't the only one, although Gino seemed unsurprised, like this was something he and Martello had discussed beforehand.

"I thought maybe Izzy's hesitation to entertain a sale had something to do with me being the would-be buyer, so I sent Eduardo to call on Izzy under the auspices of being an interested academic. He'd had some training, so I figured he could pull it off."

"What was in it for Alves?" Rodiger asked.

"If he got Izzy to sell, I was going to pay him a generous commission and give him first dibs on anything I didn't want."

"What did Alves tell you about his meeting with Weisman?" I asked.

Gino interrupted.

"Before we go any further, gentlemen, I'd like your assurance that nothing my client tells you will be used against him in a prosecution of any kind. Mr. Martello has committed no crime that I can see, but it is not hard to imagine an overzealous prosecutor attempting to spin an accessory to conspiracy charge tied to Mr. Alves' subsequent activities."

"You know we can't agree to that, counselor," I said, "but I think we can say that so long as Mr. Martello's complicity doesn't extend beyond what he has so far told us, we would have no cause to move against him."

Gino nodded at Martello. Joe glared at me but didn't say anything.

"Alright then, where were we?" Martello asked.

"Alves' meeting with Weisman," I said.

"Right. Eduardo told me he thought it went well. There were no commitments made, but Izzy agreed to keep the conversation going."

"Then what is it that you know now but didn't know before that makes you question how well you knew Alves?" I asked.

"Let's just say the timing of the fire at Izzy's place raised my suspicions."

"Of Alves?"

"Yes."

"And did you act on your suspicions?"

"After I was visited by Detective Rodiger and I realized I might be a subject of your investigation, I had my men keep an eye on him."

"And what did they learn?"

"Nothing, at first. But a couple days ago, one of my men was staking out Eduardo's apartment, and he heard some music playing. It wasn't loud, but as he moved closer to Eduardo's window, he said it sounded like a lot of the stuff I play. He also said the music kept starting and stopping, as though maybe Eduardo was taking notes or trying to find a specific section. He called me and told me what was going on, so I had him creep underneath the window and record what he was hearing on his phone."

"And?"

"And when he brought it to me and played it, you'll never guess what it was, Detective."

"Enlighten us, please."

"Antoine Dominique Domino himself, experimenting with his rolling triplets for 'Lawdy Miss Clawdy.'"

The room went silent as we absorbed what we had just heard.

"Wow!" I said finally.

"Wow indeed, Detective. It appears as though Eduardo Alves may be your arsonist thief."

The room went quiet again, until Rodiger spoke up.

"Mr. Martello, how many copies of those 'Miss Clawdy' session outtakes would you guess there are?"

"You mean, might Eduardo have gotten ahold of them from someone other than Izzy?"

"Yes."

"The chances are beyond slim, Detective. Usually, only one copy survives, if that, cut straight from the master. I suppose it's possible that there was a backup recording that could have survived, or maybe a second-generation recording or two."

"You mean a recording of the recording, made at some later point in time?" Rodiger asked.

"Yes."

"I see where you're going with this, Mike," I said, "but I'd say we've got more than enough for a warrant to search Alves' place and bring him in for questioning."

"That won't be necessary, Detective," Martello said.

"Why not?"

"Because, after some gentle persuasion, Eduardo has agreed to turn himself in. Enzo, would you be so kind as to inform our guest that we are ready for him to join us?"

"Certainly, sir," Enzo replied. Then he bowed, turned, and left the room. Not knowing what to say, we just stared at each other. Gino broke the silence.

"As you can see, gentlemen, my client has been more than simply cooperative. Without his active assistance, it is highly doubtful that you would have been able to bring your leading suspect into custody."

"So noted," I said, catching another glare from Joe.

We heard shuffling footsteps approaching. A tall, dark-haired man with his arm in a sling, a black eye, and ruffled clothes entered the room, trailed by Enzo. He looked like he hadn't slept in a week, but I recognized him from the E.R. It was Eduardo Alves, served up to us on a silver platter.

Chapter Twenty-Two

My Dearest Cheryl,

I would ask your forgiveness for lacking the courage to look you in the eye as I reveal the appalling history I am about to share with you, but there can be no forgiving the unforgivable. The fact is, Cheryl, I am a coward. And a liar, and a fraud. Worst of all, I am a murderer, if not by intent, then by way of callous recklessness. By the time you read this, I will be gone. I don't expect you to be able to make sense of what I will tell you, and I advise you not to try. My sins are too despicable and too numerous to merit an attempt at comprehension or mercy. I don't understand them myself. I know only that I owe you an honest accounting of your sweet brother Arnold's death, even if I don't know every detail myself.

Perhaps the best place to start is at the beginning. This is my confession.

Before I met Arnold or started working with musicians, I had a boyfriend who I loved very much or thought I did. His name was Andre. I was in law school, and Andre was studying to become a doctor. Looking back, there were plenty of signs that he wasn't as stuck on me as I was on him, but I couldn't see it then. When he finally broke up with me, not long after I graduated, I was devastated. I couldn't understand what I had done wrong and threw myself at his feet more than once. Eventually, I realized I had to pull myself together and get on with my life. And I did, for a while. It took some time, but gradually I built a client list and settled into a lifestyle of mingling with the music business professionals I represented. One of the places I frequented was the Dew Drop Inn, and of course, that was where I first met Arnold.

He was such a sweet boy and so much fun to be around, but you already know that. As I've told you in the past, Arnold and I were buds. I'd take him for an omelet and a shake at Camelia Grill, and he'd talk about how when he grew up, he was going to make boat loads of money and buy your mother a house. My heart breaks all over again whenever I think of him, which is pretty much every day.

There was a singer back then, named Lyla Saint-Clair. There were those among us who thought she was a major talent with a chance to make it big if only she could kick her drug habit. I wasn't in that camp. To me, she was overrated, and I took a dislike to her even before she showed up at the Dew Drop one night on my ex-boyfriend's arm. I was never a big drinker, even back then, but I got drunk and nasty that night and caused an ugly scene that got us all kicked out of the place. It wasn't my finest moment, but there was much worse yet to come.

A couple days later, I waited for Andre outside of the Charity Hospital emergency room, where he was doing his internship. When his shift ended and he came outside, I approached him and apologized for my behavior at the Dew Drop. He accepted my apology and started to leave. I should have just let him go but instead I launched into an angry tirade about Lyla being a two-bit addict and whore. Andre just shook his head, walked off, and told me to leave him and Lyla alone.

I did as he asked, but I did keep tabs on them. Sometimes I'd park down the street from Andre's apartment near the river bend and follow them when they went out. Other times, I'd find a dark corner in whatever venue Lyla was singing at and observe them from afar. I guess you could say I stalked them, but I didn't think of it that way. I just figured they would never last as a couple, and in my deluded logic, I wanted to make sure I was there to catch Andre on the rebound.

I saw enough to know that tensions had developed between Andre and Lyla. There were times when I saw Lyla run out of Andre's apartment in tears. They had arguments in public places. And it was obvious that Lyla was strung out a lot. I saw Andre pull her out of dive bars more than once.

It was June 28, 1967, when I learned from Izzy Weisman that Andre had been drafted and was due at Fort Benning on July 1. Just like that, my plan to wait out Andre's relationship with Lyla had unraveled. I panicked, desperate for one last chance to win back my man's affection. With tensions between Lyla and him running high, I reasoned that he'd be vulnerable and might come to his senses, if only I could get Lyla out of the way. But there was so little time.

The next day I purchased two dozen Quaaludes. You don't hear much about "ludes" anymore, but in those days they were ubiquitous. My plan was to put Lyla out of action long enough for me to have Andre to myself until he shipped off, but everything went wrong right from the start. I took the Quaaludes home to my apartment to grind the tablets into a powder that I could slip into Lyla's drink at whichever bar or restaurant she went to that night. But when I went back out and dropped by all her usual haunts, she was nowhere to be found. I swung by Andre's place, but the lights were off, and his motorcycle was gone. I finally found his bike outside Lyla's apartment in the Irish Channel, but by then it was too late for me to get to her. I was frustrated, but I knew I still had one more day.

The next morning, I parked outside Lyla's apartment again. Andre was no longer there. I figured he'd gone home to pack, which fit my plan perfectly. If I could neutralize Lyla, I'd have Andre all to myself in a private setting.

Lyla was up and out the door early, looking terrible. Her hair was a mess, and I could tell even from a distance that she'd been crying. I followed her as she drove downtown and parked on North Claiborne next to the Iberville projects. There was a shady-looking guy there waiting for her. They disappeared into the projects for maybe ten minutes, and when she came out, she was alone. She got back into her car, drove to Elysian Fields Avenue, and parked outside a twenty-four-

hour bar. She stayed in her car for a few minutes before getting out and disappearing into the place. I figured maybe she'd been shooting up, but I couldn't be sure. I debated following her inside, but it was a small place, and she'd recognize me, so I waited.

Maybe an hour later, Lyla emerged, stoned and drunk from the looks of it. She staggered to her car and drove aimlessly for a half hour or so, weaving all over the place. Eventually, she ended up at Izzy's house. She barely made it up the steps to his stoop. She leaned against the doorframe for support and knocked loudly. A few seconds later, Izzy appeared and saw the condition Lyla was in. He wedged his shoulder under her armpit, wrapped his arm around her waist, and walked her inside.

Now I was in a quandary. I could see that Lyla was strung out and headed for a crash landing that would put her out of commission for at least a while. I could have just headed over to Andre's then and there. But I didn't know how long Lyla might be down for. And, if I'm being honest, I wanted to punish her. So, I sat there, deliberating, until Izzy came out a short while later, got in his car, and took off. As was often the case, he didn't bother to lock his door.

Recognizing my opportunity, I grabbed my vial of ground-up Quaaludes, got out of the car, and went inside. I called out, asking if anyone was home. If Lyla answered, my plan was to play nice and offer her the powder as a palliative that would make her feel better, but she didn't. I found her asleep, lying diagonally across Izzy's bed in her underwear. I called her name and shook her a couple times. She was breathing, but unresponsive. Once again, my plan was falling apart.

Then an idea came to me. I found a lone Coke in Izzy's refrigerator. I opened it and poured half of the vial in it, thinking that would be enough to keep Lyla down for a good long while. But then I started having second thoughts. I knew that if Lyla drank the whole bottle, there was a chance it could kill her. But I figured it was more likely that she'd only take a sip or two, so I emptied the whole thing. To be honest, I didn't really care if she died. I just wanted her out of the way.

That's how out of my mind I was.

I looked around for something to stir with to dissolve the powder and spotted the straws Izzy kept around for the milkshakes he was always drinking. That worked perfectly. I took the open Coke with the straw still in it back to where Lyla lay and placed it on the bedside table right next to her. With any luck, she'd wake up thirsty, have a good long drink, and conk out all over again.

What happened next is not completely clear to me. I can piece together the gist of it, but not the details. As I was leaving Izzy's, I caught sight of Arnold in my rearview mirror, running up the steps to the house. As you know, that wasn't unusual. Izzy's place was kind of like a second home to Arnold. I breathed a sigh of relief that I'd gotten out of there before he arrived and saw me. It didn't occur to me that I might have put him in danger until I was halfway to Andre's. Only then did it hit me that not only had I left Arnold alone with a crashed addict, but that if he was thirsty, that cold Coca-Cola was going to appeal to him more than anything in Izzy's fridge. I was on St. Charles at that point, heading uptown near Napoleon, and I panicked. I pulled a U-turn without looking and came within inches of getting rammed by a trolley. The driver yelled at me, but I peeled out and raced back to Izzy's. When I got there, I was relieved to find that Izzy had returned. Telling myself that Arnold was safe now, I turned around again and headed back to find Andre.

After all this, when I finally made it to Andre's apartment, he wasn't there. I stayed outside his place until late into the night, but he never showed up. It occurred to me eventually that Izzy had probably called him to help with Lyla, and that, ironically, all my machinations to keep Andre and Lyla apart had in fact brought about the opposite result. I was tired, defeated, and an emotional basket case, so I went home.

The next morning, I found Andre at the bus station. He looked sleep-deprived, lending credence to my suspicion that he'd spent most of the night at Izzy's. I pleaded my case one final time. He listened politely and said he hoped we could be friends, but that he didn't foresee any scenario in which we would reunite as lovers. I tried to kiss him, but he gently pushed me away and boarded his bus. The finality of it all came crashing down, and I fell to my knees, sobbing.

I kept to myself for a few days following the bus station encounter, wallowing in grief and self-pity. When I did finally re-emerge and started going through the motions of everyday life, people were talking about not having seen Arnold. It wasn't long before the police started coming around, because your mother had called them to report Arnold missing. I put two and two together and was filled with dread. I dropped by Izzy's on the pretense of having some documents he needed to sign. He seemed on edge, but that wasn't unusual with him. I didn't see any evidence of Arnold having been there, or Lyla for that matter, but deep down I knew something terrible had happened, and that it was my fault.

What did I think had happened? I never knew for certain, but I felt confident that Arnold drank that Coke and died, quickly and painlessly, I tried to convince myself, and that Izzy had done something with his body to protect Lyla, probably with Andre's help. I guessed they sank him in the river or the lake or something along those lines. It wasn't until I started representing Izzy after the fire that I learned about Arnold's body having been placed inside the walls of the house.

I don't know what it says about me, or Izzy, for that matter, that we went on with our lives as though nothing had happened. Lyla killed herself, and from what I can now gather, Andre wandered in exile for most of his adult life, wracked with guilt. But Izzy and me? We just smiled at the world and kept ourselves busy. I can't speak for Izzy, but when I'm alone, especially at night, Arnold comes to me. His pleading eyes always ask the same question: why? I have no answer to give him, or myself. I cannot fathom, much less explain, how my mind could have gotten so twisted as to have not recognized at the time how deranged my behavior had become.

Many times, I have thought of ending my misery, but the one thing that always pulled me back was you. I knew I could never atone for what I had done, but in doing what I could to support you, I felt that

I was finishing the work Arnold had begun. The truth is, Cheryl, you would have made a success of yourself whether you had my help or not. Arnold would be so proud of you. In my better moods, I imagine him smiling beatifically down at you like a proud celestial father.

Now you know the truth, Cheryl. It is no longer possible for you to regard me as a friend or benefactor. There are no words that can convey the depth of my shame, or the extent of my sorrow. I have lived every day since Arnold's disappearance under a cloud of guilt and grief. I am a failed and broken wretch, undeserving even of your pity. As I go now to my final reckoning, Cheryl, know that you have been the great source of happiness in my otherwise sad and tortured life.

Your unworthy but steadfast admirer,
Bella

Chapter Twenty-Three

It was a beautiful September morning, and Sallie and I were strolling in Audubon Park enjoying the first inklings of autumnal air, when Bo called to tell me that Eduardo Alves had confessed to setting the fire that burned down Izzy Weisman's house, and that Bella Gurwitz had committed suicide after penning a note to Cheryl Bertram in which she accepted responsibility for the death of Arnold Jesse. It was a lot to take in. There were hundreds of questions I wanted to ask, but I was too stunned to form them coherently.

"How did she do it?" Sallie asked as soon as I hung up.

"How did who do what?"

"Bella? How did she kill herself?"

"I don't know. Bo didn't say, and I didn't ask. Does it matter?"

Sallie raised her hands to the sky, as if to lodge a complaint with the god of inept boyfriends.

"What about the cylinder?" she asked. "Did Alves have it or know what became of it?"

"Um…"

"Oh…my…God. Really?"

"Sorry. I guess I wasn't thinking."

Sallie took a deep breath to compose herself.

"Okay, let's try this. What *did* Bo tell you?"

"He said that Alves torched the place to cover up his theft of a handful of valuable recordings. Meaning our theory was correct."

"Uh-huh. What else?"

"He said it was Martello who turned Alves in."

"Alright, I guess that's an interesting twist. Did he say if Alves was the one who opened the safe?"

"No."

"No, he didn't say? Or no, he didn't open the safe?"

"No, he didn't say."

"Of course he didn't," Sallie said, laying on the snark.

"Did he say what Alves was looking for in my archives?"

"No."

"Jesus, Bruneau!"

"Sorry."

By this point, Sallie realized she wasn't going to get anything juicy from me.

"Whatever happened to my amateur detective, the NOPD consultant?" she asked.

"He may be in need of remedial training."

Sallie smiled and gave me a playful shove.

"Alright, let's put our planning hats on. How are we going to get all our questions answered?"

"I can't call Bo back," I said. "He said he's got a long day ahead of him, tying up two investigations."

"No doubt," Sallie said, "but that gives me an idea."

"Good. I'm glad someone has a working brain."

"Bo will be wiped out, and in the mood to kick back after work, wouldn't you think?"

"Yeah, probably."

"Probably not in the mood to deal with the kids and chaos at home? Or helping with the dishes after dinner?"

"I don't know. Maybe not, I guess."

"Alright. Give me a minute."

Sallie pulled out her phone and walked a few feet away. I heard her say hello to Angie. Then she turned her back and started talking animatedly, gesturing with her hands, but I couldn't make out the words. A couple minutes later, she hung up and spun back toward me with a big smile on her face.

"There! It's settled. Bo and Angie are coming to dinner. Sophie overheard our conversation and volunteered to cook for Bo and Monique. She's making spaghetti."

* * *

As Sallie most certainly knows, I like to plan my menus well in advance and prep what I can ahead of time to minimize last-minute stress. Her spur-of-the-moment invitation to Bo and Angie sent me reeling.

"Oh, get over yourself, Bruneau," Sallie said. "It's just Bo and Angie. It's not like we're cooking for the queen."

"Bo is one thing," I said, "Angie is another. I have a reputation to uphold."

Sallie smiled and rolled her eyes.

"C'mon, stop being an idiot and let's figure out what we're going to serve."

"How about we just whip up a quick Beef Wellington and a Baked Alaska? Maybe a spinach timbale on the side?"

Sallie ignored my sarcasm.

"We could just put steaks on the grill, bake a few potatoes, and sauté a vegetable."

"Why don't we just thaw some chicken tenders?"

"Very funny. I was being serious."

"I know," I said, "and steaks on the grill are an option. But I'd like to think we can come up with something a little more…I don't know…*impressive.*"

Sallie sighed.

"Have you ever stopped to consider the degree to which your ego is tied up with your culinary output? Don't you think it might be just a little bit unhealthy?"

"No, actually, I haven't. And no, I don't."

Sallie smirked at that and scratched my back affectionately.

"You're incorrigible, but I do eat well when I'm around you, I'll give you that," she said. "What do you have in mind?"

After some deliberation, we reached a compromise. I was to swing by Langenstein's and pick up a couple racks of lamb, which I'd roast with a wet rub of garlic, mustard, and rosemary. Sallie would sauté haricots verts with shallots and ginger and make the smashed potatoes with garlic that we both love. I was left in charge of dessert, which, after some waffling, I decided would be a simple apple crisp with lavender honey ice cream from Creole Creamery.

* * *

When Bo and Angie arrived, everything was either made or prepped. Between us it would only take Sallie and me twenty minutes or so to put dinner on the table, so we gathered in the living room with a cheese and charcuterie board Sallie had assembled. Sallie sipped a flute of prosecco while I mixed a French 75 for Angie and Boulevardiers for Bo and me. Hugo curled up at Sallie's feet, where he could keep a watchful eye on Bo. Li'l Queenie perched on her favorite windowsill, plainly uninterested in human activity.

"Alright, Bo, before we get into details that are actually important," I began, "there's one thing Sallie absolutely has to know."

"What might that be?"

"How did Bella Gurwitz kill herself?"

"Bruneau!" Sallie squealed.

"What? It's true, isn't it? That's what you want to know."

"You don't have to make me sound so crass!"

"Don't worry, baby," Angie cooed. "It was my first question too."

Bo smiled wearily.

"It's what everyone always wants to know, whether they say so or not."

"Well?" I asked.

"We don't have the toxicology report yet, but there was an empty bottle of Valium by her bedside."

"I guess there's a certain symmetry to that," Sallie said.

Bo nodded grimly.

"Who found the body?" I asked.

"A couple uniforms. Bella was supposed to have dinner with Cheryl Bertram, but she never showed up, so Cheryl went by her condo to check on her. Her car was there, and the lights were on, but she didn't answer the doorbell or her phone, so Cheryl got worried and called 9-1-1."

"Did she go in with the officers?" Angie asked.

"I don't think so. Protocol would have been to have her wait outside. I think they may have had her ID the body once they determined Bella was dead."

"That must have been rough," I said.

"Yes, I imagine so."

"And the letter to Cheryl was found near the body?"

"Yep. Along with a shorter one addressed to the police. Obviously, we had to keep both notes as evidence until an investigation is completed, but Gator did let Cheryl read the one addressed to her."

Bo took a few minutes to relate the contents of Bella's letter to Cheryl, reading from his notes.

"Bruneau and I never met Bella," Sallie said, "but from everything we've heard about her, it's hard to imagine her becoming so deranged that she couldn't untangle her obsession with Prosper. Didn't she strike you as a clear-eyed, rational person?"

"Yes," Bo said, "but looking back and thinking about some things she said, her hatred of Lyla Saint-Clair was still there, hidden beneath the surface, even now."

"Seems hard to believe."

"Oh, beware, my lord, of jealousy!" I proclaimed. "It is the green-eyed monster which doth mock the meat it feeds on."

Three blank faces stared back at me.

"That's Iago, talking to Othello," I said. "If Prosper was here, he'd get it."

Sallie patted the top of my head as she got up to pass the charcuterie board. I wasn't sure if she was patronizing me or expressing sympathy.

"Mental illness is hard to see sometimes," Angie said. "A person can seem completely normal and high functioning, but we only see the part of the iceberg that's above the surface. The turmoil going on under water is hidden from us."

"That sounds like something Prosper would say," I said. "Rather profound, Mrs. Duplessis."

Angie smiled faintly.

"Speaking of Prosper, how is he taking this?" she asked.

Bo and I looked at each other.

"Unless Bru reached out to him, I don't think he knows," Bo said.

"I haven't been in touch," I said.

"What about Cheryl?" Sallie asked, looking at Angie.

"About like you'd expect, I imagine," Angie said. "She wouldn't take my call. She texted me to thank me for my concern and to say she's not ready to talk about it. I'm sure she's angry, confused, sad. All those things and more."

Our collective mood was somber to begin with, but now a heavy gloom settled over the room. I suggested we relocate to the kitchen, where Angie and Bo could sit at the counter while Sallie and I put the finishing touches on our meal. We kept the conversation light, focused mostly on the Duplessis kids. The big news was that Little Bo had gotten into Dilliard, early action.

"That's wonderful!" Sallie said. "Is that his first choice?"

"He doesn't know," Angie said. "He's applied early action a few other places he's waiting to hear from, but at least he's in somewhere."

My lamb came out of the oven perfectly, with a fragrant, crackling crust enveloping the tender red meat. Sallie's beans and potatoes were ideal accompaniments, and the Brunello I'd been cellaring for just such an occasion delivered the goods.

As we ate, Bo filled us in on Eduardo Alves' confession. He said Alves confirmed that he'd been enlisted by Dominick Martello to pose as an academic interested in purchasing Izzy Weisman's music collection. Like Martello, Alves judged a large part of Izzy's collection to be pedestrian but knew that there were specific items that were potentially valuable. When he realized that Izzy was never going to sell, he hatched his plan. As we had speculated, he cherry-picked a half dozen recordings to abscond with and then set fire to the place. He said he was in no rush to sell his contraband.

He figured Izzy and Martello only had a few years left. Once they died, and there was no one left who would know where the recordings came from, he would go public with his "finds." He claimed he wasn't motivated by money. He was going to use the "newly discovered" recordings to drive publicity for the book he was working on.

"Is that why he was interested in my archives?" Sallie asked. "For his book?"

"Yeah, that's what he told us anyway," Bo said. "He said he was gathering information on the neighborhoods and businesses that were around at the time when this music was being made, so he could paint an accurate picture."

"Funny, that's exactly what he told me, and that actually is the kind of stuff he was looking for," Sallie said. "Once he became an arson suspect, I guess I started imagining something more sinister."

"It's an occupational hazard," Bo said. "When we investigate folks who we think did something criminal, we become suspicious of all their activity. The truth is that most criminals also do honest work. They have families to feed, and people they love, just like the rest of us."

"Why did he use an alias with me?" Sallie asked.

"I don't know, we didn't ask him that question. We probably should have. Maybe Paulo Martin was going to be his pen name."

"What about the cylinder?" I asked.

"What about it?"

"Did Alves steal it?"

"He confirmed that he was aware of its existence, but denied taking it," Bo said. "He said he didn't see the cylinder anywhere when he was searching Izzy's house, and that even if he'd come across it, he probably wouldn't have taken it."

"Why not?" Sallie asked.

"He said he wasn't convinced it was legit, and if it was, it would be too hot to handle."

Sallie frowned, looking deflated.

"Did Alves crack the safe?" I asked.

"If he did, he didn't admit to it," Bo said. "He said it was open when he got there. And empty."

There was a pause in our questioning as we took in what Bo had told us. Then Angie piped up.

"Where are the recordings Alves took?" she asked. "Have they been returned to Izzy?"

"Oh boy, wait until you get a load of this," Bo said, leaning back in his chair and clasping his hands behind his head.

"Alves told us he'd taken six recordings and stashed them in the ceiling of his apartment. But when we popped the acoustical tiles where he told us he'd hidden them, there were only four tapes."

"How did he explain that?" Angie asked.

"He didn't. He said he put them all up there."

Angie cocked her head and furrowed her brow.

"Do you think he's lying?"

"I'm not sure. Probably not."

"Then what's your explanation?"

"I think maybe somebody got there before us," Bo said.

"Like who? Do you have a suspect?"

Bo smiled faintly and looked at each of us in turn, as if to solicit a theory from the peanut gallery.

"The Dandy Duca?" I asked.

"If I was a betting man, that's where I'd put my money," Bo said.

"Can you prove it?" Angie asked.

"Prove it? That's a high bar, Ange, but he definitely had motive, means, and opportunity."

"How so?" I asked.

"Well, Martello got to Alves before we did, remember? Alves wouldn't admit it, but it was obvious that he'd been roughed up."

"Over and above the beating Bruneau gave him?" Sallie asked, smiling.

"Yeah, over and above," Bo laughed.

I ignored the fun at my expense.

"Let me make sure I'm following you. Your theory is that Martello's thugs beat the location of the recordings out of Alves, and then went to his apartment and took only two of the tapes?"

"Something along those lines, yes."

"In that case, why wouldn't Alves turn on Martello?" Angie asked. "If those recordings were missing, it would have been obvious what happened to them, right?"

"I imagine he was, shall we say, gently discouraged," Bo said. "A guy like Martello has many friends, inside and outside of prison."

Angie nodded to indicate she took Bo's meaning.

"Why take only two recordings?" Sallie asked.

Bo rested his elbows on the table and collected his thoughts.

"When we interviewed Martello, I asked him if there were specific items in Izzy's collection that he had his eyes on. He said there were a few and gave me two examples. One was a recording of outtakes from the studio sessions that produced 'Lawdy Miss Clawdy' by Lloyd Price. What was notable about them was that Fats Domino was on the piano. And then there was another from some sessions with a guy named Smiley Lewis, who he described as Fats before Fats."

"And that's important because…"

"Well, when Rodiger asked Alves if those were among the recordings he stole, he said they were. But they weren't in his ceiling."

We looked at each other with raised eyebrows as we digested Bo's latest piece of information. Then Sallie straightened up and spoke.

"That doesn't make any sense. When you interviewed Martello, he already had Alves stashed away in his house, right? Which means, if your theory is correct, he would have already been in possession of these recordings. Why would he choose as examples the two recordings he'd stolen?"

Bo smiled ruefully.

"A certain kind of man, Sallie, when he knows he's the smartest dude in the room, he gets off on proving it. Like a cat, playing with a mouse."

"Martello was playing you?" I asked.

"It didn't feel that way at the time, but looking back, he may have been."

"What's Martello like?" Angie asked.

Bo folded his arms across his chest and looked up at the ceiling.

"I'm not sure I'm qualified to say," he said after a second or two. "He was not in good health, so maybe I was more sympathetic than I should have been, but I kind of liked the guy. He answered all our questions straight up and was quite personable. Charming even. I mean there's no question the guy is crooked as can be and he got rich by running his rackets, but I'm not sure he's quite the evil villain my buddy in Vice, Joe Bailey, makes him out to be."

"Sort of an honorable scoundrel?" I suggested. "Like Jean Lafitte?"

"Yeah, something like that. Smart, and cunning, and definitely corrupt, but maybe not altogether hateful."

The table went quiet as we considered what Bo had to say about Dominick Martello. Sallie took advantage of the lull in conversation to suggest we retire to the living room for dessert. The rest of the evening passed amiably. We discussed politics, the puzzling competition Sallie was preparing for, Angie's taekwondo class, and the buying trip I was planning to Savannah.

Later, as we were seeing Bo and Angie out, Angie posed a question to the night air.

"Who's going to talk to Prosper?" she asked.

Three sets of eyes turned toward me.

"I guess I'll have to accept that assignment," I said.

Chapter Twenty-Four

When I pulled Liesel up to the curb outside Irene Coulon's Gentilly home, where Prosper lives in an apartment above the detached garage, the big man was standing in the driveway, washing his sister's car. He'd taken off his shirt, and his broad chest and shoulders glistened with suds and sweat. Prosper remains amazingly muscular for a man who turned eighty a few months back, and I felt weak and stunted as I walked up to meet him.

"Greetings, Bruneau," he bellowed.

"Good morning," I said.

"What brings you out here on this beautiful day? It's not like you to show up without calling first."

"Some difficult news, I'm afraid."

Prosper pointed to the small patio at the back of the house, where a wooden picnic table and four plastic Adirondack chairs were haphazardly arranged. We sat across from each other at the table as I delivered the news of Bella Gurwitz's suicide, and her confessional letter to Cheryl Bertram, without fanfare or preamble. Prosper sat expressionless as he listened to what I had to say, and after I was done, he paused pensively before speaking.

"I wish I could tell you all the emotions I'm feeling," he said, finally. "Then maybe I'd seem like a human being. But the truth is, I don't feel much of anything. Whatever feelings I may have once had for Bella…well…they're long gone. She was a short chapter in my life, that's all."

"But a consequential one, wouldn't you say?" I probed.

"As it turns out, yes, I guess she was, although perhaps more consequential for others than for me, unfortunately."

"Yes, I suppose so."

"I was such an idiot," Prosper said.

"How so? What do you mean?"

"I knew that Bella took our break-up hard and was having a hard time letting go, and I knew she was jealous of Lyla, but it never occurred to me that she'd gone full-fledged crazy. I should have seen it, Bruneau, but I was too wrapped up in my own little dramas to pay attention to anyone else's problems. If I hadn't been so self-absorbed, Arnold Jesse might still be alive. Maybe Lyla, too. And now Bella."

"That seems like a lot to put on yourself," I said.

"Think of all the bad things that happened. They were all because of me."

"You didn't cause Arnold Jesse's death."

"No, not directly. But Lyla almost certainly overdosed because I told her we were through. Bella accidentally killed Arnold because she was trying to neutralize or maybe even kill Lyla so she could have me to herself. Lyla's heartbreak over our break-up probably led to her death, whether accidental or intentional. And from what I can gather, I basically ruined Bella's life."

"That's ridiculous, Prosper. Bella and Lyla were grown women responsible for their own choices."

"Maybe, but they weren't the ones who decided to stash Arnold's body in the walls of Izzy's house so his sister could suffer a lifetime of misery, not knowing what had happened to him, and wondering if he might still be out there somewhere. God, she must hate me."

"She's not the hating type, from what Bo and Angie tell me."

"I don't know how she couldn't be," Prosper said.

"With time, good people have the capacity to consider context and to see the good in others. Maybe someday the two of you can be…I don't know…if not friends, cordial acquaintances at least."

"Please, don't patronize me, Bruneau."

"I'm sorry if you think that's what I'm doing. You know, Prosper, it wasn't long ago that you took me to task for being self-involved. I didn't like it at the time, but I took your words to heart, and as a result, I'm in a much better place today than I was then. Maybe it's time for you to pull yourself out of your funk and place some faith in other people."

* * *

Prosper didn't like it when I scolded him, but he gruntingly acknowledged that I had a point. By the time I left, his mood seemed marginally improved. Mine, however, was tense. I was running late for a lunch date with Angie at Queen Trini Lisa, the down-home Caribbean restaurant she'd been trying to get me to try for months, and I hate being late. Angie and I grab a bite together every so often, usually to discuss Bo or Sallie, and this appointment had been on my calendar for at least two weeks.

"I was wondering if maybe I was getting stood up," Angie said, smiling, from the corner table she'd chosen.

"I'm so sorry," I said as I approached, my arms extended in supplication. "You know I hate being late. I was delivering the news about Bella Gurwitz to Prosper, and the time got away from me."

"I do know you hate being late, and I want to hear all about Prosper, but I need to get back to work by one, so let's get our orders in first. Everything is good, so don't worry about choosing the wrong thing."

The menu was mercifully short and straightforward, and by the time Angie had summoned a waitress, I was ready to order the chicken curry. Angie asked for something called a "doubles box" and a side of cabbage stir fry.

"What's a doubles?" I asked.

"You'll see when it comes," Angie said. "Now, tell me about Prosper."

"Right. He's blaming himself for everything, basically."

"He does have a tendency to beat himself up."

"Yeah. I told him he was being ridiculous, but I'm not sure I made much of an impact."

"How old is Prosper?"

"Eighty, I think."

"Whatever mistakes he made as a young man a very long time ago, he made them for the right reasons, don't you think? I mean, he was trying to protect someone he loved, who also could have been an innocent victim in this Bella Gurwitz business had things gone differently. And God knows he paid a price for his sins, with Vietnam and the leg and all those lonely years of living by himself, drifting from place to place."

"I agree, but that's not the way he sees it," I said. "He thinks if he wasn't so 'self-absorbed,' to use his words, the whole unfortunate string of events wouldn't have happened."

"I didn't know Prosper back then," Angie said, "and I don't know him all that well now, but self-absorbed is not a term I would use to describe him. Seems to me he's unusually considerate, and he's always doing things for others. His friends, his sister, his nephews, the homeless folks at the soup kitchen where he volunteers. He's about as other-directed as you can get."

"Good point. Maybe you should have a talk with him, Angie. You have a talent for cheering people up. I didn't get that gene."

Our food arrived quickly, and it was good. I'm not much of an expert on island cuisine, but my chicken was delicious, falling off the bone tender with a heady mix of exotic spice and sweetness. But Angie's doubles, which she let me taste, were the showstopper. Two small but puffy pita-like pockets were wrapped around aromatically spiced chickpeas and a cucumber slaw. I'd never had anything quite like it, in flavor or texture, and I decided on the spot that I'd be back for more.

"I spoke with Cheryl this morning," Angie told me after we'd finished analyzing our food.

"On the phone?"

"No, in person. I didn't like the idea of her being alone at a time like this, so I dropped in on her."

"How was she?"

"She's having a really hard time. She can't reconcile the Bella she thought she knew with the person who did the awful things she did and then presented this smiling, caring face to her, knowing all the while what she'd done to her brother. She's angry, Bruneau. Really angry. And incredibly sad. She can't stop crying when she thinks about Arnold."

"Yeah, I really can't imagine being in her shoes. Will she be okay, do you think?"

"Define okay," Angie said. "Cheryl is resilient, and I'm sure she'll throw herself into her work. But okay? I don't know. I don't think I can say that."

* * *

After we said our goodbyes, Angie went back to work, and I headed back across town to the store. There was an email waiting for me when I arrived that caught my attention. It was from Izzy Weisman. He had learned about Bella Gurwitz's suicide from Joe Guidry. He said the news hit him hard and made him realize he had something he needed to show me. He asked me to meet him at Orville Whitlock's studio in Bayou St. John whenever I could shake free. He also asked me to bring Li'l Queenie with me. He'd purchased a small condo with his insurance money and was ready to take her back. I replied, saying I'd see him at four.

I caught up on a few things in my office, spent an hour or so on the floor, and then headed upstairs to pack up Li'l Queenie in the crate Annie had lent me. As much as I had complained about the cat, it felt a little strange taking her away from the home she had become comfortable in. I guess I'd gotten used to her. Even Hugo seemed a little unsettled to see his nemesis leave.

Orville Whitlock's studio was tucked away in the back of a shotgun on St. Peter Street, just a few blocks from Parkway, the famous po' boy shop. It was a spartan space with a piano, a drum kit, an assortment of chairs, tables, and music stands, some amps and speakers, and an old phonograph. When I arrived, carrying Li'l Queenie, Orville and Izzy were standing over what looked to be a piece of recording equipment, talking in low tones.

"Ah, Bruneau, so good of you to come," Orville said by way of greeting.

"Orville. Izzy. I didn't know you two were acquainted," I said.

"Everybody knows everybody in the music business," Izzy said, walking toward me with his eyes on the crate.

"Look who's here!" he cried. "Li'l Queenie, how I've missed you, my dear sweet girl."

As Izzy removed the cat from the crate and cradled her in his arms, he told me that he and Orville had been friends for years.

"When I first learned of Izzy's collection, several years ago now, I approached him about sharing some of it with my students," Orville explained. "Izzy was kind enough to agree, and it went so well that it evolved into a popular tradition. He and I would select a few items and bring them here for a few days. My students got to try out period instruments and listen to musicians in studio sessions, problem-solve, and experiment with new ideas. For the students, it made the history more immediate and accessible."

"I can see how that could be a valuable experience," I said politely. But I hadn't disrupted my afternoon for a history lesson, and the sight of the phonograph gave me an uneasy feeling.

"Izzy, you said you have something to show me," I said, looking at my watch.

"Yes. Yes, I do," Izzy said, avoiding eye contact. "But first, Orville has something he'd like to play for you."

"Very well," I said.

Orville instructed me to sit in a chair carefully placed between two speakers that were angled inward so that the chair sat at the apex of a triangle. Then he pushed the play button on a CD player. There were several seconds of silence before a familiar sound came from the speakers, but louder and cleaner, without the scratching and static I'd been conditioned to expect.

"Really?" I asked when it was over.

Orville rubbed the back of his neck, avoiding eye contact. Izzy put the cat down.

"I don't suppose you got that off my phone?"

"No," Orville said quietly.

Izzy picked up a shoe box that had been sitting by the phonograph and walked it over to me.

I didn't have to look inside to know what it was.

Chapter Twenty-Five

It has been seven months since Izzy Weisman and Orville Whitlock returned the Buddy Bolden cylinder to me. Izzy's explanation for why he kept the cylinder and lied about its whereabouts, both to me and to the police, didn't make a whole lot of sense. He said that in the beginning, he really did think someone might be trying to kill him, possibly to take possession of the cylinder, and that if it was thought that the cylinder was destroyed in the fire, then that threat would no longer exist. I pointed out that if the arsonist was after the cylinder, he would have looked for it and therefore known that it hadn't been in the house. Izzy looked at the floor and shrugged his shoulders.

"I took it with me when I left the house," he said. "I went by Orville's and asked him for his opinion. I knew I could trust Orville, and he has some experience as a sound engineer, so I left the cylinder with him to see what he could do to improve the quality. That's why there was a gap in the timeline between when the video cameras had me in the store and when the fire started."

"You could have just told me that the first time," I said.

"I'm sorry. Truly, I am Bruneau. I was scared. Once I told one lie, I felt that I had to keep lying, at least until the police arrested someone for setting the fire."

"But you just lied to me again right now."

"No, not really. I wasn't thinking clearly, that's all."

I made a face to convey my feelings about the inadequacy of that excuse and turned to address Orville.

"It would seem that when I told you about the cylinder at Commander's, and later played you the recording on my phone, you not only already knew about the cylinder, but you also actually had it in your possession."

"Yes, I'm afraid that's correct."

I was growing increasingly incensed, and it showed.

"I understand that you're angry, Bruneau, and you've every right to be," Orville said. "I didn't like keeping you in the dark, but I was worried for Izzy, and besides, I promised him I wouldn't tell anyone about the cylinder until the smoke cleared."

"So to speak…"

"Yes, so to speak."

"You do realize I could have you both arrested for theft and possession of stolen property?"

"I'm sure that's true, Bruneau," Orville said, "and you'd be well within your rights to do so. But we hope you won't. We have an idea we'd like to share with you."

"An idea?"

"Yes."

"I can hardly wait."

"You see, Bruneau, the truth is…well…the truth is I do believe that it is Buddy on that cylinder and that your discovery is a significant one. I have connections and credibility in the music business that you lack, no offense. So, I've been quietly shopping the recording around, seeing if I could get some historians to agree with me."

"And?"

"Everyone agrees our story is plausible," Orville said, "but no one is willing to stick their neck out and say for sure that it's Buddy. There's just not enough hard evidence or documentation to go on."

"That doesn't surprise me," I said. "What's your big idea, then?"

"We'd like to make a movie," Izzy announced.

"A movie?"

"Yes, a documentary," Orville said. "The idea would be to tell the story of your discovery of the cylinder and the research you and your girlfriend did, tracing the cylinder's possible origins back to Jackson State. In the process, we'd examine what is known of Buddy's life and music and ultimately let viewers decide for themselves whether the recording is legit."

"That sounds rather ambitious," I said. "Do you know anything about making movies?"

"No, not the first thing, which is why we approached a friend with deep pockets and lots of connections. He has agreed to fund the whole thing, including distribution, and has found us a filmmaker with an impressive resume."

"I see. And who might this friend be?"

"Nico Martello," Izzy said.

I raised my eyebrows.

"Let's just say he owes me."

"For tricking you with Eduardo Alves?"

"Among other things."

"The point is, Bruneau, we have everything lined up and ready to go," Orville said. "But neither of us feels comfortable moving ahead without your blessing. We'd like you to be a paid consultant or even a co-producer. We envision the film as a non-profit venture, with any net proceeds going toward local organizations and programs that promote jazz education and history."

"That's a rather audacious pitch, Orville," I said. "Why should I buy what a couple two-bit thieves are selling?"

"Call us whatever names you wish, but we're not trying to line our pockets, and the project we're proposing has obvious merit," Orville said.

"We hope you'll sleep on it and at least give our proposal some thought," Izzy said.

"I guess I can do that," I said.

Then I tucked the box with the cylinder under my arm and walked off without bothering to say goodbye.

* * *

When I got home and shared my news with her, Sallie reacted even more viscerally than me to the treachery of our would-be partners.

"Does Izzy have any idea how many rat holes we went down because we thought the cylinder was either burned or stolen?" she seethed.

"I don't think Izzy ever considers much beyond his own immediate situation," I said.

"To think that you were taking care of his cat while he sat on your cylinder!"

"Yeah, there's that too."

We took a few days to cool down before revisiting the subject. When viewed objectively, we realized, it was hard to disagree with Orville's assertion that, if done well, the movie could attract an audience and bring attention to a neglected art form. If the worst happened and the movie either didn't get made or lost money, we weren't going to be on the hook. So, in the absence of an obvious downside, and with Sallie's agreement, I gave Orville and Izzy my tepid approval to proceed with their plan. I told them I'd be happy to consult and lend them the cylinder, so long as Sallie had a voice equal to mine, but that we didn't want to be paid. The Martello connection made us uncomfortable, and if the project turned into a boondoggle, which we saw as a distinct possibility, we didn't want to be linked to it financially. If the film did make money, it would please us to see the proceeds go to the worthy causes Orville had earmarked.

Since then, to my considerable surprise, the project has proceeded smoothly and without interruption. Filming has been going on for more than a month now, and Sallie and I have both been interviewed on camera. As has Henry, who remains even more skeptical than me about the film's chances of ever making it through production.

* * *

Last week, Arnold Jesse received a proper interment. Because there was no longer an active investigation, and it was therefore a low priority, it took the police six months to compare Cheryl Betram's DNA to the genetic material extracted from the human remains found in Izzy Weisman's house. Burn damage compromised the results, but investigators found enough markers in common to conclude that the corpse likely belonged to a close relative of Cheryl's. That was good enough for the cops and good enough for Cheryl.

Cheryl chose Holt Cemetery, long a burial ground for the city's indigent population, as Arnold's final resting place. Dominick Martello footed the bill for a modest tomb that contained a second crypt, so that Cheryl can join her brother when the time comes. The inscription on the façade was written by Cheryl:

Here lies
Arnold Reginald Jesse (1954-1967)
Loving Son, Brother, Friend
Who Dances Now Among the Stars

The gathering was small and dignified, with a short but moving eulogy from the pastor at Cheryl's church. Attendees included employees, volunteers, and a few patients from the Open Arms treatment center, Bo and Angie, Mike Rodiger, Joe Guidry, and Sallie and me. Mose Adler also made an appearance, neatly coifed, in a tailored black suit and tie. He placed a pair of tap shoes at the foot of Arnold's tomb, along with a yellow gris-gris bag for good luck. Cheryl seemed touched by the gesture.

Henry Wilkins escorted Cheryl to and from the ceremony and stood by her side throughout. Henry is evasive when I ask him about it, but he has quietly let on that he and Cheryl have been spending time together.

The event was as notable for those who weren't in attendance as for those who were. Prosper Fortune was invited but declined to appear, deeming his presence inappropriate. Izzy Weisman was also a no-show, perhaps for similar reasons. Several months earlier, Izzy had paid for Bella Gurwitz's cremation and invited Prosper along to scatter Bella's ashes in the Mississippi. Prosper declined that invitation, too.

Dominick Martello was an even more notable absence. The Dandy Duca finally succumbed to cancer last month, leaving behind a complicated legacy.

He established one trust to fund our Buddy Bolden movie, and another to provide annual gifts of one million dollars to the Open Arms treatment center for the next quarter century. In addition, Martello arranged for his house on Algiers Point to be turned into a museum and educational resource center dedicated to the origins and early heyday of New Orleans rhythm and blues music. Among the future museum's many rumored one-of-a-kind possessions was a recording of outtakes from the "Lawdy Miss Clawdy" sessions featuring Fats Domino on keys. If Izzy Weisman had transferred ownership of the tape, perhaps in exchange for our movie deal, he hasn't said so.

According to Bo, the NOPD vice squad has finally infiltrated Martello's prostitution and loan sharking networks, taking advantage of the leaks, infighting, and shifting alliances that resulted from the power vacuum created by the Duca's death. Bo's friend Joe Bailey told him to expect dozens of arrests in the coming months.

As for Bo, he and Mike Rodiger are onto new cases now, including an investigation into a possible embezzlement scheme involving high-ranking individuals within city government. Bo and "Gator" Guidry worked through their past difficulties and are no longer at odds. They shared internal credit for the successful resolutions of the Arnold Jesse cold case and Eduardo Alves arson investigations, and both are scheduled to testify when the Alves prosecution goes to trial. They mutually agreed not to pursue charges against Andre Coulon and Izzy Weisman for their roles in concealing Arnold Jesse's corpse, though statutes of limitations likely would have shielded the men from prosecution anyway.

After Sallie and I said our goodbyes to Cheryl and Henry, we took a slight detour on our way back to the car. In the course of our research, we learned that Buddy Bolden was interred in an unmarked grave somewhere in Holt Cemetery. To atone for that slight, a memorial had been erected there in the 1990s, following a second-line funeral procession. We stopped by the monument to pay our respects and admire the inscription:

IN MEMORY OF

CHARLES JOSEPH "BUDDY" BOLDEN
SEPTEMBER 6, 1887-NOVEMBER 4, 1931

IN AN UNMARKED GRAVE NEAR HERE RESTS
BUDDY BOLDEN
LEGENDARY CORNET PLAYER
NEW ORLEANS JAZZ PIONEER
AND FIRST "KING OF JAZZ"

"THE BLOWINGEST MAN SINCE GABRIEL"
—JELLY ROLL MORTON

* * *

Prosper Fortune's story has taken an unforeseen turn. A few weeks after Bella Gurwitz's suicide, Prosper received a telephone call from Cheryl Bertram, who had gotten his number from Angie. She asked if he'd be willing to meet with her at Open Arms, as there was something she wanted to discuss with him. Naturally, he agreed to do so, though he later confessed to me that the thought filled him with dread.

When they met, Prosper fell all over himself apologizing for his past misdeeds, but Cheryl cut him off. She said she already knew how sorry he was, and she bore him no ill will. Her animus was reserved for Bella Gurwitz, who she said she could never forgive. What Cheryl wanted to discuss with Prosper was whether he might be interested in volunteering at Open Arms. She thought his combination of medical training, battlefield experience, and empathetic personality would make him an ideal fit for a new strategic initiative Open Arms was about to launch. She wanted him to be a van driver for a mobile medication unit she was piloting, paid for through Dominick Martello's first annual donation. The concept, basically, is to take treatment services to the neighborhoods where prospective patients live.

Prosper was hesitant at first, pointing out that, among other obstacles, he'd have to obtain a driver's license. But Cheryl persisted and eventually Prosper relented. He secured his license without difficulty and now drives the mobile unit four days a week. Once on site, he assists patients with physical needs and disabilities, provides informal counseling and encouragement, and generally helps wherever help is needed. According to what Cheryl tells Angie, the mobile unit has been a huge success and Prosper is beloved by co-workers and patients alike.

"The way Cheryl put it," Angie said, "is that patients can tell he's walked in their shoes. Maybe not with addiction, but they know he's been lost in the deepest darkness and made it through to the light. They know he cares, and they trust him."

The last time we had him for dinner, Prosper told Sallie and me that the work has given him a renewed sense of purpose.

"There's a lot of broken people in the world," he said. "Most of us can't be healed, but we can at least patch ourselves up. Sometimes all we need is a little help."

Then he looked up through watery eyes.

"And sometimes that help comes from the most unexpected of places."

* * *

A couple weekends ago, Sallie told me she had a surprise she wanted to share with me. Acting all mysterious, she piled me into her Prius and drove me uptown along Prytania, before hanging a left onto Soniat. A couple of blocks later, she pulled up in front of the same center hall cottage I had picked out for us almost two years earlier. It was back on the market, for a couple hundred thousand more than it had been when I'd looked at it before. The owners had added a few amenities and now were looking to flip the property.

"Really, you've been looking at houses without me?" I complained mockingly.

"I knew that was coming," Sallie said, smiling. "I took a walk-through with the realtor yesterday, and I love it. It's perfect, in fact. What do you say?"

CHAPTER TWENTY-FIVE

"You're kidding, right?"

"Nope."

"Can we afford it?"

"Yes, if we sell my house and rent your apartment. I've run the numbers."

"What if something goes wrong again with us?" I asked.

"If it's something that can't be healed, then we'll settle for patching it up, like Prosper says."

I couldn't believe we'd come full circle, and now it was me who was having misgivings.

"You aren't worried that I'll smother you?"

"Come on, silly. This house is big enough for both of us, don't you think? Plus, we get along best when we're working on something together. This house can be our never-ending joint project."

"What about my quirks?"

"Some I'll live with. Others I'll have to beat out of you."

Sallie placed her chin on my chest and looked up at me hopefully, her blue eyes and coral cheeks ablaze with possibility. I drew her in tight and kissed the top of her head.

"I guess I'm game if you are…"

Epilogue

Black Storyville
New Orleans, Louisiana
August 1906

The boy, just a few days removed from his fifth birthday, dashes headlong through the crowded, sodden street. Thick mud mixed with manure oozes through the holes in his shoes and cakes his bare feet, but he pays this no mind. He cannot yet see beyond the bustling traffic ahead of him as he sidesteps a mule-drawn wagon, ducks under a hitching post, and darts between men and women conducting business he is too young to understand. But he knows where he is headed.

Breathing hard, he has arrived at his destination. He climbs the steps to Zatarain's Grocery and slips inside. As he looks around, the dry, leathery smell of sawdust tickles his nostrils, but he does not see her. He shuffles uncertainly to the back of the store and cranes his neck around the end of the aisle. There, finally, he spies his mother. She is in the far corner, her broad shoulders turned away from him, examining a thick slice of fat back.

"What we having, Mayann?" he calls out, stealing up behind her. Before the woman can answer, the boy has peered into her bag, where he finds red beans, rice, a big red onion, and a stale loaf of bread from Stahle's bakery.

"Why, I reckon you already know, Louis," Mary Albert Armstrong says, smiling proudly and tussling her son's head.

"Hurry up and pay, Mayann," the boy urges. "The King's gonna play any minute now."

"The King? He and his boys settin' up across the street?"

"Yes, Mayann, at the Funky Butt. We got to hurry!"

Tugging at his mother's sleeve, the boy leads the way back to their home at Liberty and Perdido, across the street from Union Sons Hall, slowing once to maneuver around a dice game, and then stopping briefly to observe a bloody fight between two women, egged on by a raucous crowd.

"Don't you be paying no mind to none of that, Louis," his mother tells him. "Nothing good ever comes from fighting, nor gambling neither, you hear?"

"Yes, Mayann. C'mon, we're gonna miss the King."

Two blocks away, the boy still tugging at his mother's sleeve, they can see a crowd forming and hear the toots and trills of musicians tuning their instruments. A minute or two later, when they have reached their destination, his mother tells Louis to stay put while she brings the groceries inside. But by the time she comes back out, he has wormed his way to the front of the crowd, where she cannot see him.

Louis watches bug-eyed as a square-shouldered man in a black suit and white bow tie taps the wooden banquette three times with his cornet, signaling to his band that it is time to play. When the music begins, feet stomp, hands clap, and the chests of buxom women jiggle and shake as they bounce and sway to the raucous beat. But Louis barely notices. His ears are attuned to the music, decoding a language that seems as natural to him as breathing. He follows the complex interplay of horns and strings as they push and pull their way, separately and in tandem, toward a dulcet resolution. But it is when the cornet asserts itself, louder and sassier than the rest, that something stirs in the boy, deep down in his gut.

Later, when the music has ended and the band has gone inside, the boy feels the gentle clasp of his mother's hands on the back of his shoulders. He turns and looks up at her, his eyes animated by the certainty of youth.

"Someday I'm going to play like that, Mayann," he says.

"Of course you will, child," his mother softly sighs. "Of course you will."

Author's Notes

For one about whom so much has been written, it is remarkable how little is known about the life and music of Buddy Bolden. The essential source for learning what we do know remains *In Search of Buddy Bolden: First Man of Jazz,* by the late Donald M. Marquis. Bruneau Abellard paints the broad brushstrokes of Marquis' portrait of Bolden, but the book also contains quite a bit of compelling primary source material, such as birth and death records, arrest records, and correspondence between Bolden's mother and sister and officials at Jackson State Hospital. While providing numerous accounts and anecdotes from Buddy's contemporaries, Marquis is careful to separate fact from speculation, and to the extent possible, the man from the legend.

A simple Google search will return many articles about Buddy Bolden, though few provide fresh insights. One notable exception is a piece by jazz historian James Karst in the June 2020 issue of 64 Parishes, the magazine of Louisiana history and culture, which convincingly makes the case that Pellagra, the "sharecropper's disease" that resulted from a deficiency of niacin, may have been responsible for Buddy's descent into madness. Updated in 2023 and titled "Buddy Bolden's Blues," the article may be found online at https://64parishes.org/buddy-boldens-blues.

For a fictional account of Bolden's ordeal, I highly recommend *Coming Through Slaughter* by the great Canadian novelist Michael Ondaatje. Only superficially concerned with the exterior "facts" of the musician's life, Ondaatje mines the interior landscape of a disintegrating mind with remarkable insight, compassion, and artistry.

As a casual jazz fan, I had been vaguely aware of Buddy Bolden for many years, but the idea for *The Bolden Cylinder* didn't come to me until I happened upon a 2014 post on the Library of Congress Blogs site titled "The Elusive Boddy Bolden," by David Sanger (https://blogs.loc.gov/now-see-hear/20 14/11/the-elusive-buddy-bolden/), commemorating the 84th anniversary of Bolden's death. In it, Sanger mentions the "persistent rumor," reinforced by Willie Cornish and others, that Bolden's band recorded a wax cylinder in 1898; and the widely held belief that the cylinder was destroyed in the 1960s during the demolition of a storage shed owned by Oscar Zahn, a saloon owner who knew Buddy. What if there were another cylinder, as yet undiscovered, I wondered ...

The events described in *The Bolden Cylinder* are purely fictional, but in the scenes that take place during Buddy's lifetime I have strived to provide accurate historical context. The Bolden acquaintances and fellow musicians portrayed in those scenes, as well as the venues and businesses in which they occur, are real. To learn more about Bolden's musical contemporaries, I recommend visiting Tulane University's "Music Rising" website at https://m usicrising.tulane.edu/.

Lyla Saint-Clair, Mose Adler, Izzy Weisman, Arnold Jesse, and the rest of the characters who populate the sketches of New Orleans in the 1960s, are fictitious; however, the recently resurrected Dew Drop Inn and long defunct Club Tijuana were indeed the city's leading Black-owned nightclubs during the early rhythm-and-blues years. For those interested in learning more about the roots of New Orleans R&B and the many larger-than-life personalities who shaped the music and sub-cultures of the time, *Up From The Cradle of Jazz: New Orleans Music Since World War II* by Jason Berry, Jonathan Foose, and Tad Jones is both highly informative and a rollicking good read.

As Dominick Martello relates, Fats Domino plays the keyboards on Lloyd Price's "Lawdy Miss Clawdy," but I am not aware of outtakes from those sessions featuring Fats working out his rolling triplets. Likewise, Huey Smith and Frank Fields played on Smiley Lewis' "I Hear You Knocking," but the outtakes Martello mentions are my inventions.

I did not treat the conditions Buddy would have encountered at Jackson State Hospital in detail, because I thought it would distract from the story

I was trying to tell. But undoubtedly, they were abominable. This article from the nola.com website chronicles a long history of neglect, abuse, and corruption at the institution, as well as shining a light on problems that persist to this day: https://www.nola.com/news/article_bba93244-ed86-5b02-9aa1-ceaa07b16b8f.html.

To what effect, I know not, but Dr. E.M. Robards did introduce music therapy at Jackson State in the late 1920's. According to the Marquis book, the hospital's chaplain at the time, Sebe Bradham, remembered Buddy playing a horn every so often, and as quoted in *The Bolden Cylinder*, said that "you could tell [Bolden] was better than the rest. He played over the rest and louder than most people."

Finally, Louis Armstrong did in fact tell a story of listening to Buddy play the cornet at Funky Butt Hall when he was five years old. The year would have been 1906. "He blew so hard," he said, "that I used to wonder if I would ever have enough lung power to fill one of those cornets."

It is tempting, but ultimately folly, I think, to draw a straight line from Buddy to Satchmo. Marquis deserves the last word on this front. In the preface to a 2005 revised edition of *In Search of Buddy Bolden*, he wrote the following:

"[Bolden] did not influence many cornetists directly by his playing, but he did influence the style of their music. He contributed only what he was capable of contributing. If he had not done what he did, someone else eventually would have. He was a man a short step ahead of his time, and time for him was so limited that that step was all he needed to achieve what he did."

Acknowledgments

As with my first novel, I circulated chapters of *The Bolden Cylinder* to a trusted inner circle of readers as I completed them. The steadfast encouragement, discerning judgment, and occasional unvarnished candor served up by these kind souls are more appreciated than they can possibly know.

My family, both nuclear and extended, was a bulwark of support throughout the writing process, and a source of valued feedback. I send love and thanks to my wife Lori; children Nathalie, Alexander, and Rachel; daughter-in-law Meghan; son-in-law Chris; brothers Eric, Tim, and Steve; mothers-in-law Sue and Eunie; brother-in-law Wright; sister-in-law Drake; nephew Isaac. During the writing of this book, Lori and I became grandparents to Tristan, a most welcome addition to our fold and a source of endless amusement and delight.

I remain likewise indebted to my honorary literary family, listed here in alphabetical order: Thierry Drapanas; Sarah Gorman; Proal Heartwell; Claire Holman-Thompson; Barbara Kessler; Nancy Joe Krueger; Connie Weck; Winifred Wegmann. And once again, I owe special thanks to my closest reader and most skilled editor, Cullen Couch, who I depended upon to flag abuses of the king's English while policing integrity of plot and character.

My brother Steve is a thought leader in the field of opioid addiction therapy, and I am indebted to his subject matter expertise, of which he shared generously as I endeavored to plausibly portray the Open Arms Treatment Center and the scene in which Andre Coulon ministers to Lyla Saint-Clair's overdose. Any errors, in fact or judgment, are mine alone.

I am grateful to Verena Rose, Shawn Reilly Simmons, Deb Well and the rest of the hard-working team at Level Best Books. I am simply amazed at the volume of high-quality titles this "small" publisher puts out, while responding with courtesy and care to such needy scribes as I.

I owe special thanks to Ann-Marie Nieves and her associates at Get Red PR, who got *The Lafitte Affair* into the hands of readers I never could have found on my own, and who are doing the same for *The Bolden Cylinder.* In a similar vein, I am grateful to Molly Wraight-Ring for skillfully maintaining my website at www.normanwoolworth.com, while gracefully juggling young motherhood and a full-time job.

Finally, I owe my deepest thanks to Lori for her patient indulgence of my authorial itch, and for so very much else.

About the Author

The Bolden Cylinder is the second novel in author Norman Woolworth's Bruneau Abellard series. His first book, *The Lafitte Affair,* was a Kirkus Reviews 2024 "Best of Indie" selection. Woolworth is a retired corporate executive who lives in Charlottesville, Virginia, with his wife Lori and their dog Nola. A father of three grown children and now a grandfather, Woolworth is a graduate of Tulane University and holds a M.A. in English Literature from the University of Virginia.

AUTHOR WEBSITE:

https://www.normanwoolworth.com/

SOCIAL MEDIA HANDLES:

https://www.linkedin.com/in/norman-woolworth-7803884/
https://www.facebook.com/norman.woolworth.2024/
https://www.instagram.com/woolwonj56/?hl=en
https://www.amazon.com/stores/Norman-Woolworth/author/B0DB1144NX?isDramIntegrated=true&shoppingPortalEnabled=true
https://www.goodreads.com/author/show/51115315.Norman_Woolworth
https://www.bookbub.com/profile/1056201728

Also by Norman Woolworth

The Lafitte Affair: A Bruneau Abellard Novel